AMERICUS

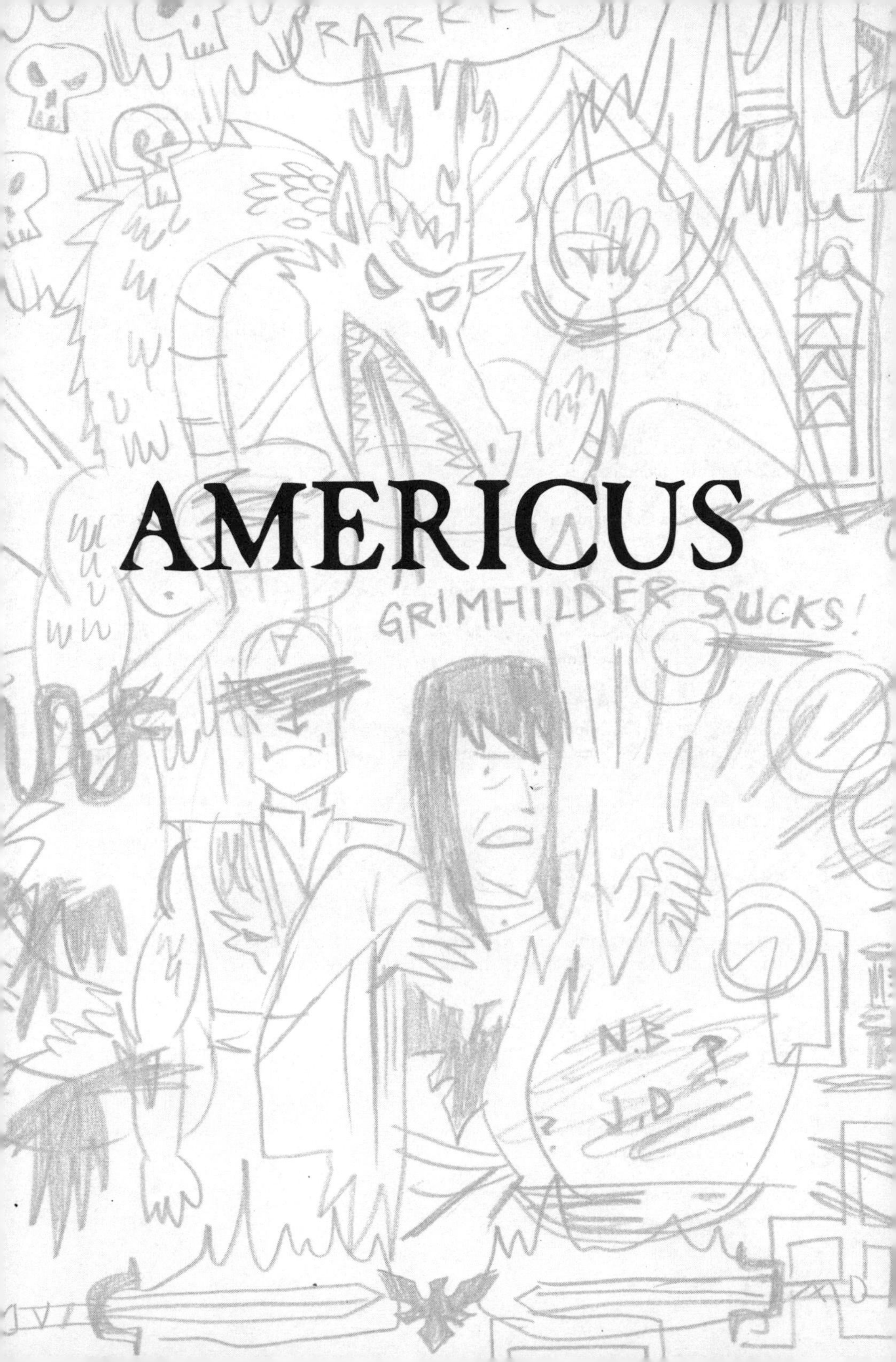
GRIMHILDER SUCKS!

First Second

New York & London

Thanks to Galen Longstreth, Greg Means, and Jason Rainey for their parts in making this book.

Text copyright © 2011 by MK Reed
Illustrations copyright © 2011 by Jonathan Hill
Published by First Second
First Second is an imprint of Roaring Brook Press, a division of Holtzbrinck Publishing
Holdings Limited Partnership
175 Fifth Avenue, New York, New York 10010
All rights reserved

Distributed in the United Kingdom by Macmillan Children's Books,
a division of Pan Macmillan.

Library of Congress Cataloging-in-Publication Data

Reed, M. K.
    Americus / MK Reed ; [illustrations by] Jonathan David Hill.—1st ed.
       p. cm.
    Summary: Oklahoma teen Neil Barton stands up for his favorite fantasy series, The
Chronicles of Apathea Ravenchilde, when conservative Christians try to bully the town of
Americus into banning it from the public library.
    ISBN 978-1-59643-601-5
    1. Graphic novels. [1. Graphic novels. 2. Books and reading—Fiction. 3. Censorship—
Fiction. 4. Libraries—Fiction. 5. Fundamentalism—Fiction.] I. Hill, Jonathan David, ill.
II. Title.
    PZ7.7.R42Ame 2011
    741.5'973—dc22

                                                                              2010051586

Hardcover ISBN: 978-1-59643-768-5

First Second books are available for special promotions and premiums.
For details, contact: Director of Special Markets, Holtzbrinck Publishers.

First edition 2011
Book design by Colleen AF Venable
Printed in the United States of America

Paperback: 10 9 8 7 6 5 4 3 2 1
Hardcover: 10 9 8 7 6 5 4 3 2 1

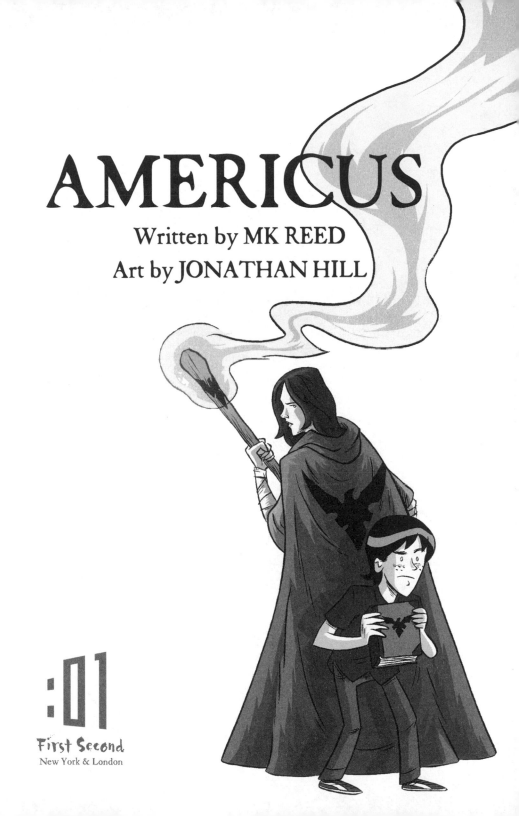

AMERICUS

Written by MK REED
Art by JONATHAN HILL

:01

First Second
New York & London

CHAPTER 1

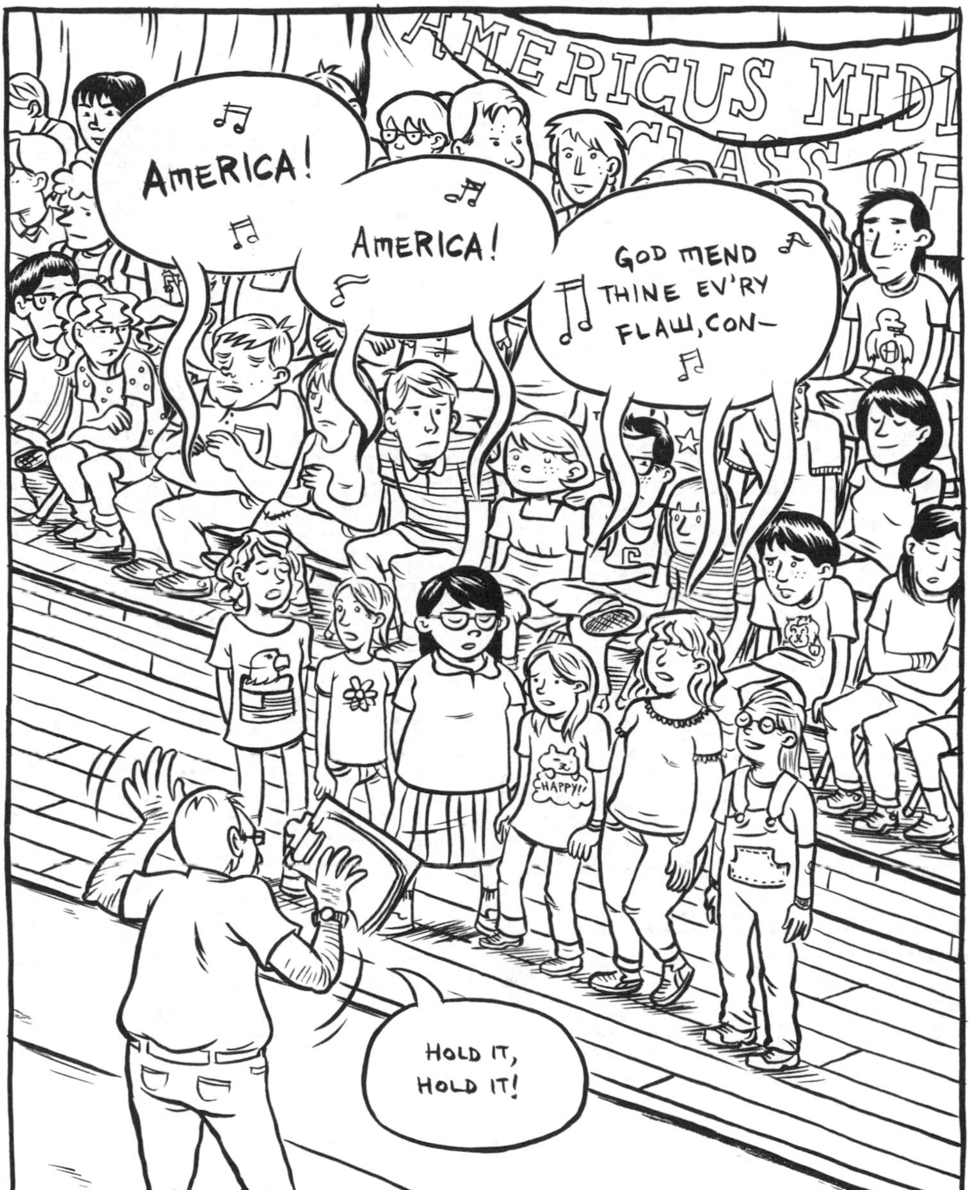
AMERICUS MIDD
CLASS OF
AMERICA!
AMERICA!
GOD MEND THINE EV'RY FLAW, CON—
HAPPY!!
HOLD IT, HOLD IT!

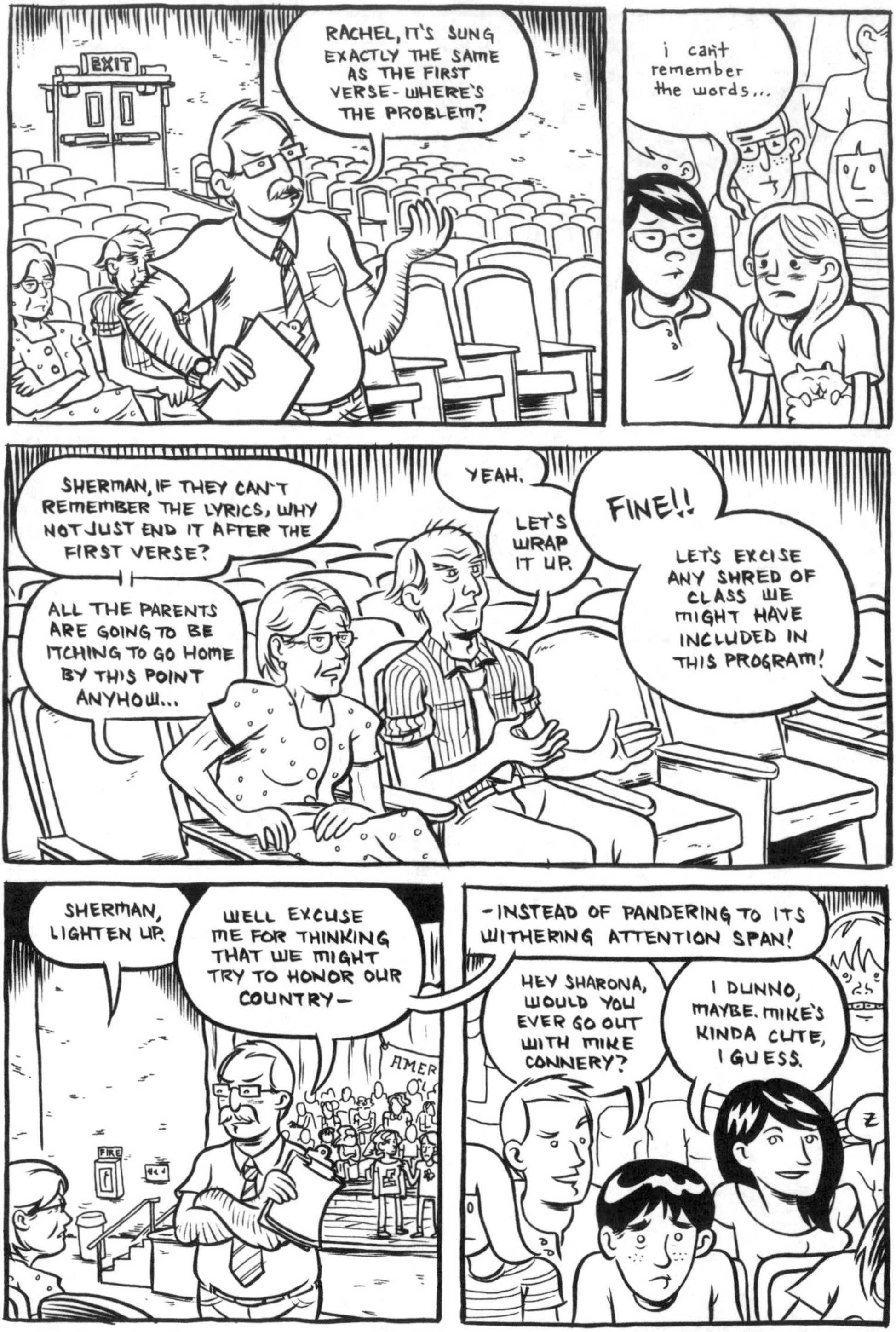
RACHEL, IT'S SUNG EXACTLY THE SAME AS THE FIRST VERSE- WHERE'S THE PROBLEM?
i can't remember the words...
SHERMAN, IF THEY CAN'T REMEMBER THE LYRICS, WHY NOT JUST END IT AFTER THE FIRST VERSE?
ALL THE PARENTS ARE GOING TO BE ITCHING TO GO HOME BY THIS POINT ANYHOW...
YEAH.
LET'S WRAP IT UP.
FINE!!
LET'S EXCISE ANY SHRED OF CLASS WE MIGHT HAVE INCLUDED IN THIS PROGRAM!
SHERMAN, LIGHTEN UP.
WELL EXCUSE ME FOR THINKING THAT WE MIGHT TRY TO HONOR OUR COUNTRY-
-INSTEAD OF PANDERING TO ITS WITHERING ATTENTION SPAN!
HEY SHARONA, WOULD YOU EVER GO OUT WITH MIKE CONNERY?
I DUNNO, MAYBE. MIKE'S KINDA CUTE, I GUESS.

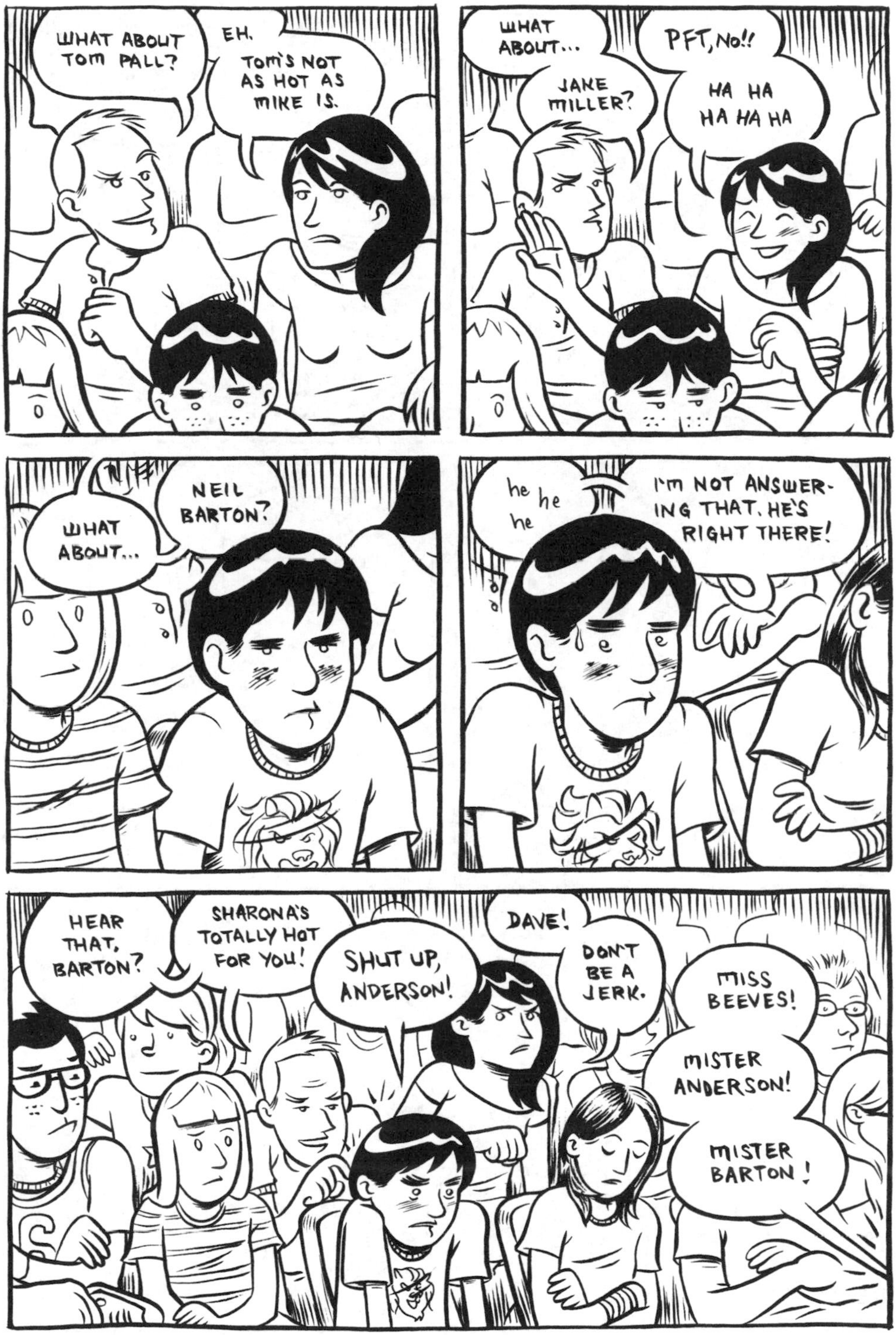
WHAT ABOUT TOM PALL?
EH.
TOM'S NOT AS HOT AS MIKE IS.
WHAT ABOUT...
JAKE MILLER?
PFT, NO!!
HA HA HA HA HA
WHAT ABOUT...
NEIL BARTON?
he he he
I'M NOT ANSWERING THAT. HE'S RIGHT THERE!
HEAR THAT, BARTON?
SHARONA'S TOTALLY HOT FOR YOU!
SHUT UP, ANDERSON!
DAVE!
DON'T BE A JERK.
MISS BEEVES!
MISTER ANDERSON!
MISTER BARTON!

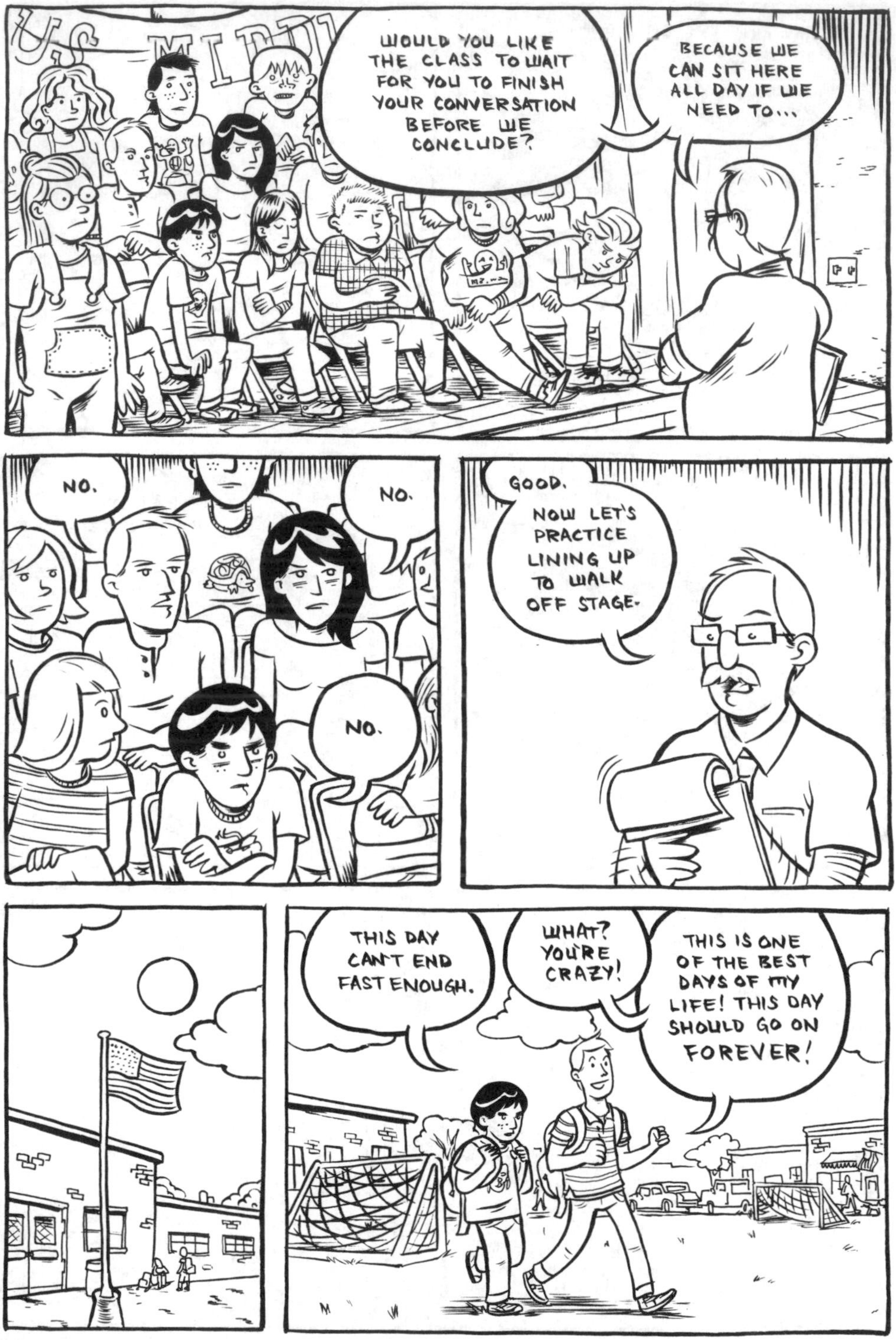

WOULD YOU LIKE THE CLASS TO WAIT FOR YOU TO FINISH YOUR CONVERSATION BEFORE WE CONCLUDE?
BECAUSE WE CAN SIT HERE ALL DAY IF WE NEED TO...
NO.
NO.
NO.
GOOD.
NOW LET'S PRACTICE LINING UP TO WALK OFF STAGE.
THIS DAY CAN'T END FAST ENOUGH.
WHAT? YOU'RE CRAZY!
THIS IS ONE OF THE BEST DAYS OF MY LIFE! THIS DAY SHOULD GO ON FOREVER!

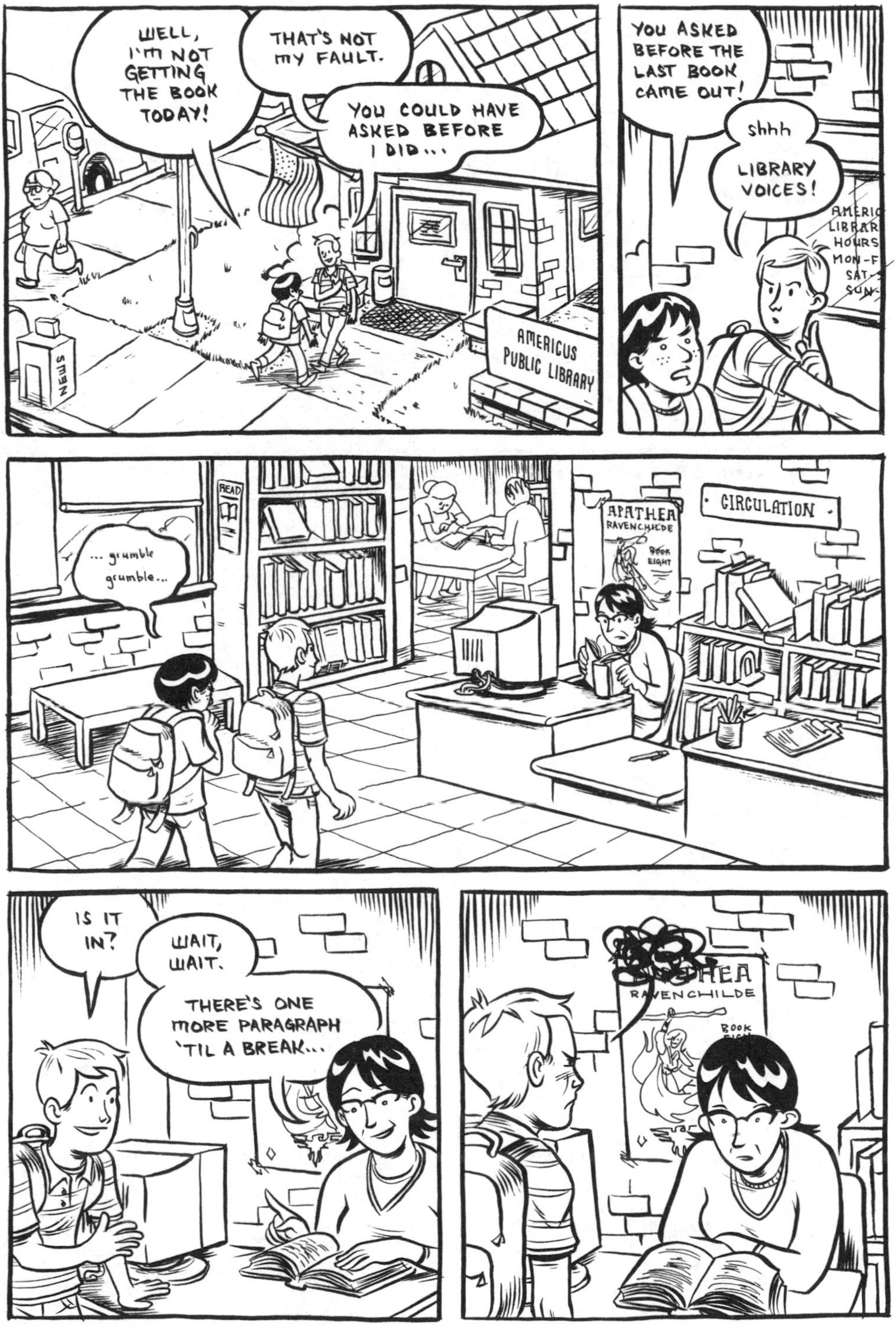
WELL, I'M NOT GETTING THE BOOK TODAY!
THAT'S NOT MY FAULT.
YOU COULD HAVE ASKED BEFORE I DID...
AMERICUS PUBLIC LIBRARY
YOU ASKED BEFORE THE LAST BOOK CAME OUT!
shhh
LIBRARY VOICES!
READ
...grumble grumble...
APATHEA RAVENCHILDE BOOK EIGHT
CIRCULATION
IS IT IN?
WAIT, WAIT.
THERE'S ONE MORE PARAGRAPH 'TIL A BREAK...
RAVENCHILDE

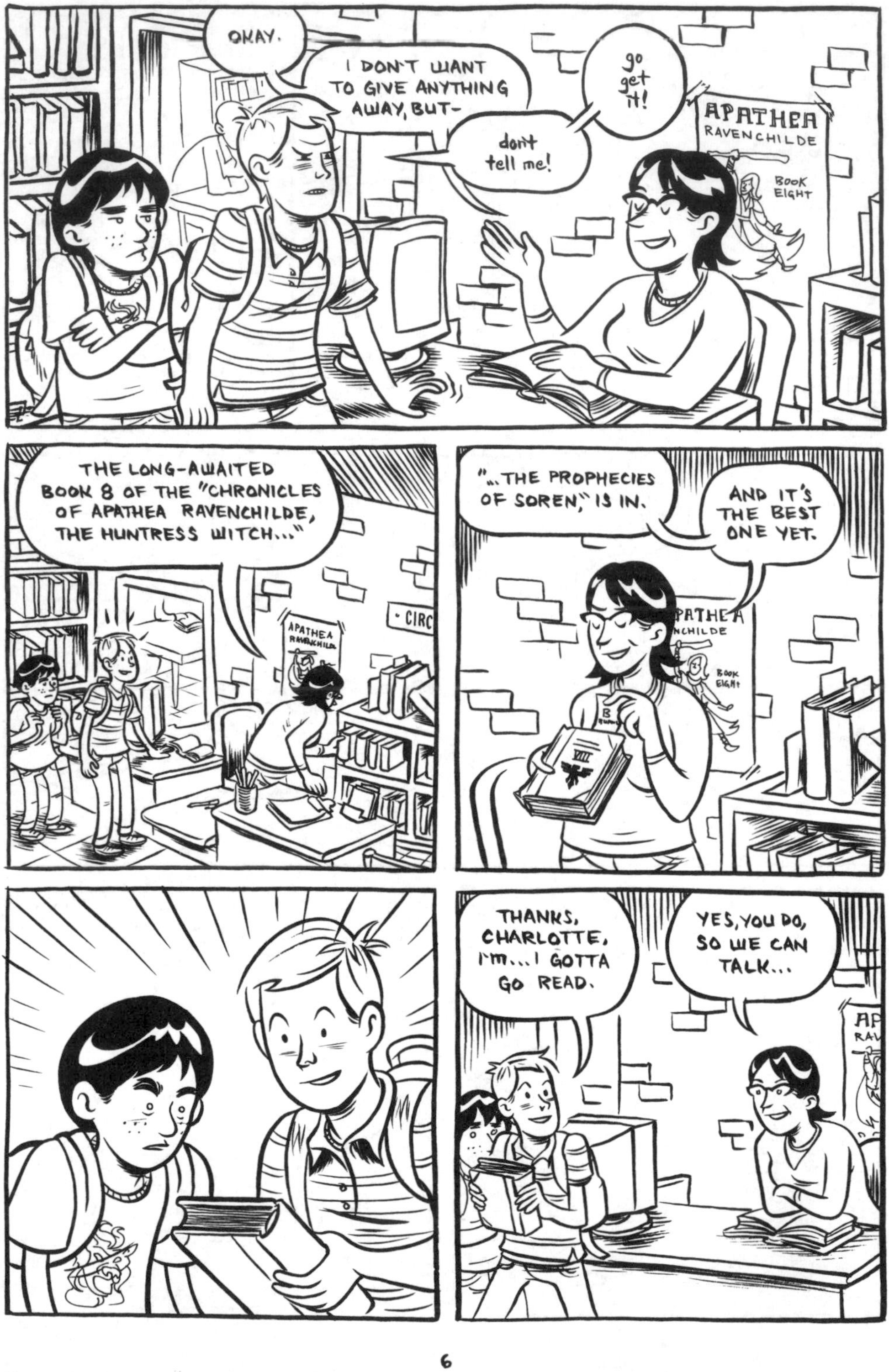
OKAY.
I DON'T WANT TO GIVE ANYTHING AWAY, BUT-
go get it!
don't tell me!
APATHEA RAVENCHILDE
BOOK EIGHT
THE LONG-AWAITED BOOK 8 OF THE "CHRONICLES OF APATHEA RAVENCHILDE, THE HUNTRESS WITCH..."
APATHEA RAVENCHILDE
CIRC
"...THE PROPHECIES OF SOREN," IS IN.
AND IT'S THE BEST ONE YET.
THANKS, CHARLOTTE. I'M... I GOTTA GO READ.
YES, YOU DO, SO WE CAN TALK...

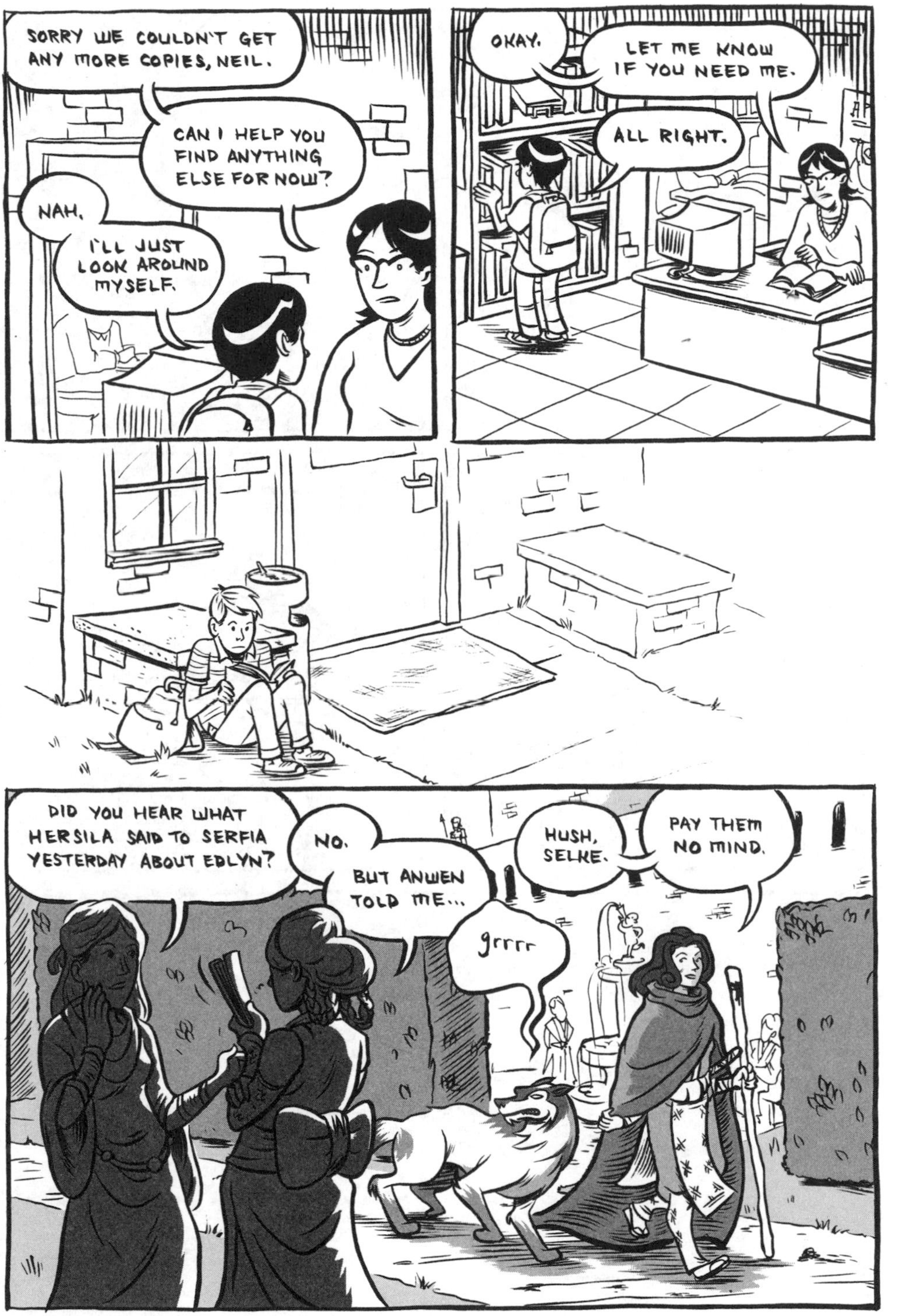
SORRY WE COULDN'T GET ANY MORE COPIES, NEIL.
CAN I HELP YOU FIND ANYTHING ELSE FOR NOW?
NAH.
I'LL JUST LOOK AROUND MYSELF.
OKAY.
LET ME KNOW IF YOU NEED ME.
ALL RIGHT.
DID YOU HEAR WHAT HERSILA SAID TO SERFIA YESTERDAY ABOUT EDLYN?
NO.
BUT ANWEN TOLD ME...
grrrr
HUSH, SELKE.
PAY THEM NO MIND.

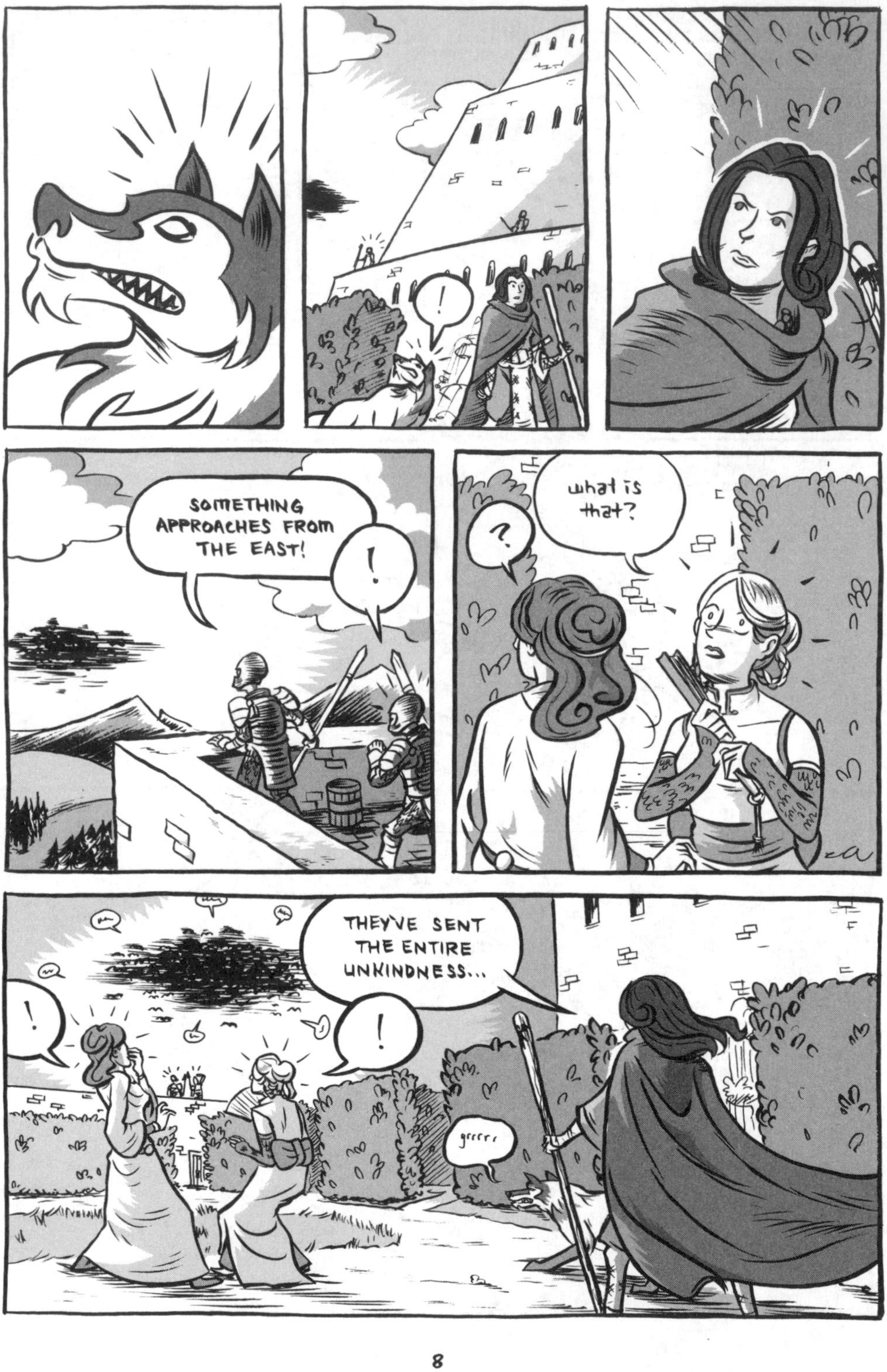
!
SOMETHING APPROACHES FROM THE EAST!
!
?
what is that?
!
THEY'VE SENT THE ENTIRE UNKINDNESS...
!
grrrr.

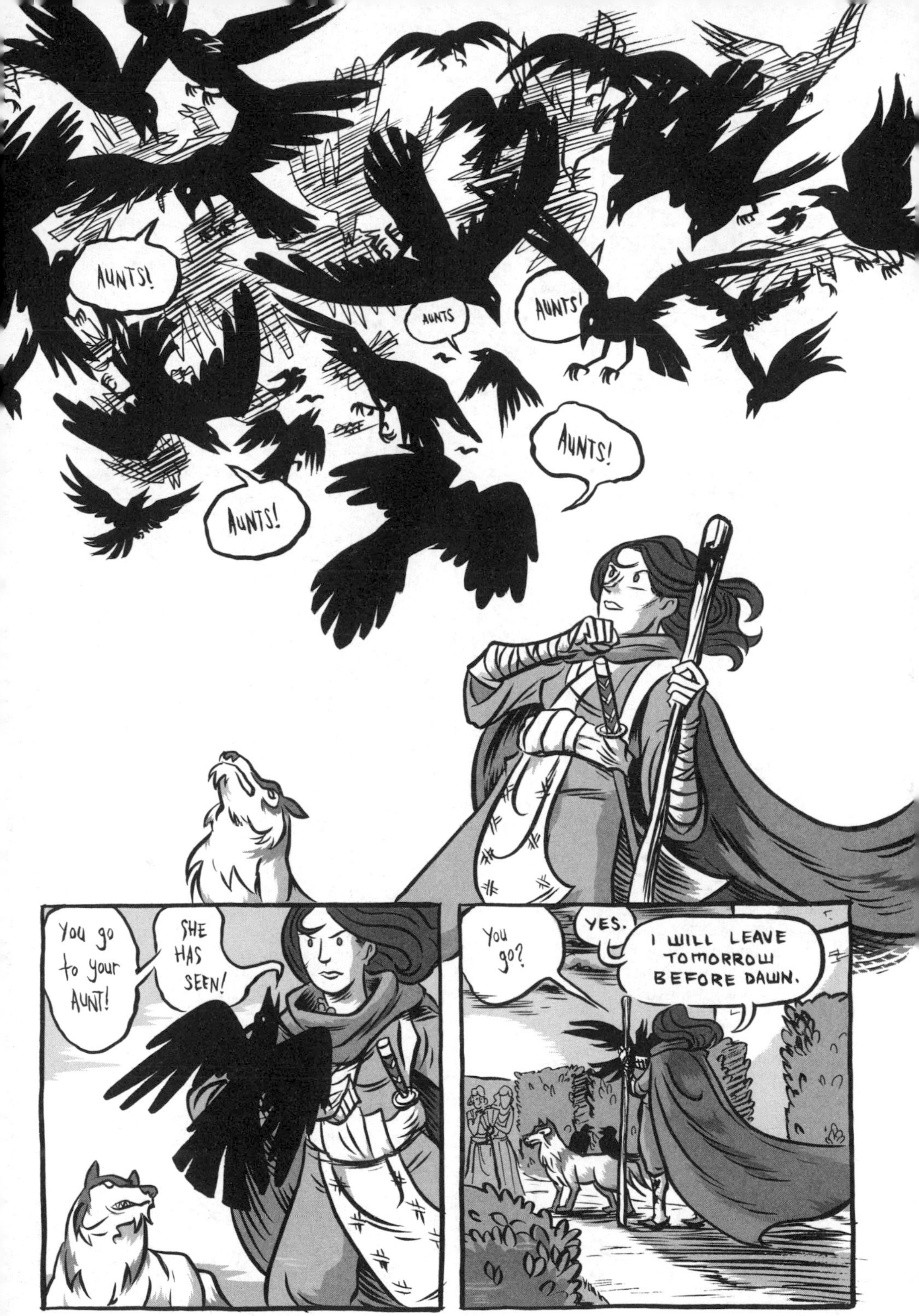
AUNTS!
AUNTS
AUNTS!
AUNTS!
AUNTS!
You go to your AUNT!
SHE HAS SEEN!
You go?
YES.
I WILL LEAVE TOMORROW BEFORE DAWN.

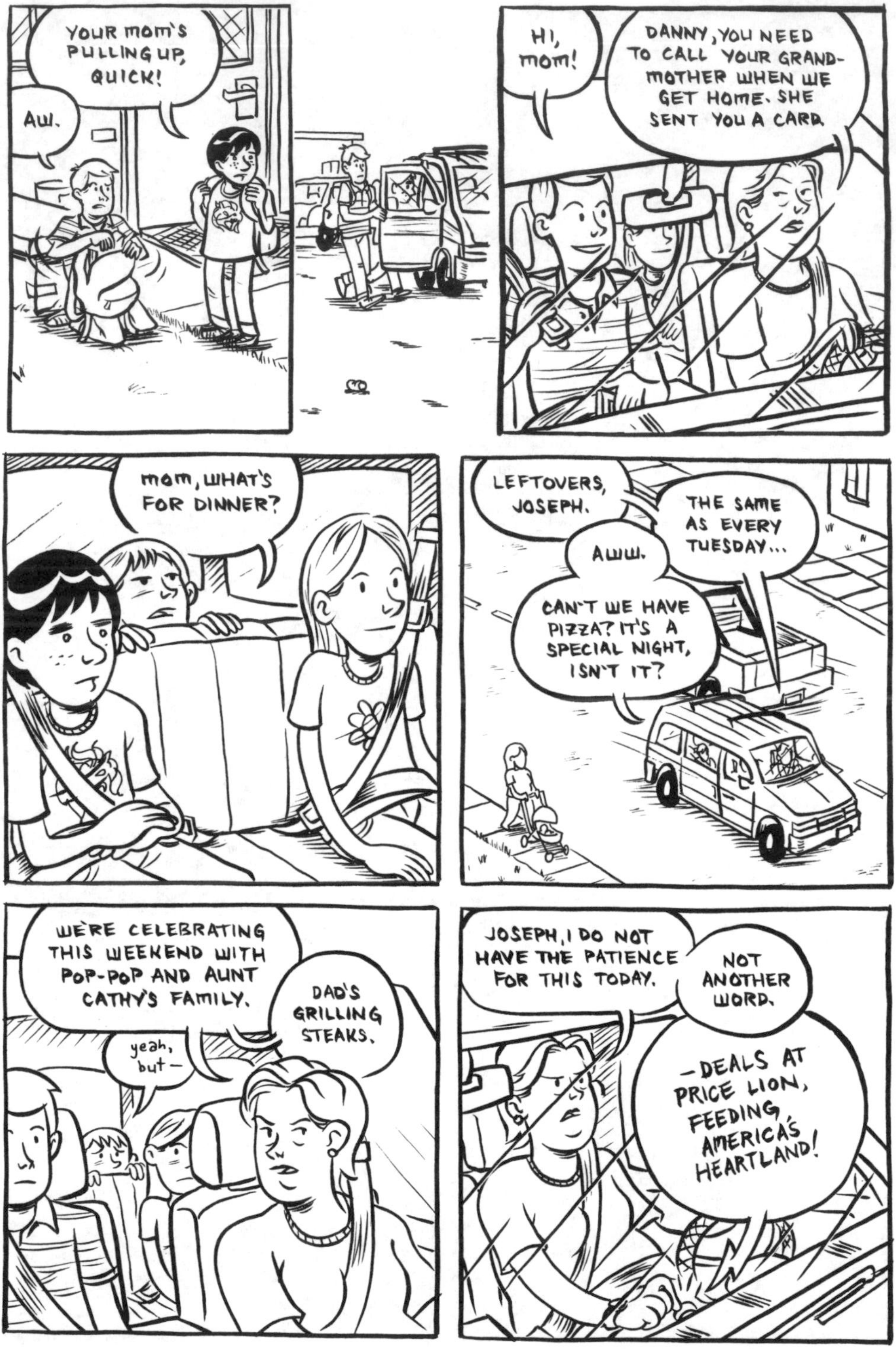
YOUR MOM'S PULLING UP, QUICK!
AW.
HI, MOM!
DANNY, YOU NEED TO CALL YOUR GRAND-MOTHER WHEN WE GET HOME. SHE SENT YOU A CARD.
MOM, WHAT'S FOR DINNER?
LEFTOVERS, JOSEPH.
THE SAME AS EVERY TUESDAY...
AWW.
CAN'T WE HAVE PIZZA? IT'S A SPECIAL NIGHT, ISN'T IT?
WE'RE CELEBRATING THIS WEEKEND WITH POP-POP AND AUNT CATHY'S FAMILY.
DAD'S GRILLING STEAKS.
yeah, but—
JOSEPH, I DO NOT HAVE THE PATIENCE FOR THIS TODAY.
NOT ANOTHER WORD.
—DEALS AT PRICE LION, FEEDING AMERICA'S HEARTLAND!

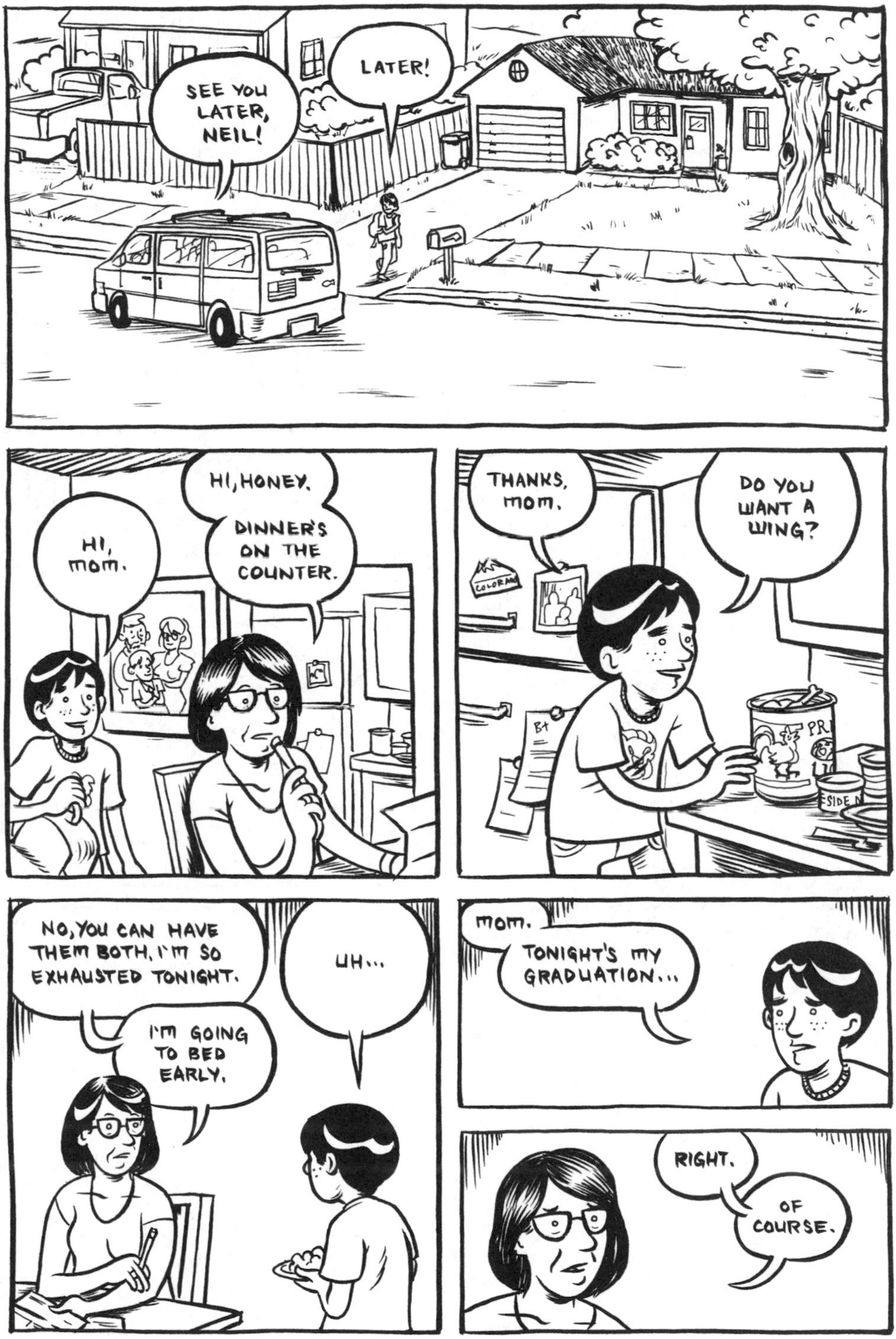
SEE YOU LATER, NEIL!
LATER!
HI, HONEY.
DINNER'S ON THE COUNTER.
HI, MOM.
THANKS, MOM.
DO YOU WANT A WING?
NO, YOU CAN HAVE THEM BOTH, I'M SO EXHAUSTED TONIGHT.
I'M GOING TO BED EARLY.
UH...
MOM.
TONIGHT'S MY GRADUATION...
RIGHT.
OF COURSE.

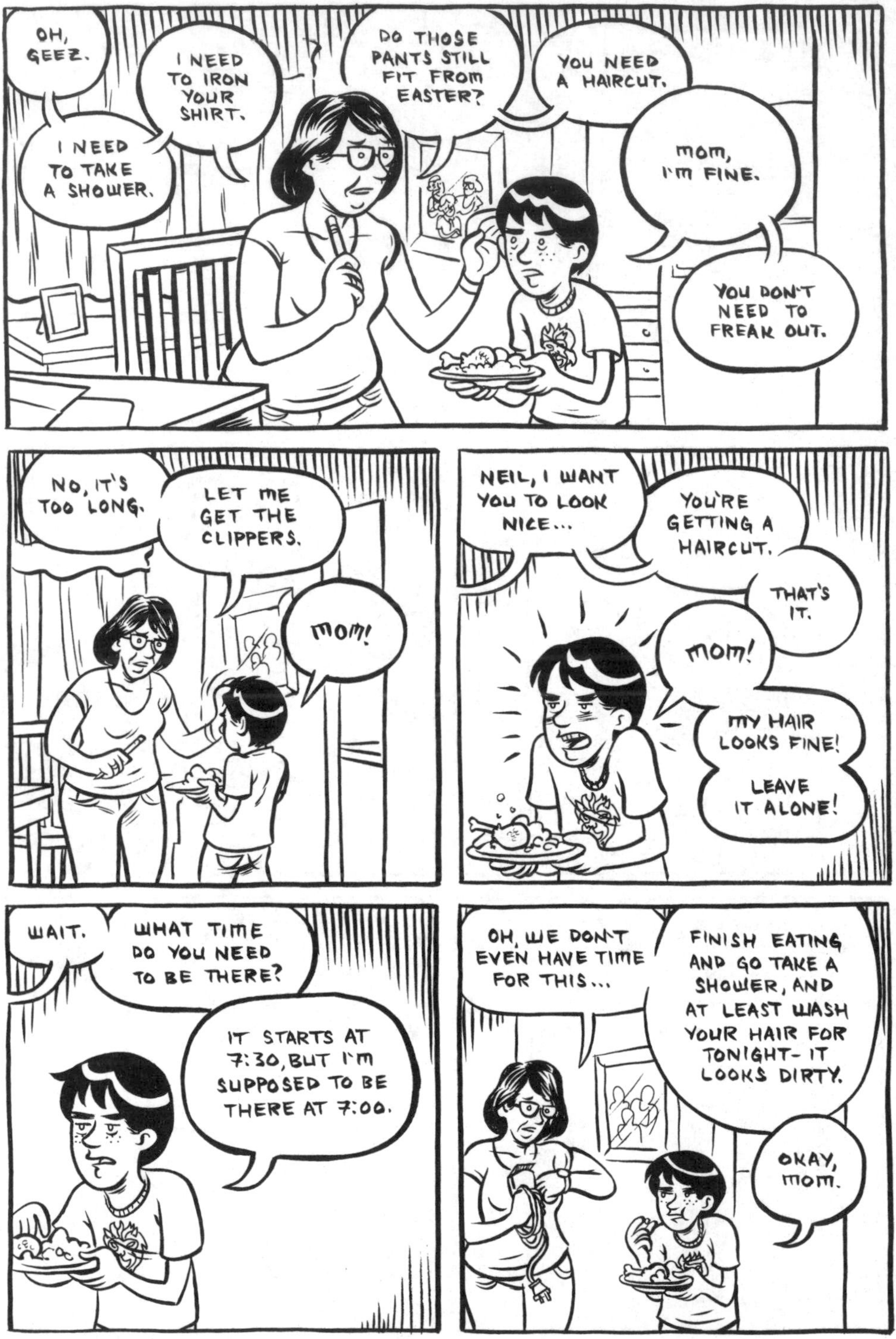
OH, GEEZ.
I NEED TO TAKE A SHOWER.
I NEED TO IRON YOUR SHIRT.
DO THOSE PANTS STILL FIT FROM EASTER?
YOU NEED A HAIRCUT.
MOM, I'M FINE.
YOU DON'T NEED TO FREAK OUT.
NO, IT'S TOO LONG.
LET ME GET THE CLIPPERS.
MOM!
NEIL, I WANT YOU TO LOOK NICE...
YOU'RE GETTING A HAIRCUT.
THAT'S IT.
MOM!
MY HAIR LOOKS FINE!
LEAVE IT ALONE!
WAIT.
WHAT TIME DO YOU NEED TO BE THERE?
IT STARTS AT 7:30, BUT I'M SUPPOSED TO BE THERE AT 7:00.
OH, WE DON'T EVEN HAVE TIME FOR THIS...
FINISH EATING AND GO TAKE A SHOWER, AND AT LEAST WASH YOUR HAIR FOR TONIGHT- IT LOOKS DIRTY.
OKAY, MOM.

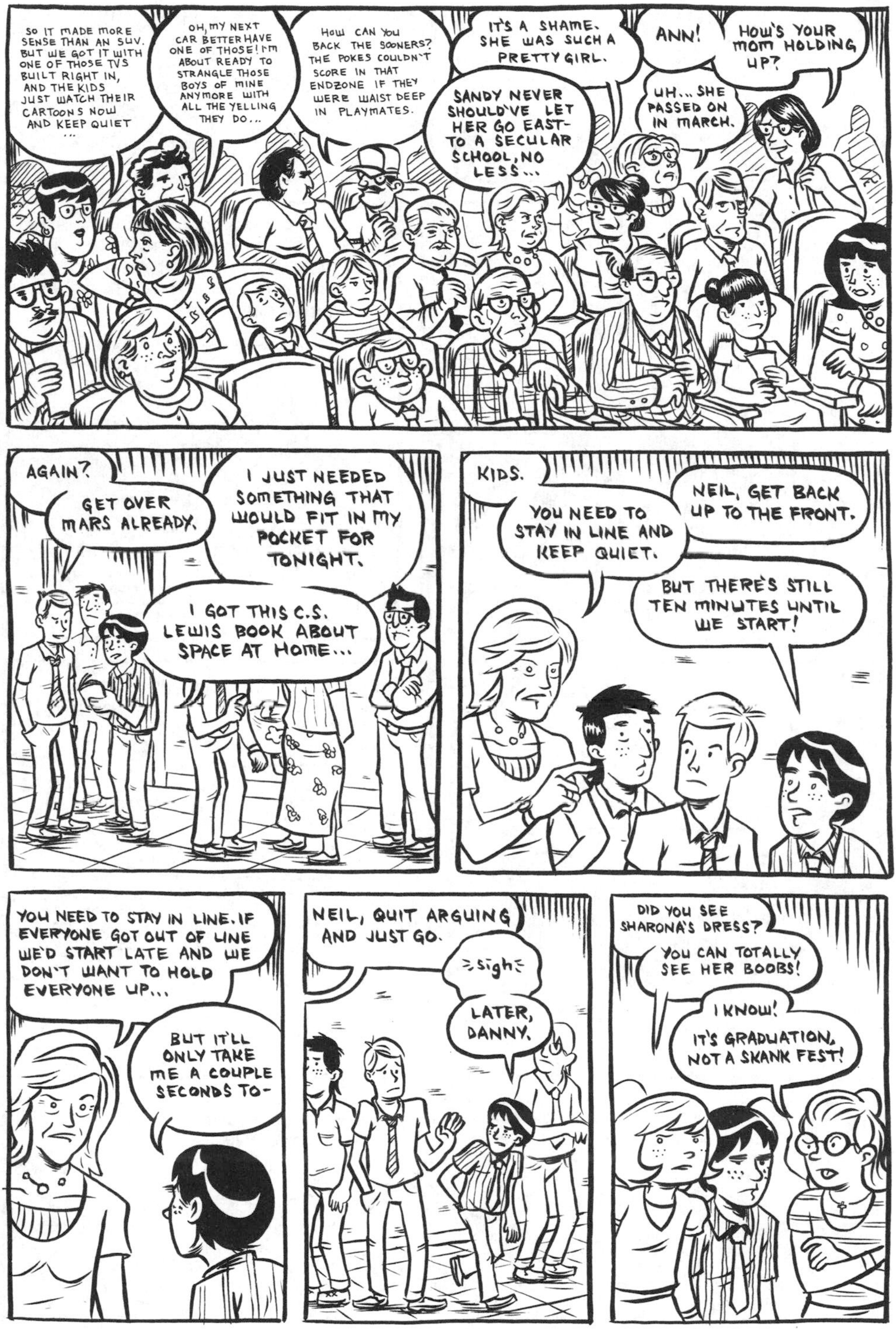
SO IT MADE MORE SENSE THAN AN SUV. BUT WE GOT IT WITH ONE OF THOSE TVS BUILT RIGHT IN, AND THE KIDS JUST WATCH THEIR CARTOONS NOW AND KEEP QUIET...
OH, MY NEXT CAR BETTER HAVE ONE OF THOSE! I'M ABOUT READY TO STRANGLE THOSE BOYS OF MINE ANYMORE WITH ALL THE YELLING THEY DO...
HOW CAN YOU BACK THE SOONERS? THE POKES COULDN'T SCORE IN THAT ENDZONE IF THEY WERE WAIST DEEP IN PLAYMATES.
IT'S A SHAME. SHE WAS SUCH A PRETTY GIRL.
SANDY NEVER SHOULD'VE LET HER GO EAST- TO A SECULAR SCHOOL, NO LESS...
ANN!
HOW'S YOUR MOM HOLDING UP?
UH... SHE PASSED ON IN MARCH.
AGAIN?
GET OVER MARS ALREADY.
I JUST NEEDED SOMETHING THAT WOULD FIT IN MY POCKET FOR TONIGHT.
I GOT THIS C.S. LEWIS BOOK ABOUT SPACE AT HOME...
KIDS.
YOU NEED TO STAY IN LINE AND KEEP QUIET.
NEIL, GET BACK UP TO THE FRONT.
BUT THERE'S STILL TEN MINUTES UNTIL WE START!
YOU NEED TO STAY IN LINE. IF EVERYONE GOT OUT OF LINE WE'D START LATE AND WE DON'T WANT TO HOLD EVERYONE UP...
BUT IT'LL ONLY TAKE ME A COUPLE SECONDS TO-
NEIL, QUIT ARGUING AND JUST GO.
sigh
LATER, DANNY.
DID YOU SEE SHARONA'S DRESS?
YOU CAN TOTALLY SEE HER BOOBS!
I KNOW!
IT'S GRADUATION, NOT A SKANK FEST!

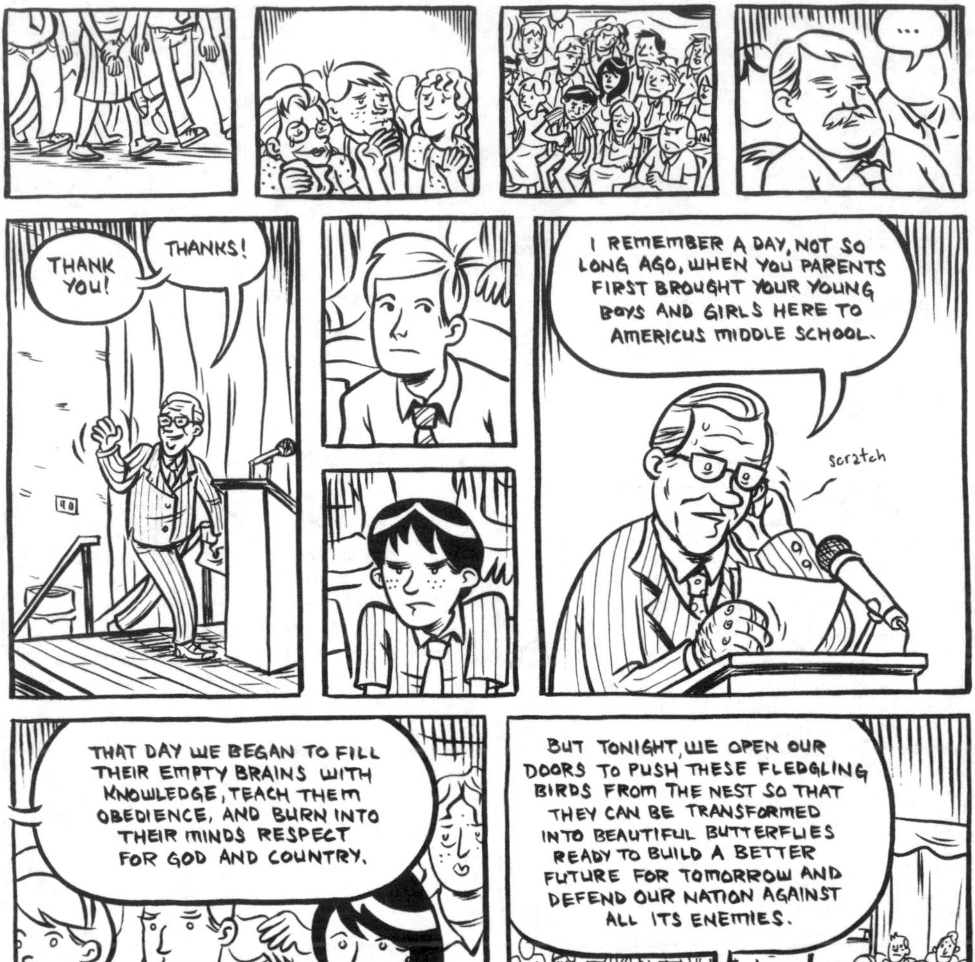
...
THANK YOU!
THANKS!
I REMEMBER A DAY, NOT SO LONG AGO, WHEN YOU PARENTS FIRST BROUGHT YOUR YOUNG BOYS AND GIRLS HERE TO AMERICUS MIDDLE SCHOOL.
scratch
THAT DAY WE BEGAN TO FILL THEIR EMPTY BRAINS WITH KNOWLEDGE, TEACH THEM OBEDIENCE, AND BURN INTO THEIR MINDS RESPECT FOR GOD AND COUNTRY.
BUT TONIGHT, WE OPEN OUR DOORS TO PUSH THESE FLEDGLING BIRDS FROM THE NEST SO THAT THEY CAN BE TRANSFORMED INTO BEAUTIFUL BUTTERFLIES READY TO BUILD A BETTER FUTURE FOR TOMORROW AND DEFEND OUR NATION AGAINST ALL ITS ENEMIES.
AS OUR LITTLE PIONEERS SETTLE THE NEW FRONTIER OF MCGRAW-COYNE HIGH SCHOOL THIS FALL, THEY WILL BRING WITH THEM THE GAME PLAN FOR SUCCESS.

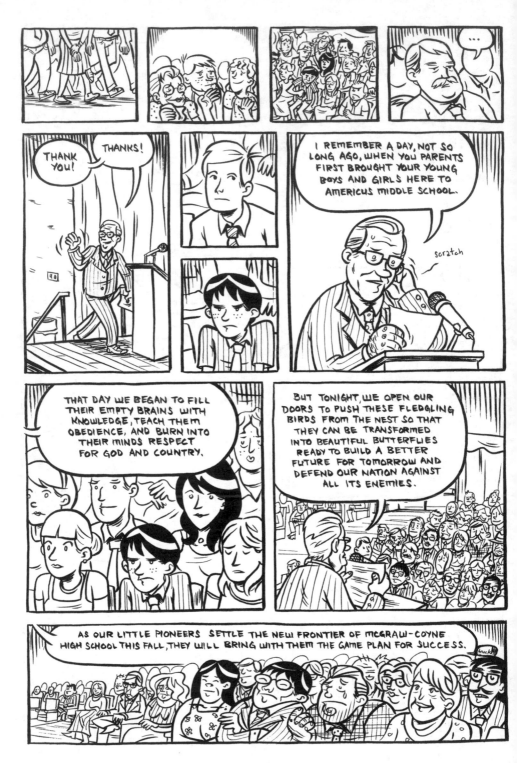

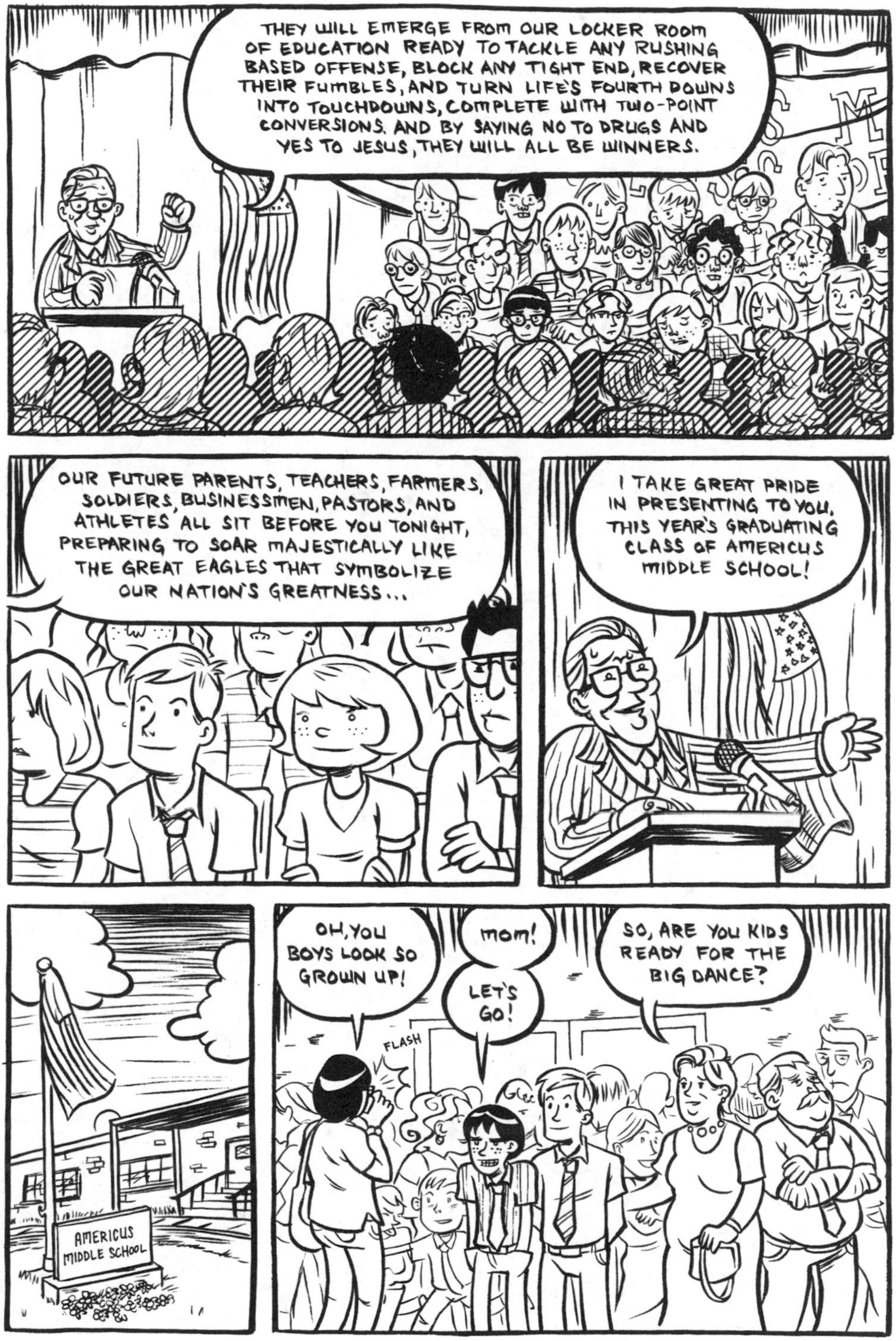
THEY WILL EMERGE FROM OUR LOCKER ROOM OF EDUCATION READY TO TACKLE ANY RUSHING BASED OFFENSE, BLOCK ANY TIGHT END, RECOVER THEIR FUMBLES, AND TURN LIFE'S FOURTH DOWNS INTO TOUCHDOWNS, COMPLETE WITH TWO-POINT CONVERSIONS. AND BY SAYING NO TO DRUGS AND YES TO JESUS, THEY WILL ALL BE WINNERS.
OUR FUTURE PARENTS, TEACHERS, FARMERS, SOLDIERS, BUSINESSMEN, PASTORS, AND ATHLETES ALL SIT BEFORE YOU TONIGHT, PREPARING TO SOAR MAJESTICALLY LIKE THE GREAT EAGLES THAT SYMBOLIZE OUR NATION'S GREATNESS...
I TAKE GREAT PRIDE IN PRESENTING TO YOU, THIS YEAR'S GRADUATING CLASS OF AMERICUS MIDDLE SCHOOL!
AMERICUS MIDDLE SCHOOL
OH, YOU BOYS LOOK SO GROWN UP!
FLASH
MOM!
LET'S GO!
SO, ARE YOU KIDS READY FOR THE BIG DANCE?

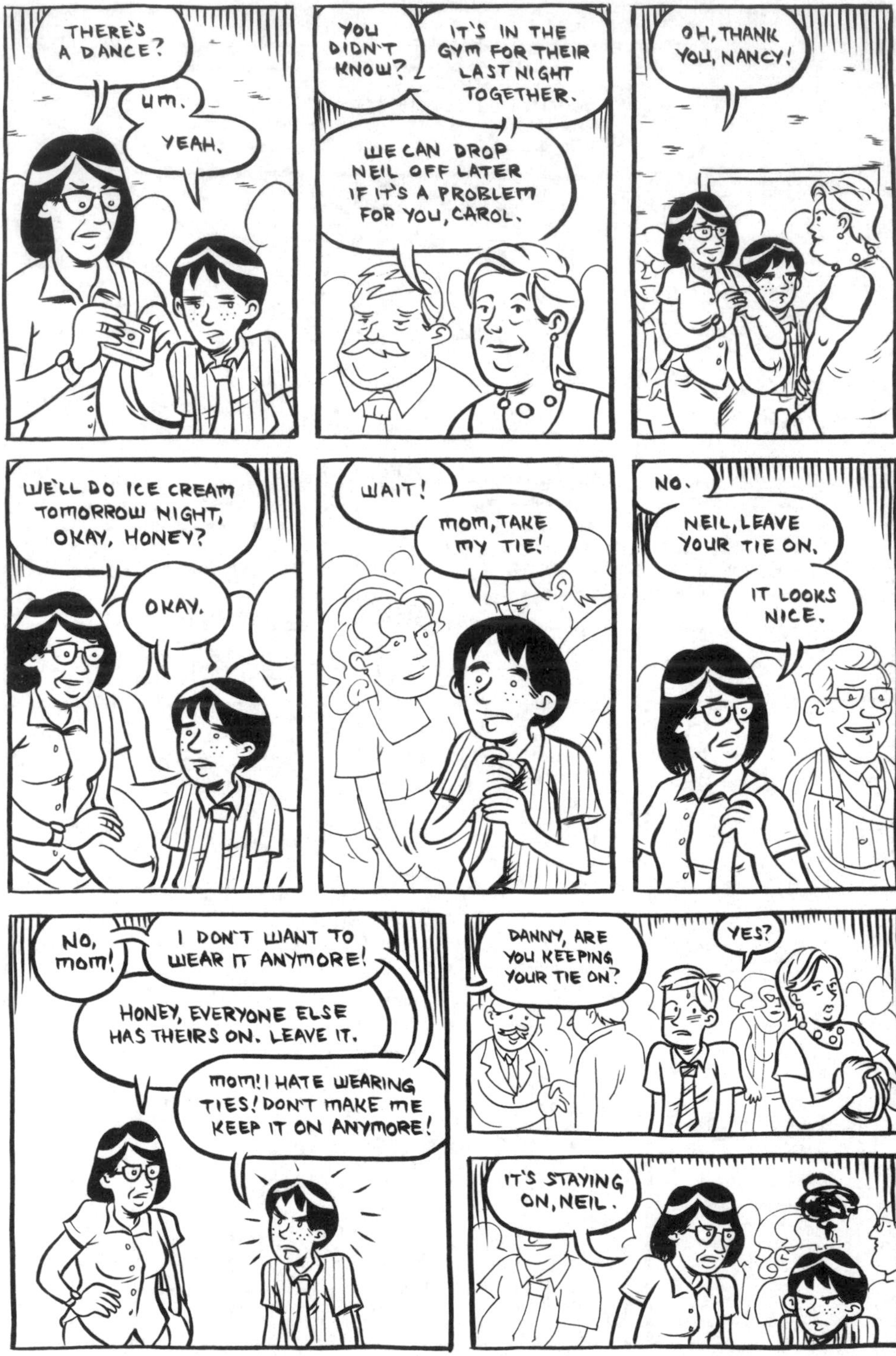

THERE'S A DANCE?
UM.
YEAH.
YOU DIDN'T KNOW?
IT'S IN THE GYM FOR THEIR LAST NIGHT TOGETHER.
WE CAN DROP NEIL OFF LATER IF IT'S A PROBLEM FOR YOU, CAROL.
OH, THANK YOU, NANCY!
WE'LL DO ICE CREAM TOMORROW NIGHT, OKAY, HONEY?
OKAY.
WAIT!
MOM, TAKE MY TIE!
NO.
NEIL, LEAVE YOUR TIE ON.
IT LOOKS NICE.
NO, MOM!
I DON'T WANT TO WEAR IT ANYMORE!
HONEY, EVERYONE ELSE HAS THEIRS ON. LEAVE IT.
MOM! I HATE WEARING TIES! DON'T MAKE ME KEEP IT ON ANYMORE!
DANNY, ARE YOU KEEPING YOUR TIE ON?
YES?
IT'S STAYING ON, NEIL.

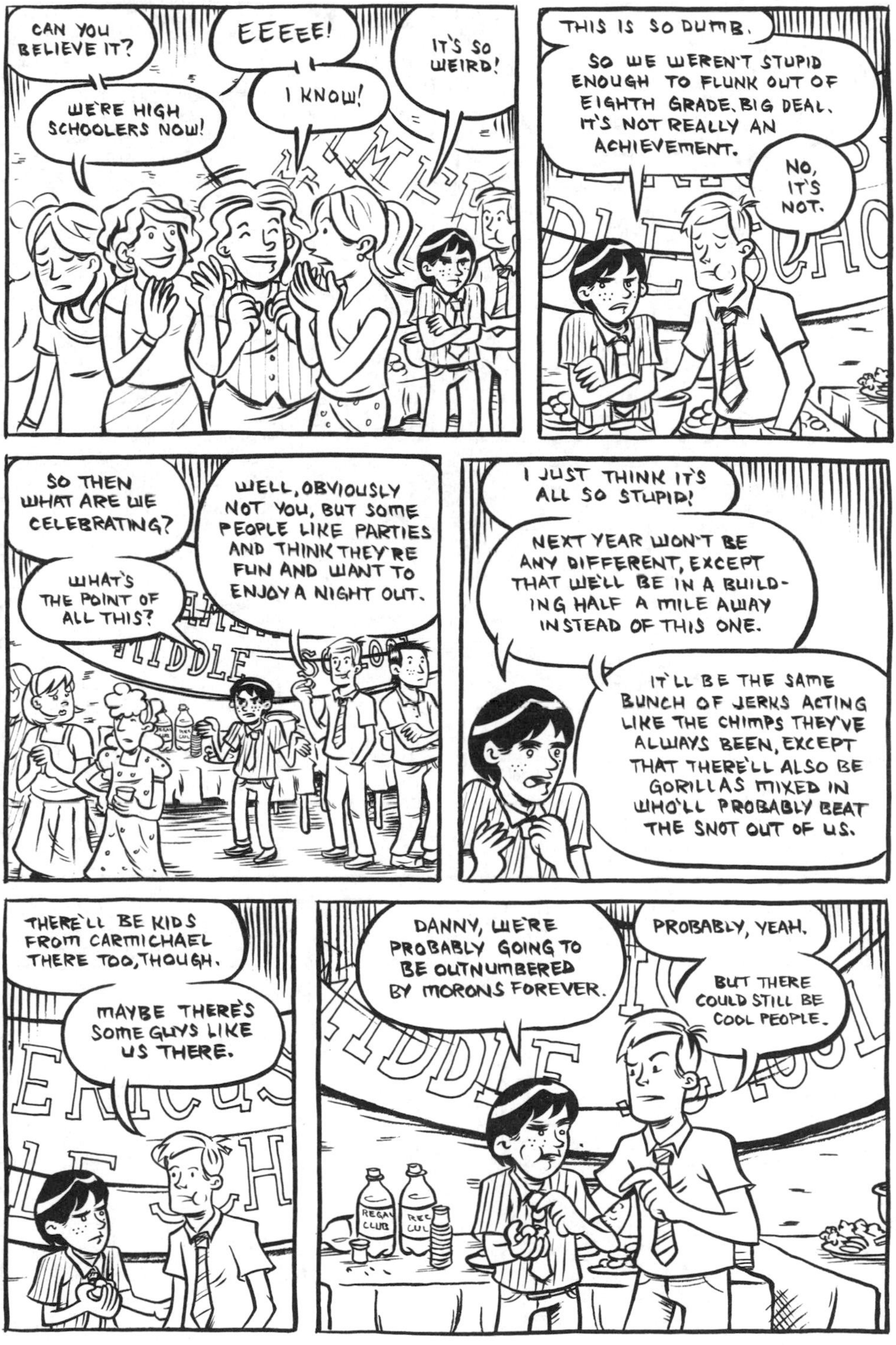
CAN YOU BELIEVE IT?
WE'RE HIGH SCHOOLERS NOW!
EEEEE!
I KNOW!
IT'S SO WEIRD!
THIS IS SO DUMB.
SO WE WEREN'T STUPID ENOUGH TO FLUNK OUT OF EIGHTH GRADE. BIG DEAL. IT'S NOT REALLY AN ACHIEVEMENT.
NO, IT'S NOT.
SO THEN WHAT ARE WE CELEBRATING?
WHAT'S THE POINT OF ALL THIS?
WELL, OBVIOUSLY NOT YOU, BUT SOME PEOPLE LIKE PARTIES AND THINK THEY'RE FUN AND WANT TO ENJOY A NIGHT OUT.
I JUST THINK IT'S ALL SO STUPID!
NEXT YEAR WON'T BE ANY DIFFERENT, EXCEPT THAT WE'LL BE IN A BUILD-ING HALF A MILE AWAY INSTEAD OF THIS ONE.
IT'LL BE THE SAME BUNCH OF JERKS ACTING LIKE THE CHIMPS THEY'VE ALWAYS BEEN, EXCEPT THAT THERE'LL ALSO BE GORILLAS MIXED IN WHO'LL PROBABLY BEAT THE SNOT OUT OF US.
THERE'LL BE KIDS FROM CARMICHAEL THERE TOO, THOUGH.
MAYBE THERE'S SOME GUYS LIKE US THERE.
DANNY, WE'RE PROBABLY GOING TO BE OUTNUMBERED BY MORONS FOREVER.
PROBABLY, YEAH.
BUT THERE COULD STILL BE COOL PEOPLE.

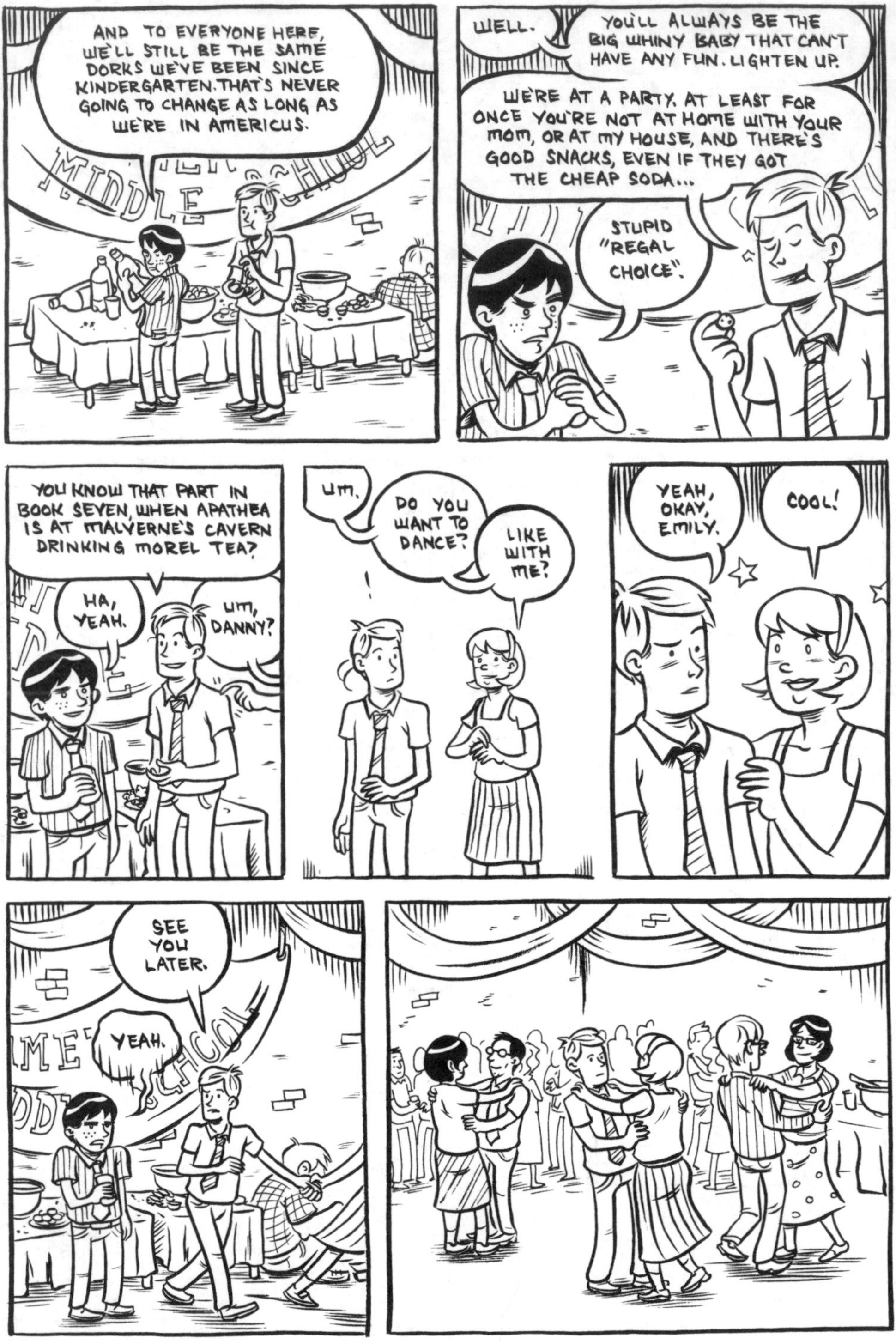

AND TO EVERYONE HERE, WE'LL STILL BE THE SAME DORKS WE'VE BEEN SINCE KINDERGARTEN. THAT'S NEVER GOING TO CHANGE AS LONG AS WE'RE IN AMERICUS.
MIDDLE SCHOOL
WELL.
YOU'LL ALWAYS BE THE BIG WHINY BABY THAT CAN'T HAVE ANY FUN. LIGHTEN UP.
WE'RE AT A PARTY. AT LEAST FOR ONCE YOU'RE NOT AT HOME WITH YOUR MOM, OR AT MY HOUSE, AND THERE'S GOOD SNACKS, EVEN IF THEY GOT THE CHEAP SODA...
STUPID "REGAL CHOICE".
YOU KNOW THAT PART IN BOOK SEVEN, WHEN APATHEA IS AT MALVERNE'S CAVERN DRINKING MOREL TEA?
HA, YEAH.
UM, DANNY?
UM.
DO YOU WANT TO DANCE?
LIKE WITH ME?
!
YEAH, OKAY, EMILY.
COOL!
SEE YOU LATER.
YEAH.

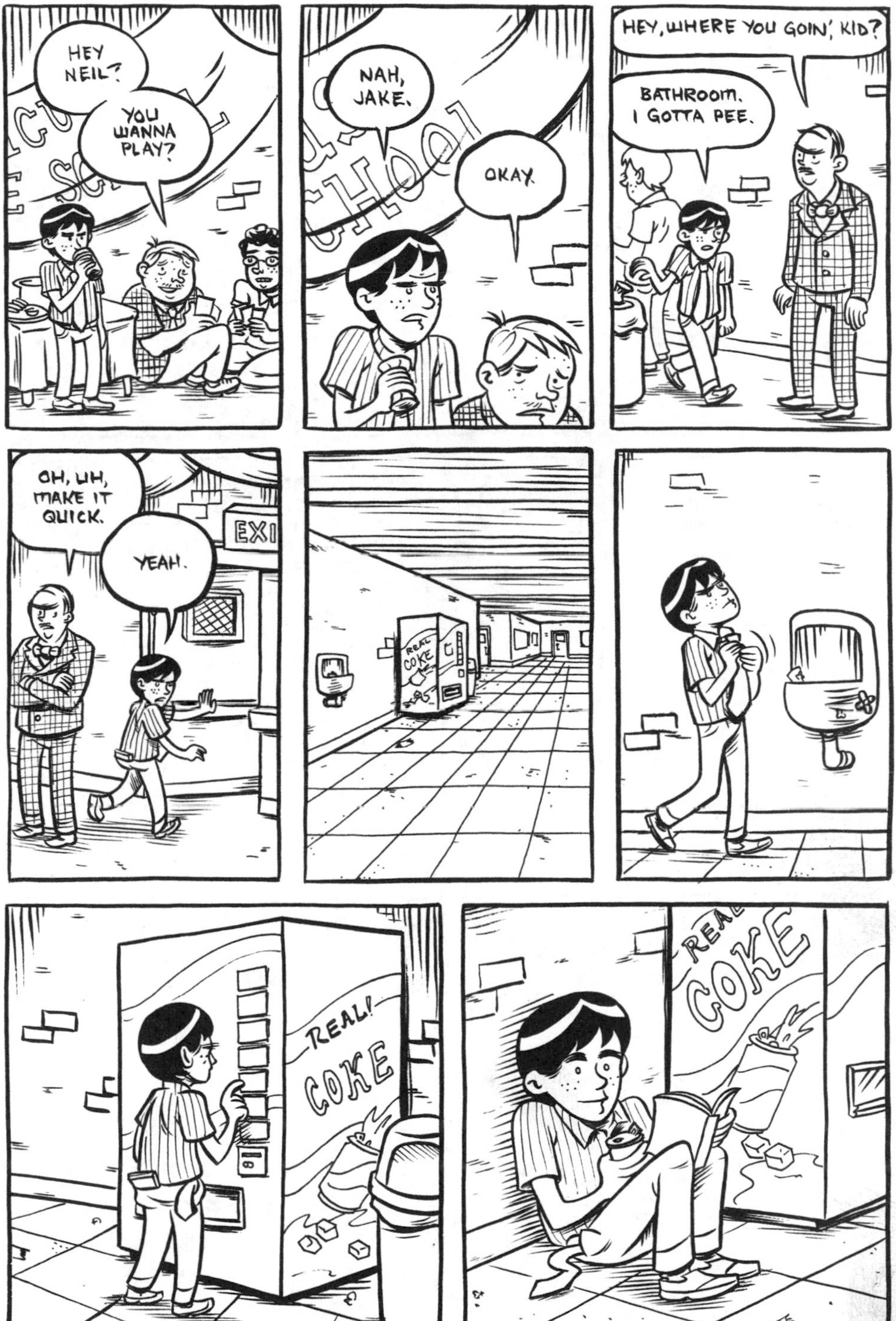

HEY NEIL?
YOU WANNA PLAY?
NAH, JAKE.
OKAY.
HEY, WHERE YOU GOIN', KID?
BATHROOM. I GOTTA PEE.
OH, UH, MAKE IT QUICK.
YEAH.
EXI
REAL COKE
REAL! COKE
REAL COKE

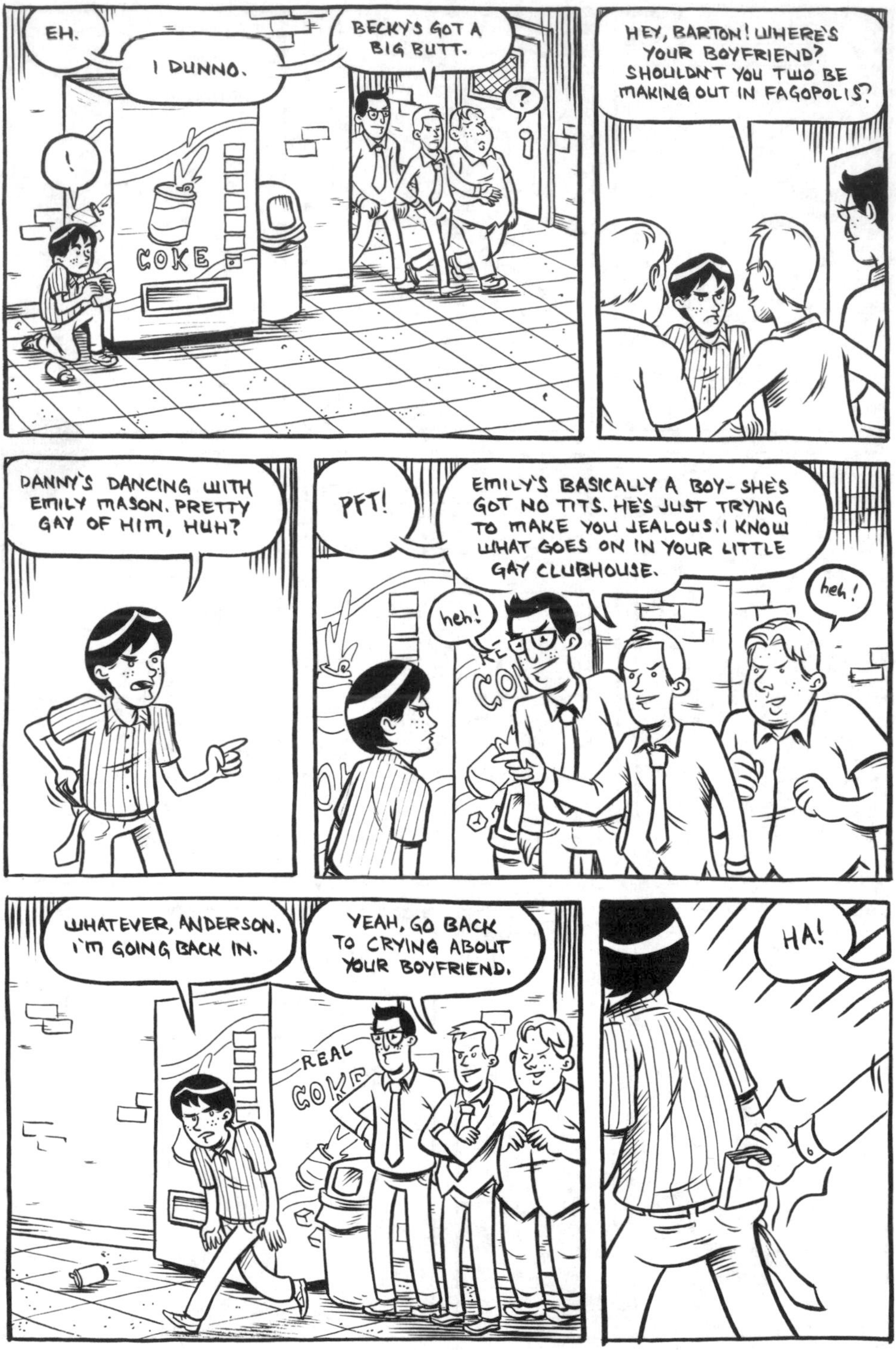
EH.
I DUNNO.
BECKY'S GOT A BIG BUTT.
?
!
COKE
HEY, BARTON! WHERE'S YOUR BOYFRIEND? SHOULDN'T YOU TWO BE MAKING OUT IN FAGOPOLIS?
DANNY'S DANCING WITH EMILY MASON. PRETTY GAY OF HIM, HUH?
PFT!
EMILY'S BASICALLY A BOY- SHE'S GOT NO TITS. HE'S JUST TRYING TO MAKE YOU JEALOUS. I KNOW WHAT GOES ON IN YOUR LITTLE GAY CLUBHOUSE.
heh!
heh!
WHATEVER, ANDERSON. I'M GOING BACK IN.
YEAH, GO BACK TO CRYING ABOUT YOUR BOYFRIEND.
REAL
COKE
HA!

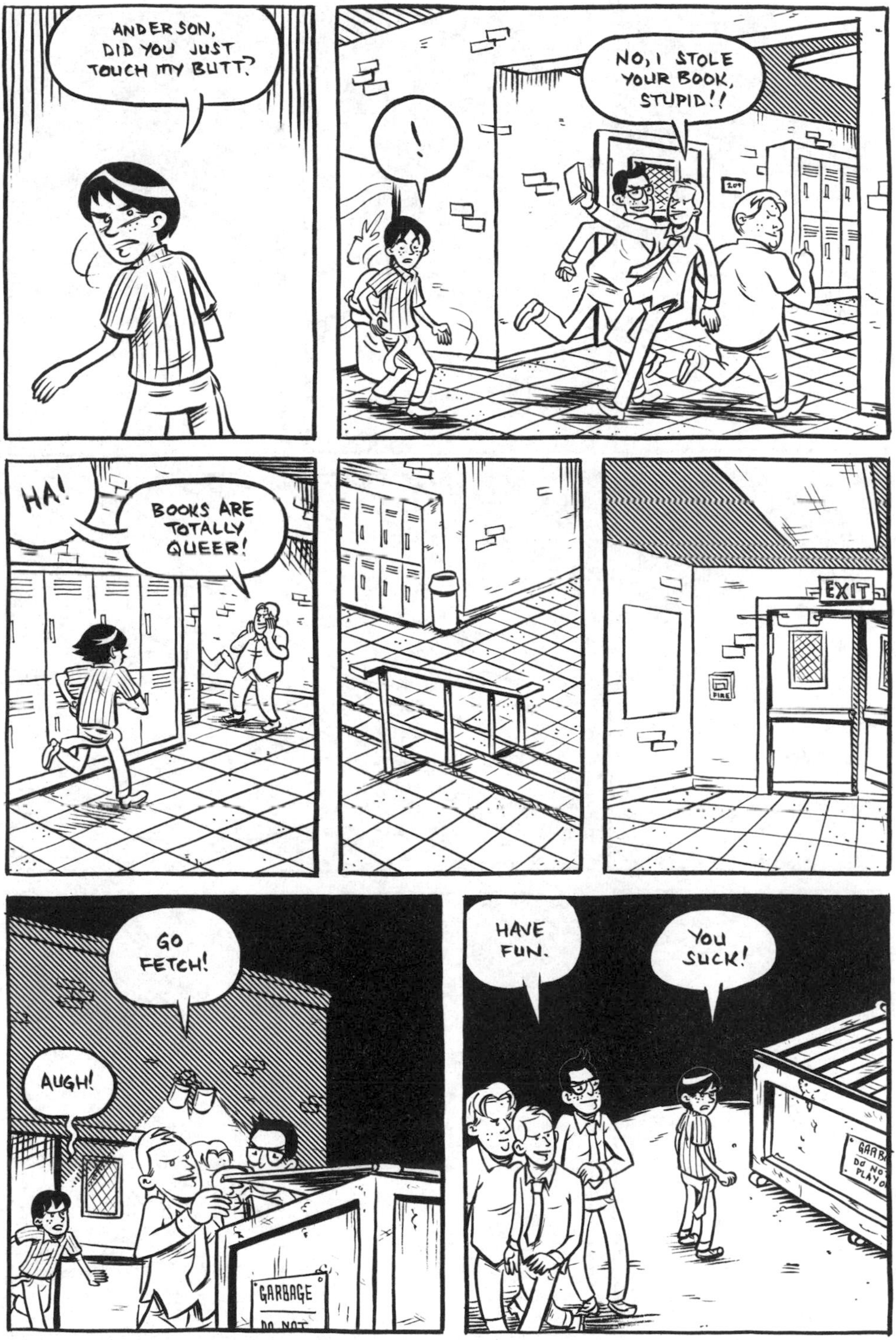
ANDERSON, DID YOU JUST TOUCH MY BUTT?
!
NO, I STOLE YOUR BOOK, STUPID!!
HA!
BOOKS ARE TOTALLY QUEER!
EXIT
FIRE
GO FETCH!
AUGH!
GARBAGE
HAVE FUN.
YOU SUCK!

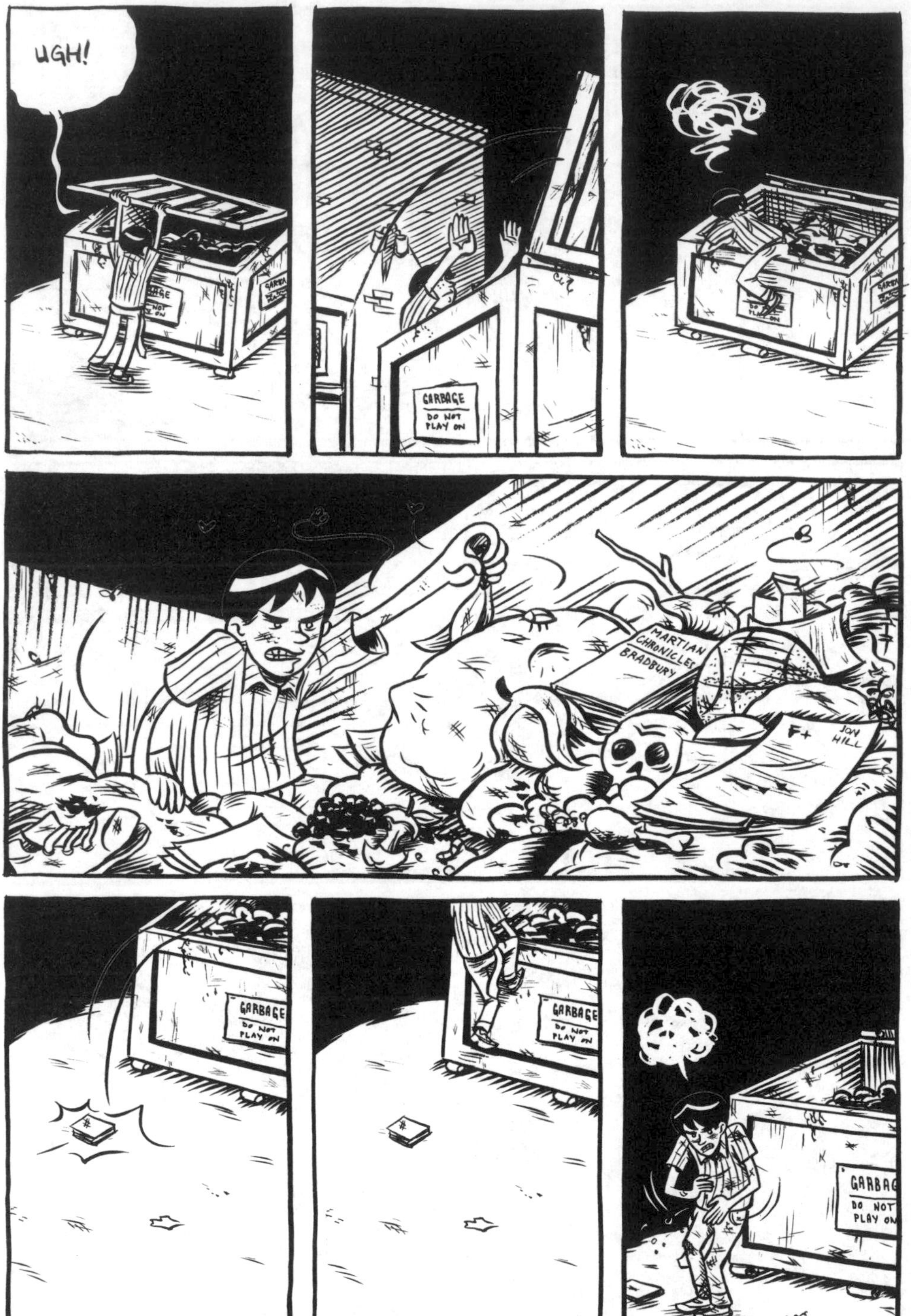
UGH!
GARBAGE
DO NOT PLAY ON
MARTIAN CHRONICLES BRADBURY
F+
JON HILL
GARBAGE
DO NOT PLAY ON
GARBAGE
DO NOT PLAY ON
GARBAGE
DO NOT PLAY ON

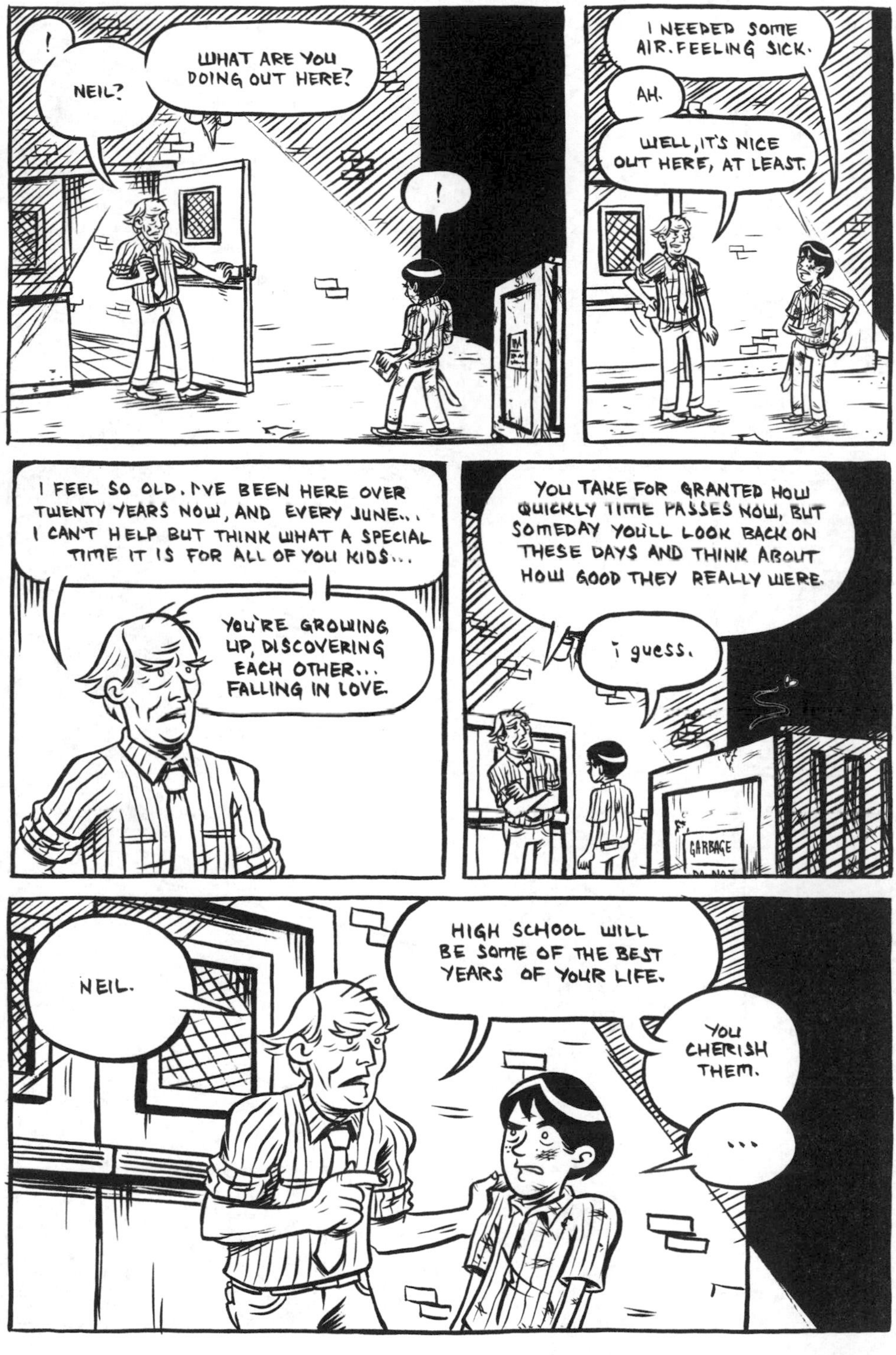
!
NEIL?
WHAT ARE YOU DOING OUT HERE?
!
I NEEDED SOME AIR. FEELING SICK.
AH.
WELL, IT'S NICE OUT HERE, AT LEAST.
I FEEL SO OLD. I'VE BEEN HERE OVER TWENTY YEARS NOW, AND EVERY JUNE... I CAN'T HELP BUT THINK WHAT A SPECIAL TIME IT IS FOR ALL OF YOU KIDS...
YOU'RE GROWING UP, DISCOVERING EACH OTHER... FALLING IN LOVE.
YOU TAKE FOR GRANTED HOW QUICKLY TIME PASSES NOW, BUT SOMEDAY YOU'LL LOOK BACK ON THESE DAYS AND THINK ABOUT HOW GOOD THEY REALLY WERE.
i guess.
GARBAGE
NEIL.
HIGH SCHOOL WILL BE SOME OF THE BEST YEARS OF YOUR LIFE.
YOU CHERISH THEM.
...

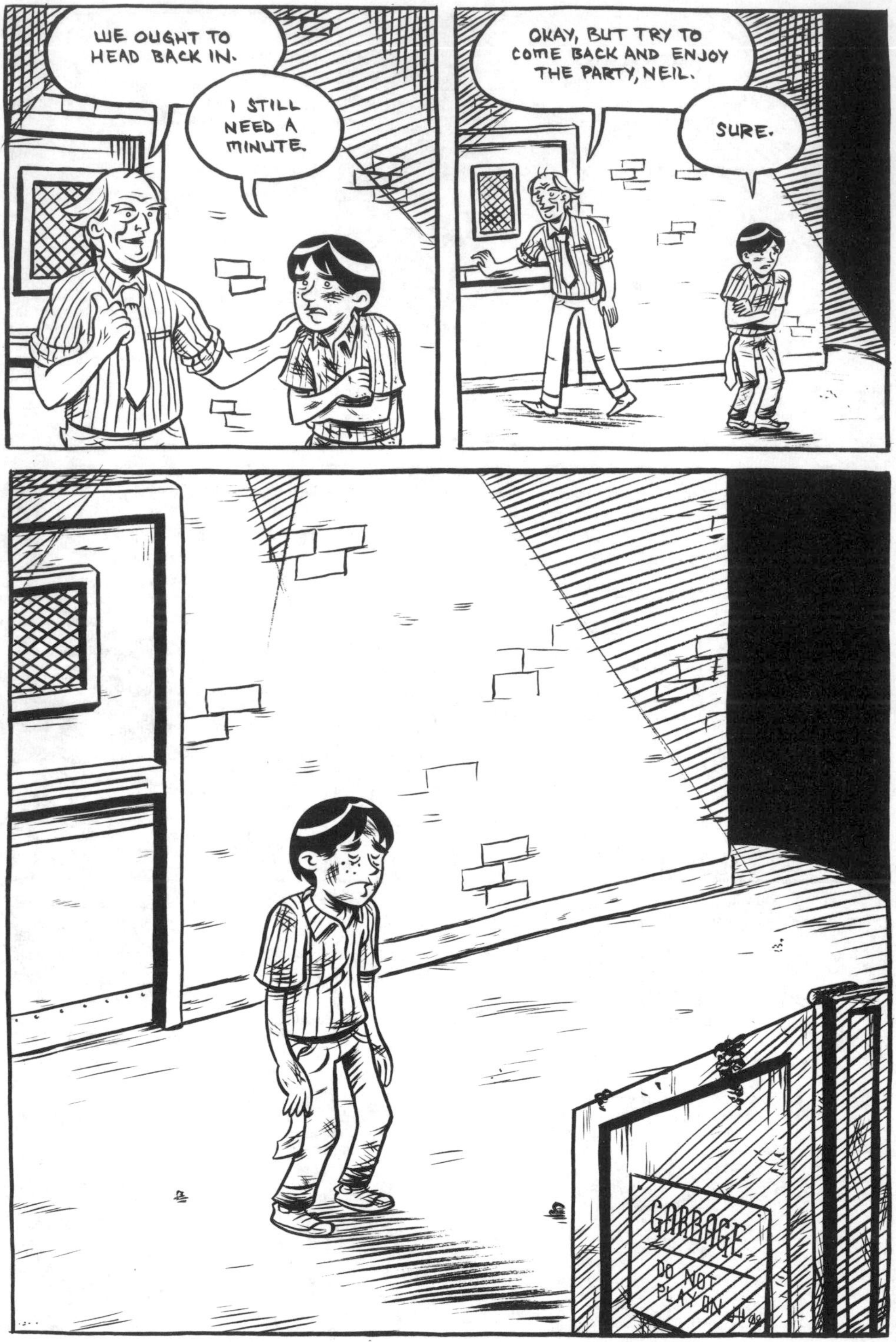
WE OUGHT TO HEAD BACK IN.
I STILL NEED A MINUTE.
OKAY, BUT TRY TO COME BACK AND ENJOY THE PARTY, NEIL.
SURE.
GARBAGE
DO NOT PLAY ON

CHAPTER 2

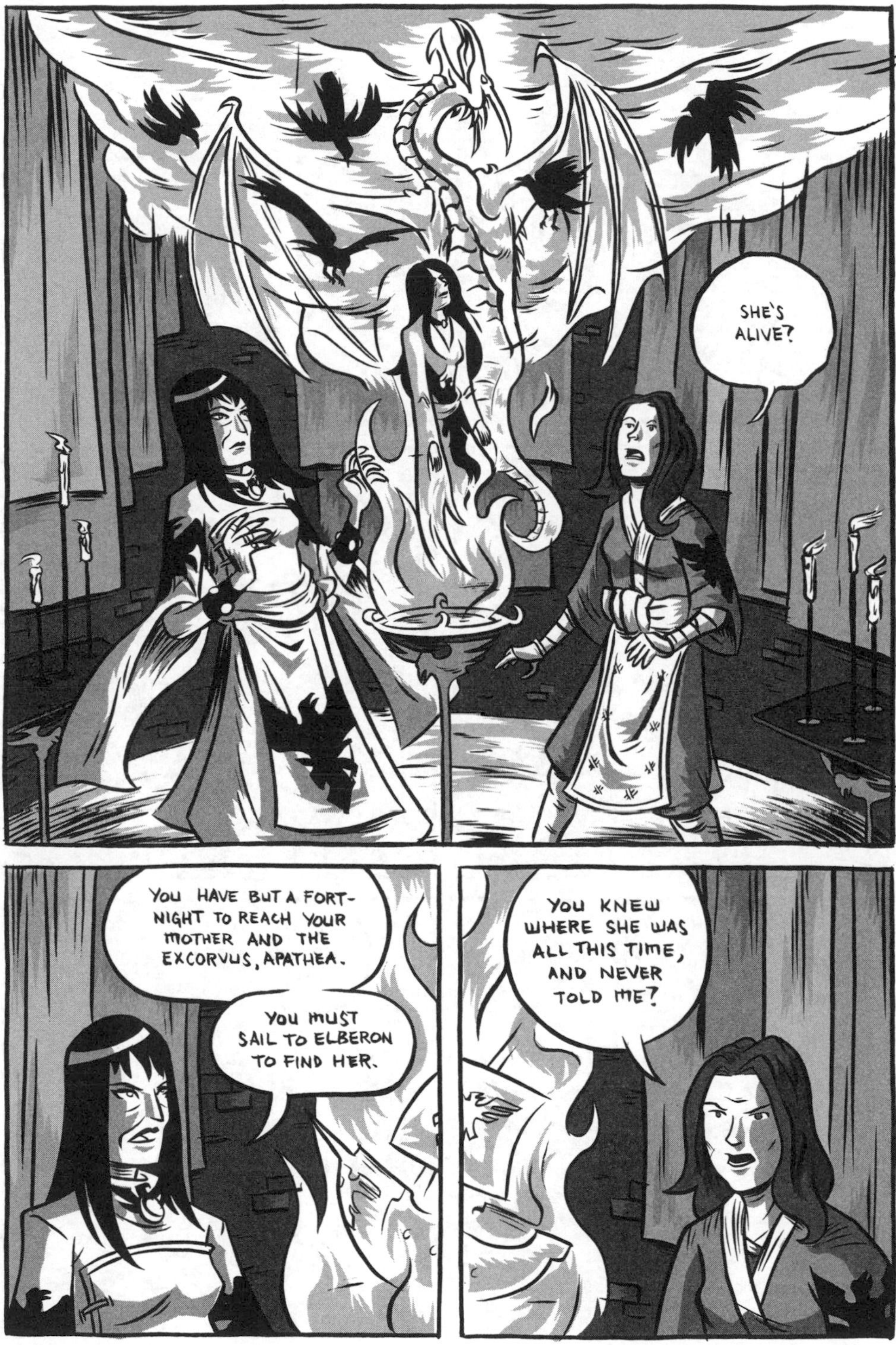
SHE'S ALIVE?
YOU HAVE BUT A FORTNIGHT TO REACH YOUR MOTHER AND THE EXCORVUS, APATHEA.
YOU MUST SAIL TO ELBERON TO FIND HER.
YOU KNEW WHERE SHE WAS ALL THIS TIME, AND NEVER TOLD ME?

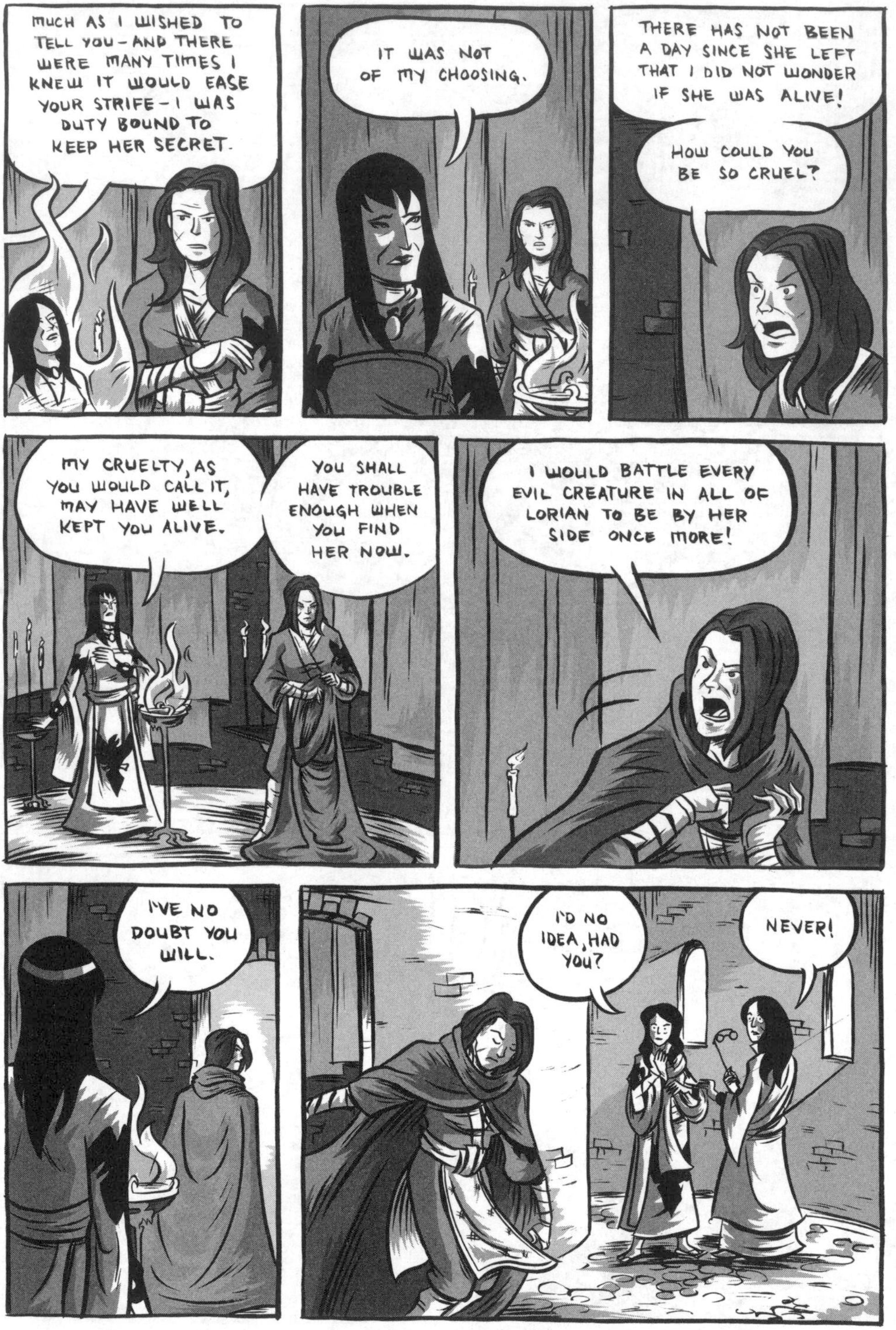
MUCH AS I WISHED TO TELL YOU - AND THERE WERE MANY TIMES I KNEW IT WOULD EASE YOUR STRIFE - I WAS DUTY BOUND TO KEEP HER SECRET.
IT WAS NOT OF MY CHOOSING.
THERE HAS NOT BEEN A DAY SINCE SHE LEFT THAT I DID NOT WONDER IF SHE WAS ALIVE!
HOW COULD YOU BE SO CRUEL?
MY CRUELTY, AS YOU WOULD CALL IT, MAY HAVE WELL KEPT YOU ALIVE.
YOU SHALL HAVE TROUBLE ENOUGH WHEN YOU FIND HER NOW.
I WOULD BATTLE EVERY EVIL CREATURE IN ALL OF LORIAN TO BE BY HER SIDE ONCE MORE!
I'VE NO DOUBT YOU WILL.
I'D NO IDEA, HAD YOU?
NEVER!

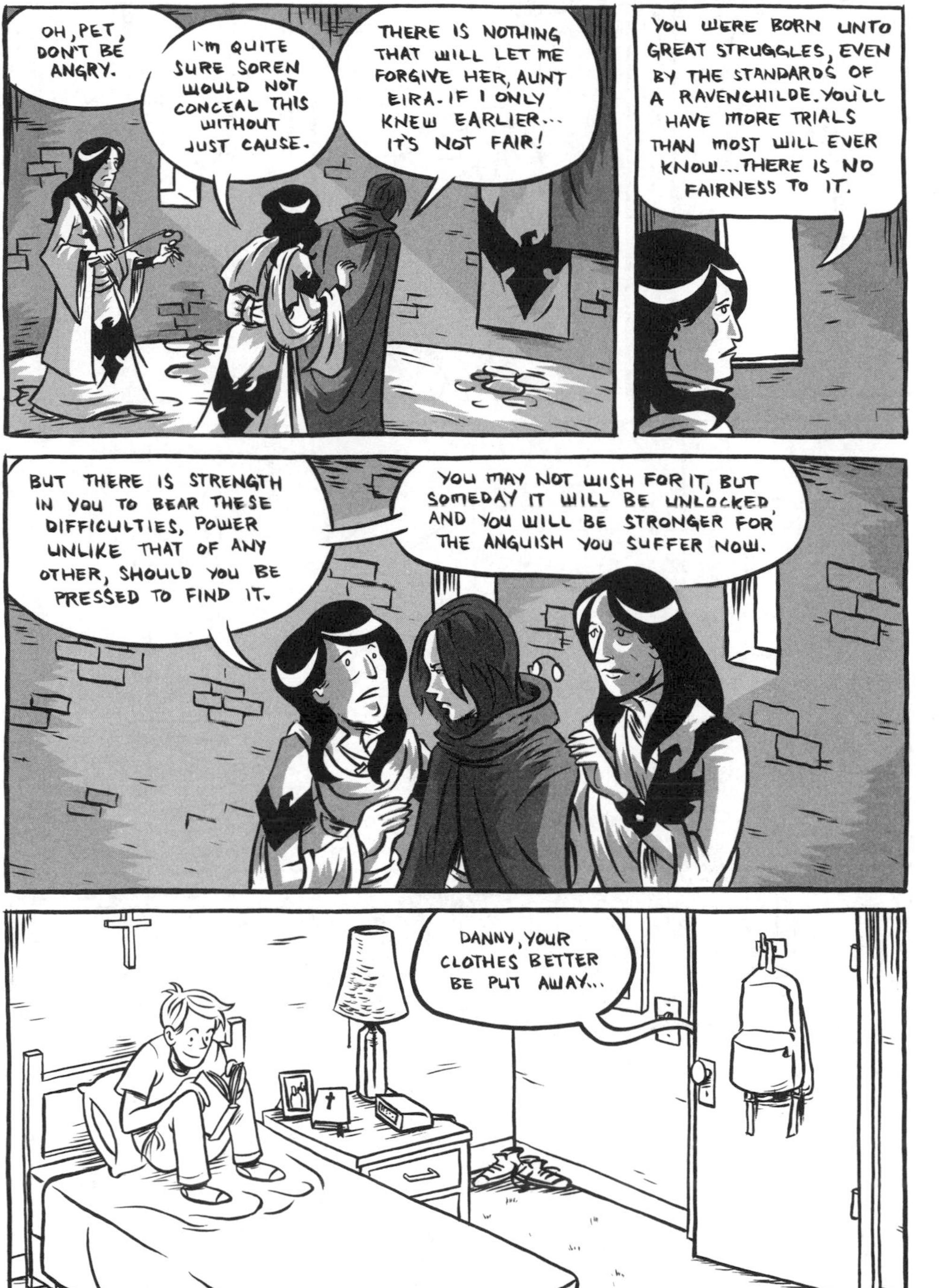
OH, PET, DON'T BE ANGRY.
I'M QUITE SURE SOREN WOULD NOT CONCEAL THIS WITHOUT JUST CAUSE.
THERE IS NOTHING THAT WILL LET ME FORGIVE HER, AUNT EIRA. IF I ONLY KNEW EARLIER... IT'S NOT FAIR!
YOU WERE BORN UNTO GREAT STRUGGLES, EVEN BY THE STANDARDS OF A RAVENCHILDE. YOU'LL HAVE MORE TRIALS THAN MOST WILL EVER KNOW... THERE IS NO FAIRNESS TO IT.
BUT THERE IS STRENGTH IN YOU TO BEAR THESE DIFFICULTIES, POWER UNLIKE THAT OF ANY OTHER, SHOULD YOU BE PRESSED TO FIND IT.
YOU MAY NOT WISH FOR IT, BUT SOMEDAY IT WILL BE UNLOCKED, AND YOU WILL BE STRONGER FOR THE ANGUISH YOU SUFFER NOW.
DANNY, YOUR CLOTHES BETTER BE PUT AWAY...

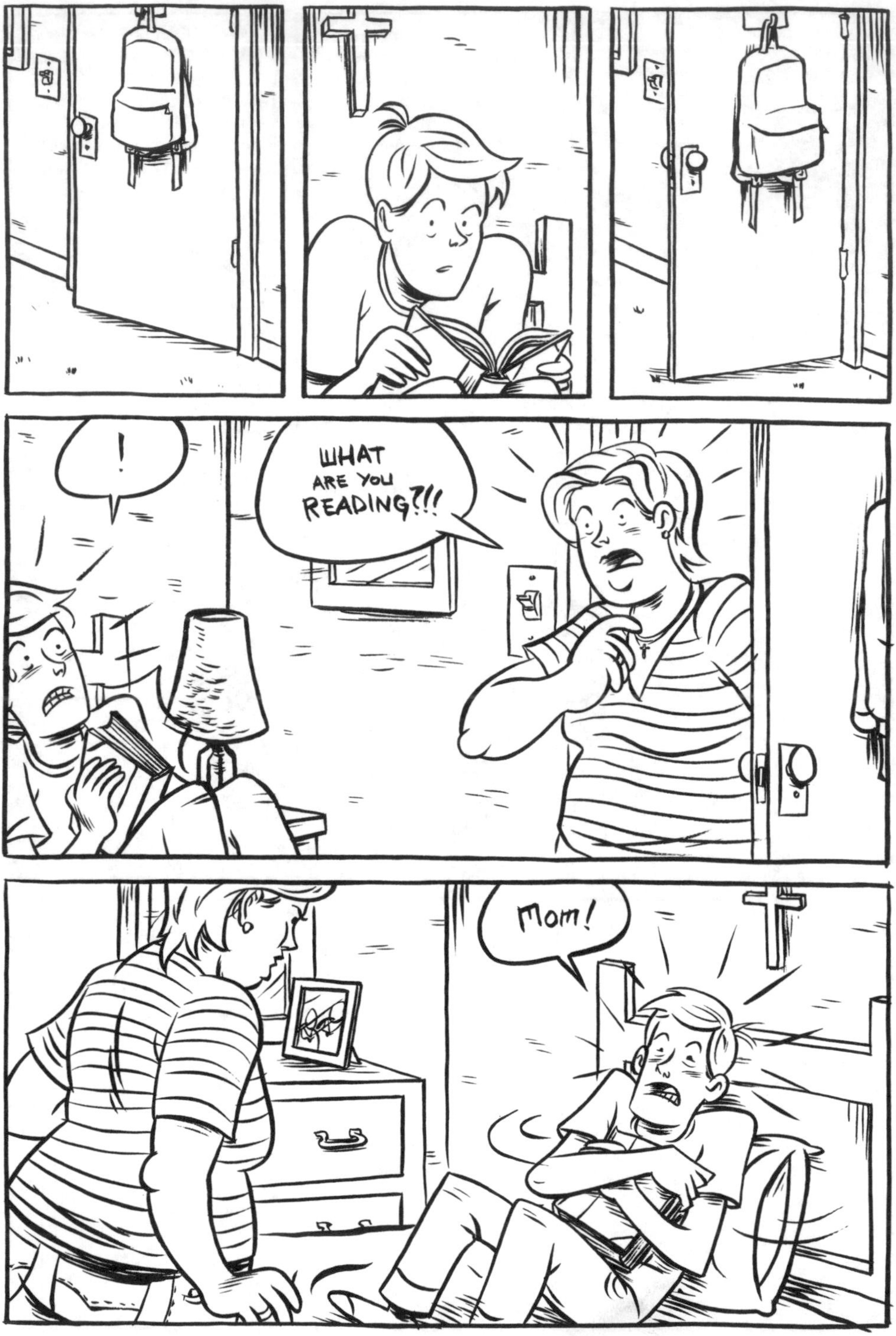
!
WHAT ARE YOU READING?!!
Mom!

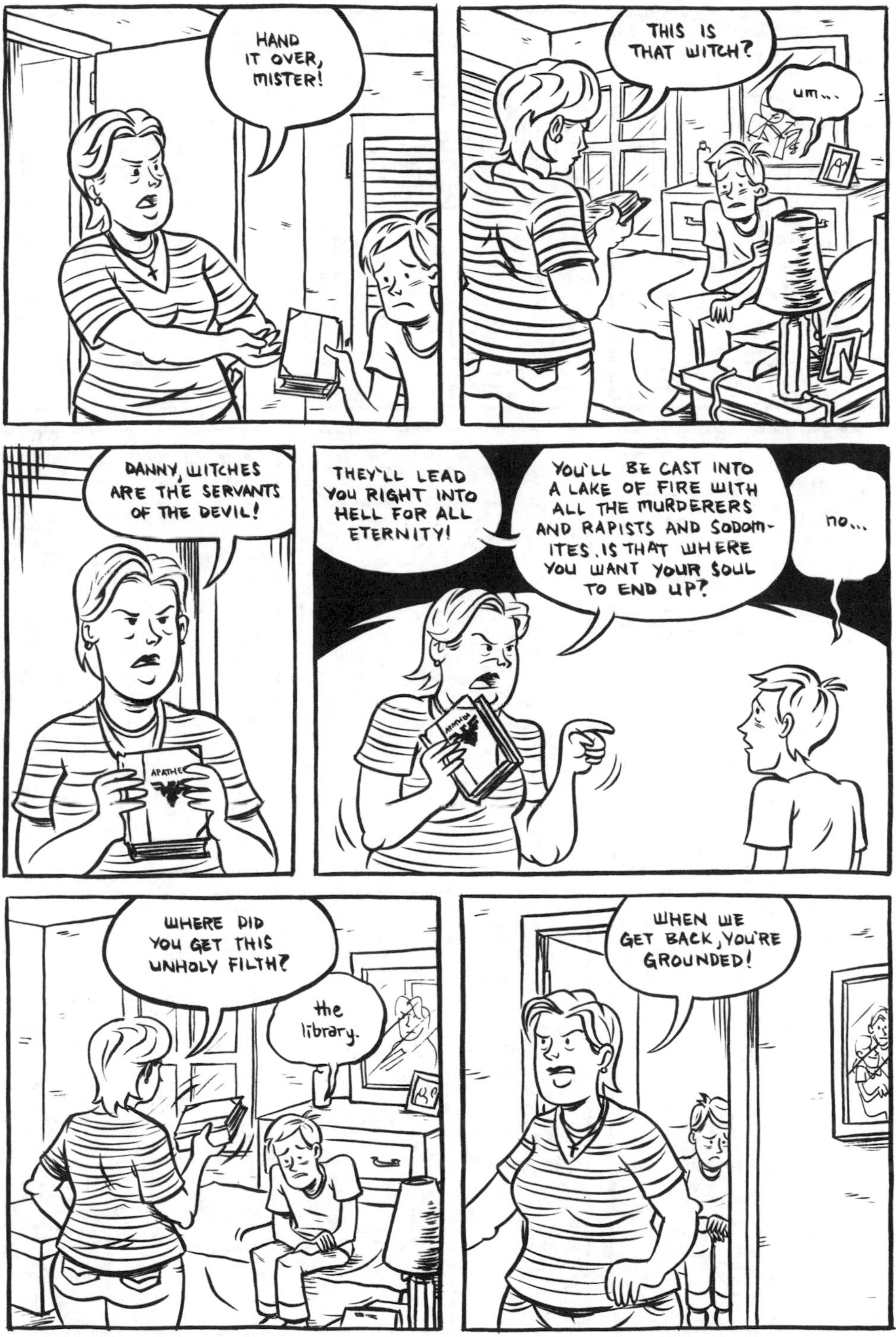
HAND IT OVER, MISTER!
THIS IS THAT WITCH?
um...
DANNY, WITCHES ARE THE SERVANTS OF THE DEVIL!
APATHE
THEY'LL LEAD YOU RIGHT INTO HELL FOR ALL ETERNITY!
YOU'LL BE CAST INTO A LAKE OF FIRE WITH ALL THE MURDERERS AND RAPISTS AND SODOMITES. IS THAT WHERE YOU WANT YOUR SOUL TO END UP?
no...
WHERE DID YOU GET THIS UNHOLY FILTH?
the library.
WHEN WE GET BACK, YOU'RE GROUNDED!

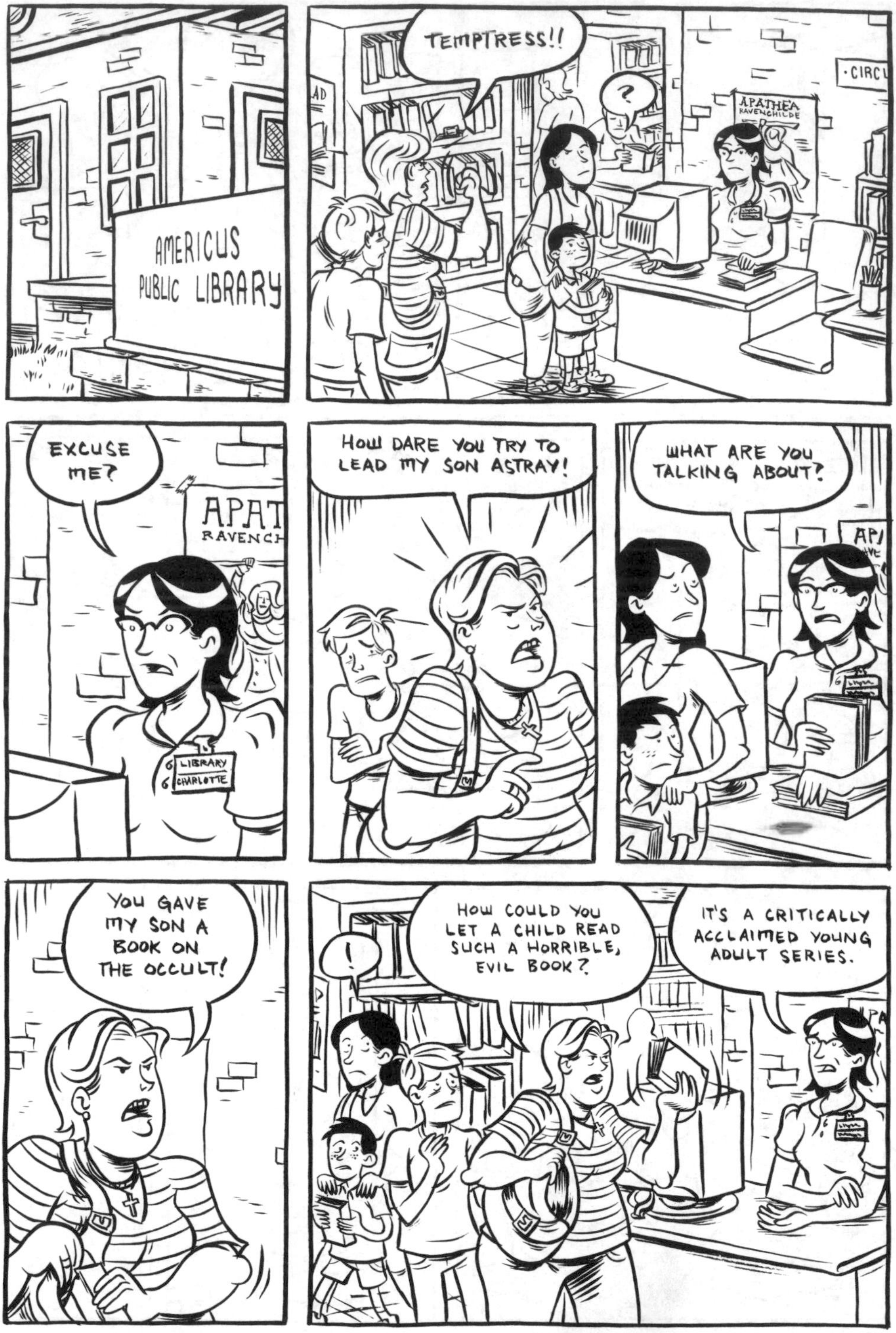
AMERICUS PUBLIC LIBRARY
TEMPTRESS!!
?
APATHEA RAVENCHILDE
·CIRCU
EXCUSE ME?
LIBRARY
CHARLOTTE
HOW DARE YOU TRY TO LEAD MY SON ASTRAY!
WHAT ARE YOU TALKING ABOUT?
YOU GAVE MY SON A BOOK ON THE OCCULT!
!
HOW COULD YOU LET A CHILD READ SUCH A HORRIBLE, EVIL BOOK?
IT'S A CRITICALLY ACCLAIMED YOUNG ADULT SERIES.

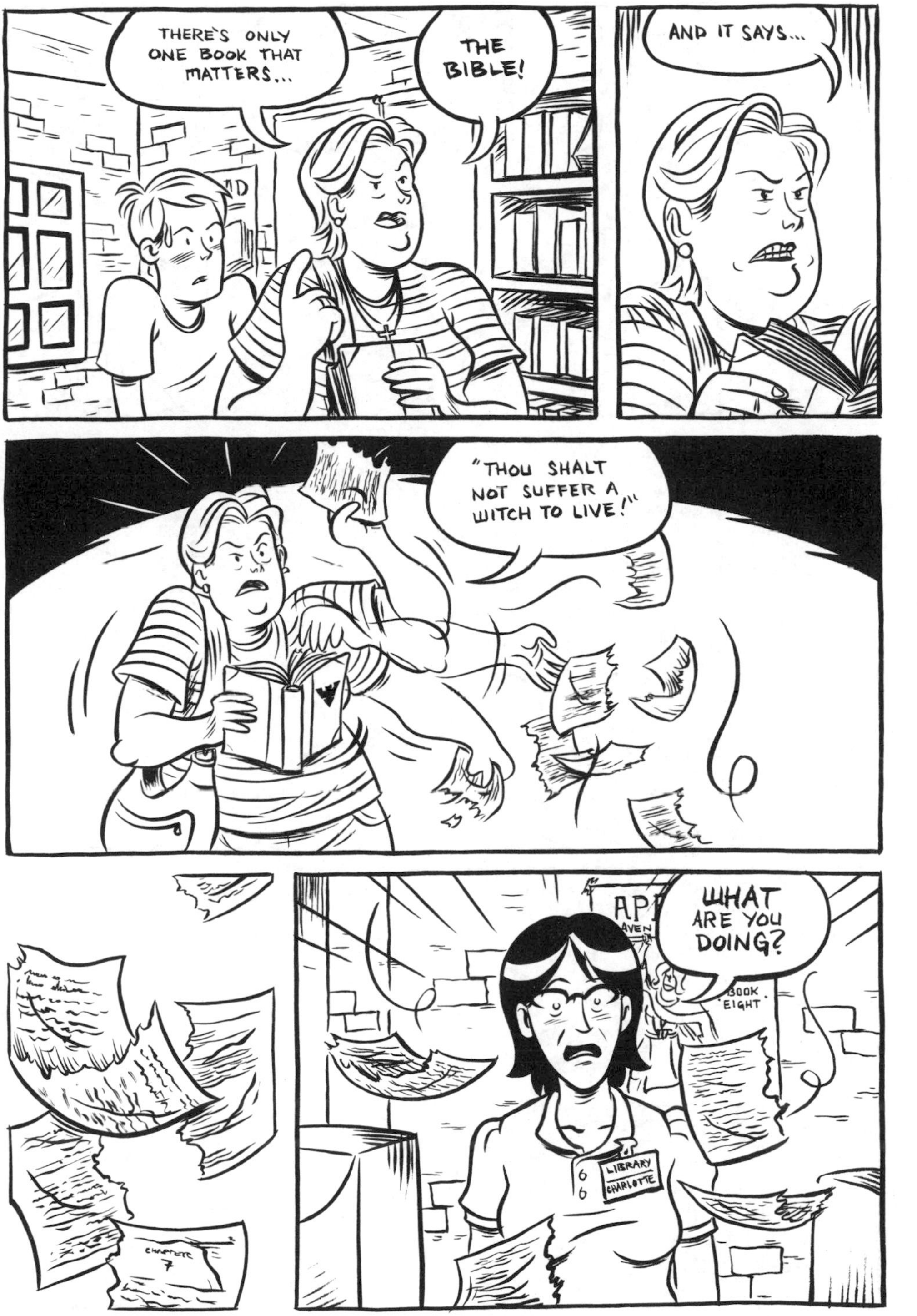
THERE'S ONLY ONE BOOK THAT MATTERS...
THE BIBLE!
AND IT SAYS...
"THOU SHALT NOT SUFFER A WITCH TO LIVE!"
CHAPTER 7
WHAT ARE YOU DOING?
BOOK EIGHT
LIBRARY
CHARLOTTE

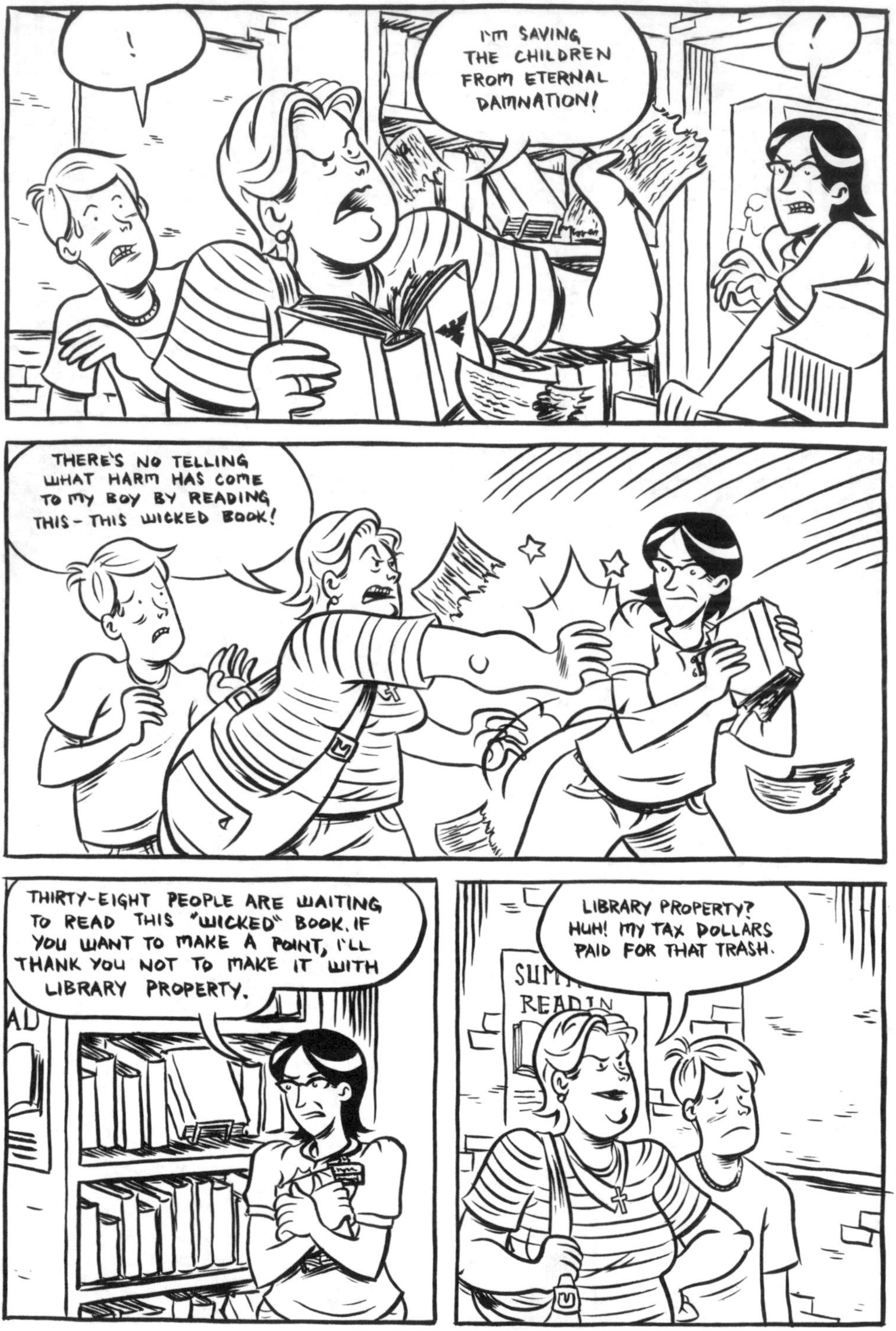
!
I'M SAVING THE CHILDREN FROM ETERNAL DAMNATION!
!
THERE'S NO TELLING WHAT HARM HAS COME TO MY BOY BY READING THIS - THIS WICKED BOOK!
THIRTY-EIGHT PEOPLE ARE WAITING TO READ THIS "WICKED" BOOK. IF YOU WANT TO MAKE A POINT, I'LL THANK YOU NOT TO MAKE IT WITH LIBRARY PROPERTY.
LIBRARY PROPERTY? HUH! MY TAX DOLLARS PAID FOR THAT TRASH.

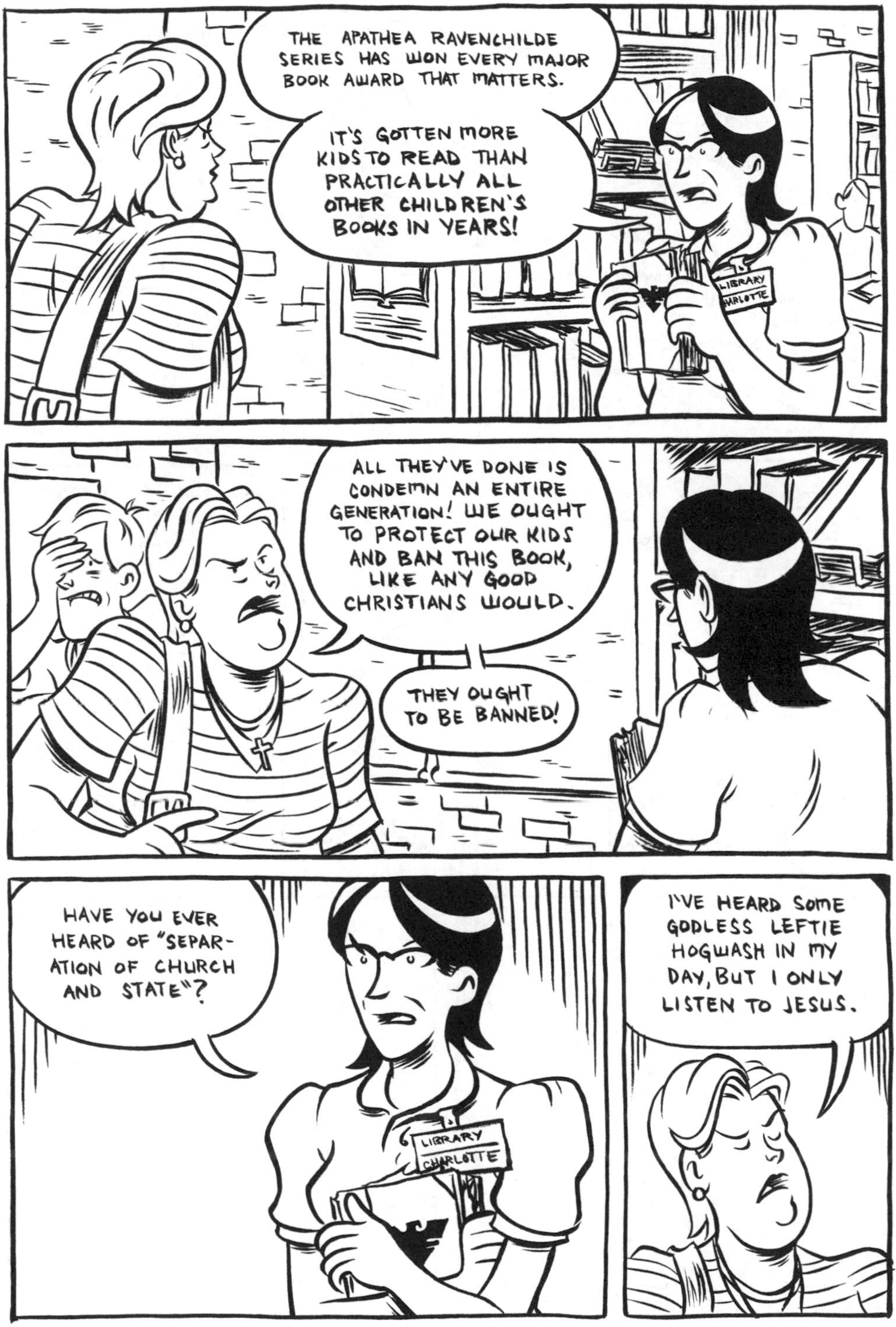
THE APATHEA RAVENCHILDE SERIES HAS WON EVERY MAJOR BOOK AWARD THAT MATTERS.
IT'S GOTTEN MORE KIDS TO READ THAN PRACTICALLY ALL OTHER CHILDREN'S BOOKS IN YEARS!
LIBRARY CHARLOTTE
ALL THEY'VE DONE IS CONDEMN AN ENTIRE GENERATION! WE OUGHT TO PROTECT OUR KIDS AND BAN THIS BOOK, LIKE ANY GOOD CHRISTIANS WOULD.
THEY OUGHT TO BE BANNED!
HAVE YOU EVER HEARD OF "SEPARATION OF CHURCH AND STATE"?
LIBRARY CHARLOTTE
I'VE HEARD SOME GODLESS LEFTIE HOGWASH IN MY DAY, BUT I ONLY LISTEN TO JESUS.

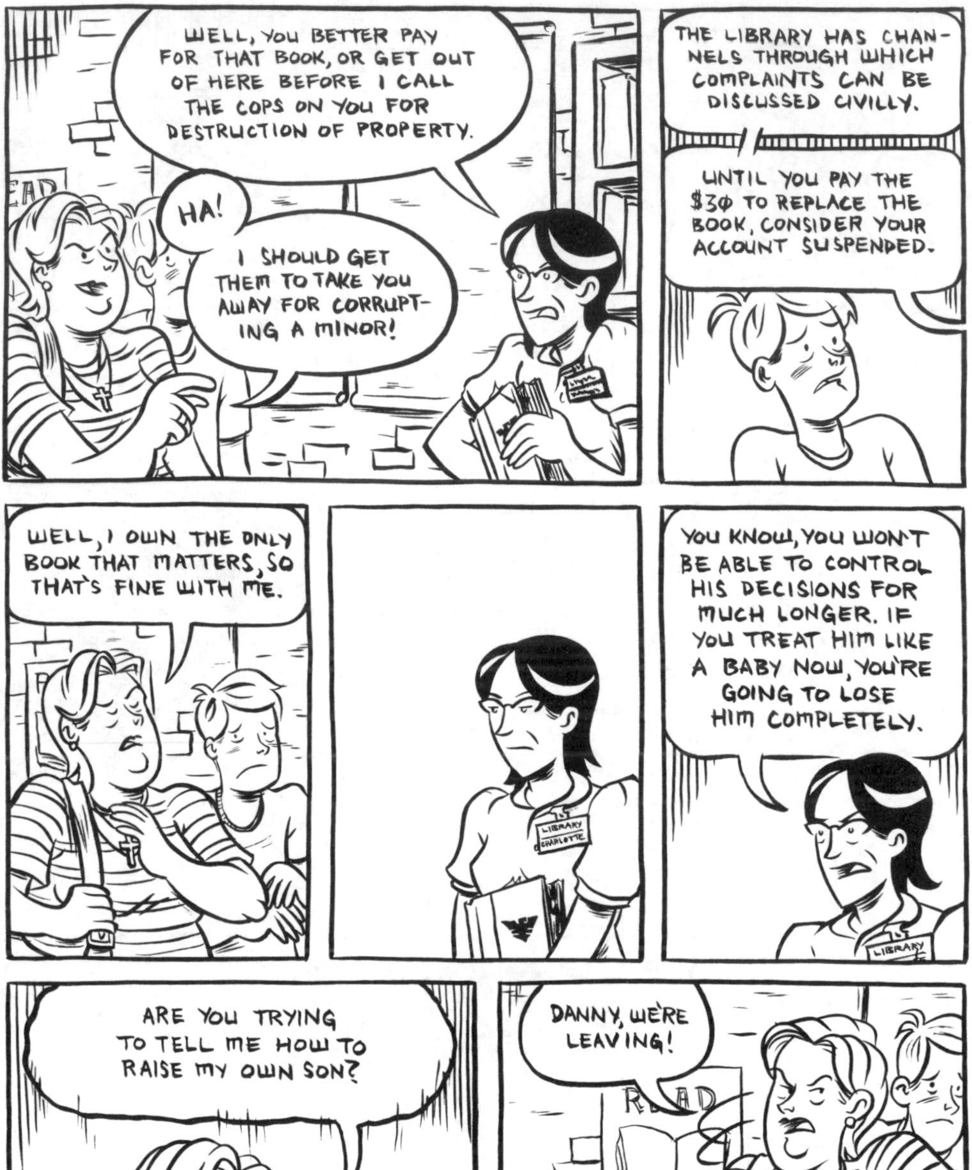
WELL, YOU BETTER PAY FOR THAT BOOK, OR GET OUT OF HERE BEFORE I CALL THE COPS ON YOU FOR DESTRUCTION OF PROPERTY.
HA!
I SHOULD GET THEM TO TAKE YOU AWAY FOR CORRUPTING A MINOR!
THE LIBRARY HAS CHANNELS THROUGH WHICH COMPLAINTS CAN BE DISCUSSED CIVILLY.
UNTIL YOU PAY THE $30 TO REPLACE THE BOOK, CONSIDER YOUR ACCOUNT SUSPENDED.
WELL, I OWN THE ONLY BOOK THAT MATTERS, SO THAT'S FINE WITH ME.
LIBRARY
CHARLOTTE
YOU KNOW, YOU WON'T BE ABLE TO CONTROL HIS DECISIONS FOR MUCH LONGER. IF YOU TREAT HIM LIKE A BABY NOW, YOU'RE GOING TO LOSE HIM COMPLETELY.
LIBRARY
ARE YOU TRYING TO TELL ME HOW TO RAISE MY OWN SON?
DANNY, WE'RE LEAVING!
READ

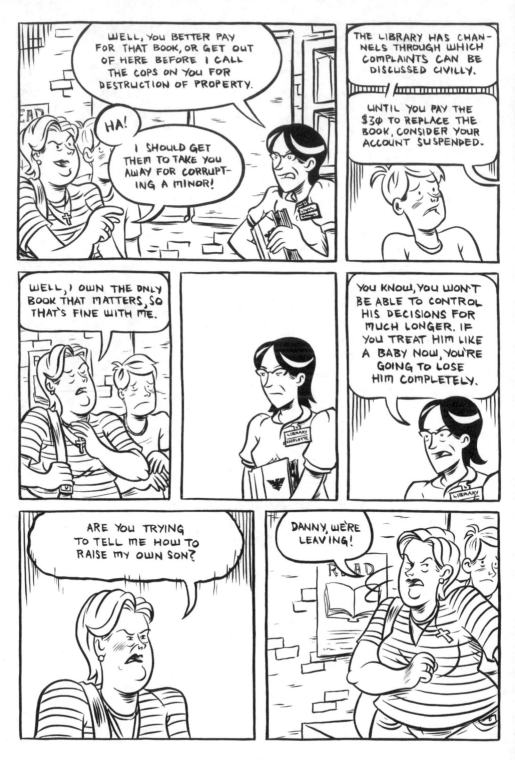

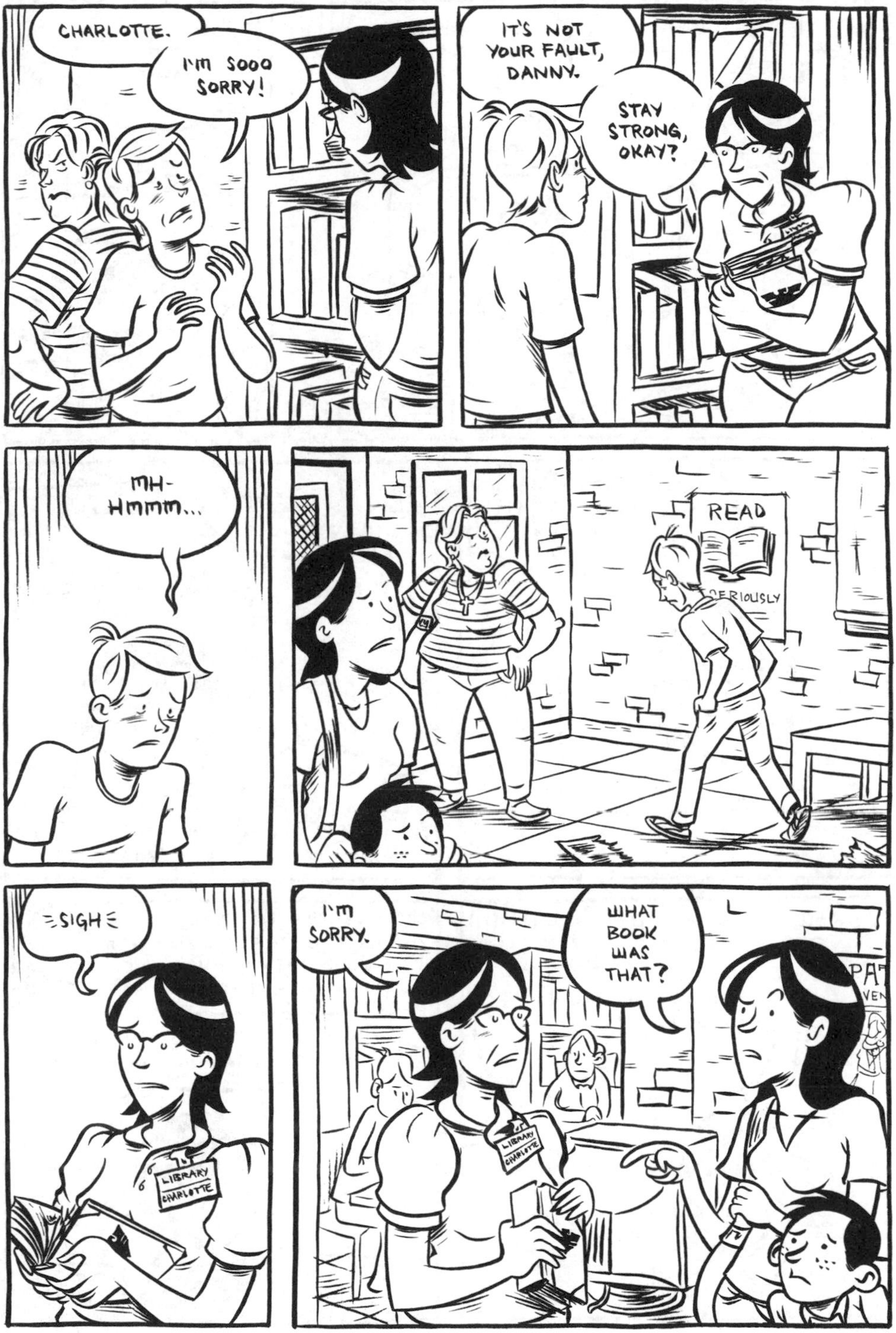
CHARLOTTE.
I'M SOOO SORRY!
IT'S NOT YOUR FAULT, DANNY.
STAY STRONG, OKAY?
MH-HMMM...
READ
SERIOUSLY
≡SIGH≡
LIBRARY CHARLOTTE
I'M SORRY.
WHAT BOOK WAS THAT?
LIBRARY CHARLOTTE

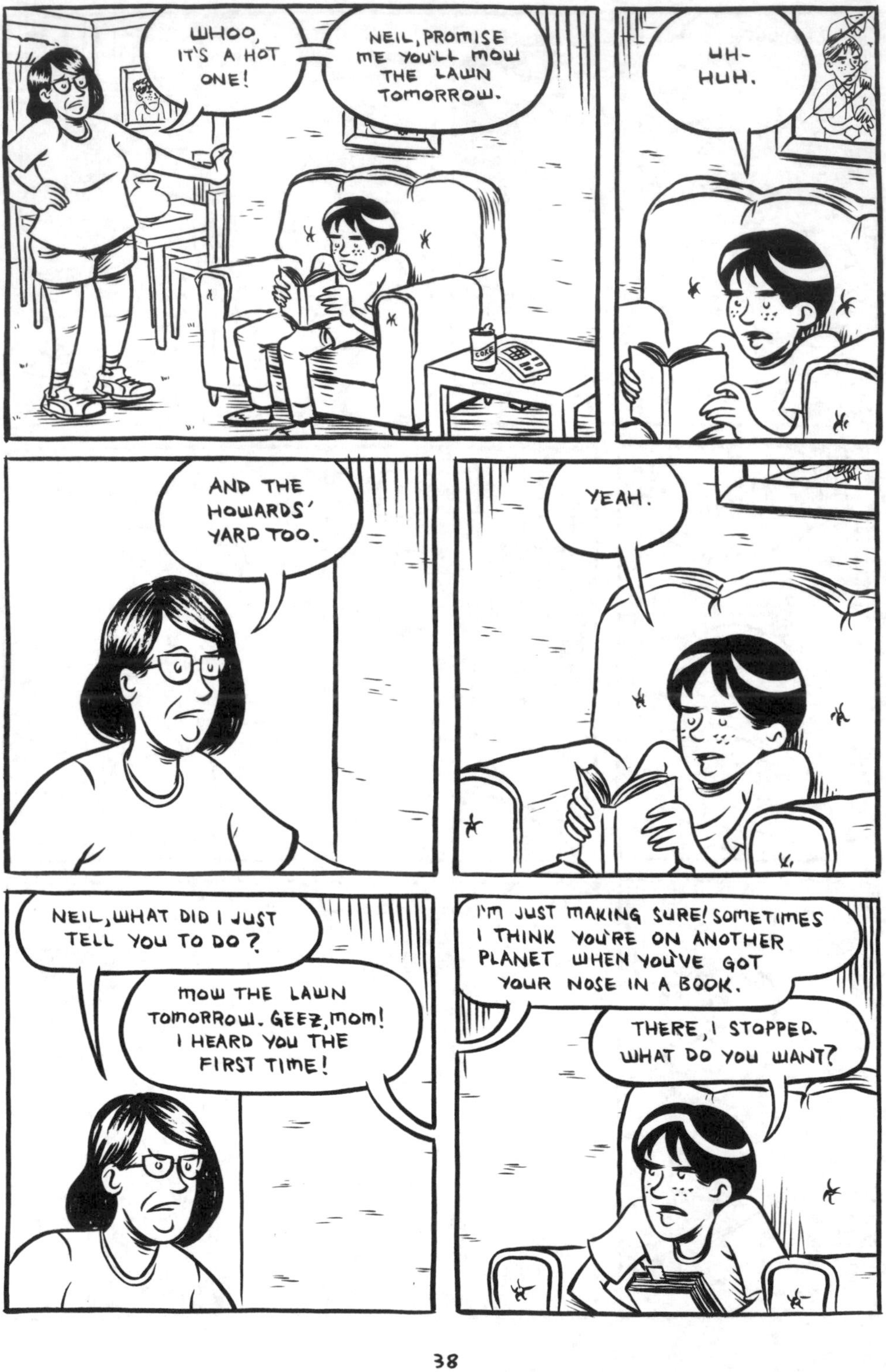

WHOO, IT'S A HOT ONE!
NEIL, PROMISE ME YOU'LL MOW THE LAWN TOMORROW.
COKE
UH-HUH.
AND THE HOWARDS' YARD TOO.
YEAH.
NEIL, WHAT DID I JUST TELL YOU TO DO?
MOW THE LAWN TOMORROW. GEEZ, MOM! I HEARD YOU THE FIRST TIME!
I'M JUST MAKING SURE! SOMETIMES I THINK YOU'RE ON ANOTHER PLANET WHEN YOU'VE GOT YOUR NOSE IN A BOOK.
THERE, I STOPPED. WHAT DO YOU WANT?

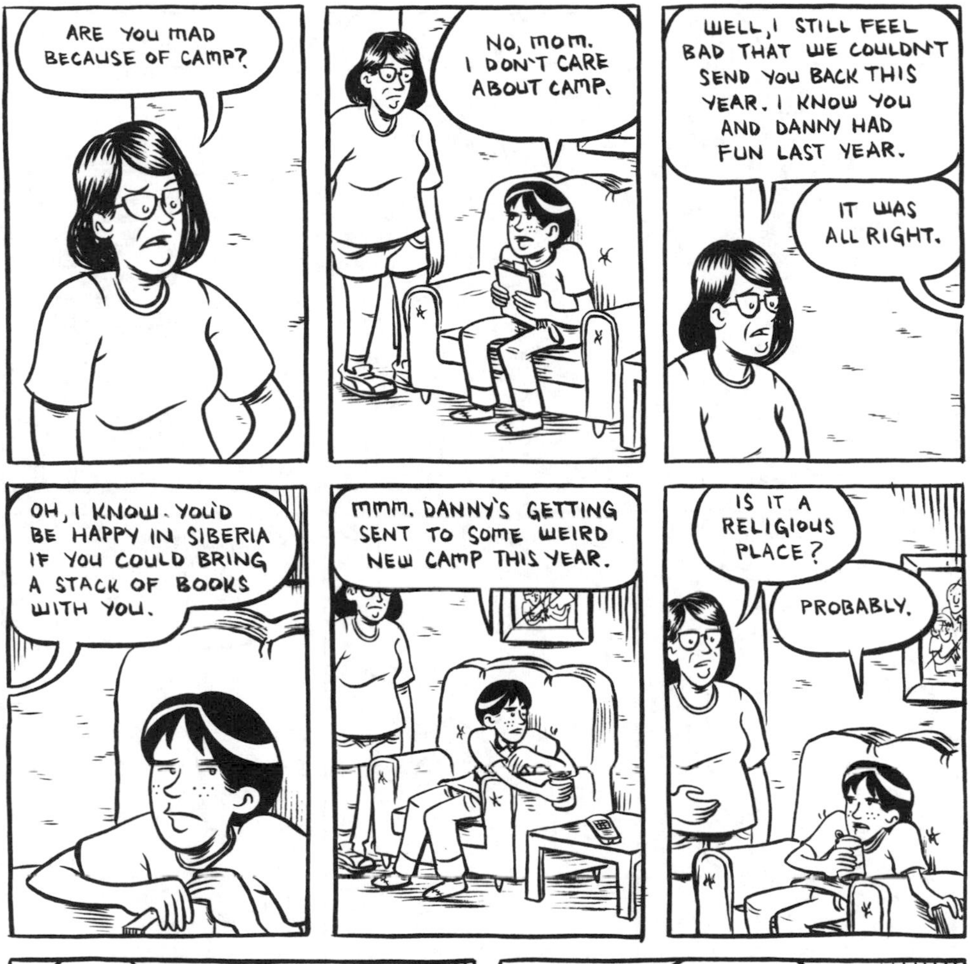
ARE YOU MAD BECAUSE OF CAMP?
NO, MOM. I DON'T CARE ABOUT CAMP.
WELL, I STILL FEEL BAD THAT WE COULDN'T SEND YOU BACK THIS YEAR. I KNOW YOU AND DANNY HAD FUN LAST YEAR.
IT WAS ALL RIGHT.
OH, I KNOW. YOU'D BE HAPPY IN SIBERIA IF YOU COULD BRING A STACK OF BOOKS WITH YOU.
MMM. DANNY'S GETTING SENT TO SOME WEIRD NEW CAMP THIS YEAR.
IS IT A RELIGIOUS PLACE?
PROBABLY.
HM
IS HE EXCITED ABOUT IT?
NOT REALLY.
. . . .

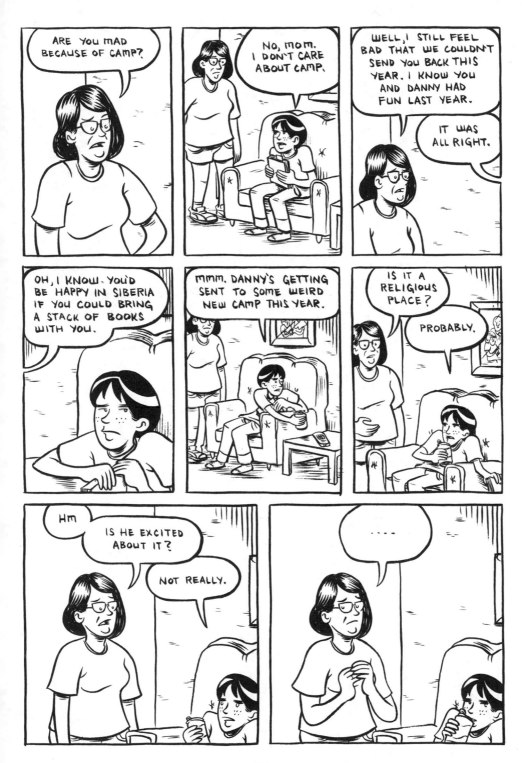

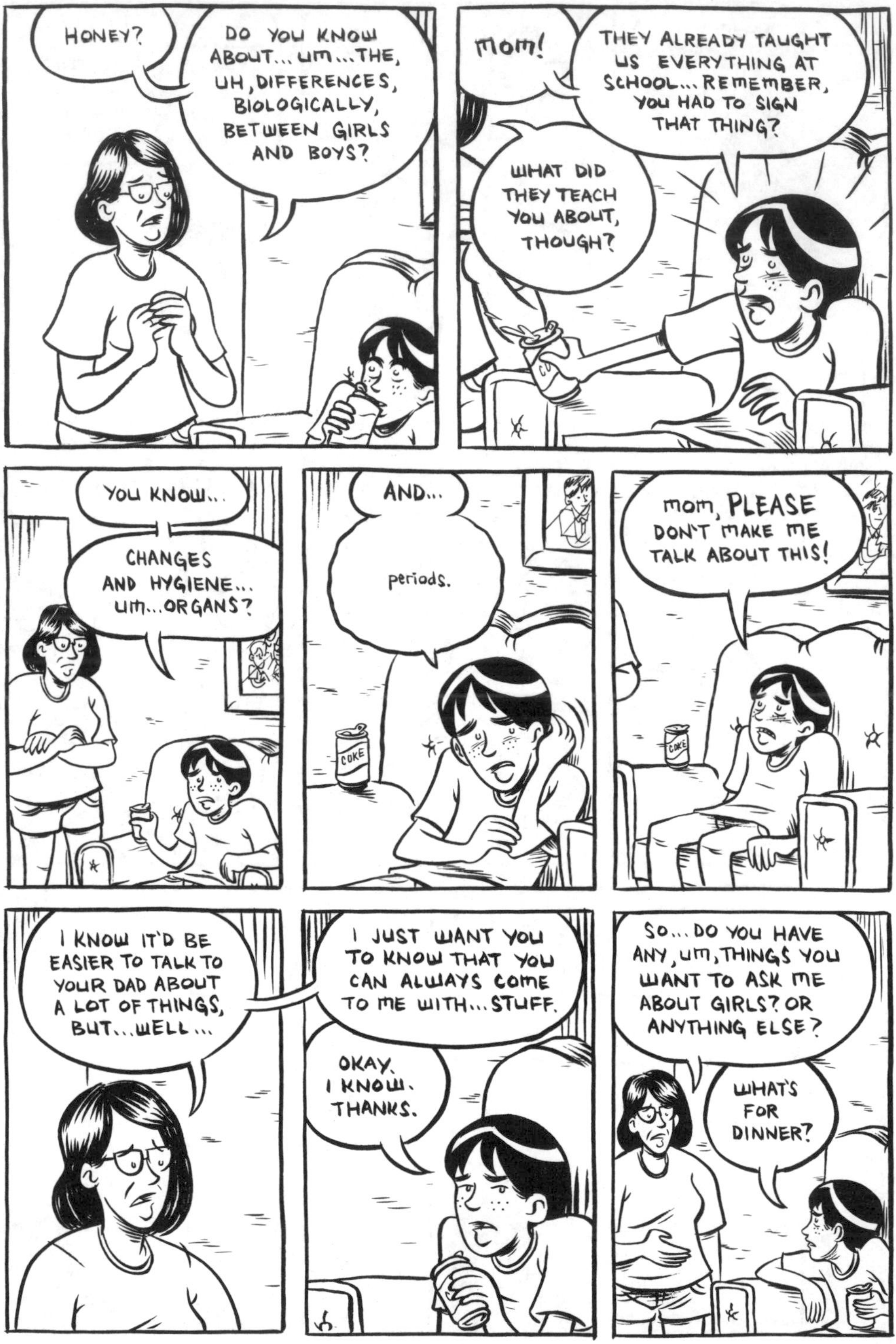
HONEY?
DO YOU KNOW ABOUT... UM... THE, UH, DIFFERENCES, BIOLOGICALLY, BETWEEN GIRLS AND BOYS?
MOM!
THEY ALREADY TAUGHT US EVERYTHING AT SCHOOL... REMEMBER, YOU HAD TO SIGN THAT THING?
WHAT DID THEY TEACH YOU ABOUT, THOUGH?
YOU KNOW...
CHANGES AND HYGIENE... UM...ORGANS?
AND...
periods.
COKE
MOM, PLEASE DON'T MAKE ME TALK ABOUT THIS!
COKE
I KNOW IT'D BE EASIER TO TALK TO YOUR DAD ABOUT A LOT OF THINGS, BUT...WELL...
I JUST WANT YOU TO KNOW THAT YOU CAN ALWAYS COME TO ME WITH...STUFF.
OKAY. I KNOW. THANKS.
SO... DO YOU HAVE ANY, UM, THINGS YOU WANT TO ASK ME ABOUT GIRLS? OR ANYTHING ELSE?
WHAT'S FOR DINNER?

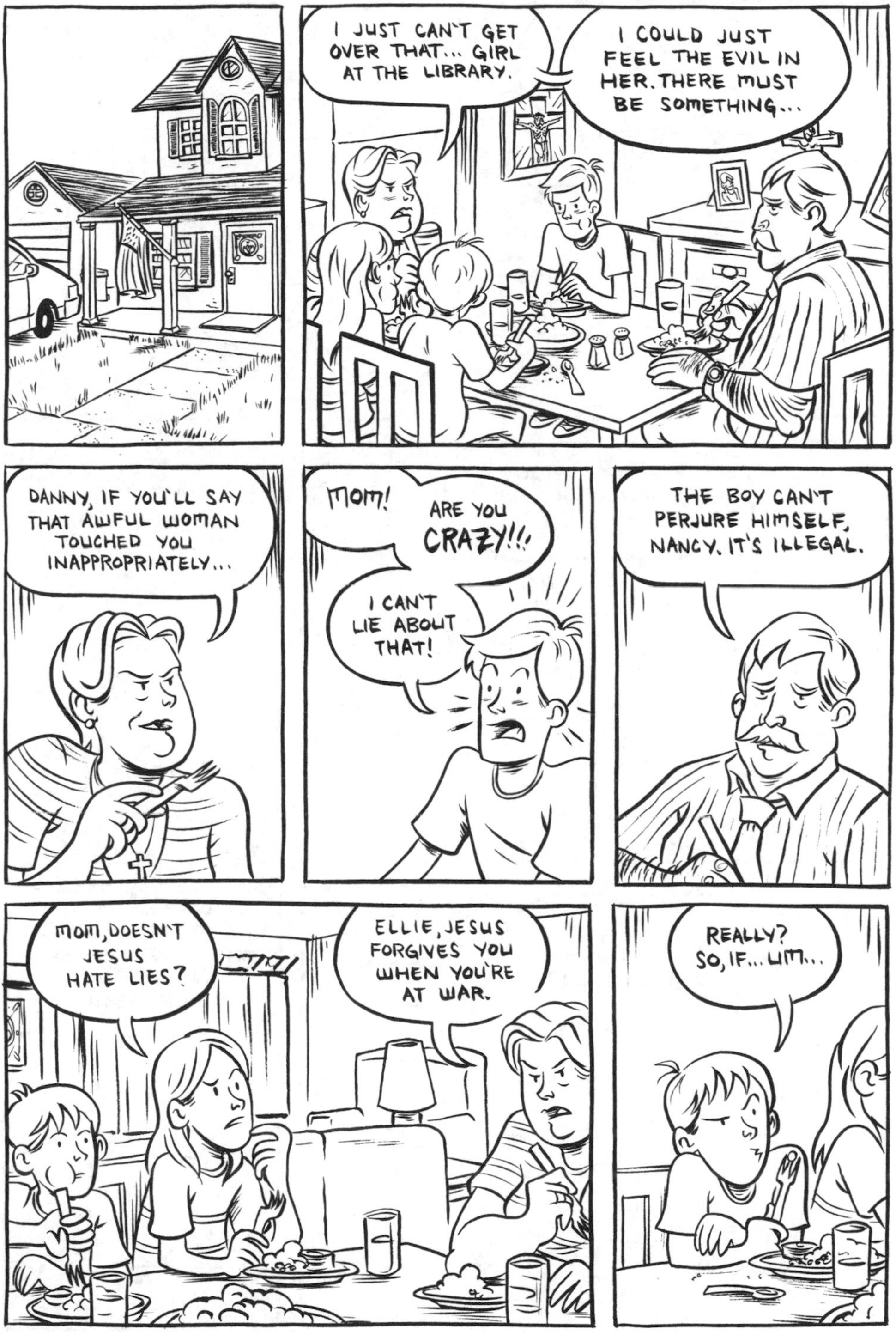
I JUST CAN'T GET OVER THAT... GIRL AT THE LIBRARY.
I COULD JUST FEEL THE EVIL IN HER. THERE MUST BE SOMETHING...
DANNY, IF YOU'LL SAY THAT AWFUL WOMAN TOUCHED YOU INAPPROPRIATELY...
MOM!
ARE YOU CRAZY!!!
I CAN'T LIE ABOUT THAT!
THE BOY CAN'T PERJURE HIMSELF, NANCY. IT'S ILLEGAL.
MOM, DOESN'T JESUS HATE LIES?
ELLIE, JESUS FORGIVES YOU WHEN YOU'RE AT WAR.
REALLY? SO, IF... UM...

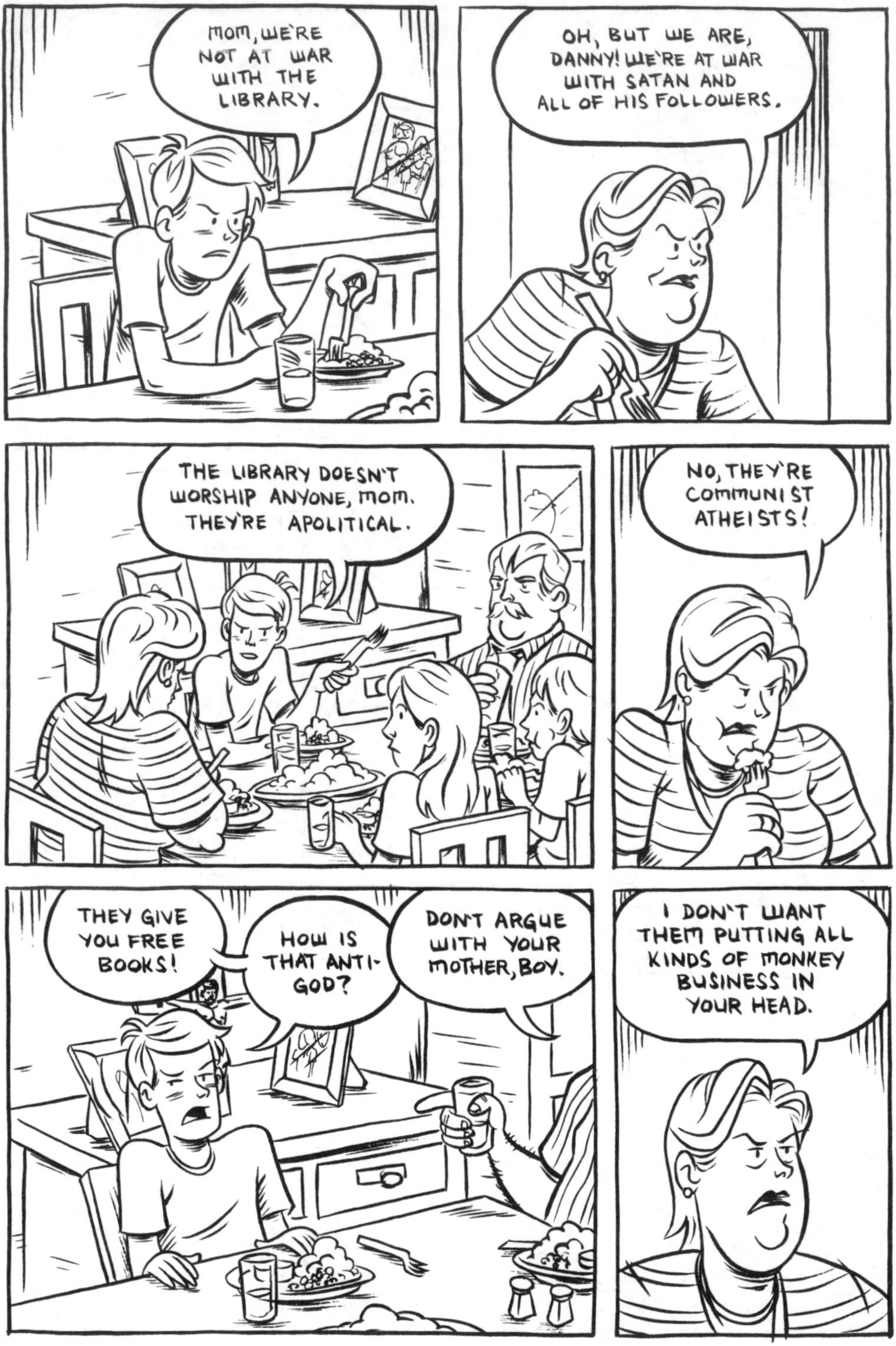
MOM, WE'RE NOT AT WAR WITH THE LIBRARY.
OH, BUT WE ARE, DANNY! WE'RE AT WAR WITH SATAN AND ALL OF HIS FOLLOWERS.
THE LIBRARY DOESN'T WORSHIP ANYONE, MOM. THEY'RE APOLITICAL.
NO, THEY'RE COMMUNIST ATHEISTS!
THEY GIVE YOU FREE BOOKS!
HOW IS THAT ANTI-GOD?
DON'T ARGUE WITH YOUR MOTHER, BOY.
I DON'T WANT THEM PUTTING ALL KINDS OF MONKEY BUSINESS IN YOUR HEAD.

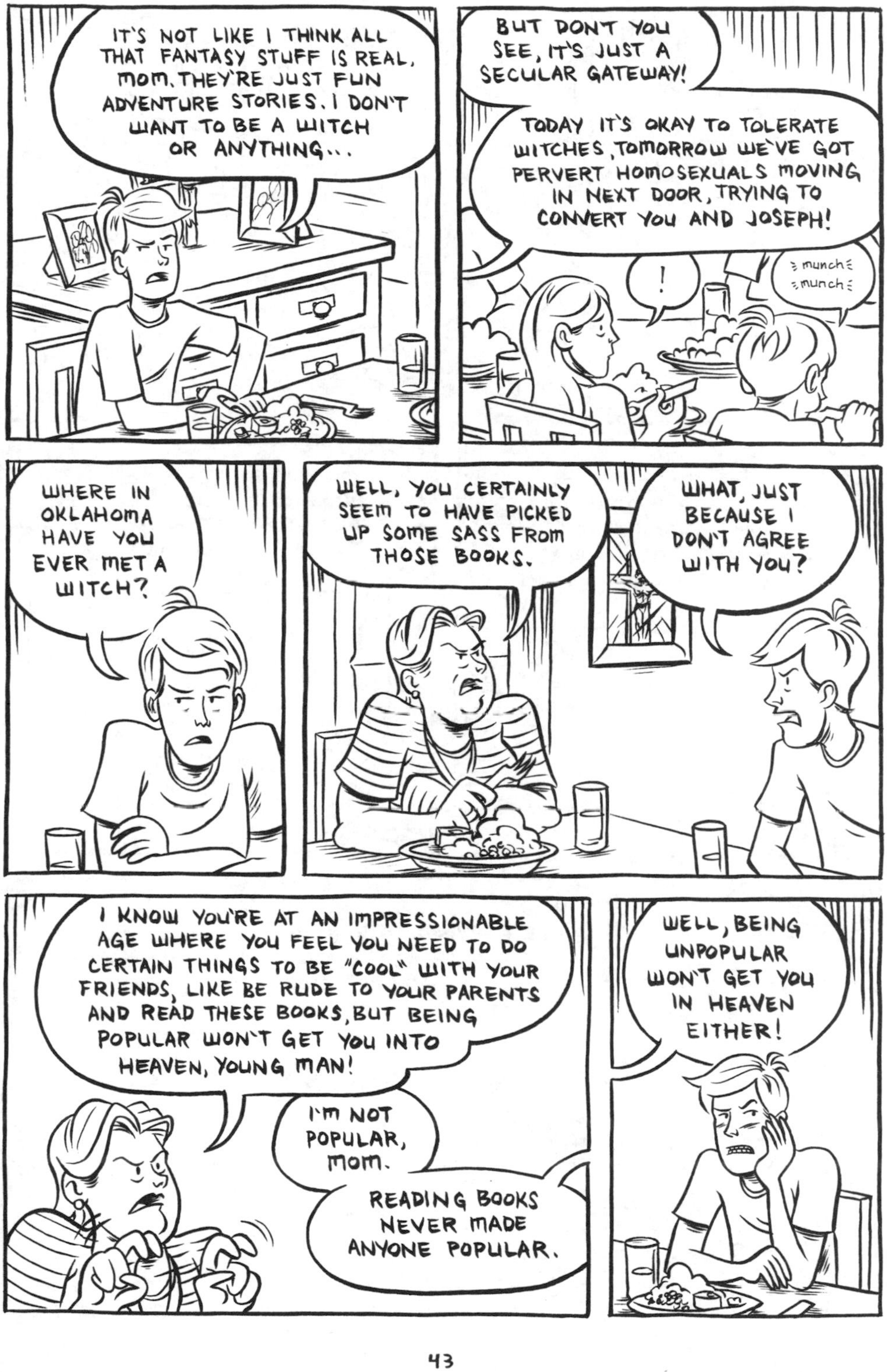
IT'S NOT LIKE I THINK ALL THAT FANTASY STUFF IS REAL, MOM. THEY'RE JUST FUN ADVENTURE STORIES. I DON'T WANT TO BE A WITCH OR ANYTHING...
BUT DON'T YOU SEE, IT'S JUST A SECULAR GATEWAY!
TODAY IT'S OKAY TO TOLERATE WITCHES, TOMORROW WE'VE GOT PERVERT HOMOSEXUALS MOVING IN NEXT DOOR, TRYING TO CONVERT YOU AND JOSEPH!
!
munch munch
WHERE IN OKLAHOMA HAVE YOU EVER MET A WITCH?
WELL, YOU CERTAINLY SEEM TO HAVE PICKED UP SOME SASS FROM THOSE BOOKS.
WHAT, JUST BECAUSE I DON'T AGREE WITH YOU?
I KNOW YOU'RE AT AN IMPRESSIONABLE AGE WHERE YOU FEEL YOU NEED TO DO CERTAIN THINGS TO BE "COOL" WITH YOUR FRIENDS, LIKE BE RUDE TO YOUR PARENTS AND READ THESE BOOKS, BUT BEING POPULAR WON'T GET YOU INTO HEAVEN, YOUNG MAN!
I'M NOT POPULAR, MOM.
READING BOOKS NEVER MADE ANYONE POPULAR.
WELL, BEING UNPOPULAR WON'T GET YOU IN HEAVEN EITHER!

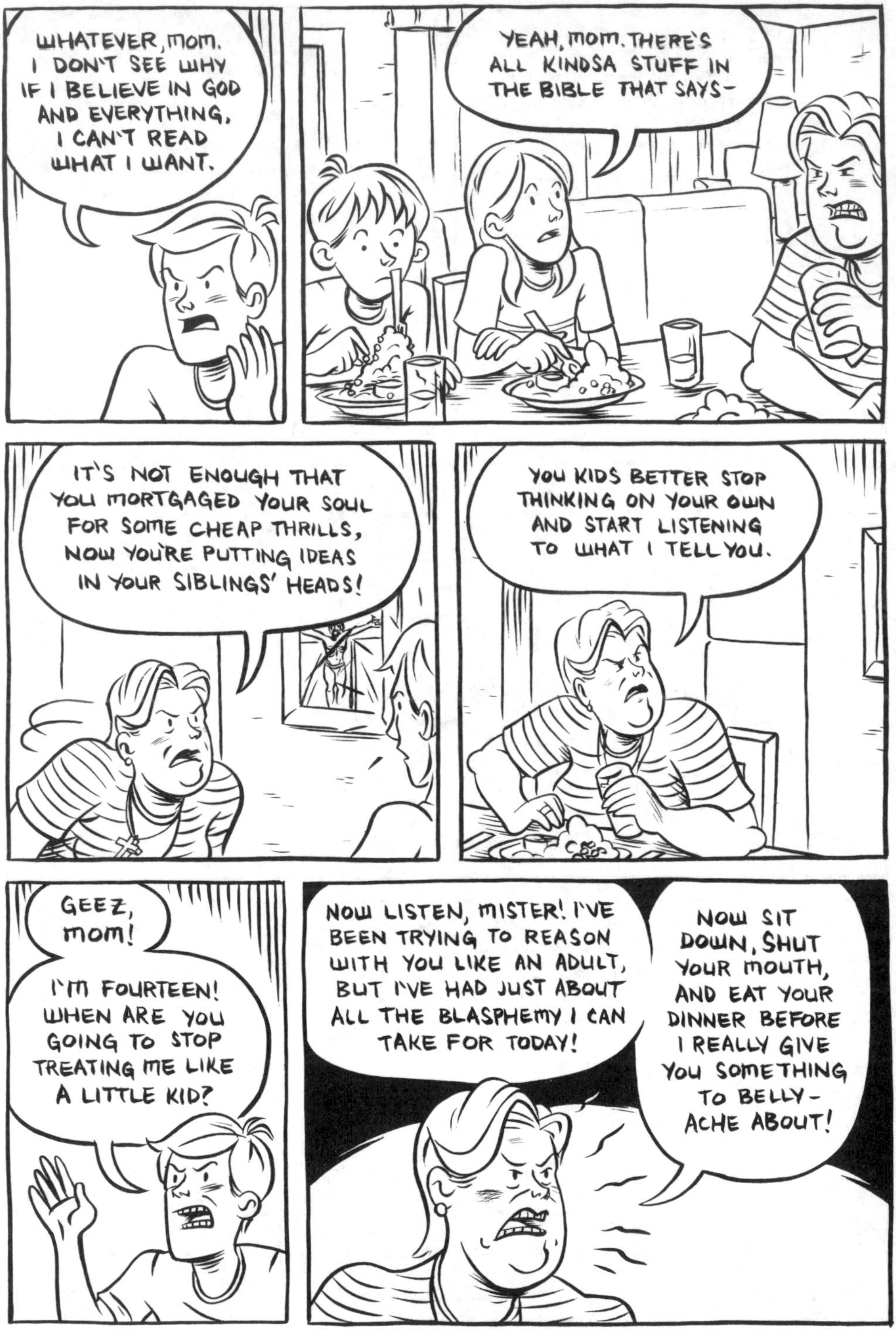
WHATEVER, MOM. I DON'T SEE WHY IF I BELIEVE IN GOD AND EVERYTHING, I CAN'T READ WHAT I WANT.
YEAH, MOM. THERE'S ALL KINDSA STUFF IN THE BIBLE THAT SAYS-
IT'S NOT ENOUGH THAT YOU MORTGAGED YOUR SOUL FOR SOME CHEAP THRILLS, NOW YOU'RE PUTTING IDEAS IN YOUR SIBLINGS' HEADS!
YOU KIDS BETTER STOP THINKING ON YOUR OWN AND START LISTENING TO WHAT I TELL YOU.
GEEZ, MOM!
I'M FOURTEEN! WHEN ARE YOU GOING TO STOP TREATING ME LIKE A LITTLE KID?
NOW LISTEN, MISTER! I'VE BEEN TRYING TO REASON WITH YOU LIKE AN ADULT, BUT I'VE HAD JUST ABOUT ALL THE BLASPHEMY I CAN TAKE FOR TODAY!
NOW SIT DOWN, SHUT YOUR MOUTH, AND EAT YOUR DINNER BEFORE I REALLY GIVE YOU SOMETHING TO BELLY-ACHE ABOUT!

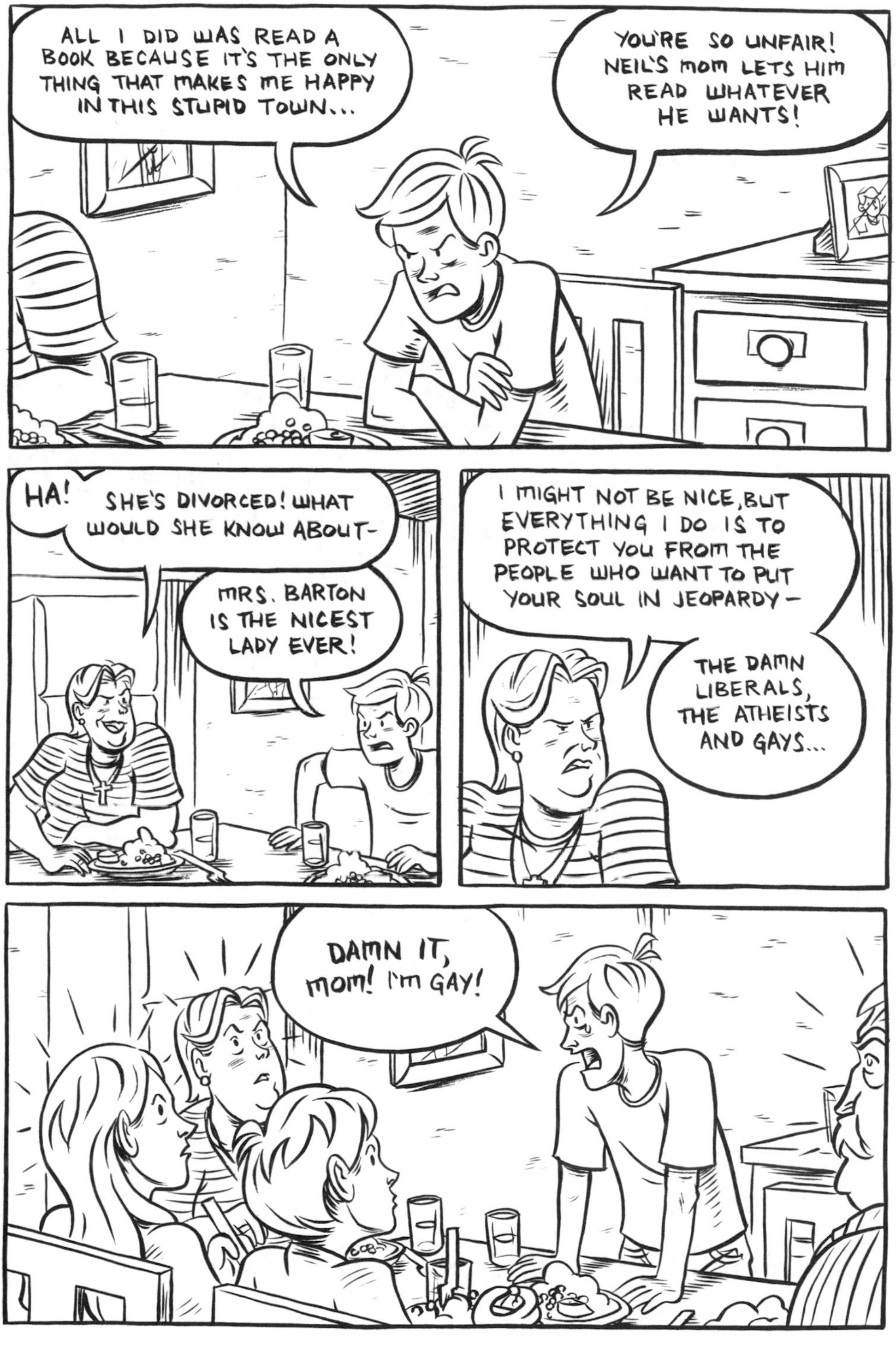
ALL I DID WAS READ A BOOK BECAUSE IT'S THE ONLY THING THAT MAKES ME HAPPY IN THIS STUPID TOWN...
YOU'RE SO UNFAIR! NEIL'S MOM LETS HIM READ WHATEVER HE WANTS!
HA!
SHE'S DIVORCED! WHAT WOULD SHE KNOW ABOUT-
MRS. BARTON IS THE NICEST LADY EVER!
I MIGHT NOT BE NICE, BUT EVERYTHING I DO IS TO PROTECT YOU FROM THE PEOPLE WHO WANT TO PUT YOUR SOUL IN JEOPARDY-
THE DAMN LIBERALS, THE ATHEISTS AND GAYS...
DAMN IT, MOM! I'M GAY!

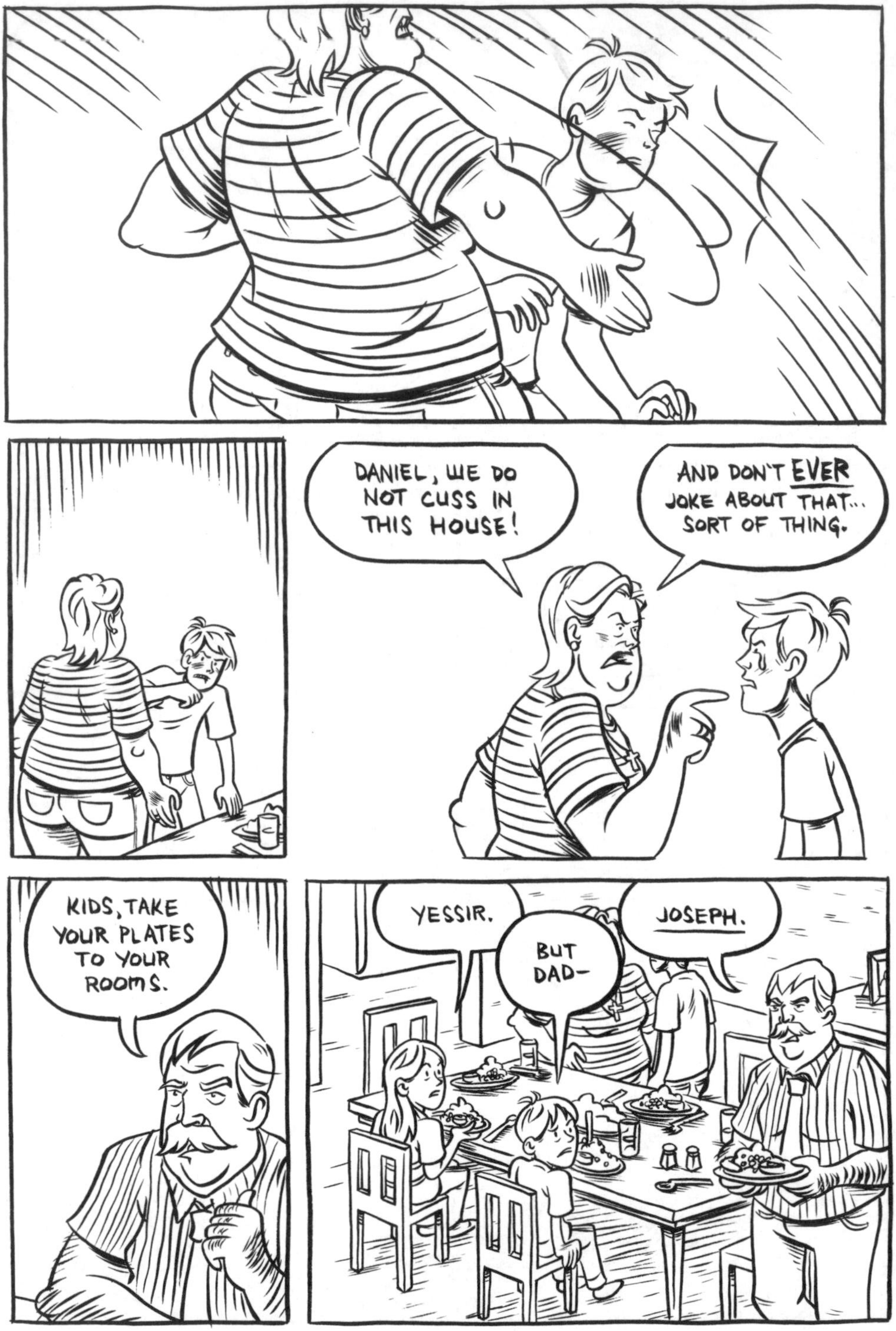
DANIEL, WE DO NOT CUSS IN THIS HOUSE!
AND DON'T EVER JOKE ABOUT THAT... SORT OF THING.
KIDS, TAKE YOUR PLATES TO YOUR ROOMS.
YESSIR.
BUT DAD-
JOSEPH.

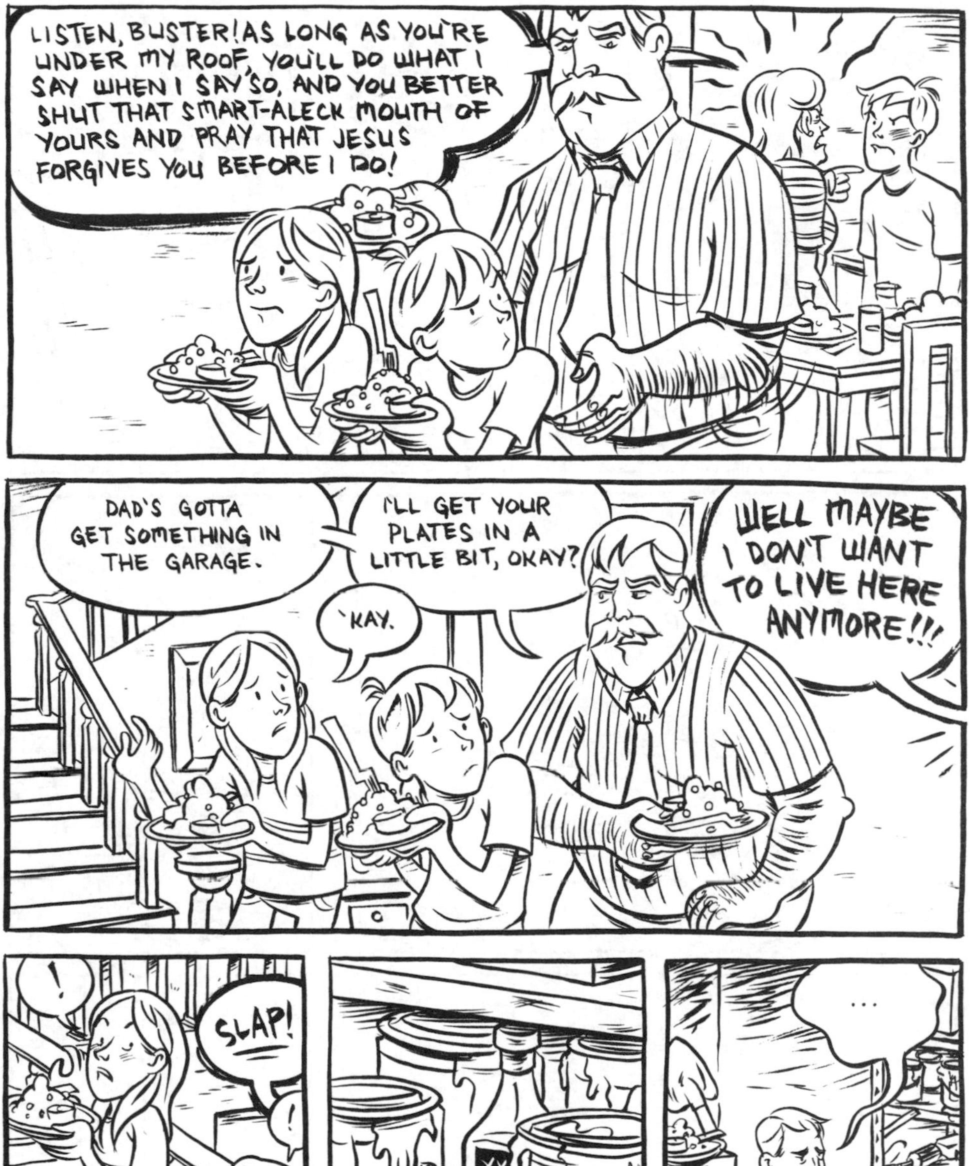
LISTEN, BUSTER! AS LONG AS YOU'RE UNDER MY ROOF, YOU'LL DO WHAT I SAY WHEN I SAY SO, AND YOU BETTER SHUT THAT SMART-ALECK MOUTH OF YOURS AND PRAY THAT JESUS FORGIVES YOU BEFORE I DO!
DAD'S GOTTA GET SOMETHING IN THE GARAGE.
I'LL GET YOUR PLATES IN A LITTLE BIT, OKAY?
`KAY.
WELL MAYBE I DON'T WANT TO LIVE HERE ANYMORE!!!
!
SLAP!
!
JACK DANIEL
...
UP

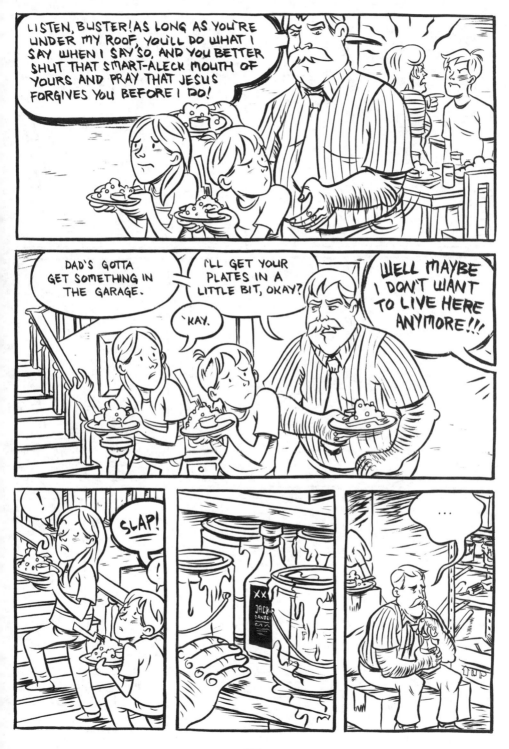

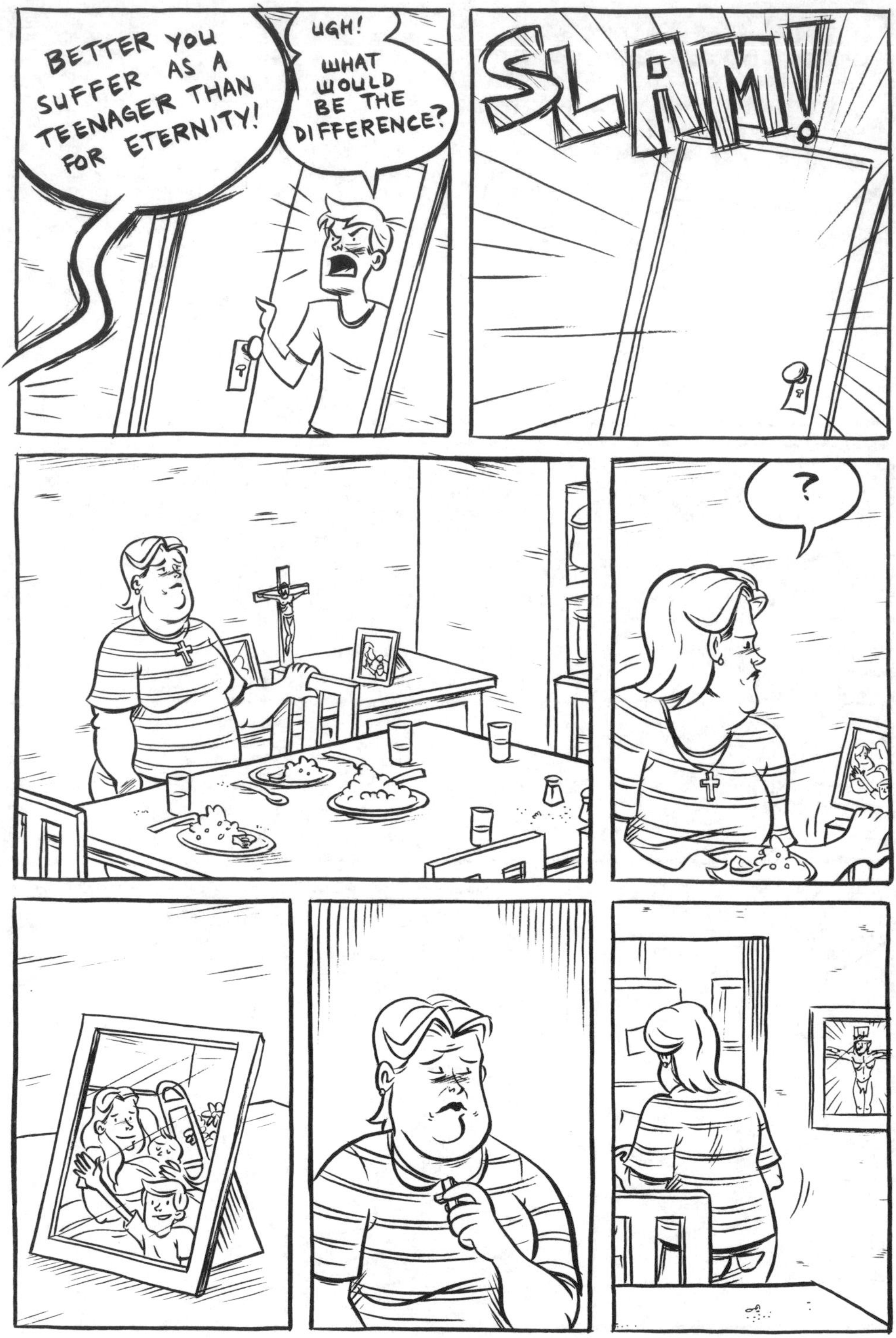
BETTER YOU SUFFER AS A TEENAGER THAN FOR ETERNITY!
UGH!
WHAT WOULD BE THE DIFFERENCE?
SLAM!
?

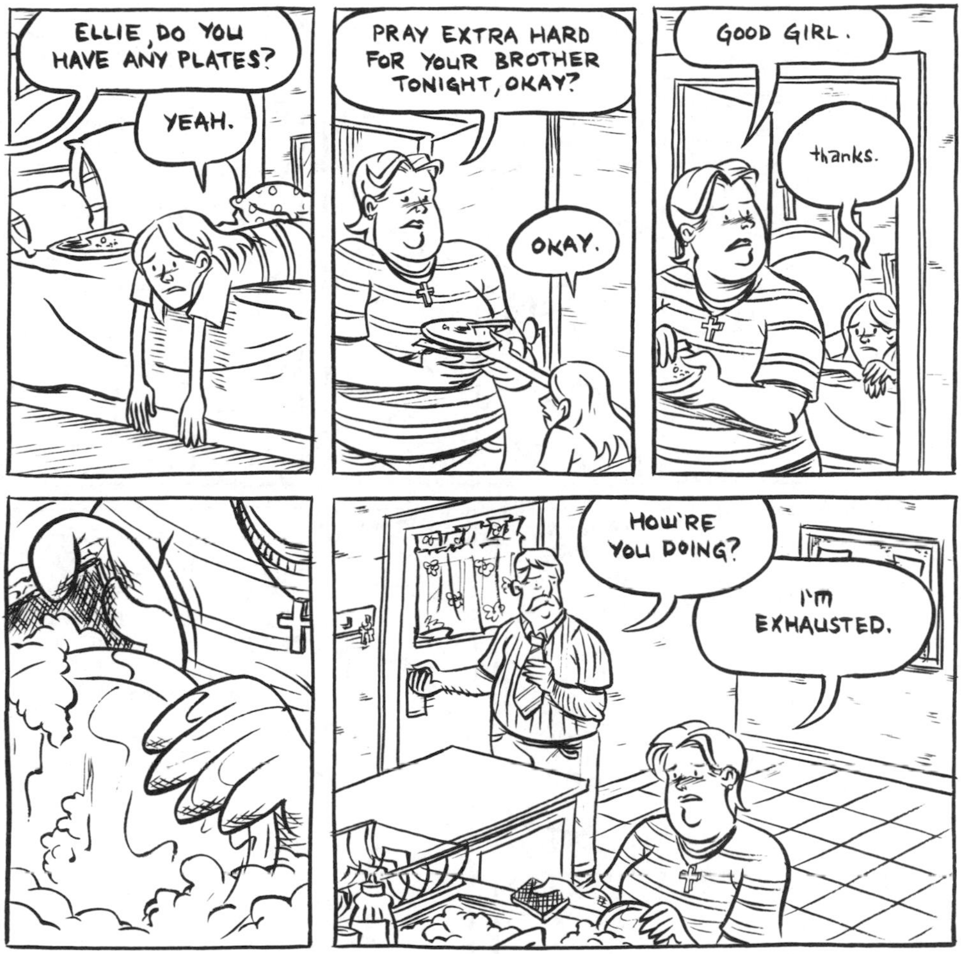
ELLIE, DO YOU HAVE ANY PLATES?
YEAH.
PRAY EXTRA HARD FOR YOUR BROTHER TONIGHT, OKAY?
OKAY.
GOOD GIRL.
thanks.
HOW'RE YOU DOING?
I'M EXHAUSTED.
THAT GOT UGLIER THAN I EXPECTED.
TOUGH LOVE ISN'T PRETTY.
HM.
BETTER THAT HE HATES ME NOW AND TURNS OUT RIGHT.

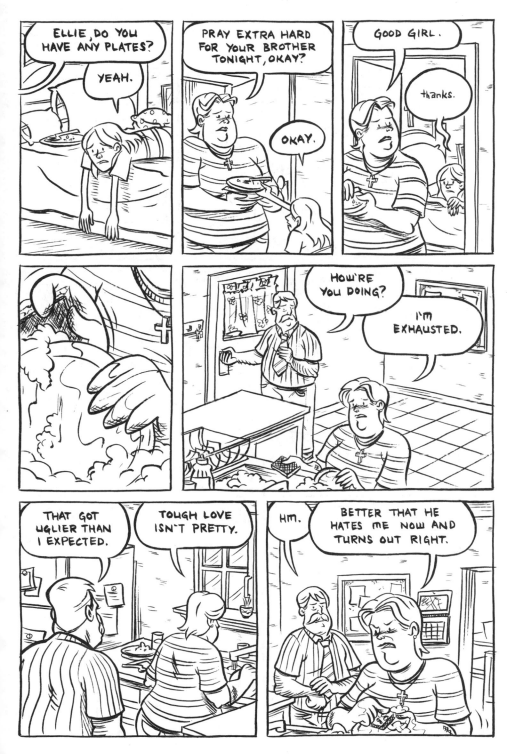

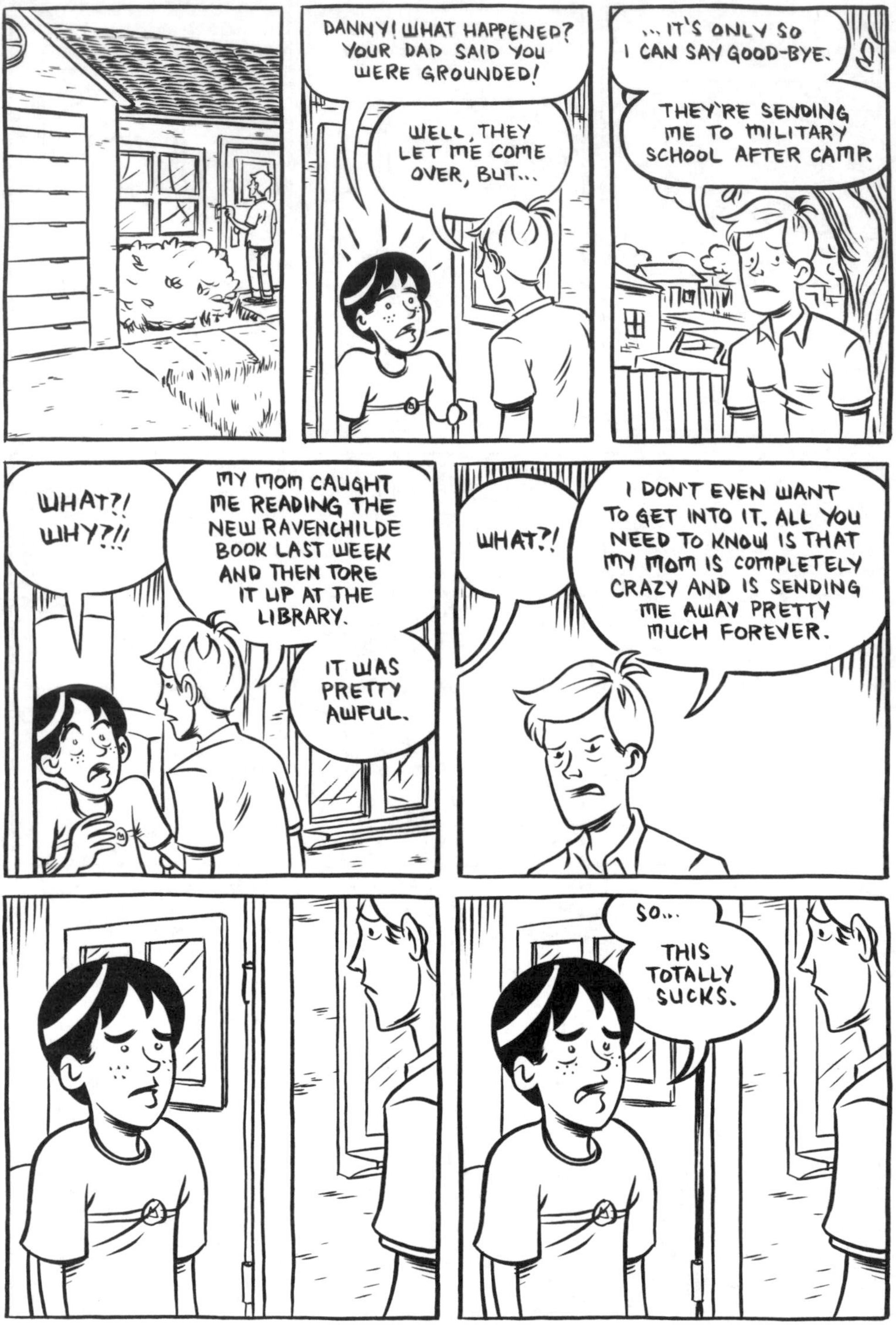
DANNY! WHAT HAPPENED? YOUR DAD SAID YOU WERE GROUNDED!
WELL, THEY LET ME COME OVER, BUT...
... IT'S ONLY SO I CAN SAY GOOD-BYE.
THEY'RE SENDING ME TO MILITARY SCHOOL AFTER CAMP.
WHAT?! WHY?!!
MY MOM CAUGHT ME READING THE NEW RAVENCHILDE BOOK LAST WEEK AND THEN TORE IT UP AT THE LIBRARY.
IT WAS PRETTY AWFUL.
WHAT?!
I DON'T EVEN WANT TO GET INTO IT. ALL YOU NEED TO KNOW IS THAT MY MOM IS COMPLETELY CRAZY AND IS SENDING ME AWAY PRETTY MUCH FOREVER.
SO...
THIS TOTALLY SUCKS.

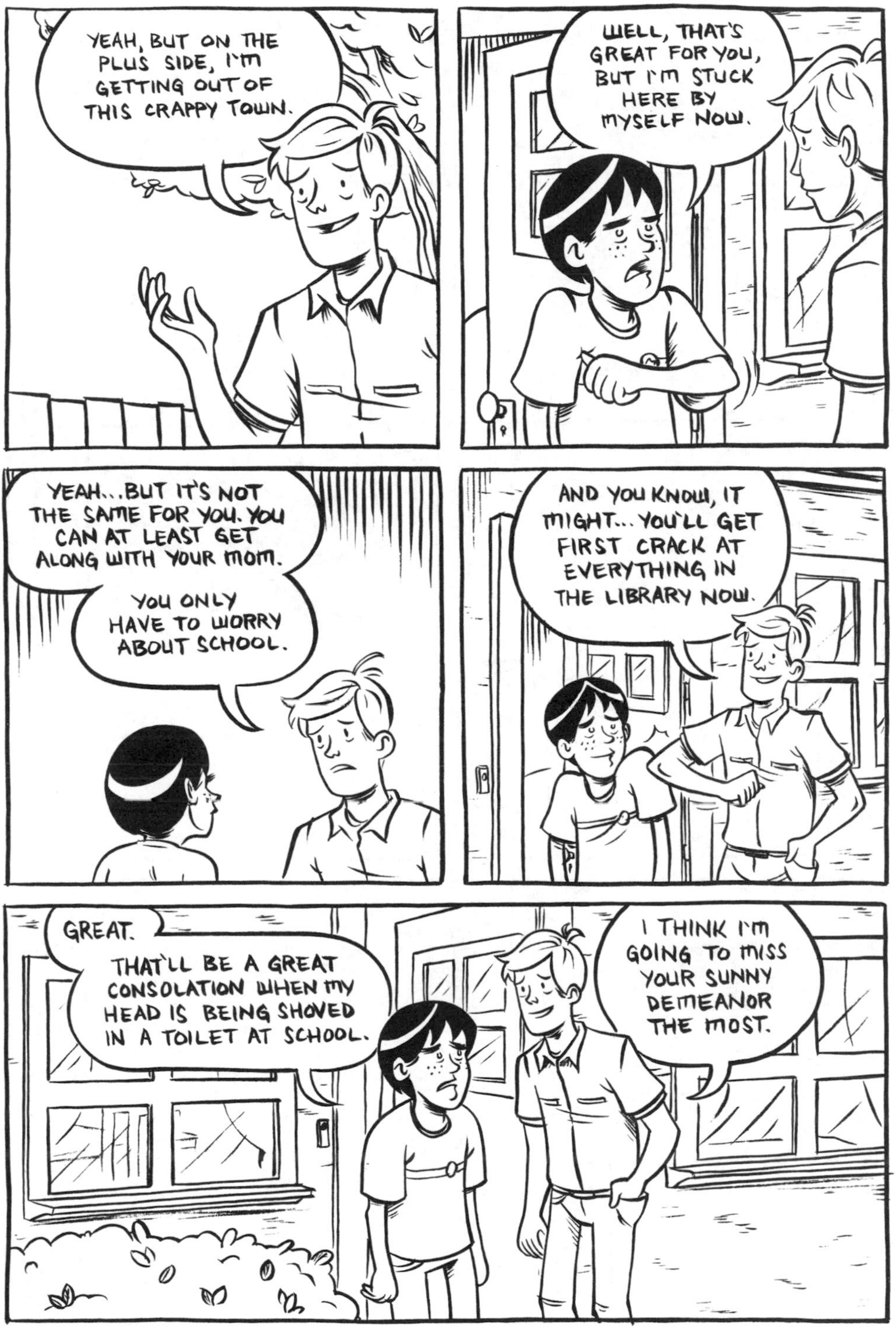
YEAH, BUT ON THE PLUS SIDE, I'M GETTING OUT OF THIS CRAPPY TOWN.
WELL, THAT'S GREAT FOR YOU, BUT I'M STUCK HERE BY MYSELF NOW.
YEAH...BUT IT'S NOT THE SAME FOR YOU. YOU CAN AT LEAST GET ALONG WITH YOUR MOM.
YOU ONLY HAVE TO WORRY ABOUT SCHOOL.
AND YOU KNOW, IT MIGHT... YOU'LL GET FIRST CRACK AT EVERYTHING IN THE LIBRARY NOW.
GREAT.
THAT'LL BE A GREAT CONSOLATION WHEN MY HEAD IS BEING SHOVED IN A TOILET AT SCHOOL.
I THINK I'M GOING TO MISS YOUR SUNNY DEMEANOR THE MOST.

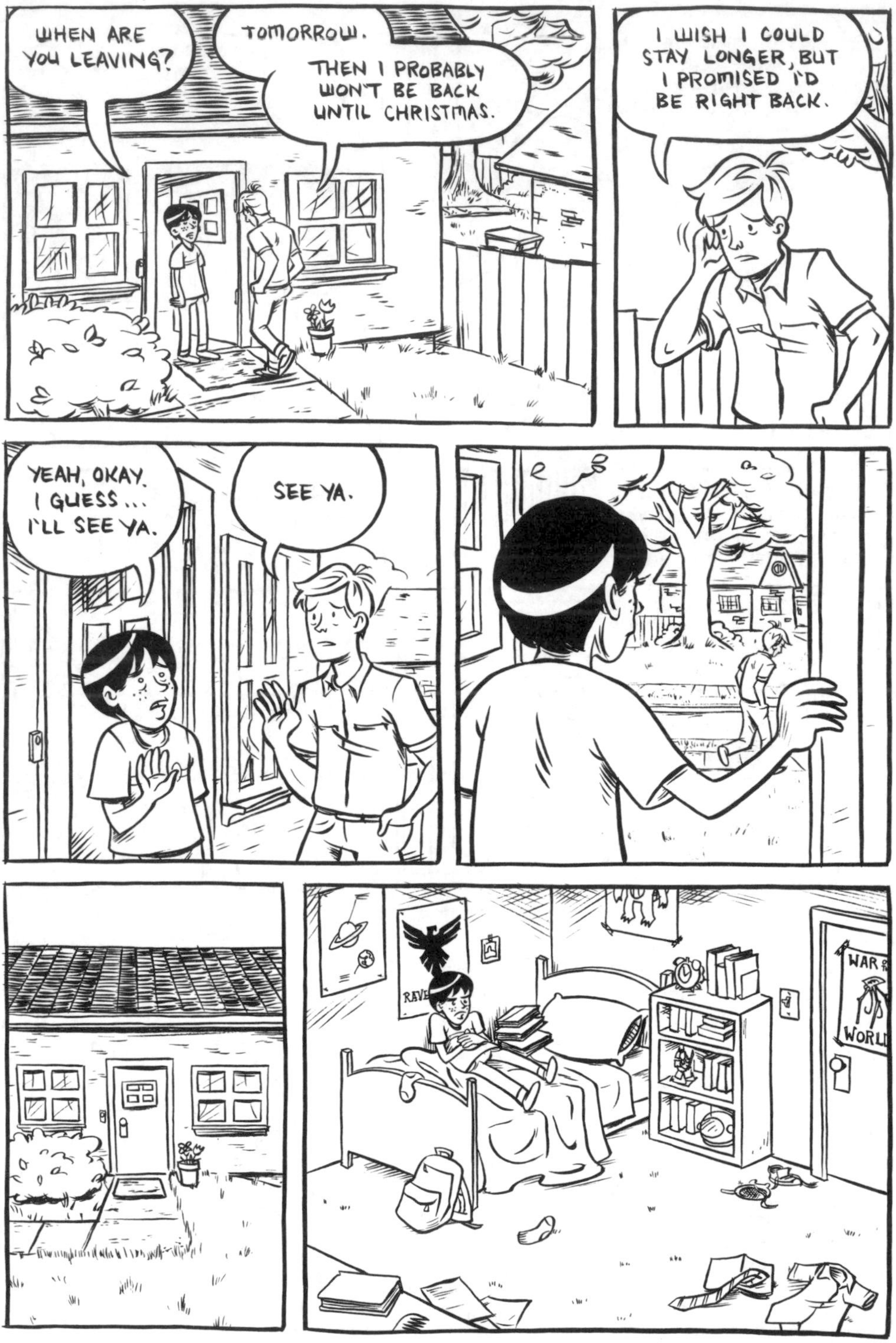
WHEN ARE YOU LEAVING?
TOMORROW.
THEN I PROBABLY WON'T BE BACK UNTIL CHRISTMAS.
I WISH I COULD STAY LONGER, BUT I PROMISED I'D BE RIGHT BACK.
YEAH, OKAY. I GUESS... I'LL SEE YA.
SEE YA.
RAVE
WAR
WORL

CHAPTER 3

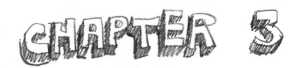

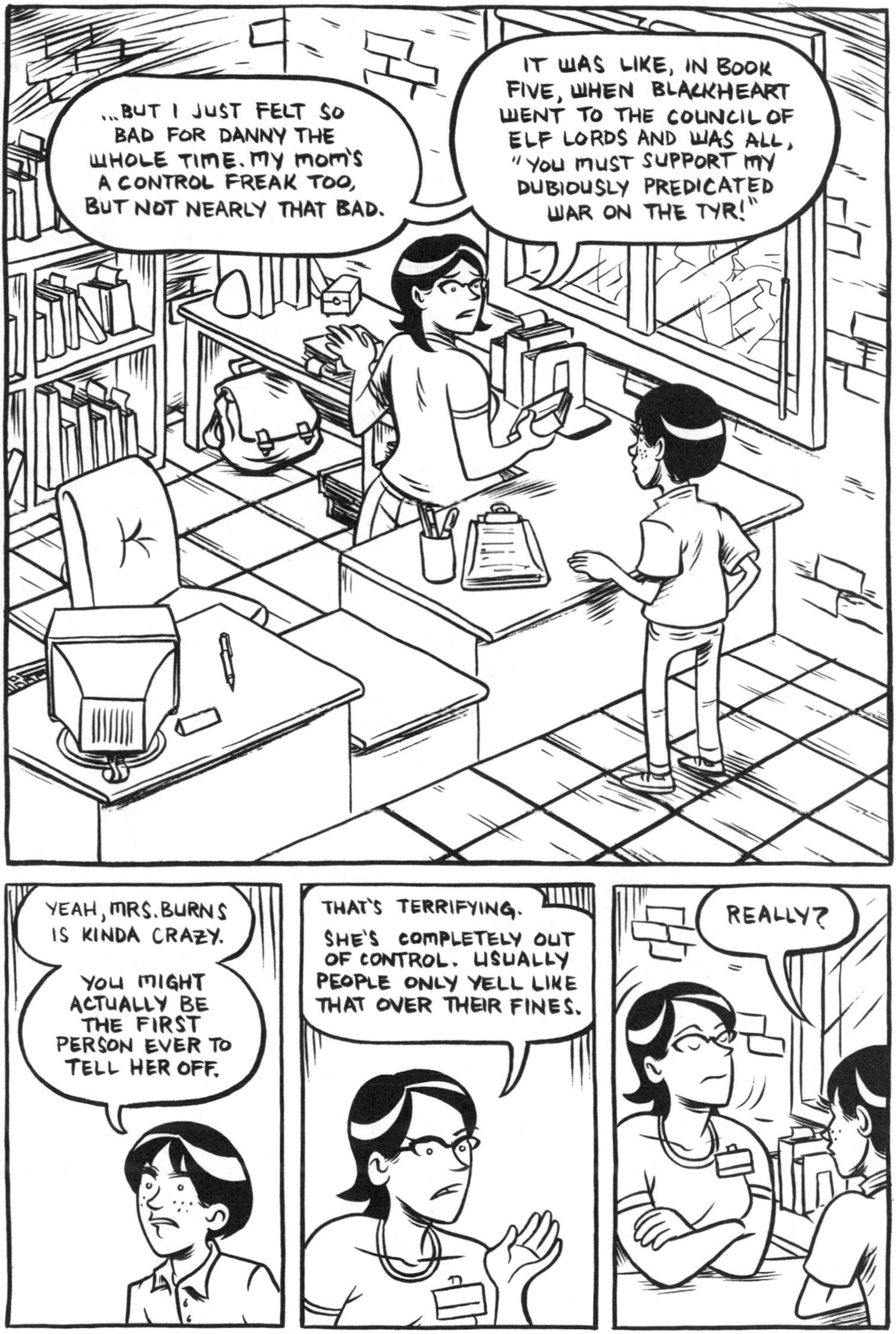
...BUT I JUST FELT SO BAD FOR DANNY THE WHOLE TIME. MY MOM'S A CONTROL FREAK TOO, BUT NOT NEARLY THAT BAD.
IT WAS LIKE, IN BOOK FIVE, WHEN BLACKHEART WENT TO THE COUNCIL OF ELF LORDS AND WAS ALL, "YOU MUST SUPPORT MY DUBIOUSLY PREDICATED WAR ON THE TYR!"
YEAH, MRS. BURNS IS KINDA CRAZY.
YOU MIGHT ACTUALLY BE THE FIRST PERSON EVER TO TELL HER OFF.
THAT'S TERRIFYING.
SHE'S COMPLETELY OUT OF CONTROL. USUALLY PEOPLE ONLY YELL LIKE THAT OVER THEIR FINES.
REALLY?

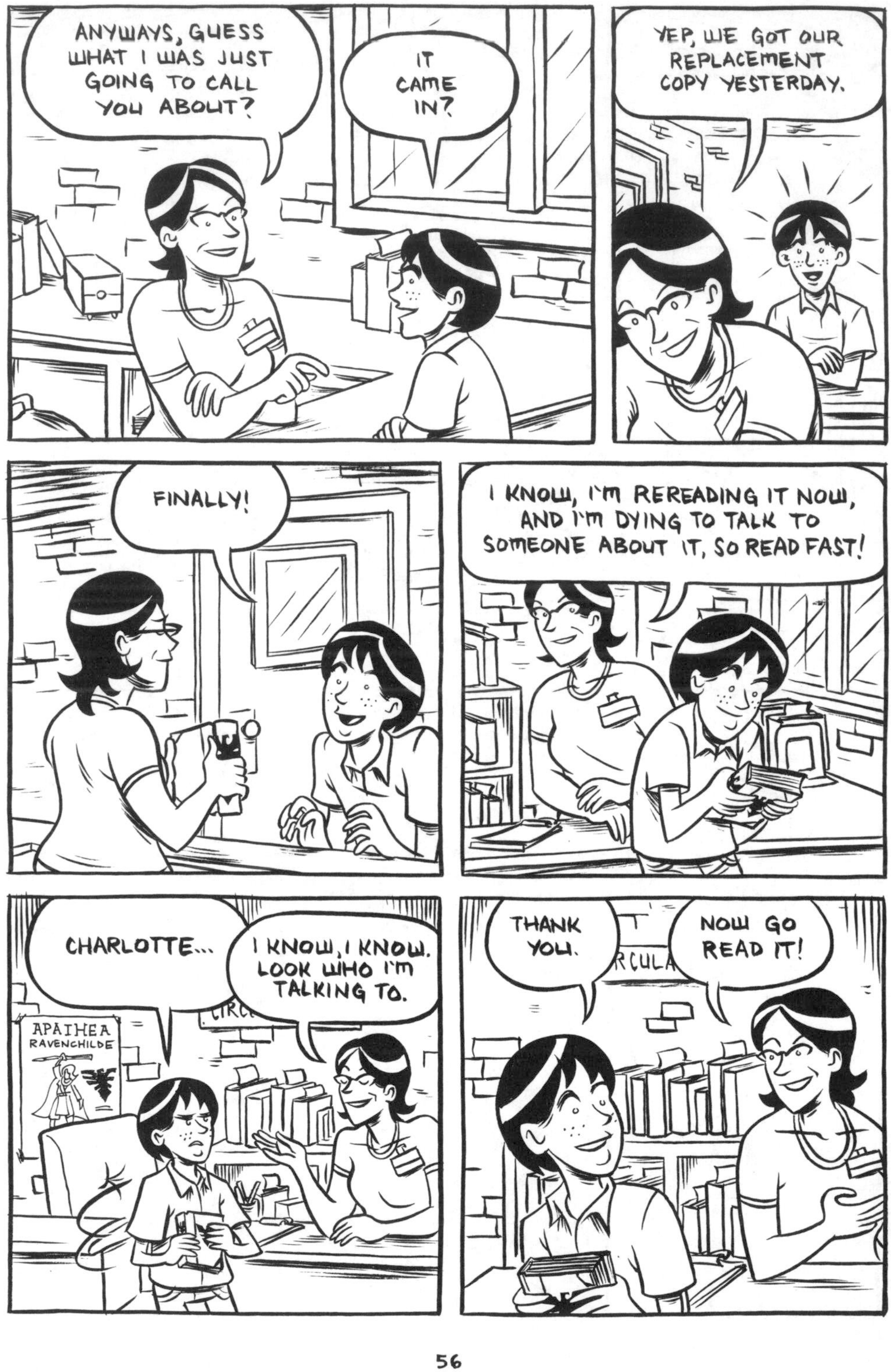
ANYWAYS, GUESS WHAT I WAS JUST GOING TO CALL YOU ABOUT?
IT CAME IN?
YEP, WE GOT OUR REPLACEMENT COPY YESTERDAY.
FINALLY!
I KNOW, I'M REREADING IT NOW, AND I'M DYING TO TALK TO SOMEONE ABOUT IT, SO READ FAST!
CHARLOTTE...
I KNOW, I KNOW. LOOK WHO I'M TALKING TO.
APAIHEA RAVENCHILDE
THANK YOU.
NOW GO READ IT!

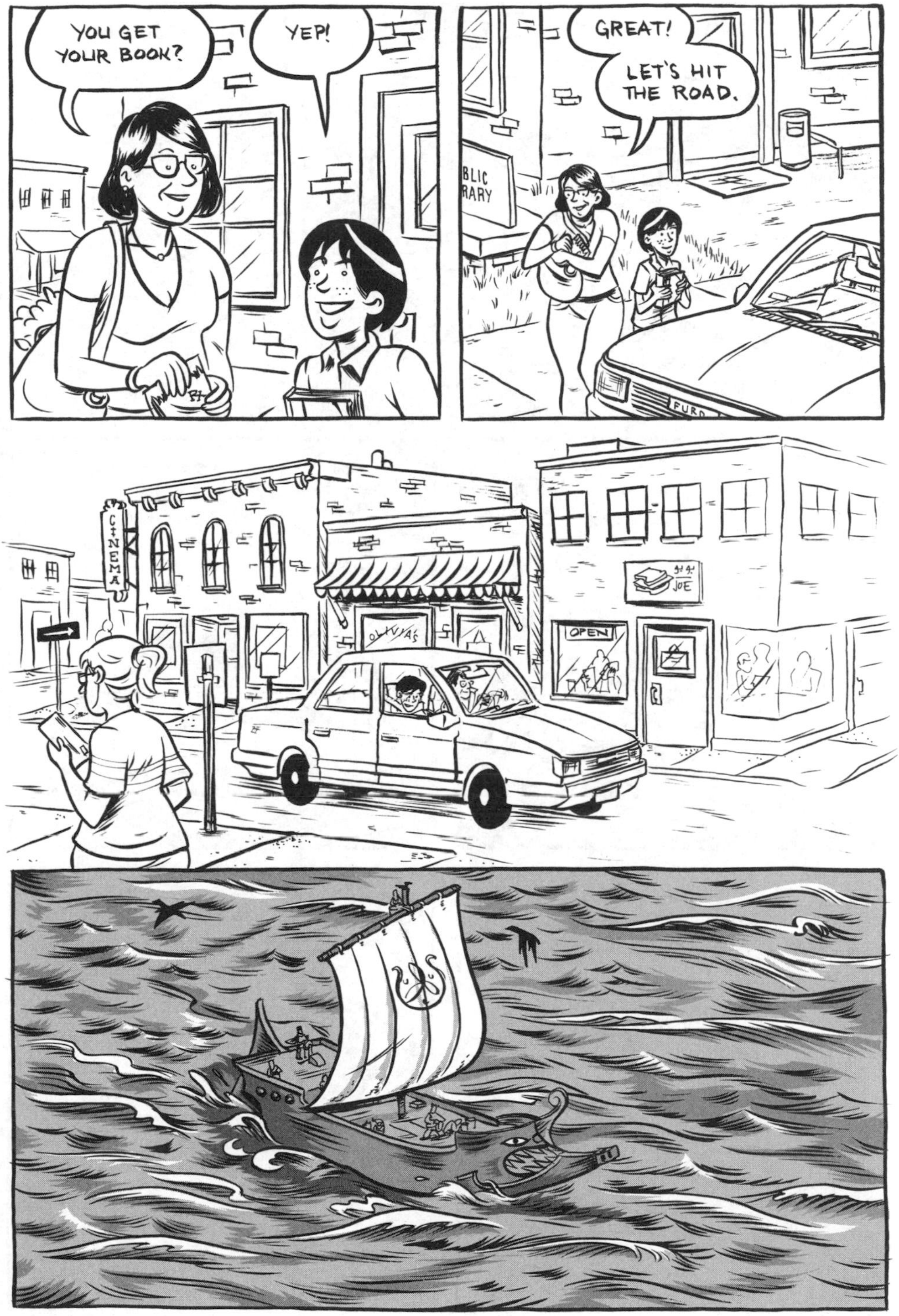
YOU GET YOUR BOOK?
YEP!
GREAT!
LET'S HIT THE ROAD.
CINEMA
OLIVIA'S
OPEN
JOE

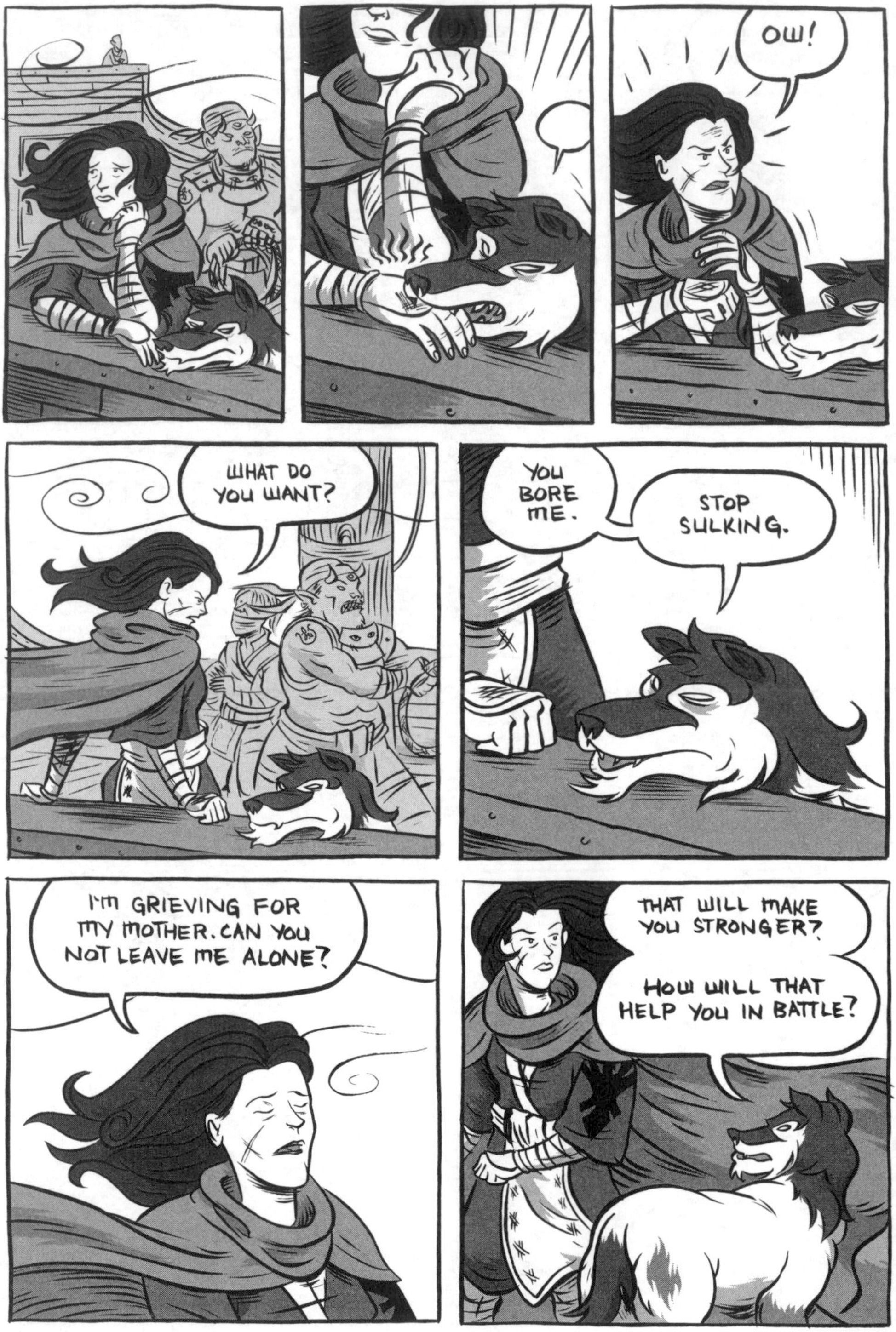
OW!
WHAT DO YOU WANT?
YOU BORE ME.
STOP SULKING.
I'M GRIEVING FOR MY MOTHER. CAN YOU NOT LEAVE ME ALONE?
THAT WILL MAKE YOU STRONGER?
HOW WILL THAT HELP YOU IN BATTLE?

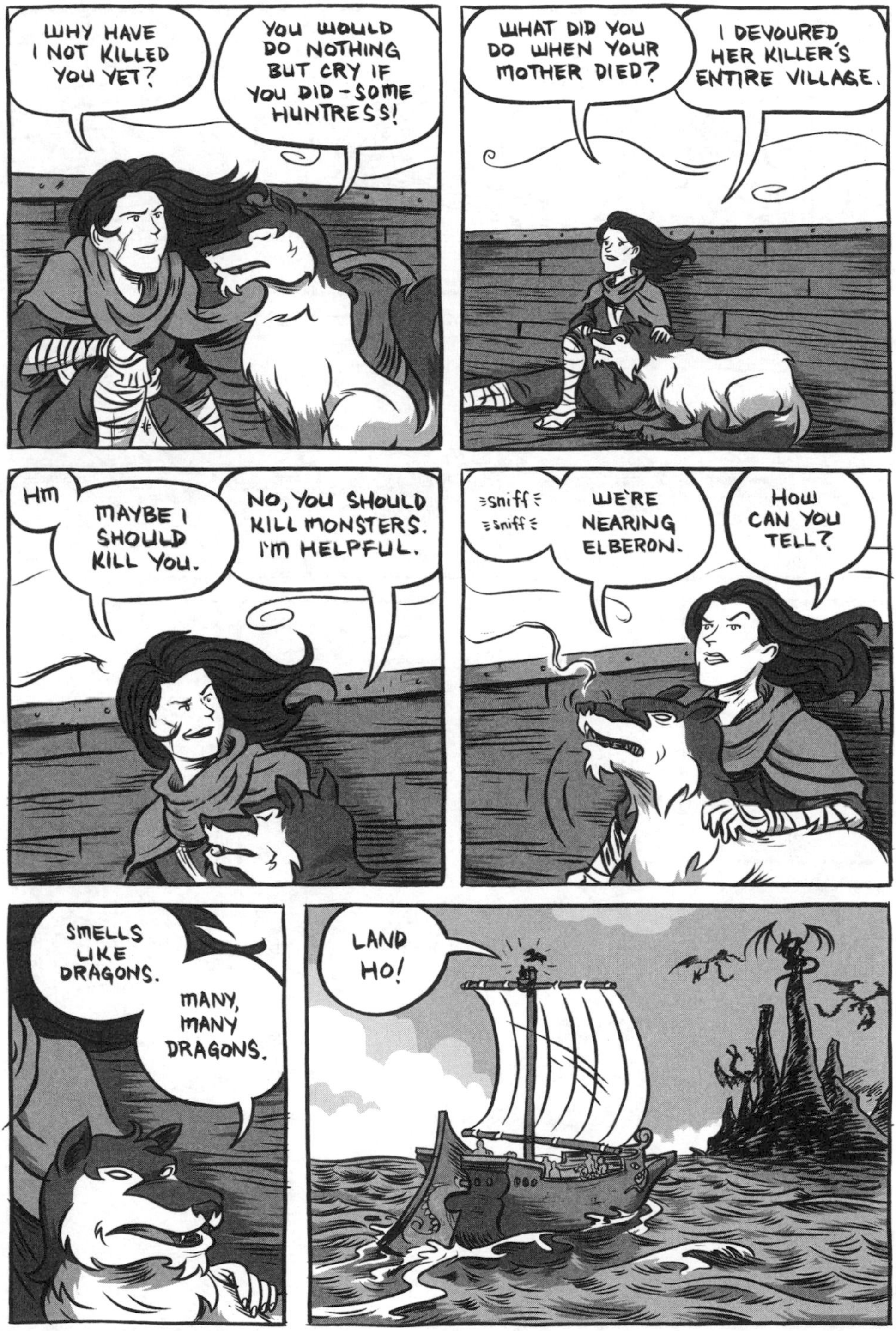
WHY HAVE I NOT KILLED YOU YET?
YOU WOULD DO NOTHING BUT CRY IF YOU DID-SOME HUNTRESS!
WHAT DID YOU DO WHEN YOUR MOTHER DIED?
I DEVOURED HER KILLER'S ENTIRE VILLAGE.
Hm
MAYBE I SHOULD KILL YOU.
NO, YOU SHOULD KILL MONSTERS. I'M HELPFUL.
sniff
sniff
WE'RE NEARING ELBERON.
HOW CAN YOU TELL?
SMELLS LIKE DRAGONS.
MANY, MANY DRAGONS.
LAND HO!

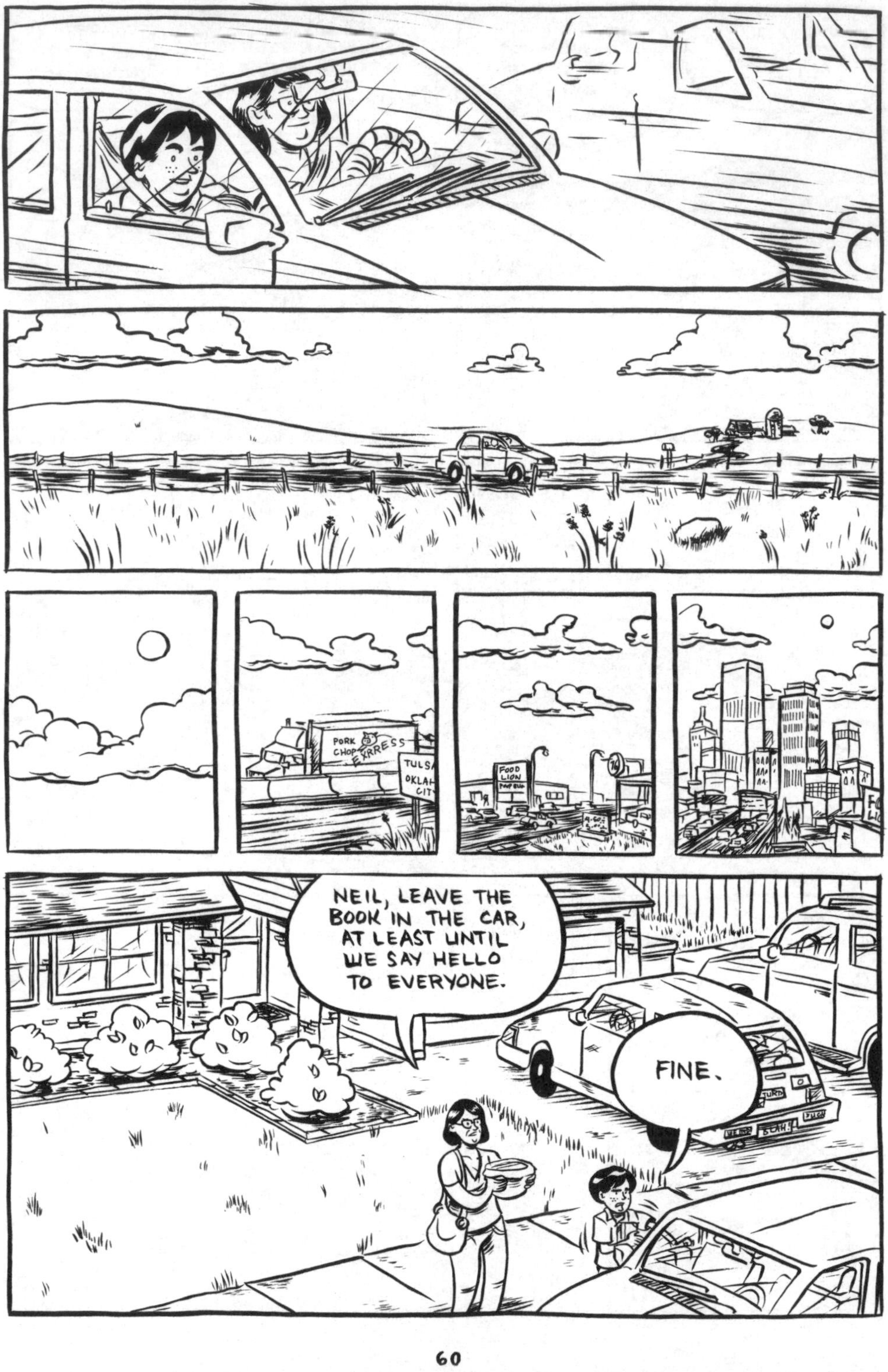
FOOD LION
NEIL, LEAVE THE BOOK IN THE CAR, AT LEAST UNTIL WE SAY HELLO TO EVERYONE.
FINE.

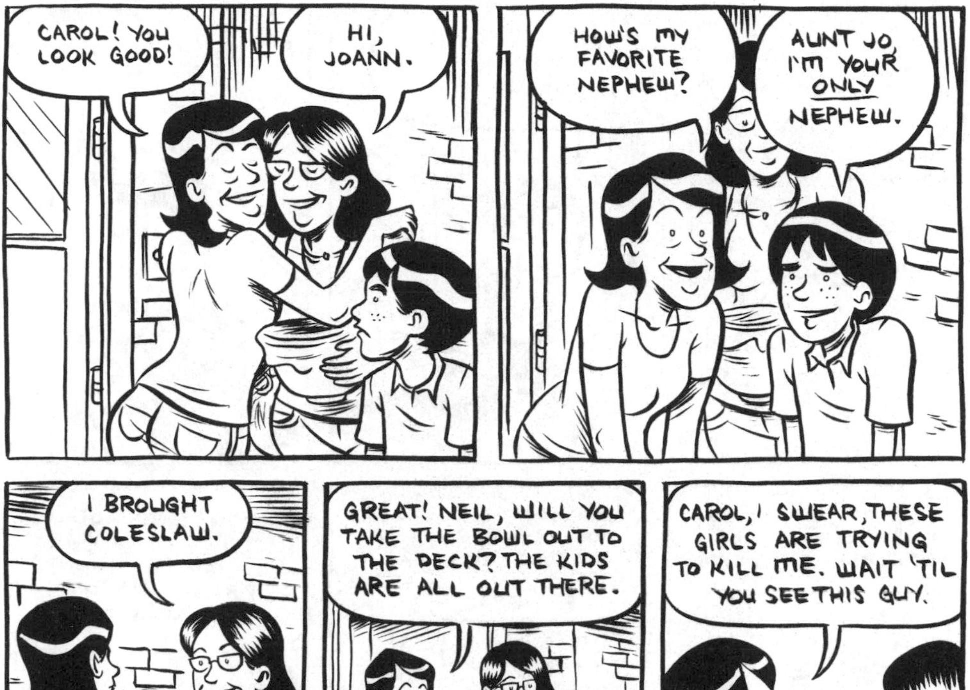
CAROL! YOU LOOK GOOD!
HI, JOANN.
HOW'S MY FAVORITE NEPHEW?
AUNT JO, I'M YOUR ONLY NEPHEW.
I BROUGHT COLESLAW.
GREAT! NEIL, WILL YOU TAKE THE BOWL OUT TO THE DECK? THE KIDS ARE ALL OUT THERE.
CAROL, I SWEAR, THESE GIRLS ARE TRYING TO KILL ME. WAIT 'TIL YOU SEE THIS GUY.
HEY, UNCLE BILL.
HELLO, NEIL! HELP YOURSELF TO A POP.
SO SHE SAID KATHLEEN WASN'T EVEN AT THE PARTY, BUT SHE TOTALLY POSTED LIKE FIFTY PICTURES FROM IT, AND HE'S LIKE IN HALF OF THEM!
YOU KNOW, IT'S KINDA TELLING THAT HE DIDN'T BRING YOU WITH HIM IN THE FIRST PLACE.
...

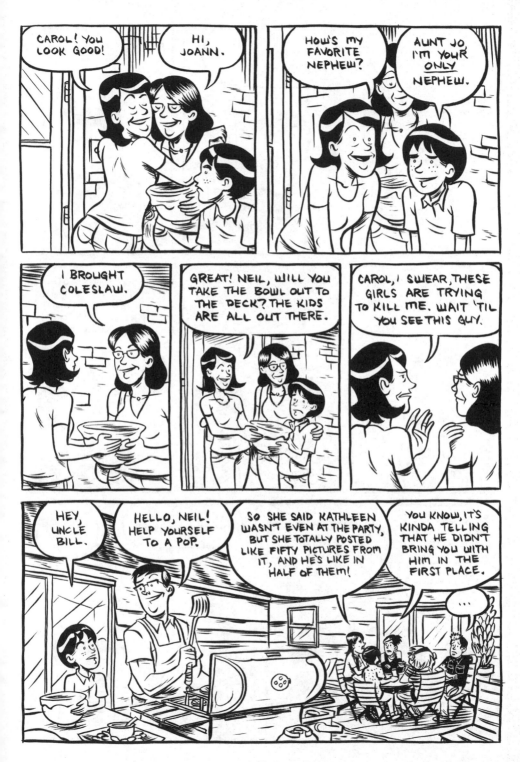

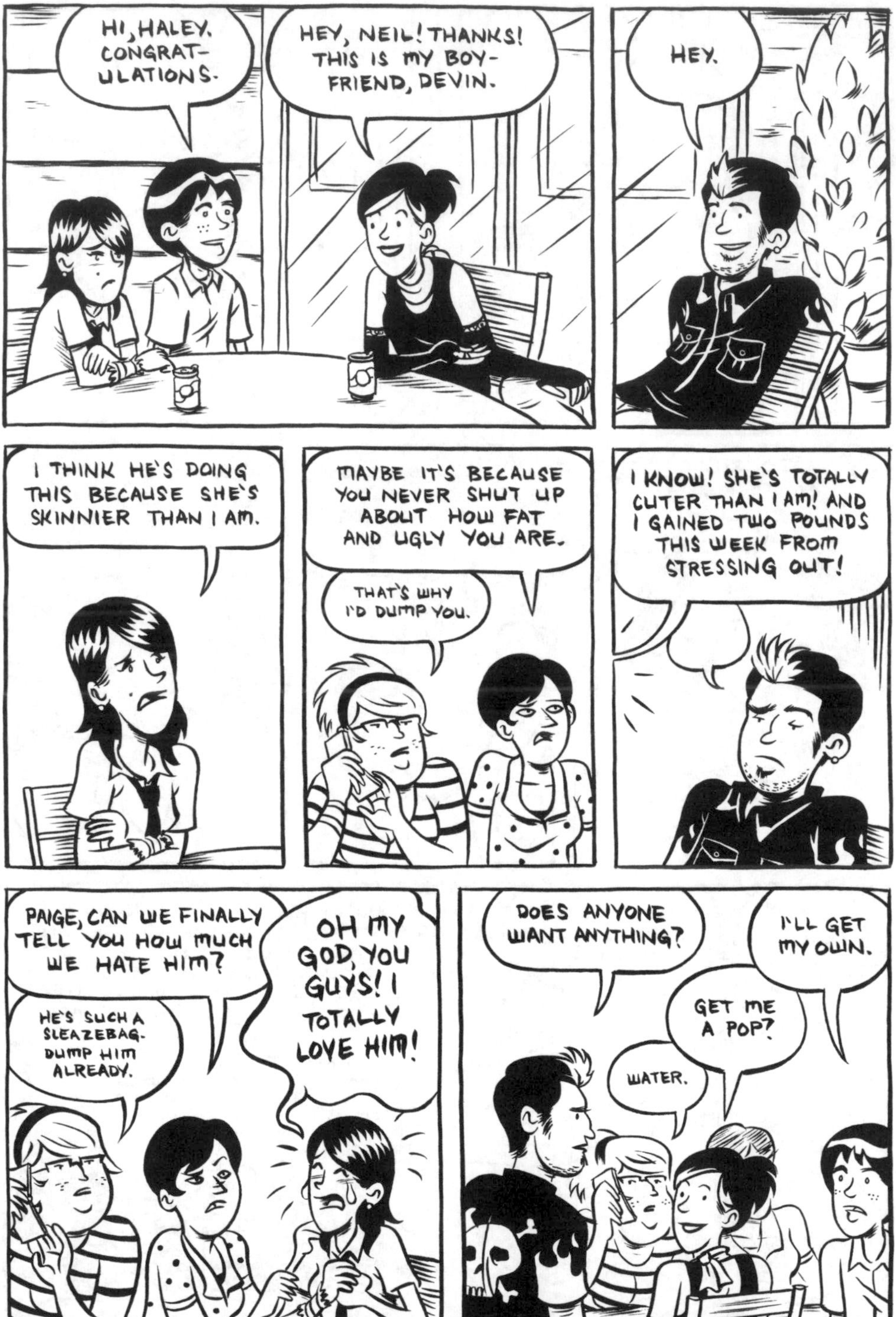
HI, HALEY. CONGRAT-ULATIONS.
HEY, NEIL! THANKS! THIS IS MY BOY-FRIEND, DEVIN.
HEY.
I THINK HE'S DOING THIS BECAUSE SHE'S SKINNIER THAN I AM.
MAYBE IT'S BECAUSE YOU NEVER SHUT UP ABOUT HOW FAT AND UGLY YOU ARE.
THAT'S WHY I'D DUMP YOU.
I KNOW! SHE'S TOTALLY CUTER THAN I AM! AND I GAINED TWO POUNDS THIS WEEK FROM STRESSING OUT!
PAIGE, CAN WE FINALLY TELL YOU HOW MUCH WE HATE HIM?
HE'S SUCH A SLEAZEBAG. DUMP HIM ALREADY.
OH MY GOD, YOU GUYS! I TOTALLY LOVE HIM!
DOES ANYONE WANT ANYTHING?
I'LL GET MY OWN.
GET ME A POP?
WATER.

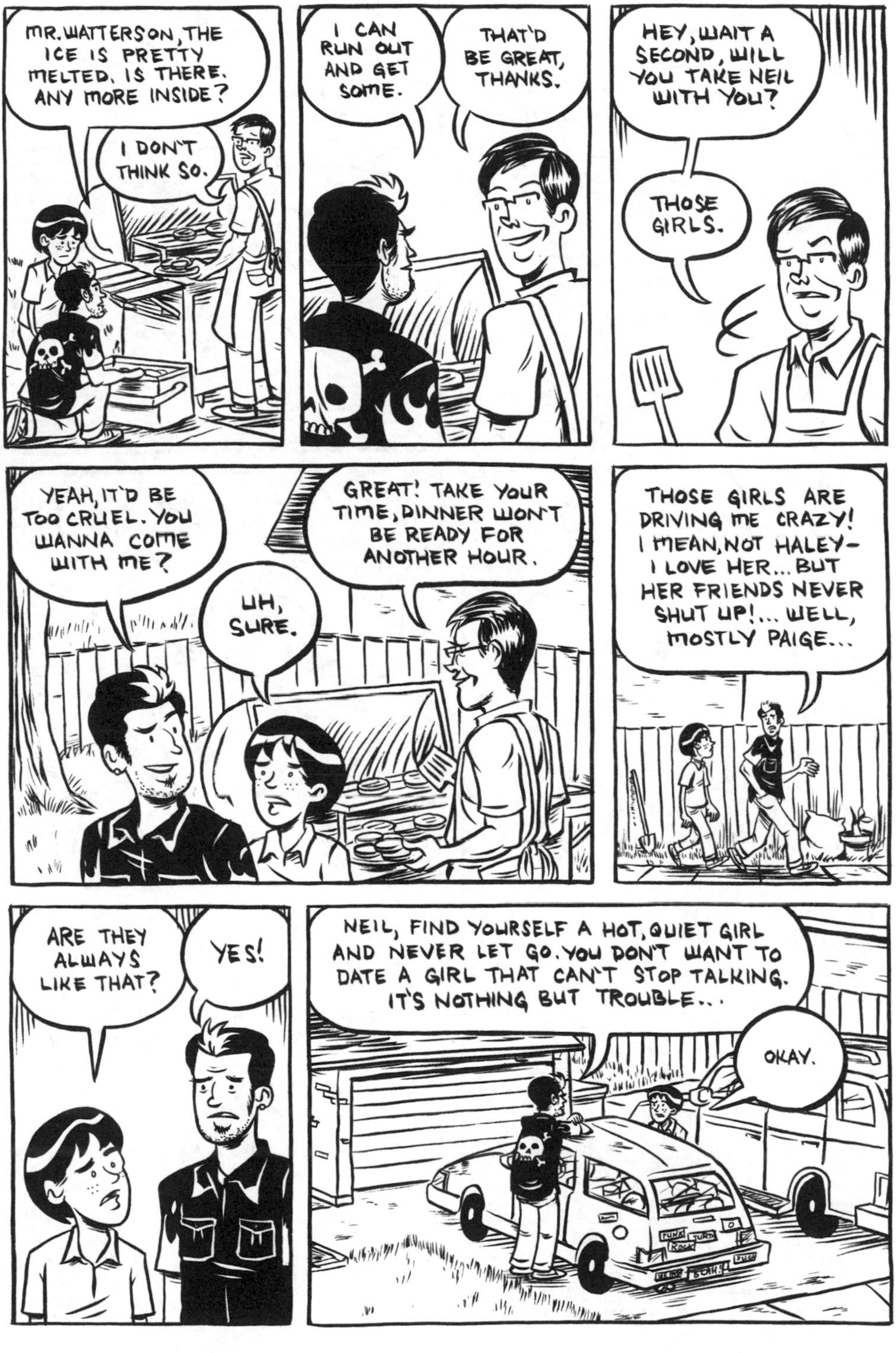
MR. WATTERSON, THE ICE IS PRETTY MELTED. IS THERE ANY MORE INSIDE?
I DON'T THINK SO.
I CAN RUN OUT AND GET SOME.
THAT'D BE GREAT, THANKS.
HEY, WAIT A SECOND, WILL YOU TAKE NEIL WITH YOU?
THOSE GIRLS.
YEAH, IT'D BE TOO CRUEL. YOU WANNA COME WITH ME?
UH, SURE.
GREAT! TAKE YOUR TIME, DINNER WON'T BE READY FOR ANOTHER HOUR.
THOSE GIRLS ARE DRIVING ME CRAZY! I MEAN, NOT HALEY- I LOVE HER... BUT HER FRIENDS NEVER SHUT UP!... WELL, MOSTLY PAIGE...
ARE THEY ALWAYS LIKE THAT?
YES!
NEIL, FIND YOURSELF A HOT, QUIET GIRL AND NEVER LET GO. YOU DON'T WANT TO DATE A GIRL THAT CAN'T STOP TALKING. IT'S NOTHING BUT TROUBLE...
OKAY.

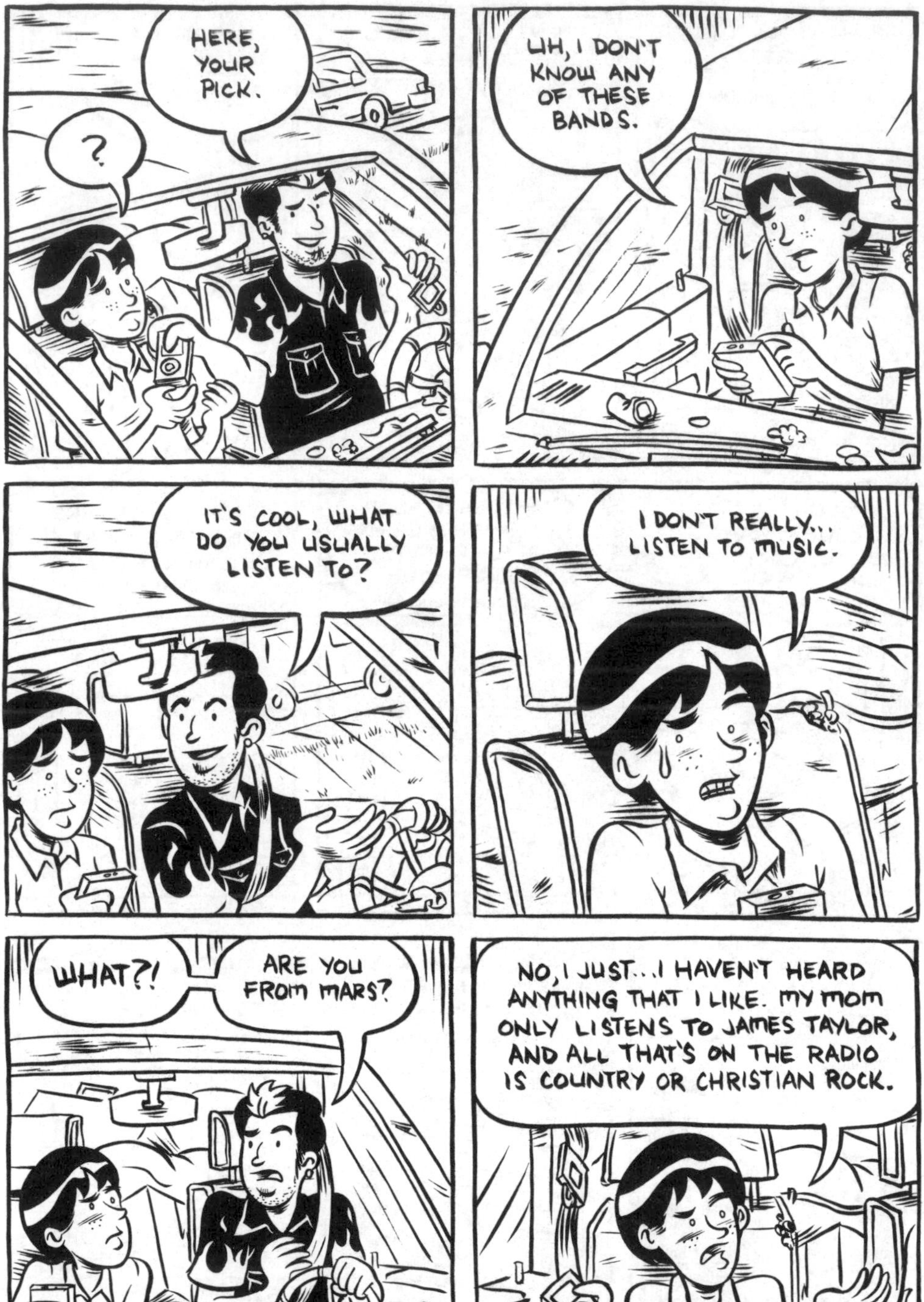
HERE, YOUR PICK.
?
UH, I DON'T KNOW ANY OF THESE BANDS.
IT'S COOL, WHAT DO YOU USUALLY LISTEN TO?
I DON'T REALLY... LISTEN TO MUSIC.
WHAT?!
ARE YOU FROM MARS?
NO, I JUST...I HAVEN'T HEARD ANYTHING THAT I LIKE. MY MOM ONLY LISTENS TO JAMES TAYLOR, AND ALL THAT'S ON THE RADIO IS COUNTRY OR CHRISTIAN ROCK.

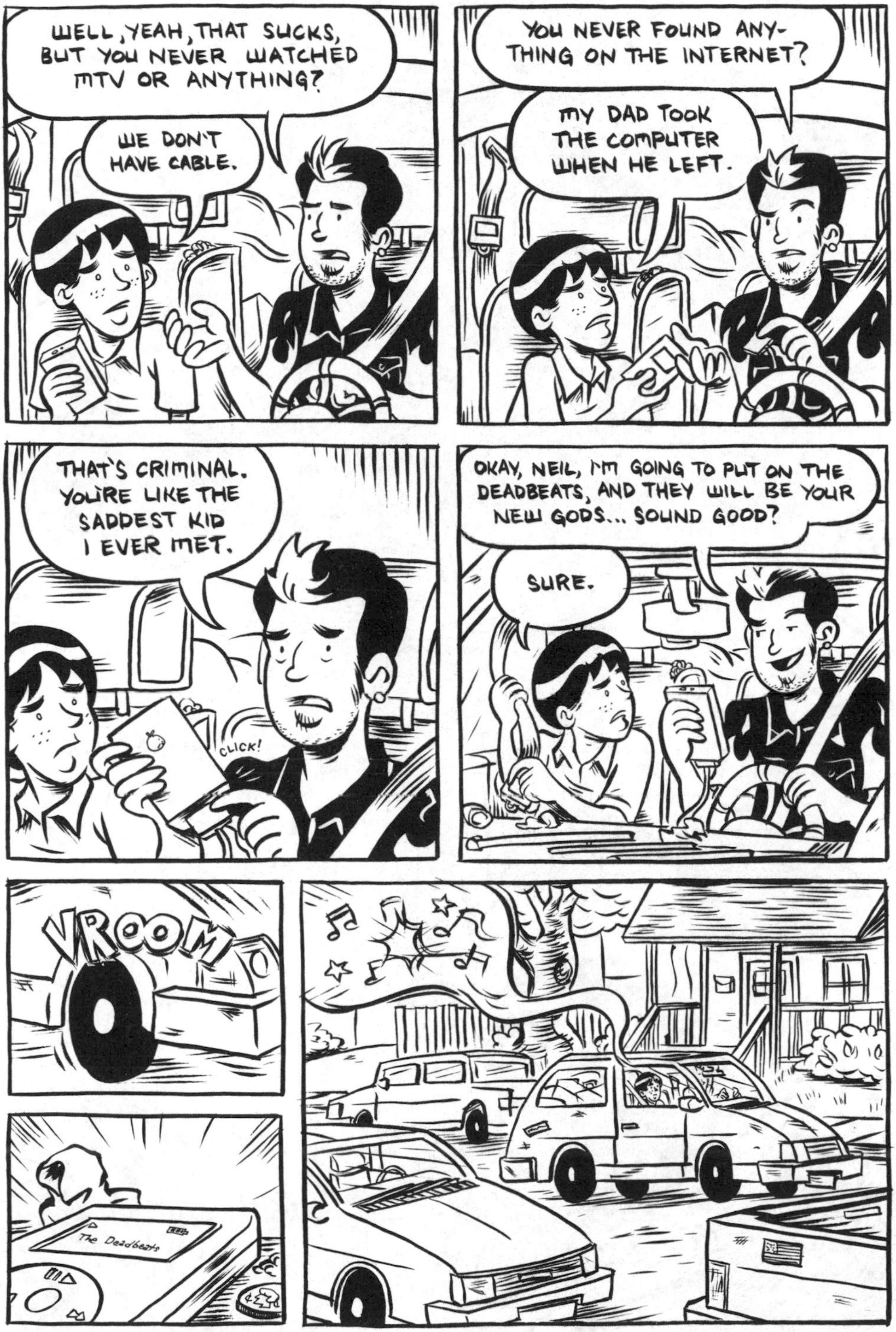

WELL, YEAH, THAT SUCKS, BUT YOU NEVER WATCHED MTV OR ANYTHING?
WE DON'T HAVE CABLE.
YOU NEVER FOUND ANYTHING ON THE INTERNET?
MY DAD TOOK THE COMPUTER WHEN HE LEFT.
THAT'S CRIMINAL. YOU'RE LIKE THE SADDEST KID I EVER MET.
CLICK!
OKAY, NEIL, I'M GOING TO PUT ON THE DEADBEATS, AND THEY WILL BE YOUR NEW GODS... SOUND GOOD?
SURE.
VROOM
The Deadbeats

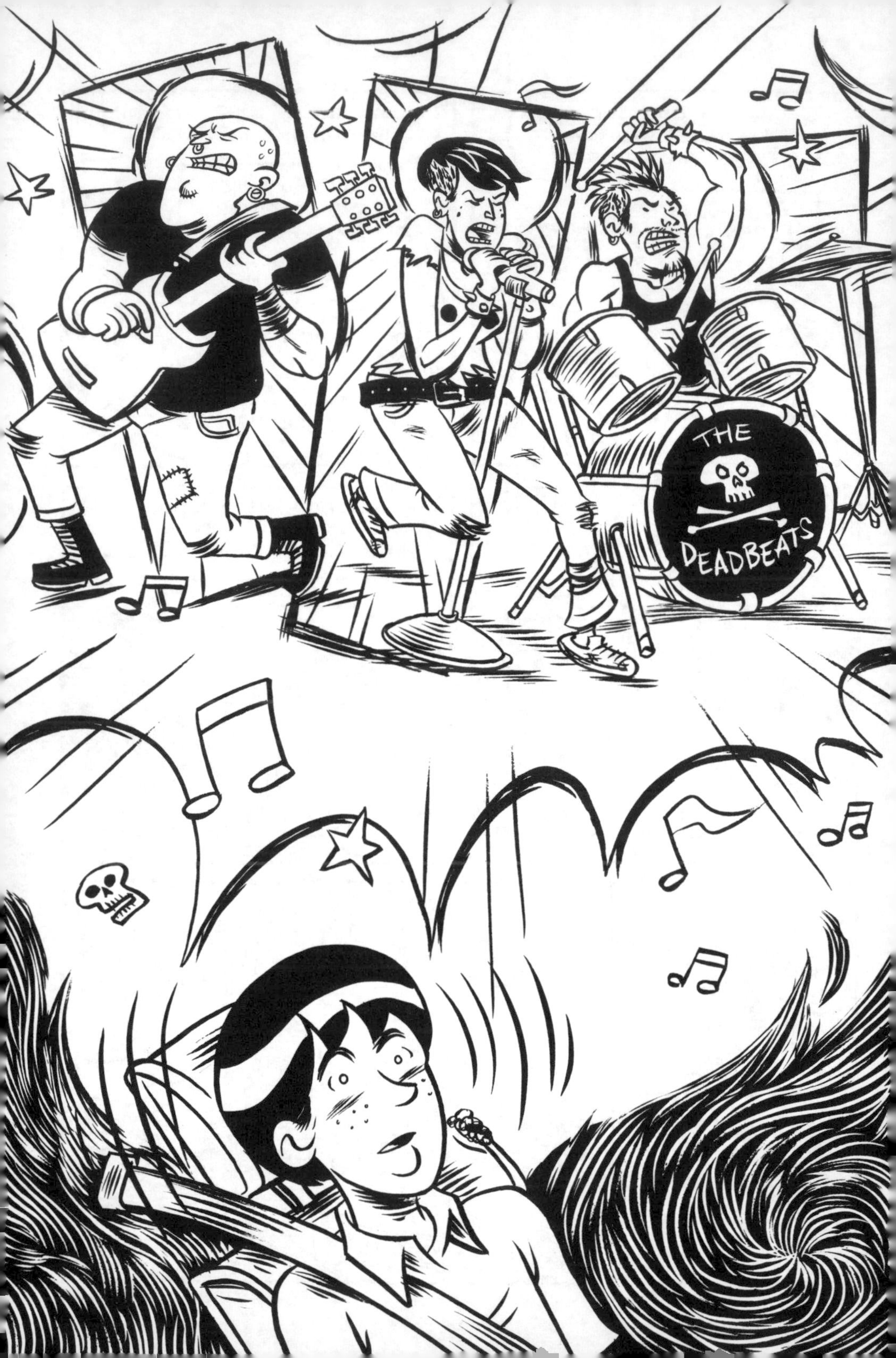
THE DEADBEATS

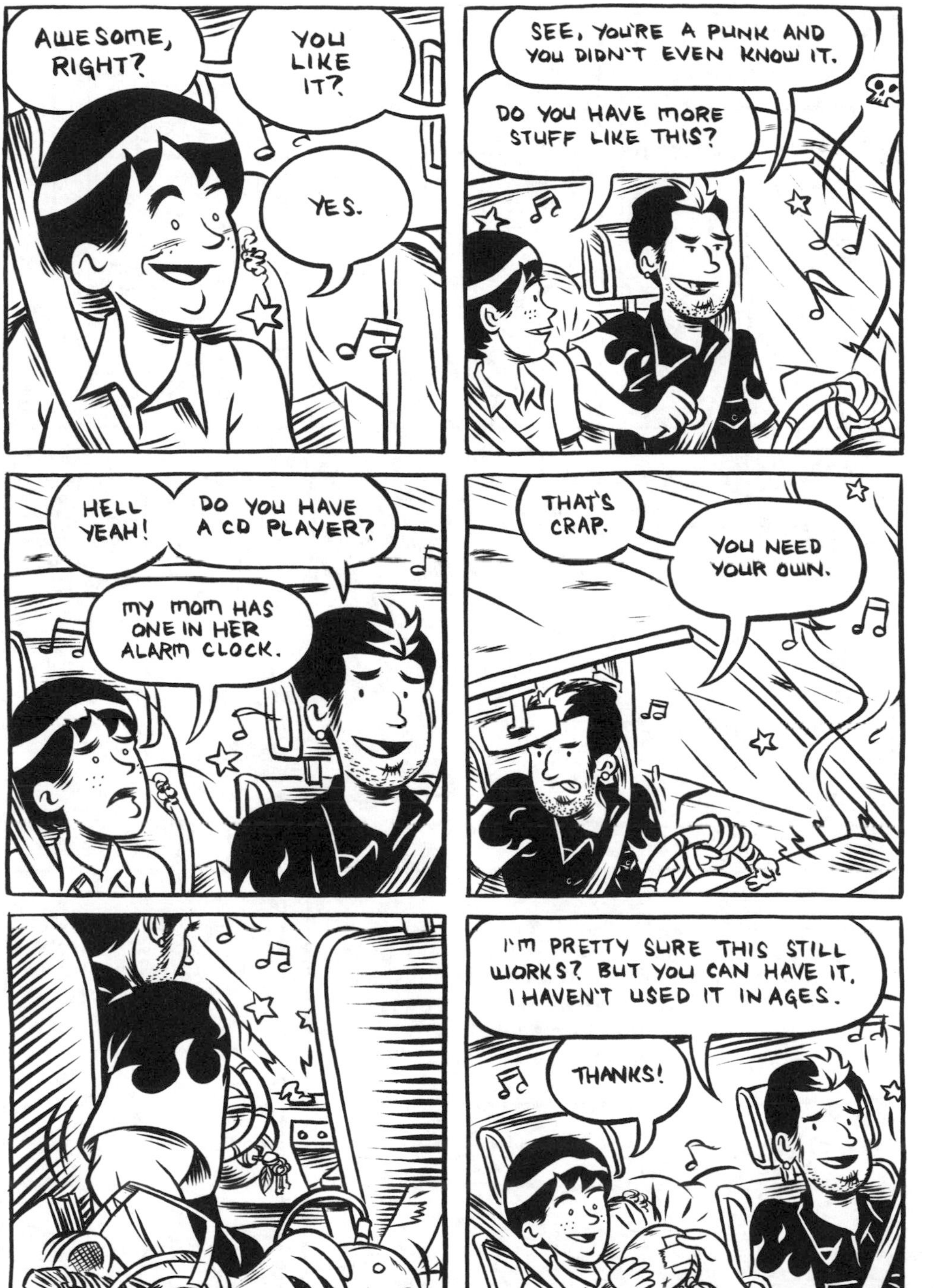
AWESOME, RIGHT?
YOU LIKE IT?
YES.
SEE, YOU'RE A PUNK AND YOU DIDN'T EVEN KNOW IT.
DO YOU HAVE MORE STUFF LIKE THIS?
HELL YEAH!
DO YOU HAVE A CD PLAYER?
MY MOM HAS ONE IN HER ALARM CLOCK.
THAT'S CRAP.
YOU NEED YOUR OWN.
I'M PRETTY SURE THIS STILL WORKS? BUT YOU CAN HAVE IT. I HAVEN'T USED IT IN AGES.
THANKS!

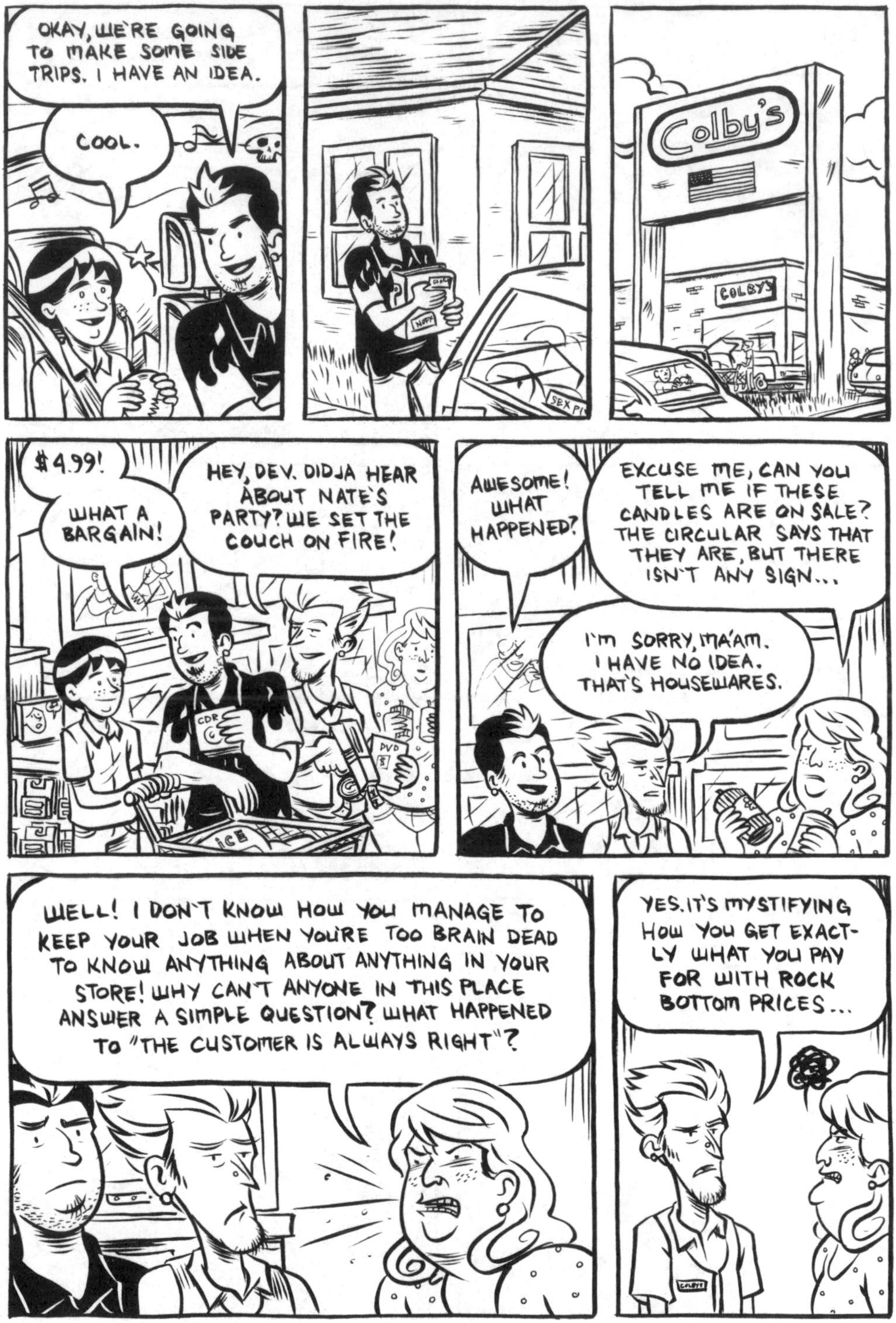
OKAY, WE'RE GOING TO MAKE SOME SIDE TRIPS. I HAVE AN IDEA.
COOL.
Colby's
COLBY'S
$4.99!
WHAT A BARGAIN!
HEY, DEV. DIDJA HEAR ABOUT NATE'S PARTY? WE SET THE COUCH ON FIRE!
AWESOME! WHAT HAPPENED?
EXCUSE ME, CAN YOU TELL ME IF THESE CANDLES ARE ON SALE? THE CIRCULAR SAYS THAT THEY ARE, BUT THERE ISN'T ANY SIGN...
I'M SORRY, MA'AM. I HAVE NO IDEA. THAT'S HOUSEWARES.
WELL! I DON'T KNOW HOW YOU MANAGE TO KEEP YOUR JOB WHEN YOU'RE TOO BRAIN DEAD TO KNOW ANYTHING ABOUT ANYTHING IN YOUR STORE! WHY CAN'T ANYONE IN THIS PLACE ANSWER A SIMPLE QUESTION? WHAT HAPPENED TO "THE CUSTOMER IS ALWAYS RIGHT"?
YES. IT'S MYSTIFYING HOW YOU GET EXACTLY WHAT YOU PAY FOR WITH ROCK BOTTOM PRICES...

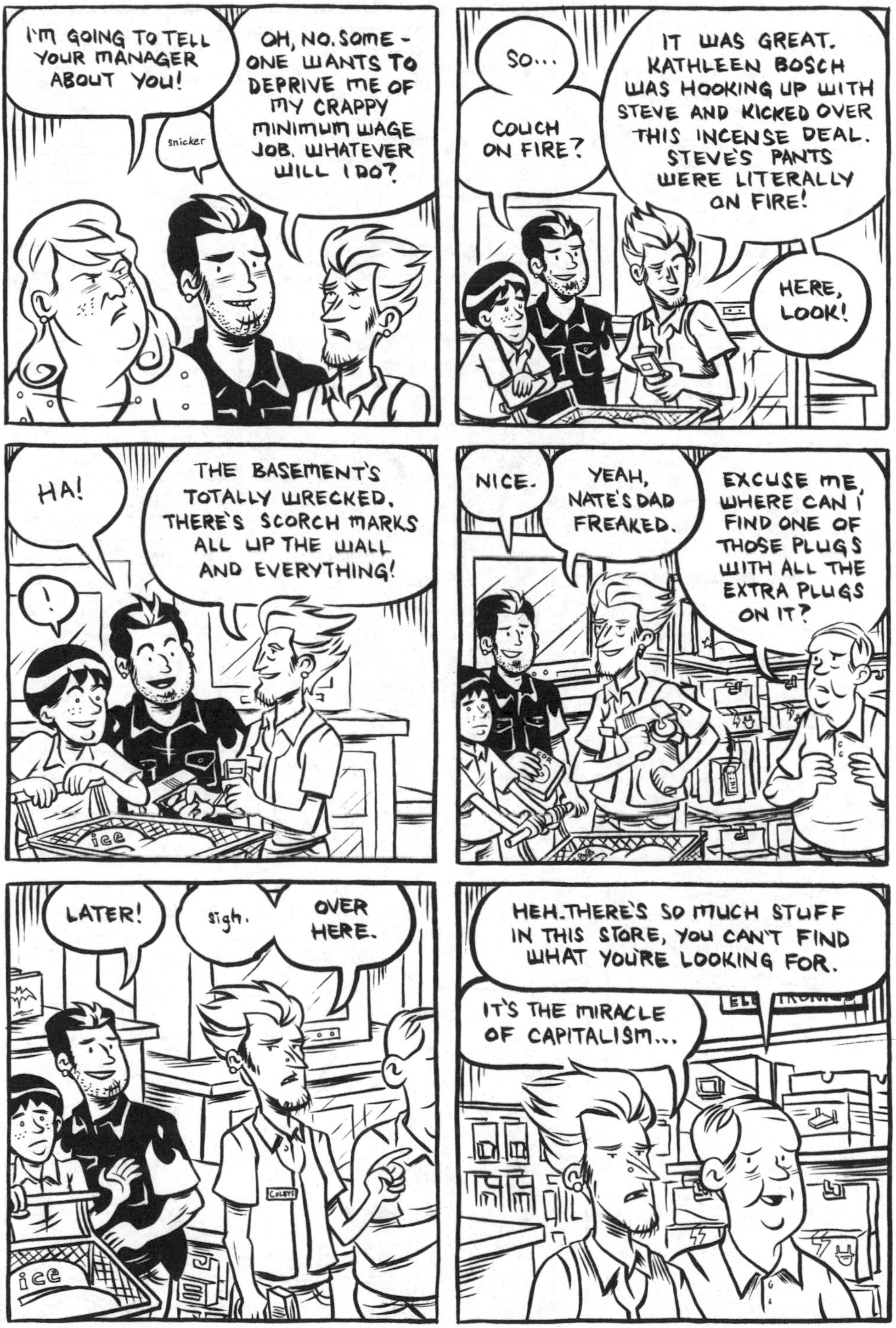
I'M GOING TO TELL YOUR MANAGER ABOUT YOU!
snicker
OH, NO. SOME-ONE WANTS TO DEPRIVE ME OF MY CRAPPY MINIMUM WAGE JOB. WHATEVER WILL I DO?
SO...
COUCH ON FIRE?
IT WAS GREAT. KATHLEEN BOSCH WAS HOOKING UP WITH STEVE AND KICKED OVER THIS INCENSE DEAL. STEVE'S PANTS WERE LITERALLY ON FIRE!
HERE, LOOK!
HA!
!
THE BASEMENT'S TOTALLY WRECKED. THERE'S SCORCH MARKS ALL UP THE WALL AND EVERYTHING!
ice
NICE.
YEAH, NATE'S DAD FREAKED.
EXCUSE ME, WHERE CAN I FIND ONE OF THOSE PLUGS WITH ALL THE EXTRA PLUGS ON IT?
LATER!
sigh.
OVER HERE.
ice
HEH. THERE'S SO MUCH STUFF IN THIS STORE, YOU CAN'T FIND WHAT YOU'RE LOOKING FOR.
IT'S THE MIRACLE OF CAPITALISM...

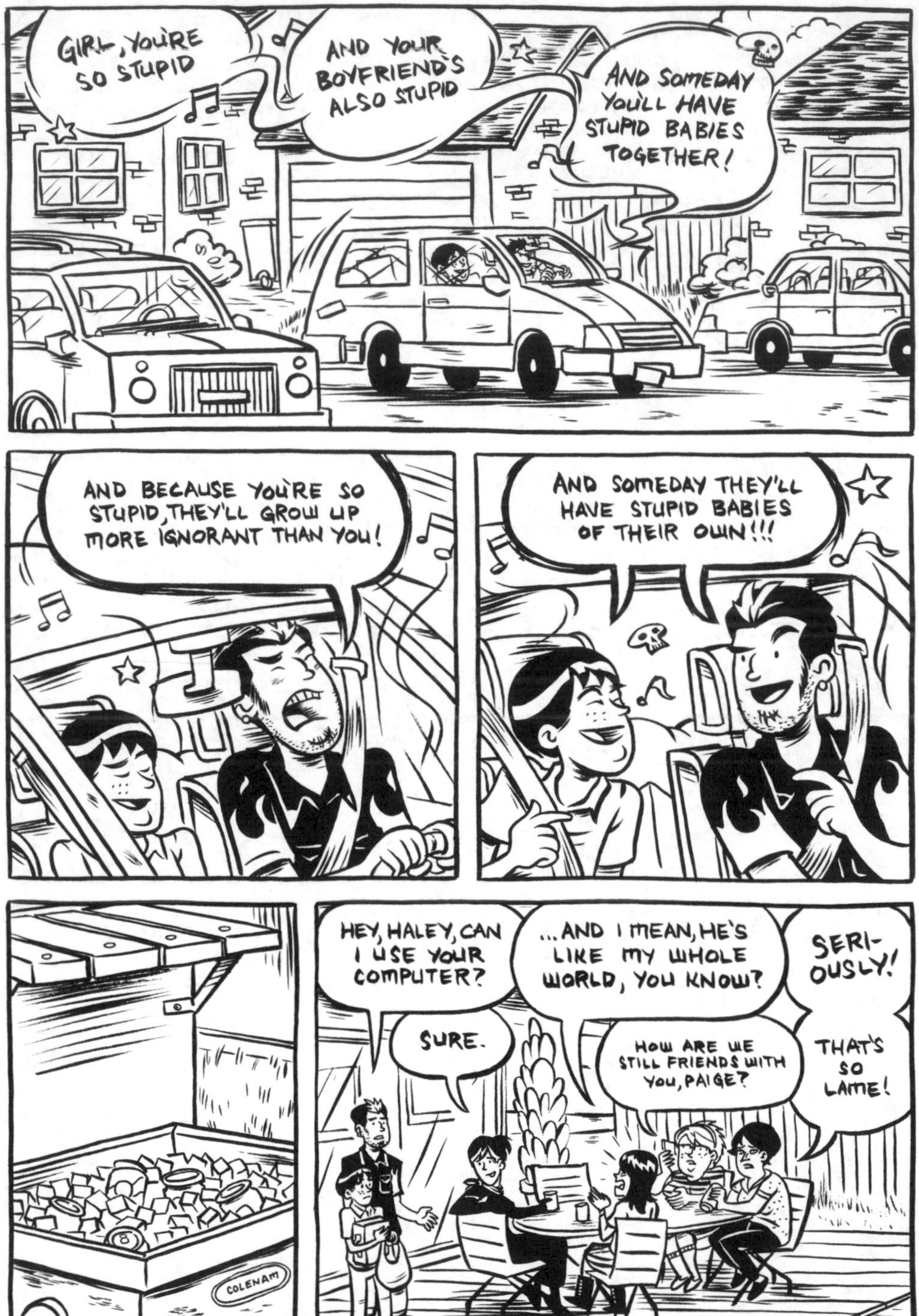
GIRL, YOU'RE SO STUPID
AND YOUR BOYFRIEND'S ALSO STUPID
AND SOMEDAY YOU'LL HAVE STUPID BABIES TOGETHER!
AND BECAUSE YOU'RE SO STUPID, THEY'LL GROW UP MORE IGNORANT THAN YOU!
AND SOMEDAY THEY'LL HAVE STUPID BABIES OF THEIR OWN!!!
COLENAM
HEY, HALEY, CAN I USE YOUR COMPUTER?
SURE.
...AND I MEAN, HE'S LIKE MY WHOLE WORLD, YOU KNOW?
HOW ARE WE STILL FRIENDS WITH YOU, PAIGE?
SERI-OUSLY!
THAT'S SO LAME!

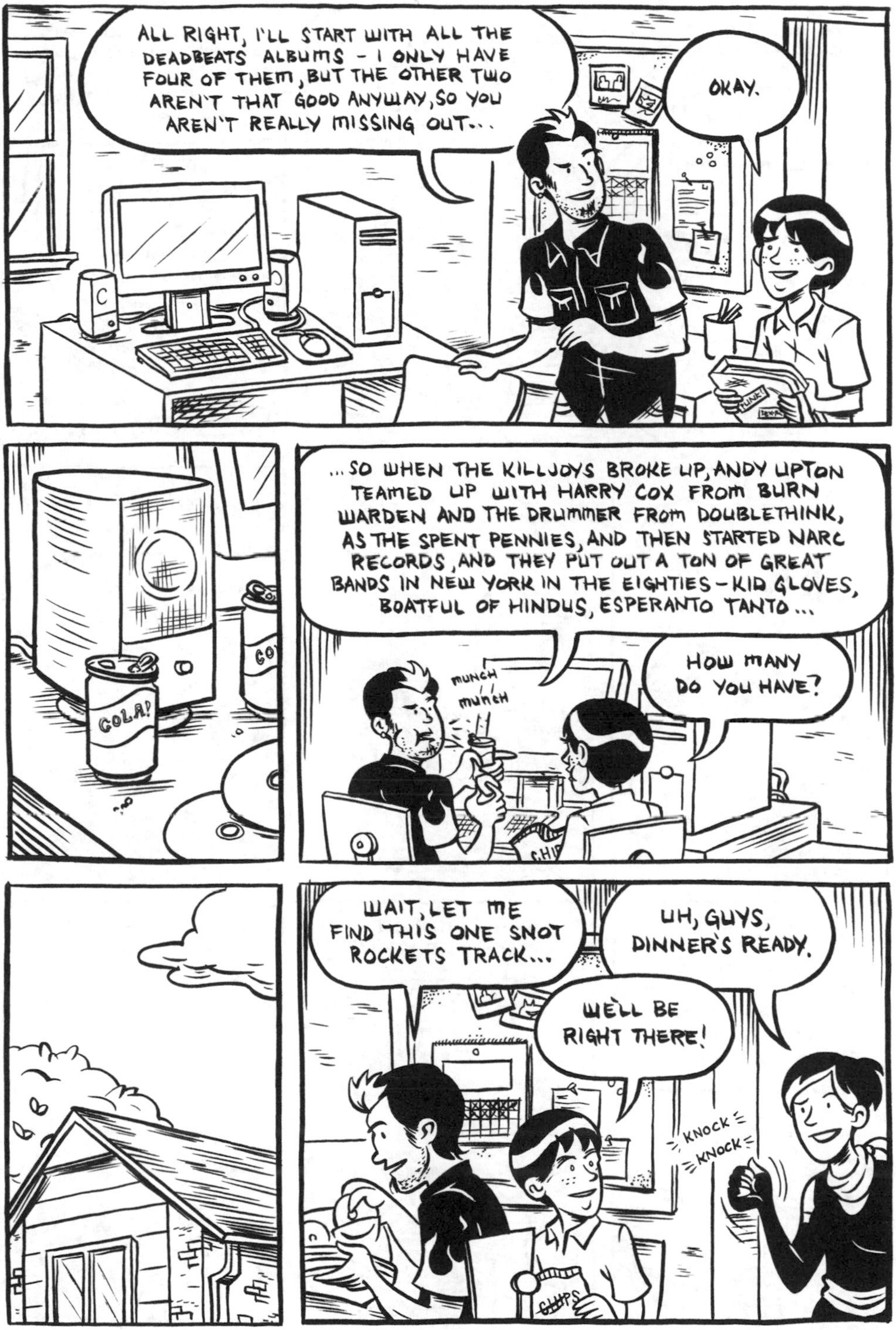
ALL RIGHT, I'LL START WITH ALL THE DEADBEATS ALBUMS - I ONLY HAVE FOUR OF THEM, BUT THE OTHER TWO AREN'T THAT GOOD ANYWAY, SO YOU AREN'T REALLY MISSING OUT...
OKAY.
COLA!
...SO WHEN THE KILLJOYS BROKE UP, ANDY UPTON TEAMED UP WITH HARRY COX FROM BURN WARDEN AND THE DRUMMER FROM DOUBLETHINK, AS THE SPENT PENNIES, AND THEN STARTED NARC RECORDS, AND THEY PUT OUT A TON OF GREAT BANDS IN NEW YORK IN THE EIGHTIES - KID GLOVES, BOATFUL OF HINDUS, ESPERANTO TANTO...
MUNCH MUNCH
HOW MANY DO YOU HAVE?
WAIT, LET ME FIND THIS ONE SNOT ROCKETS TRACK...
UH, GUYS, DINNER'S READY.
WE'LL BE RIGHT THERE!
KNOCK KNOCK
CHIPS

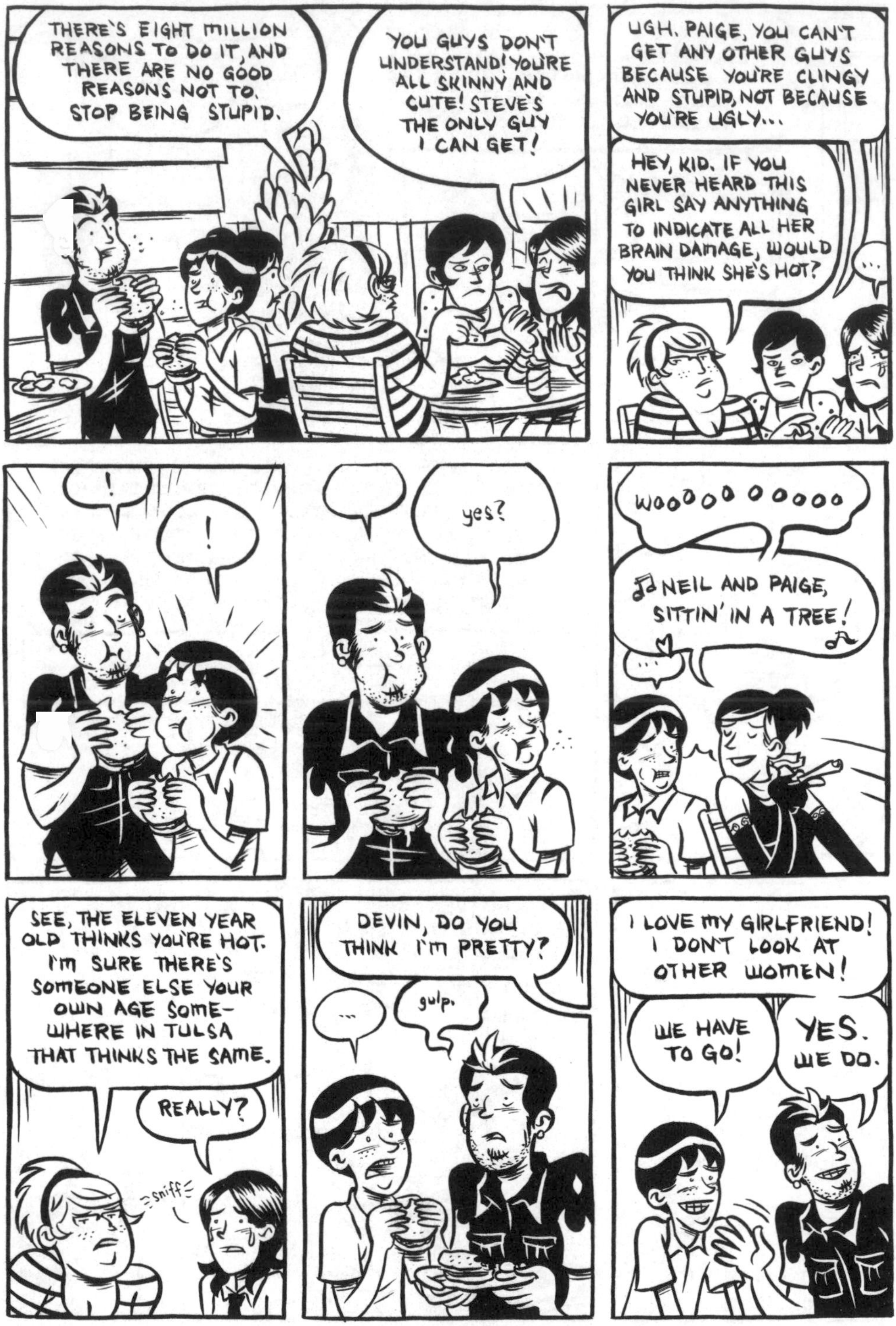
THERE'S EIGHT MILLION REASONS TO DO IT, AND THERE ARE NO GOOD REASONS NOT TO. STOP BEING STUPID.
YOU GUYS DON'T UNDERSTAND! YOU'RE ALL SKINNY AND CUTE! STEVE'S THE ONLY GUY I CAN GET!
UGH. PAIGE, YOU CAN'T GET ANY OTHER GUYS BECAUSE YOU'RE CLINGY AND STUPID, NOT BECAUSE YOU'RE UGLY...
HEY, KID. IF YOU NEVER HEARD THIS GIRL SAY ANYTHING TO INDICATE ALL HER BRAIN DAMAGE, WOULD YOU THINK SHE'S HOT?
...
!
!
yes?
WOOOOO OOOOO
NEIL AND PAIGE, SITTIN' IN A TREE!
...
SEE, THE ELEVEN YEAR OLD THINKS YOU'RE HOT. I'M SURE THERE'S SOMEONE ELSE YOUR OWN AGE SOMEWHERE IN TULSA THAT THINKS THE SAME.
REALLY?
sniff
DEVIN, DO YOU THINK I'M PRETTY?
...
gulp.
I LOVE MY GIRLFRIEND! I DON'T LOOK AT OTHER WOMEN!
WE HAVE TO GO!
YES. WE DO.

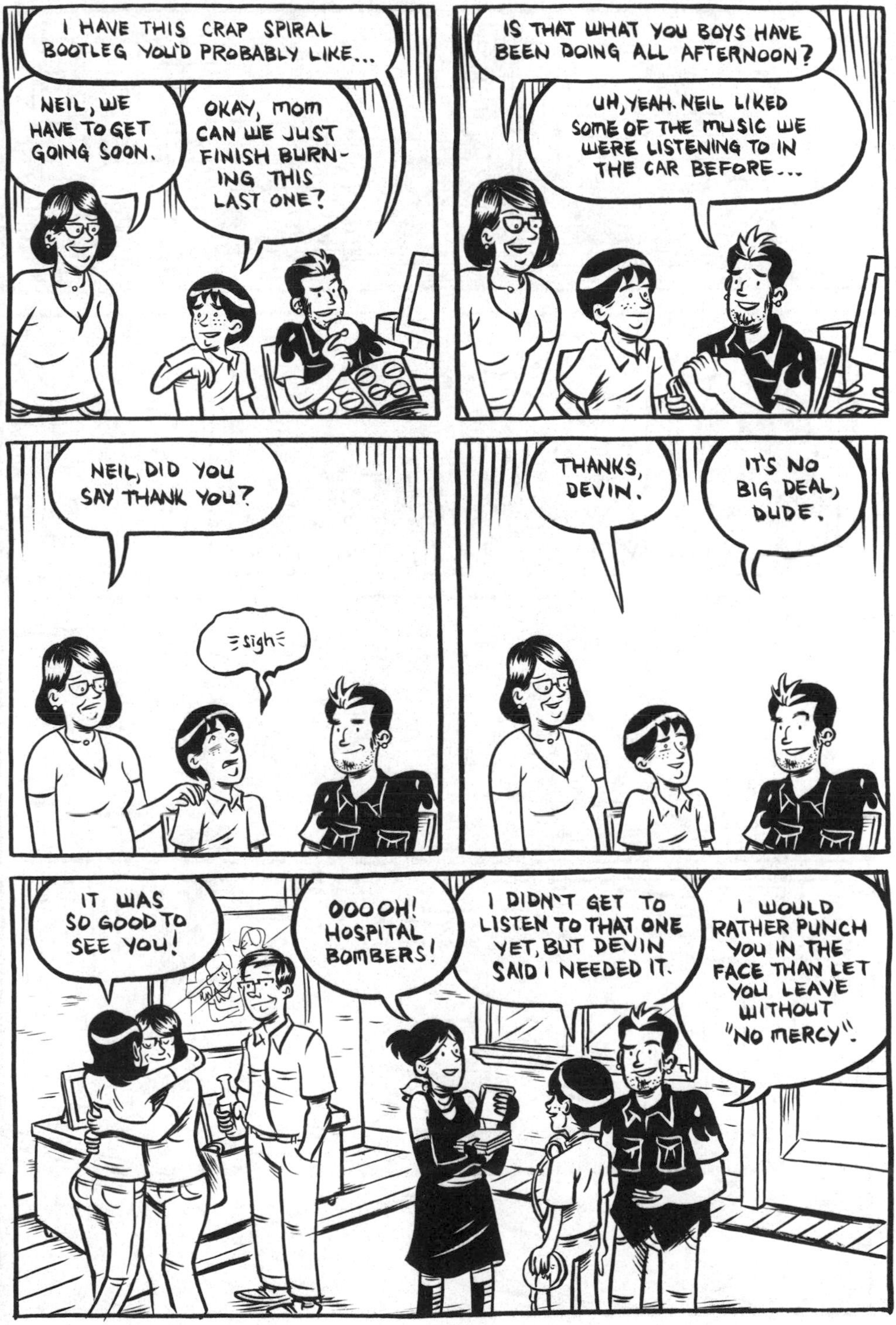
I HAVE THIS CRAP SPIRAL BOOTLEG YOU'D PROBABLY LIKE...
NEIL, WE HAVE TO GET GOING SOON.
OKAY, MOM CAN WE JUST FINISH BURNING THIS LAST ONE?
IS THAT WHAT YOU BOYS HAVE BEEN DOING ALL AFTERNOON?
UH, YEAH. NEIL LIKED SOME OF THE MUSIC WE WERE LISTENING TO IN THE CAR BEFORE...
NEIL, DID YOU SAY THANK YOU?
sigh
THANKS, DEVIN.
IT'S NO BIG DEAL, DUDE.
IT WAS SO GOOD TO SEE YOU!
OOOOH! HOSPITAL BOMBERS!
I DIDN'T GET TO LISTEN TO THAT ONE YET, BUT DEVIN SAID I NEEDED IT.
I WOULD RATHER PUNCH YOU IN THE FACE THAN LET YOU LEAVE WITHOUT "NO MERCY"!

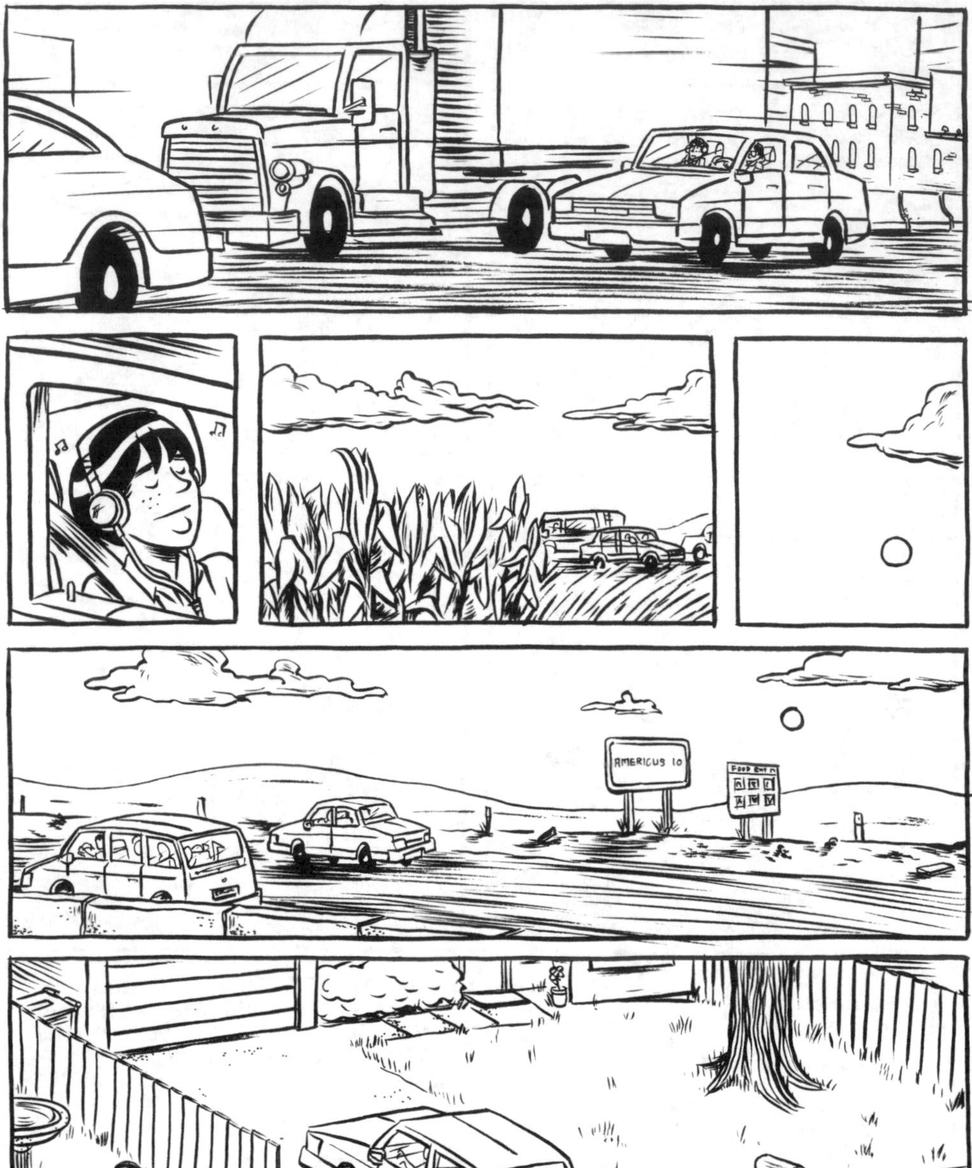
AMERICUS 10

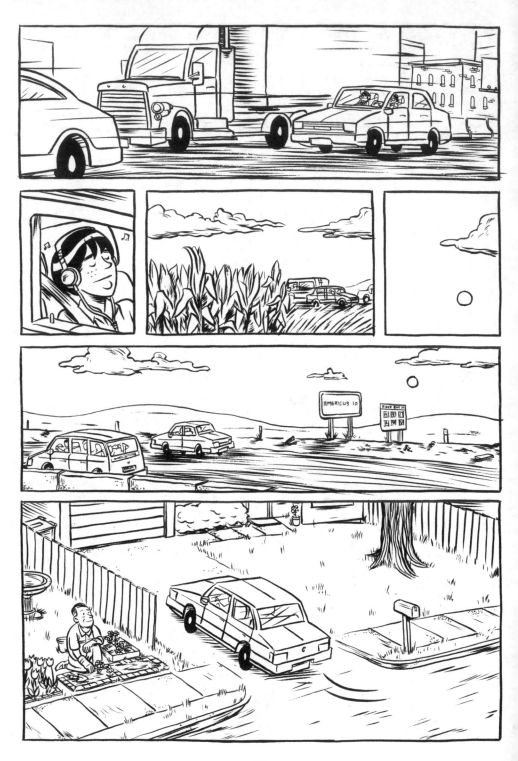

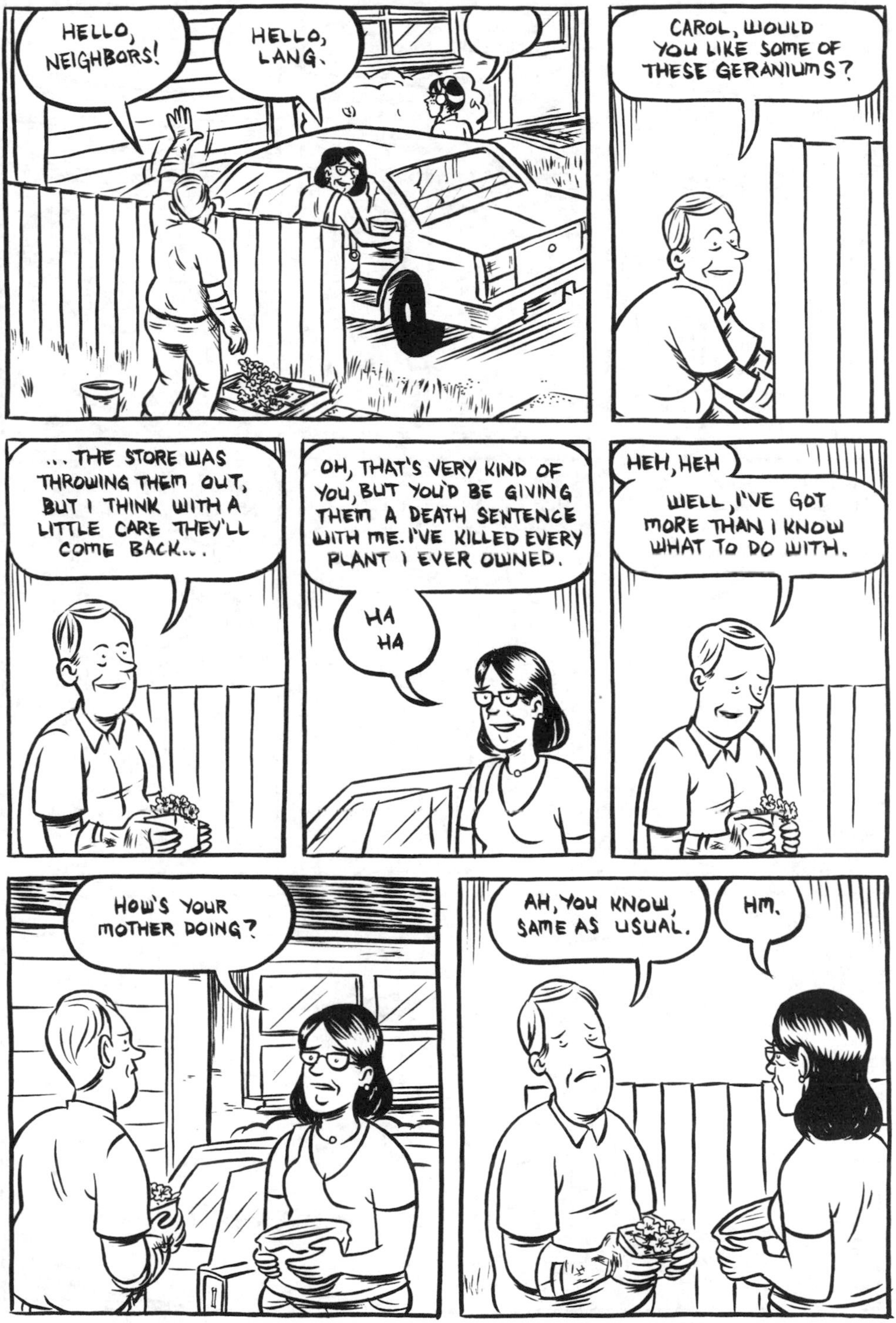

HELLO, NEIGHBORS!
HELLO, LANG.
CAROL, WOULD YOU LIKE SOME OF THESE GERANIUMS?
... THE STORE WAS THROWING THEM OUT, BUT I THINK WITH A LITTLE CARE THEY'LL COME BACK...
OH, THAT'S VERY KIND OF YOU, BUT YOU'D BE GIVING THEM A DEATH SENTENCE WITH ME. I'VE KILLED EVERY PLANT I EVER OWNED.
HA HA
HEH, HEH
WELL, I'VE GOT MORE THAN I KNOW WHAT TO DO WITH.
HOW'S YOUR MOTHER DOING?
AH, YOU KNOW, SAME AS USUAL.
HM.

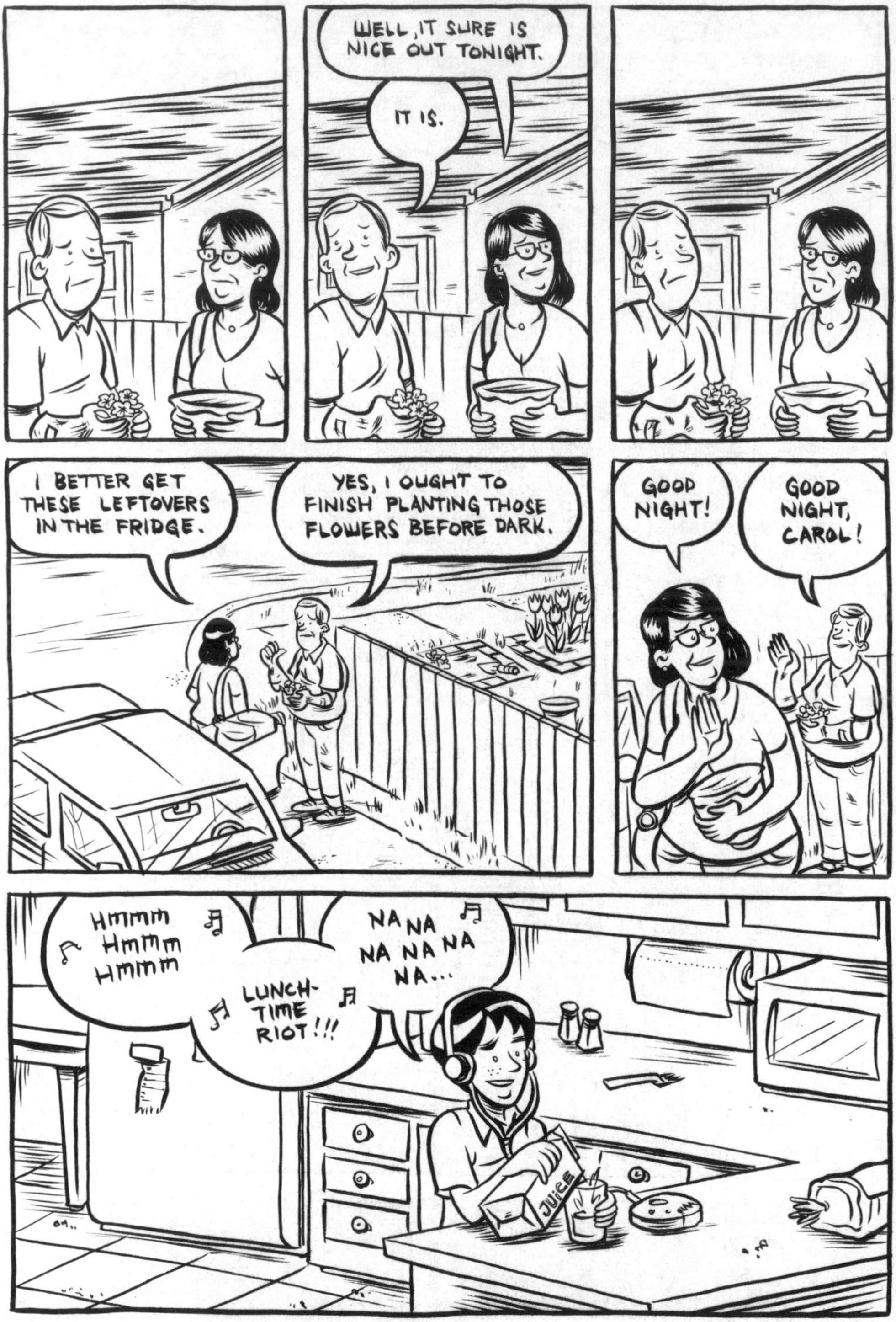
WELL, IT SURE IS NICE OUT TONIGHT.
IT IS.
I BETTER GET THESE LEFTOVERS IN THE FRIDGE.
YES, I OUGHT TO FINISH PLANTING THOSE FLOWERS BEFORE DARK.
GOOD NIGHT!
GOOD NIGHT, CAROL!
HMMM HMMM HMMM
NA NA NA NA NA NA...
LUNCH-TIME RIOT!!!
JUICE

CHAPTER 4

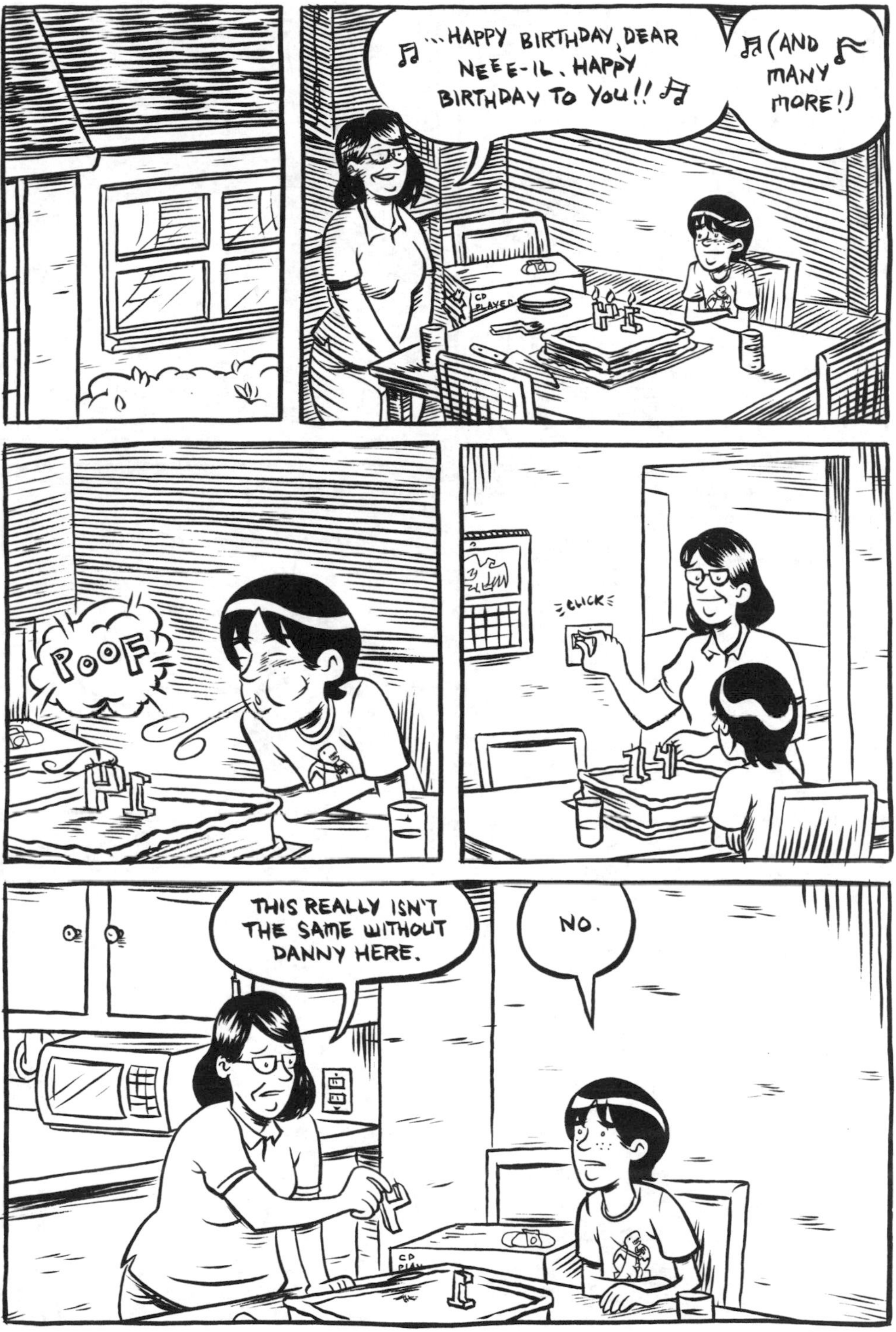
...HAPPY BIRTHDAY, DEAR NEEE-IL. HAPPY BIRTHDAY TO YOU!!
(AND MANY MORE!)
CD PLAYER
POOF
CLICK
THIS REALLY ISN'T THE SAME WITHOUT DANNY HERE.
NO.
CD PLAY

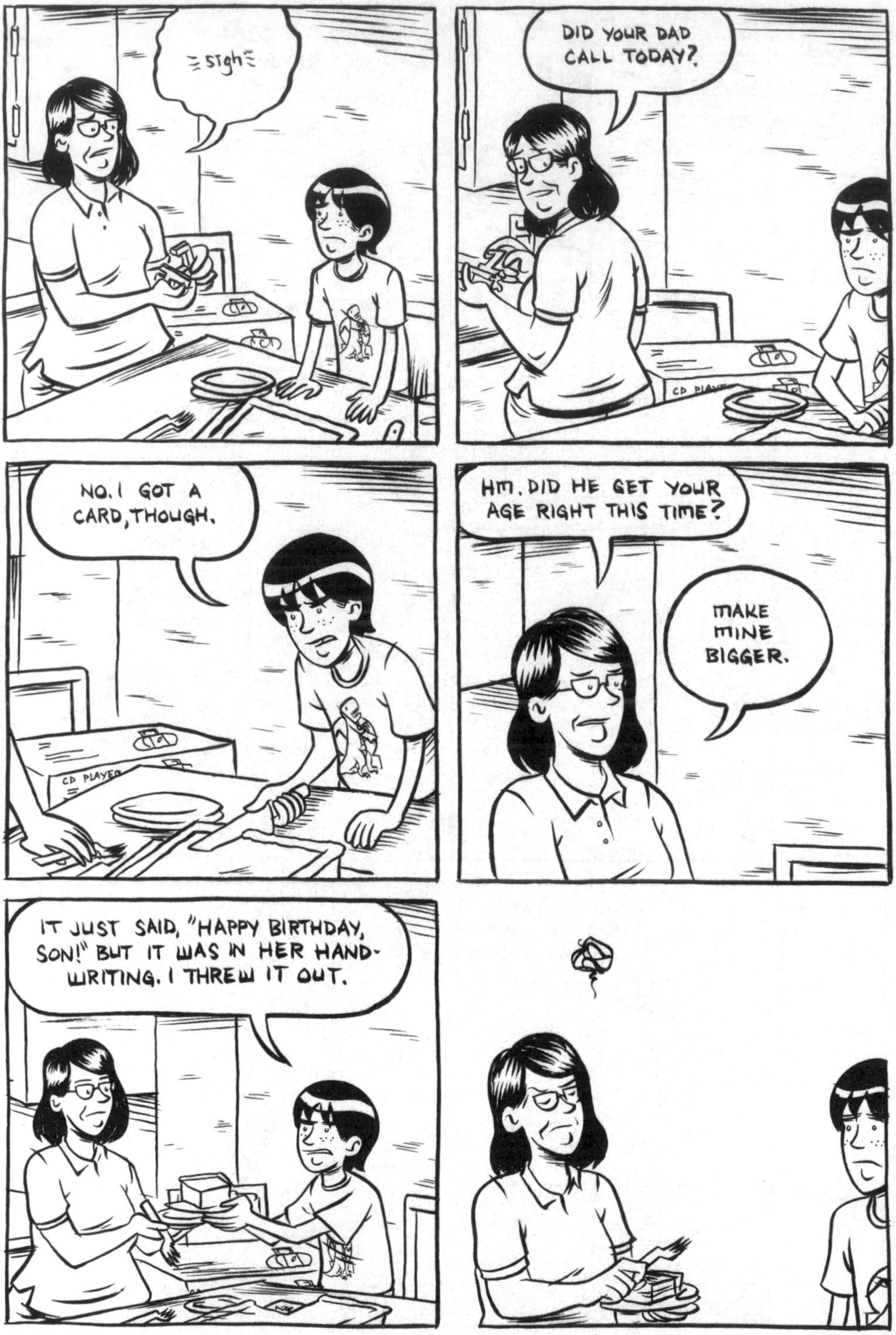
sigh
DID YOUR DAD CALL TODAY?
NO. I GOT A CARD, THOUGH.
HM. DID HE GET YOUR AGE RIGHT THIS TIME?
MAKE MINE BIGGER.
IT JUST SAID, "HAPPY BIRTHDAY, SON!" BUT IT WAS IN HER HAND-WRITING. I THREW IT OUT.

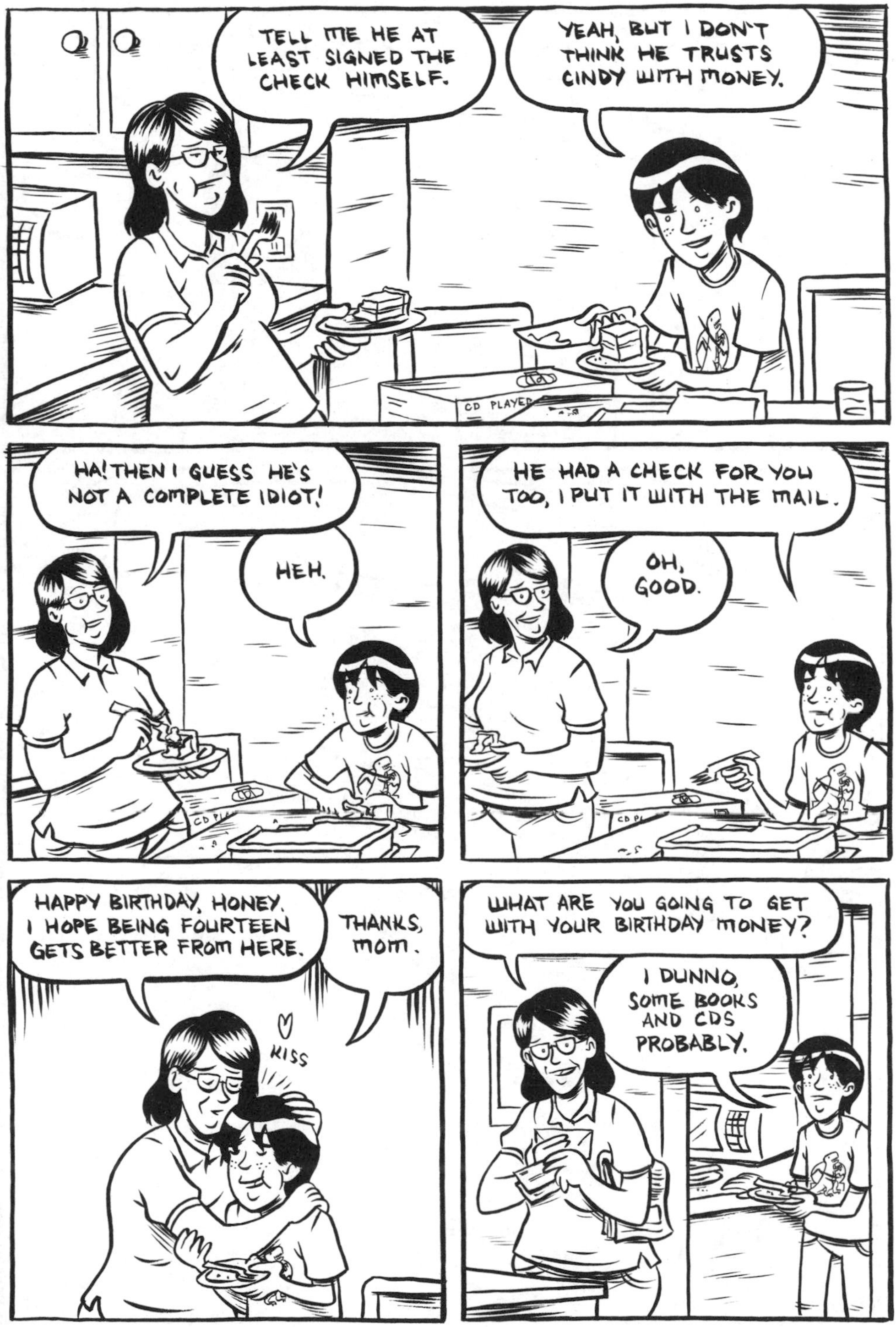
TELL ME HE AT LEAST SIGNED THE CHECK HIMSELF.
YEAH, BUT I DON'T THINK HE TRUSTS CINDY WITH MONEY.
CD PLAYER
HA! THEN I GUESS HE'S NOT A COMPLETE IDIOT!
HEH.
HE HAD A CHECK FOR YOU TOO, I PUT IT WITH THE MAIL.
OH, GOOD.
HAPPY BIRTHDAY, HONEY. I HOPE BEING FOURTEEN GETS BETTER FROM HERE.
THANKS, MOM.
KISS
WHAT ARE YOU GOING TO GET WITH YOUR BIRTHDAY MONEY?
I DUNNO, SOME BOOKS AND CDS PROBABLY.

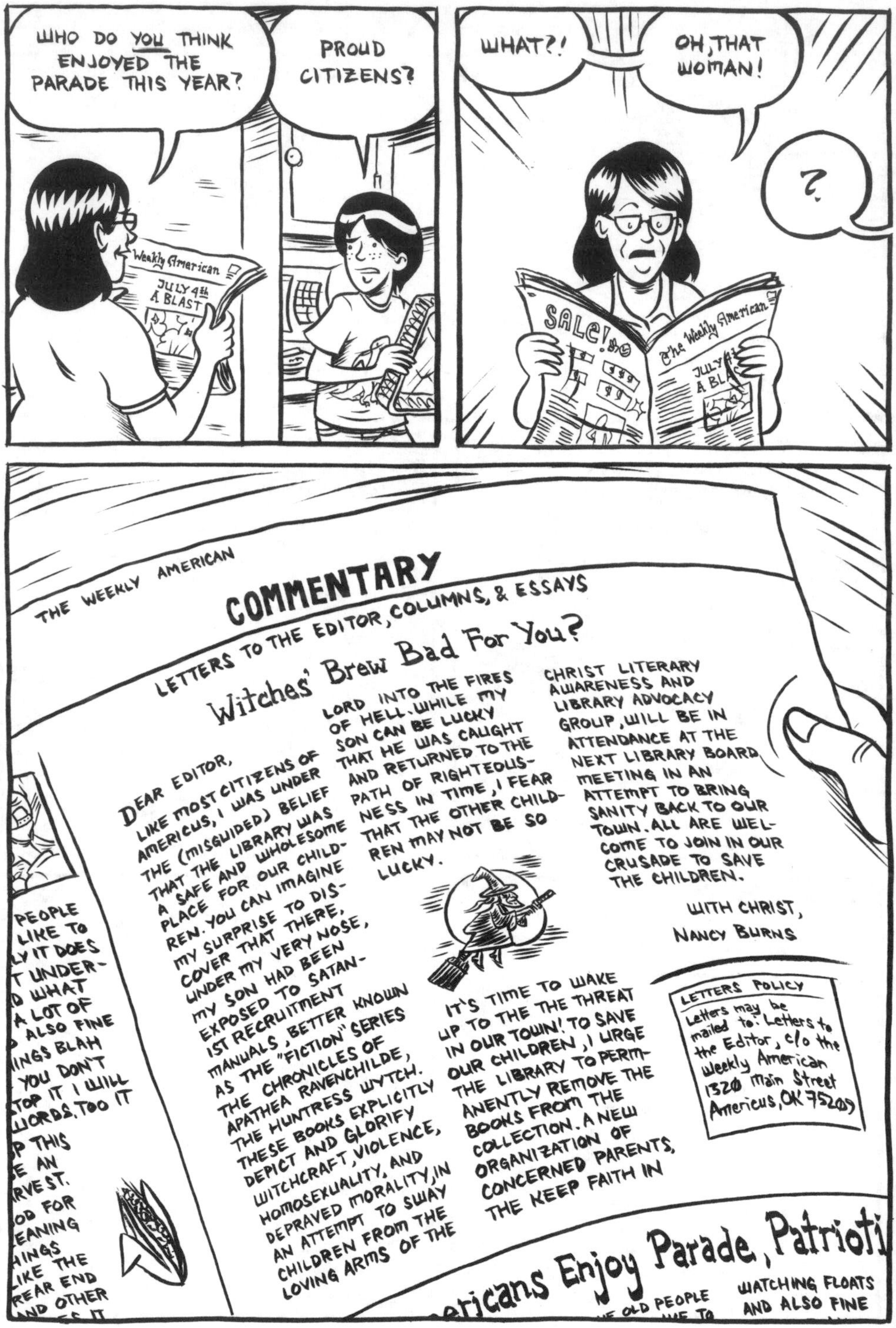
WHO DO YOU THINK ENJOYED THE PARADE THIS YEAR?
PROUD CITIZENS?
Weekly American
JULY 4th A BLAST
WHAT?!
OH, THAT WOMAN!
?
SALE!
The Weekly American
THE WEEKLY AMERICAN
COMMENTARY
LETTERS TO THE EDITOR, COLUMNS, & ESSAYS
Witches' Brew Bad For You?
DEAR EDITOR,
LIKE MOST CITIZENS OF AMERICUS, I WAS UNDER THE (MISGUIDED) BELIEF THAT THE LIBRARY WAS A SAFE AND WHOLESOME PLACE FOR OUR CHILDREN. YOU CAN IMAGINE MY SURPRISE TO DISCOVER THAT THERE, UNDER MY VERY NOSE, MY SON HAD BEEN EXPOSED TO SATANIST RECRUITMENT MANUALS, BETTER KNOWN AS THE "FICTION" SERIES THE CHRONICLES OF APATHEA RAVENCHILDE, THE HUNTRESS WYTCH. THESE BOOKS EXPLICITLY DEPICT AND GLORIFY WITCHCRAFT, VIOLENCE, HOMOSEXUALITY, AND DEPRAVED MORALITY, IN AN ATTEMPT TO SWAY CHILDREN FROM THE LOVING ARMS OF THE LORD INTO THE FIRES OF HELL. WHILE MY SON CAN BE LUCKY THAT HE WAS CAUGHT AND RETURNED TO THE PATH OF RIGHTEOUSNESS IN TIME, I FEAR THAT THE OTHER CHILDREN MAY NOT BE SO LUCKY.
IT'S TIME TO WAKE UP TO THE THE THREAT IN OUR TOWN! TO SAVE OUR CHILDREN, I URGE THE LIBRARY TO PERMANENTLY REMOVE THE BOOKS FROM THE COLLECTION. A NEW ORGANIZATION OF CONCERNED PARENTS, THE KEEP FAITH IN CHRIST LITERARY AWARENESS AND LIBRARY ADVOCACY GROUP, WILL BE IN ATTENDANCE AT THE NEXT LIBRARY BOARD MEETING IN AN ATTEMPT TO BRING SANITY BACK TO OUR TOWN. ALL ARE WELCOME TO JOIN IN OUR CRUSADE TO SAVE THE CHILDREN.
WITH CHRIST,
NANCY BURNS
LETTERS POLICY
Letters may be mailed to: Letters to the Editor, c/o the Weekly American 1320 Main Street Americus, OK 75209
...ericans Enjoy Parade, Patrioti...
WATCHING FLOATS AND ALSO FINE

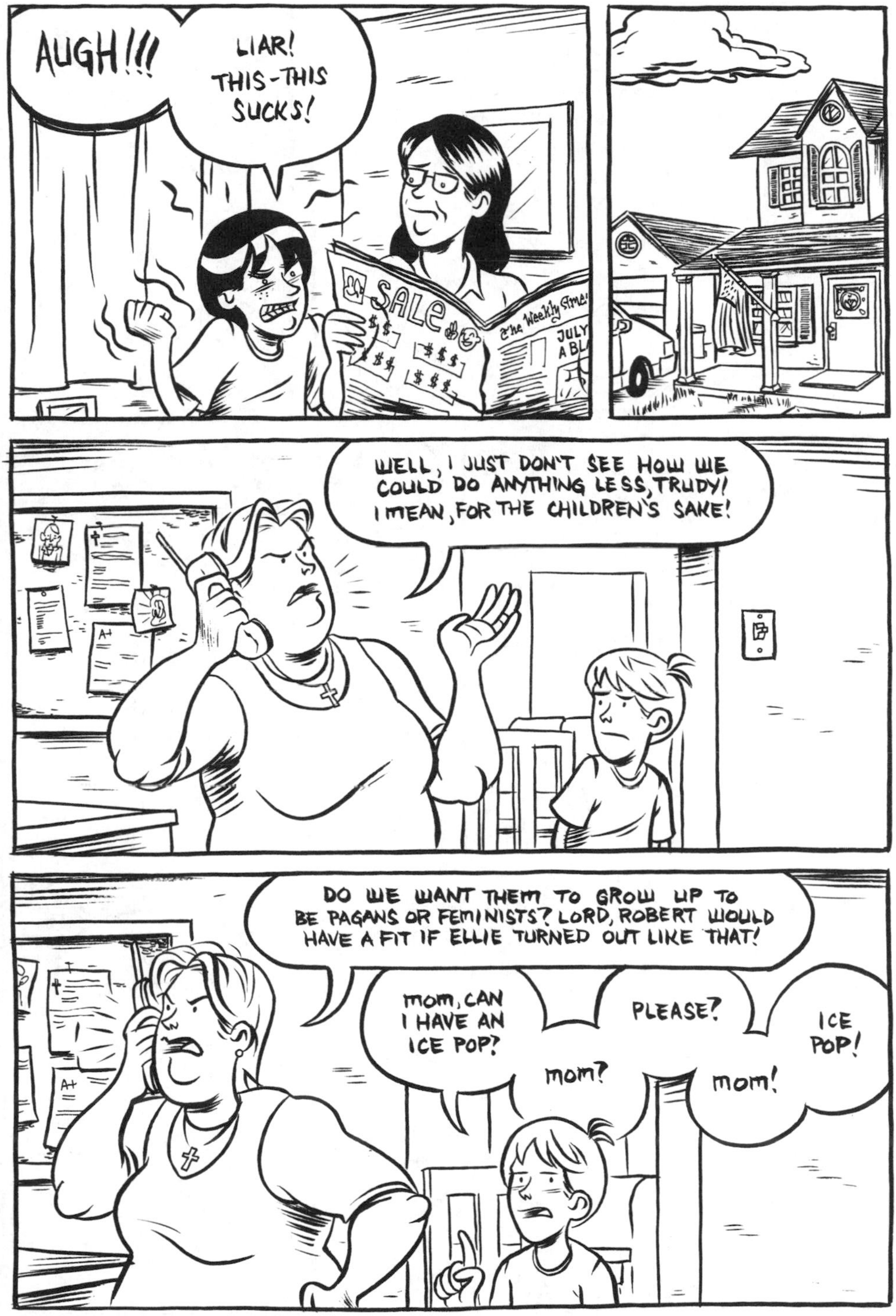
AUGH!!!
LIAR! THIS-THIS SUCKS!
SALE
$$ $$$ $$$ $$$
The Weekly Times
JULY
A BLA
WELL, I JUST DON'T SEE HOW WE COULD DO ANYTHING LESS, TRUDY! I MEAN, FOR THE CHILDREN'S SAKE!
A+
DO WE WANT THEM TO GROW UP TO BE PAGANS OR FEMINISTS? LORD, ROBERT WOULD HAVE A FIT IF ELLIE TURNED OUT LIKE THAT!
MOM, CAN I HAVE AN ICE POP?
PLEASE?
ICE POP!
MOM?
MOM!
A+

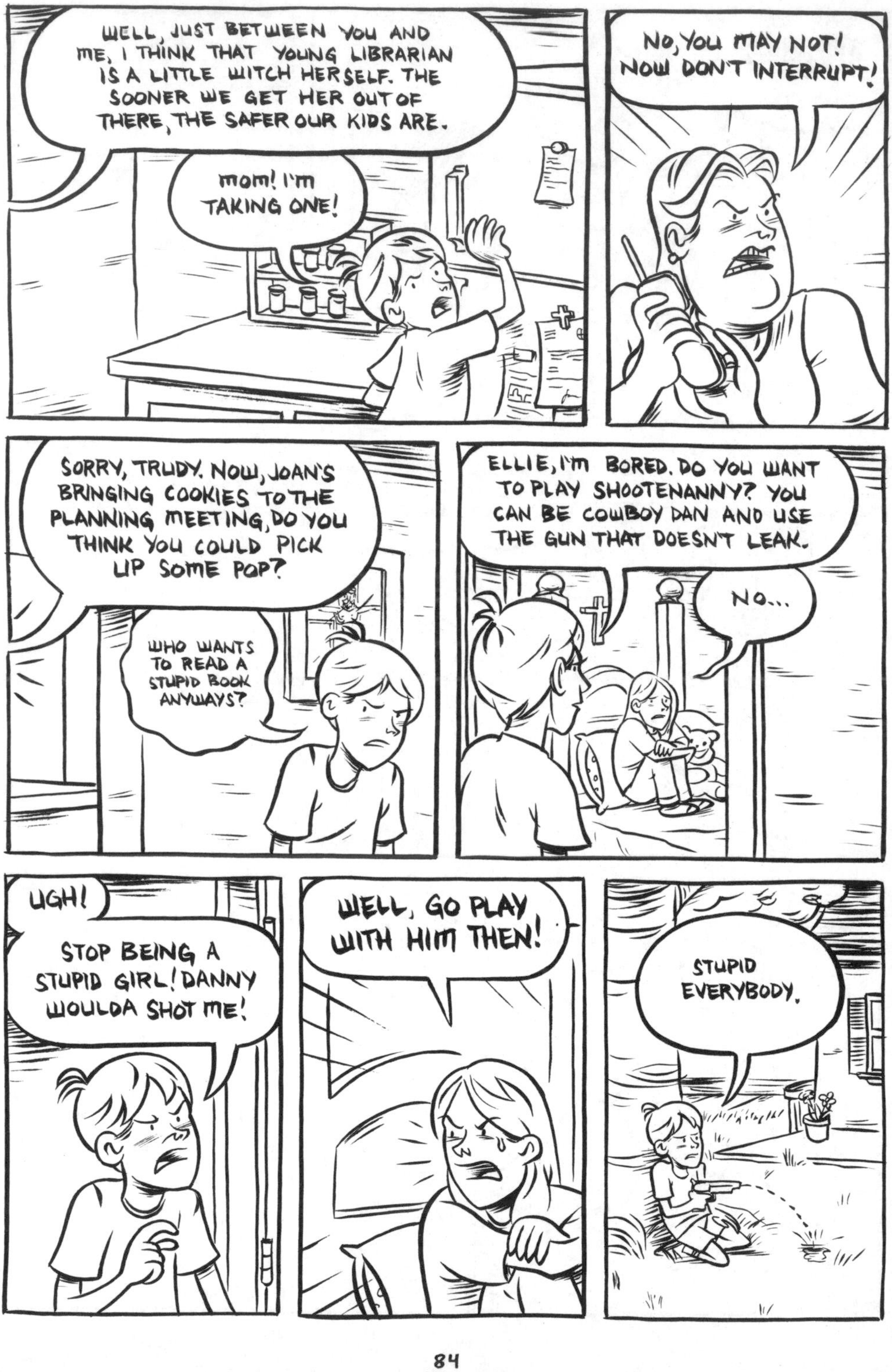
WELL, JUST BETWEEN YOU AND ME, I THINK THAT YOUNG LIBRARIAN IS A LITTLE WITCH HERSELF. THE SOONER WE GET HER OUT OF THERE, THE SAFER OUR KIDS ARE.
MOM! I'M TAKING ONE!
NO, YOU MAY NOT! NOW DON'T INTERRUPT!
SORRY, TRUDY. NOW, JOAN'S BRINGING COOKIES TO THE PLANNING MEETING, DO YOU THINK YOU COULD PICK UP SOME POP?
WHO WANTS TO READ A STUPID BOOK ANYWAYS?
ELLIE, I'M BORED. DO YOU WANT TO PLAY SHOOTENANNY? YOU CAN BE COWBOY DAN AND USE THE GUN THAT DOESN'T LEAK.
NO...
UGH!
STOP BEING A STUPID GIRL! DANNY WOULDA SHOT ME!
WELL, GO PLAY WITH HIM THEN!
STUPID EVERYBODY.

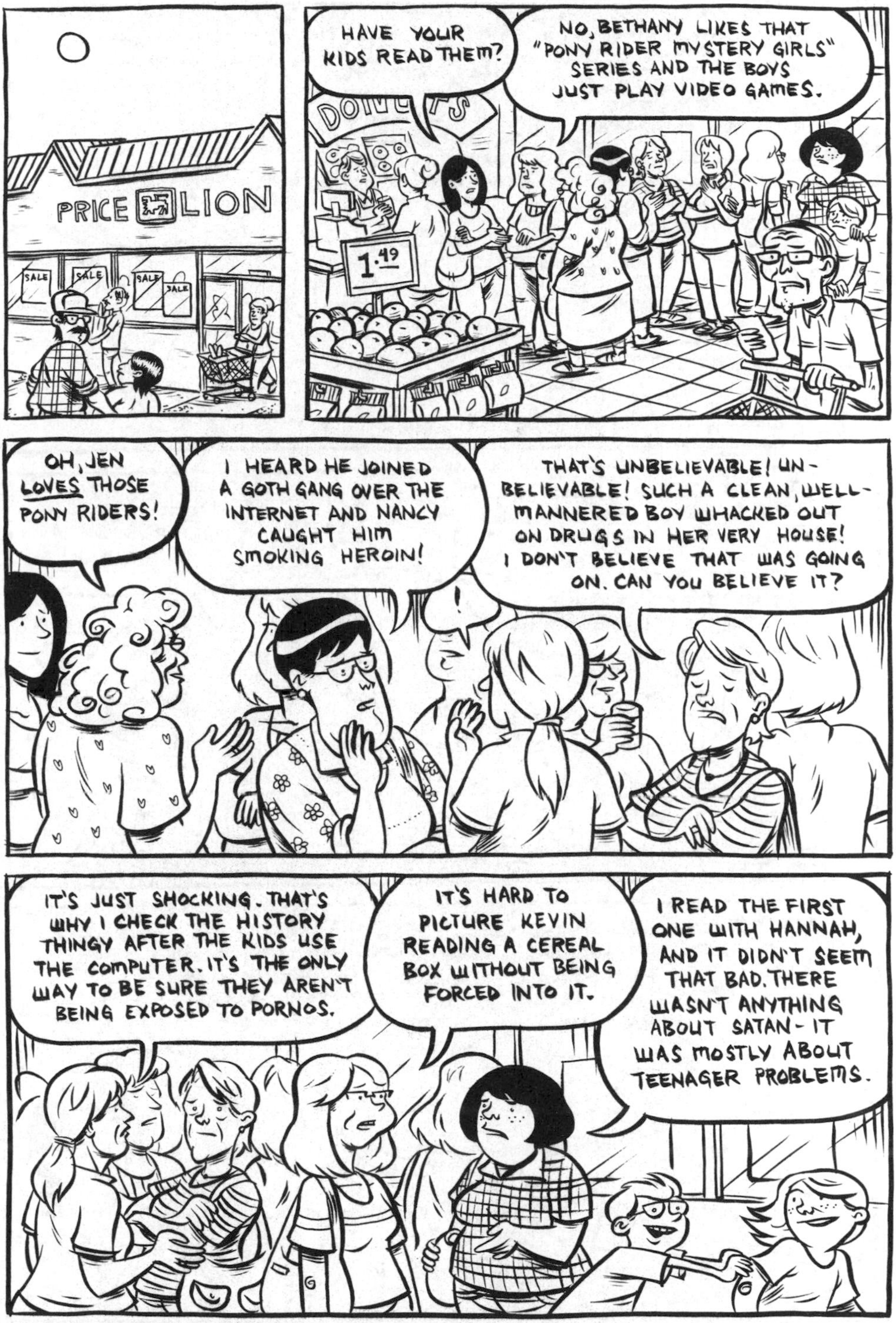
PRICE LION
SALE
SALE
SALE
SALE
DONUTS
1.49
HAVE YOUR KIDS READ THEM?
NO, BETHANY LIKES THAT "PONY RIDER MYSTERY GIRLS" SERIES AND THE BOYS JUST PLAY VIDEO GAMES.
OH, JEN LOVES THOSE PONY RIDERS!
I HEARD HE JOINED A GOTH GANG OVER THE INTERNET AND NANCY CAUGHT HIM SMOKING HEROIN!
!
THAT'S UNBELIEVABLE! UN-BELIEVABLE! SUCH A CLEAN, WELL-MANNERED BOY WHACKED OUT ON DRUGS IN HER VERY HOUSE! I DON'T BELIEVE THAT WAS GOING ON. CAN YOU BELIEVE IT?
IT'S JUST SHOCKING. THAT'S WHY I CHECK THE HISTORY THINGY AFTER THE KIDS USE THE COMPUTER. IT'S THE ONLY WAY TO BE SURE THEY AREN'T BEING EXPOSED TO PORNOS.
IT'S HARD TO PICTURE KEVIN READING A CEREAL BOX WITHOUT BEING FORCED INTO IT.
I READ THE FIRST ONE WITH HANNAH, AND IT DIDN'T SEEM THAT BAD. THERE WASN'T ANYTHING ABOUT SATAN - IT WAS MOSTLY ABOUT TEENAGER PROBLEMS.

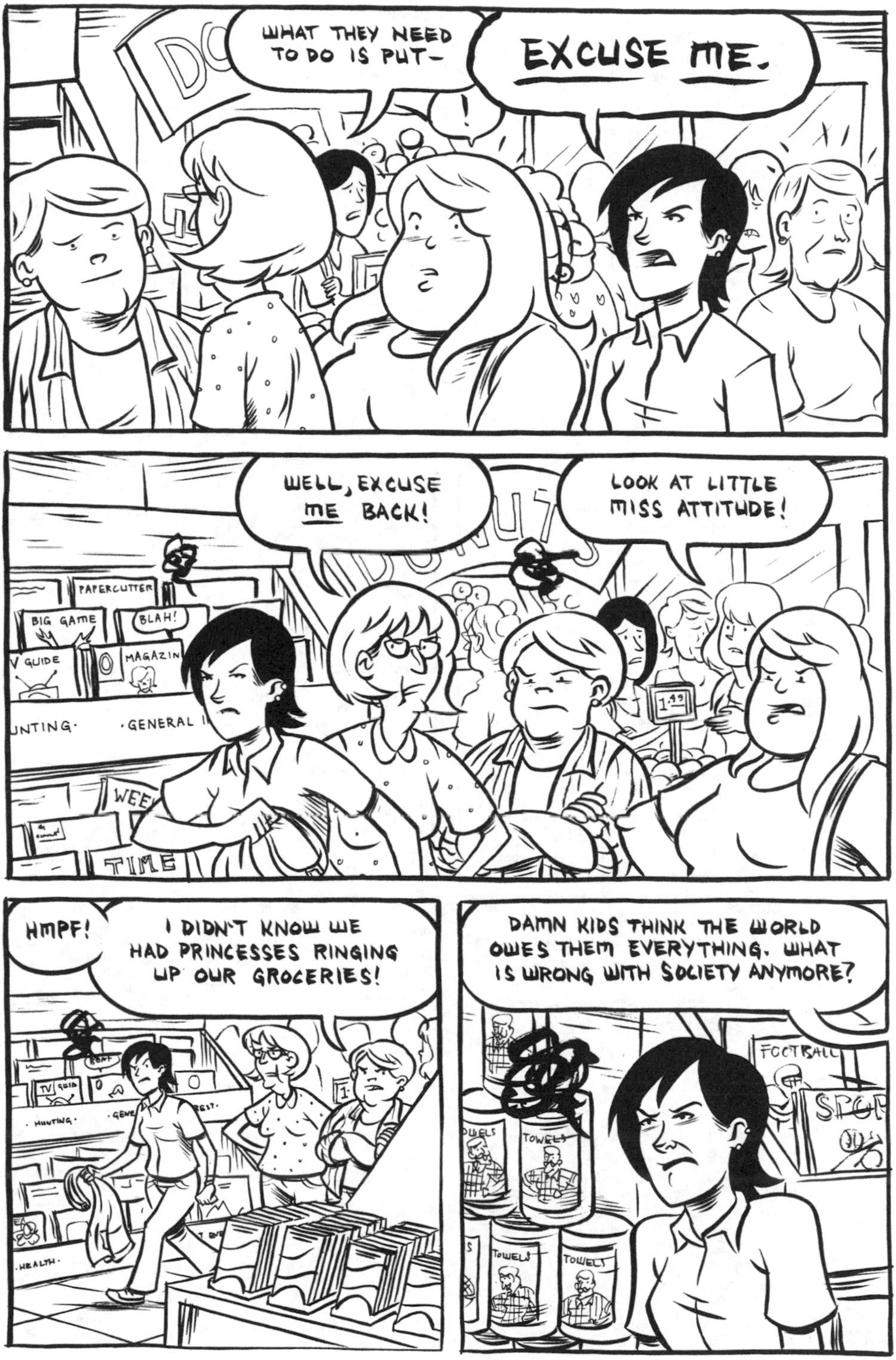
WHAT THEY NEED TO DO IS PUT-
EXCUSE ME.
!
WELL, EXCUSE ME BACK!
LOOK AT LITTLE MISS ATTITUDE!
PAPERCUTTER
BIG GAME
BLAH!
TV GUIDE
MAGAZIN
HUNTING
GENERAL I
1.49
TIME
HMPF!
I DIDN'T KNOW WE HAD PRINCESSES RINGING UP OUR GROCERIES!
HUNTING
HEALTH
DAMN KIDS THINK THE WORLD OWES THEM EVERYTHING. WHAT IS WRONG WITH SOCIETY ANYMORE?
FOOTBALL
TOWELS
TOWELS
TOWELS

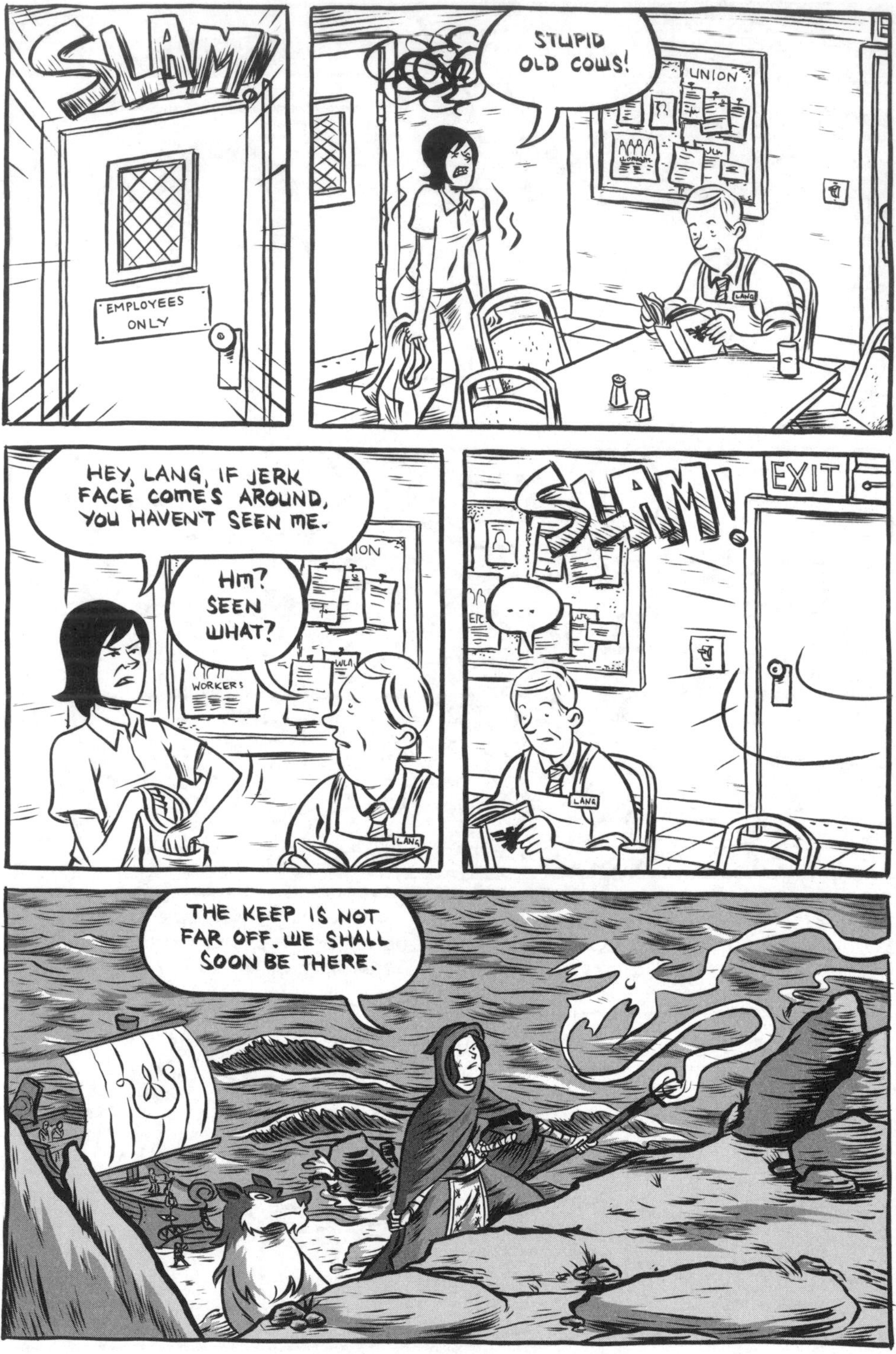
SLAM!
EMPLOYEES ONLY
STUPID OLD COWS!
UNION
LANG
HEY, LANG, IF JERK FACE COMES AROUND, YOU HAVEN'T SEEN ME.
HM? SEEN WHAT?
WORKERS
LANG
SLAM!
EXIT
...
LANG
THE KEEP IS NOT FAR OFF. WE SHALL SOON BE THERE.

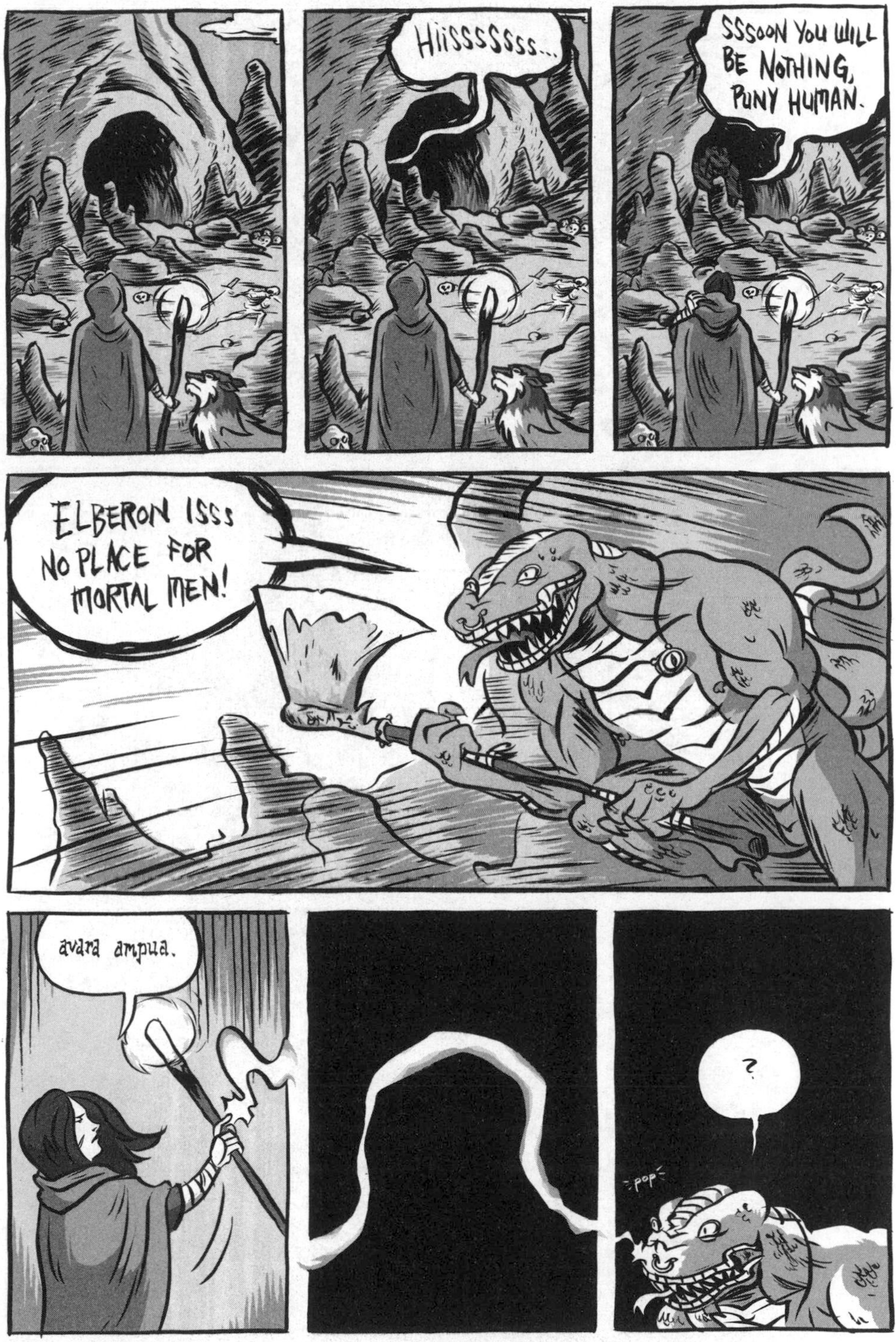

HiissssSsss...
SSsoon you will be nothing, puny human.
ELBERON ISSs NO PLACE FOR MORTAL MEN!
avara ampua.
?
pop

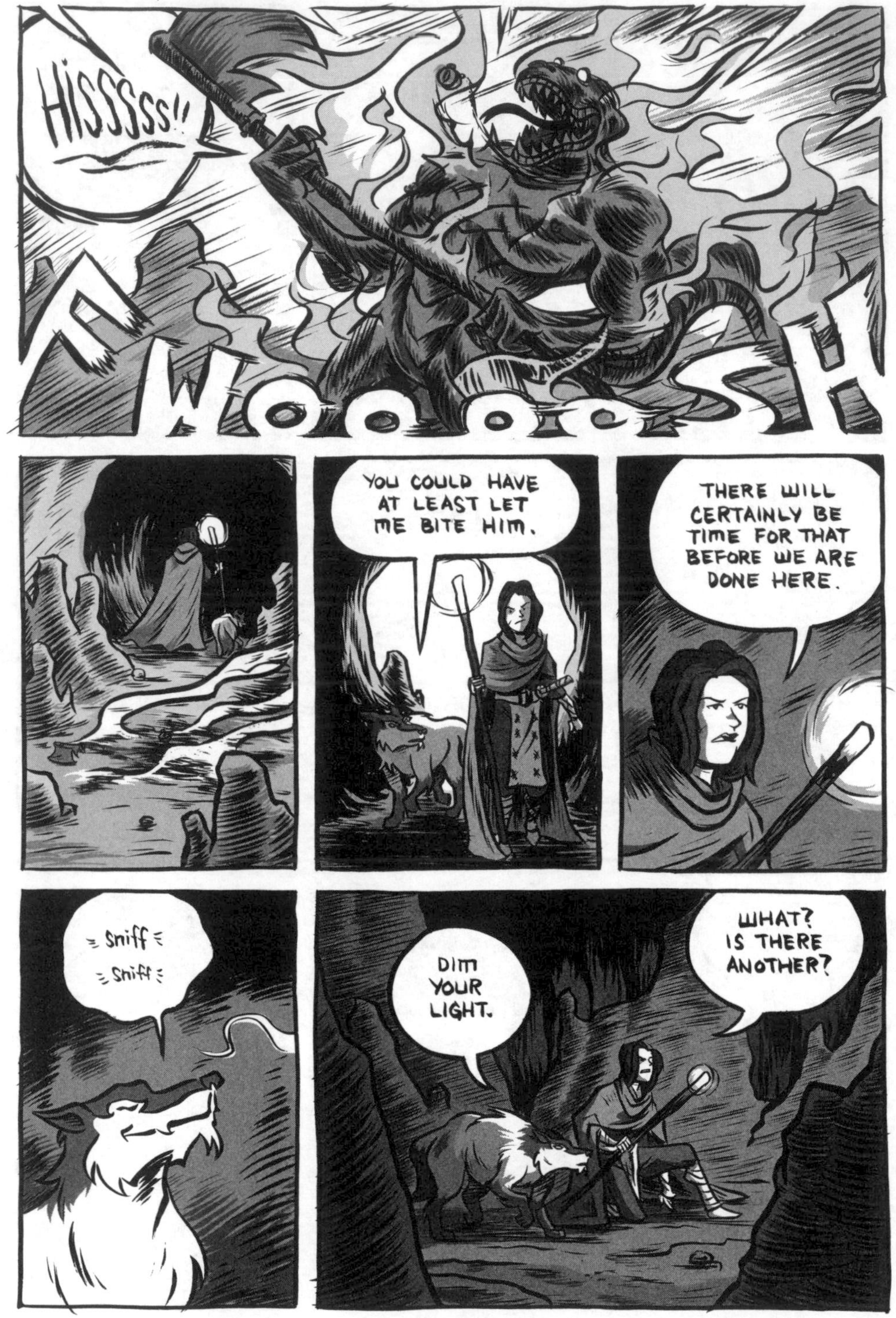
HISSSSS!!
WOOOOSSH!
YOU COULD HAVE AT LEAST LET ME BITE HIM.
THERE WILL CERTAINLY BE TIME FOR THAT BEFORE WE ARE DONE HERE.
sniff
sniff
DIM YOUR LIGHT.
WHAT? IS THERE ANOTHER?

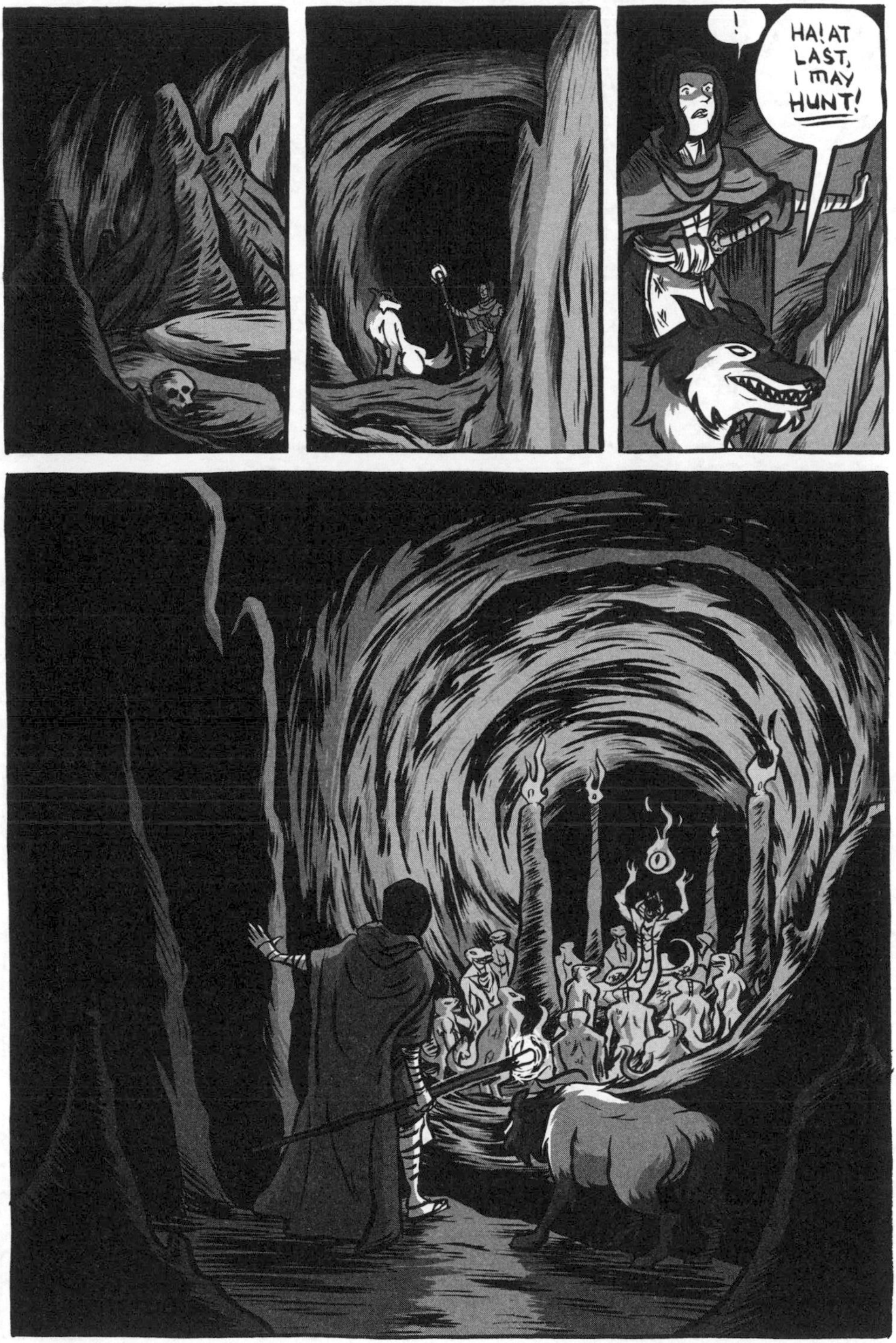
!
HA! AT LAST, I MAY HUNT!

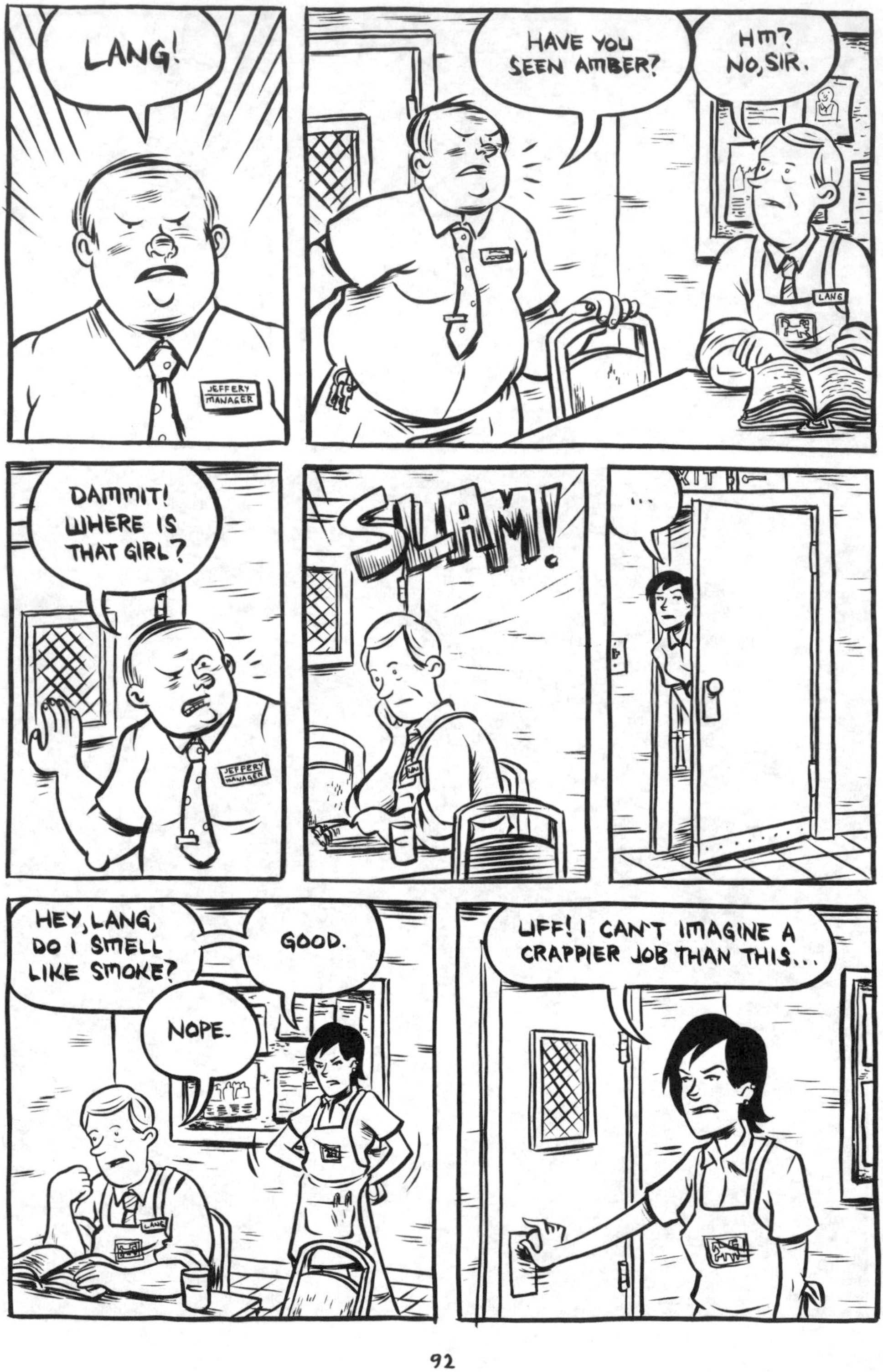
LANG!
JEFFERY MANAGER
HAVE YOU SEEN AMBER?
Hm? NO, SIR.
LANG
DAMMIT! WHERE IS THAT GIRL?
JEFFERY MANAGER
SLAM!
...
HEY, LANG, DO I SMELL LIKE SMOKE?
NOPE.
GOOD.
LANG
UFF! I CAN'T IMAGINE A CRAPPIER JOB THAN THIS...

93

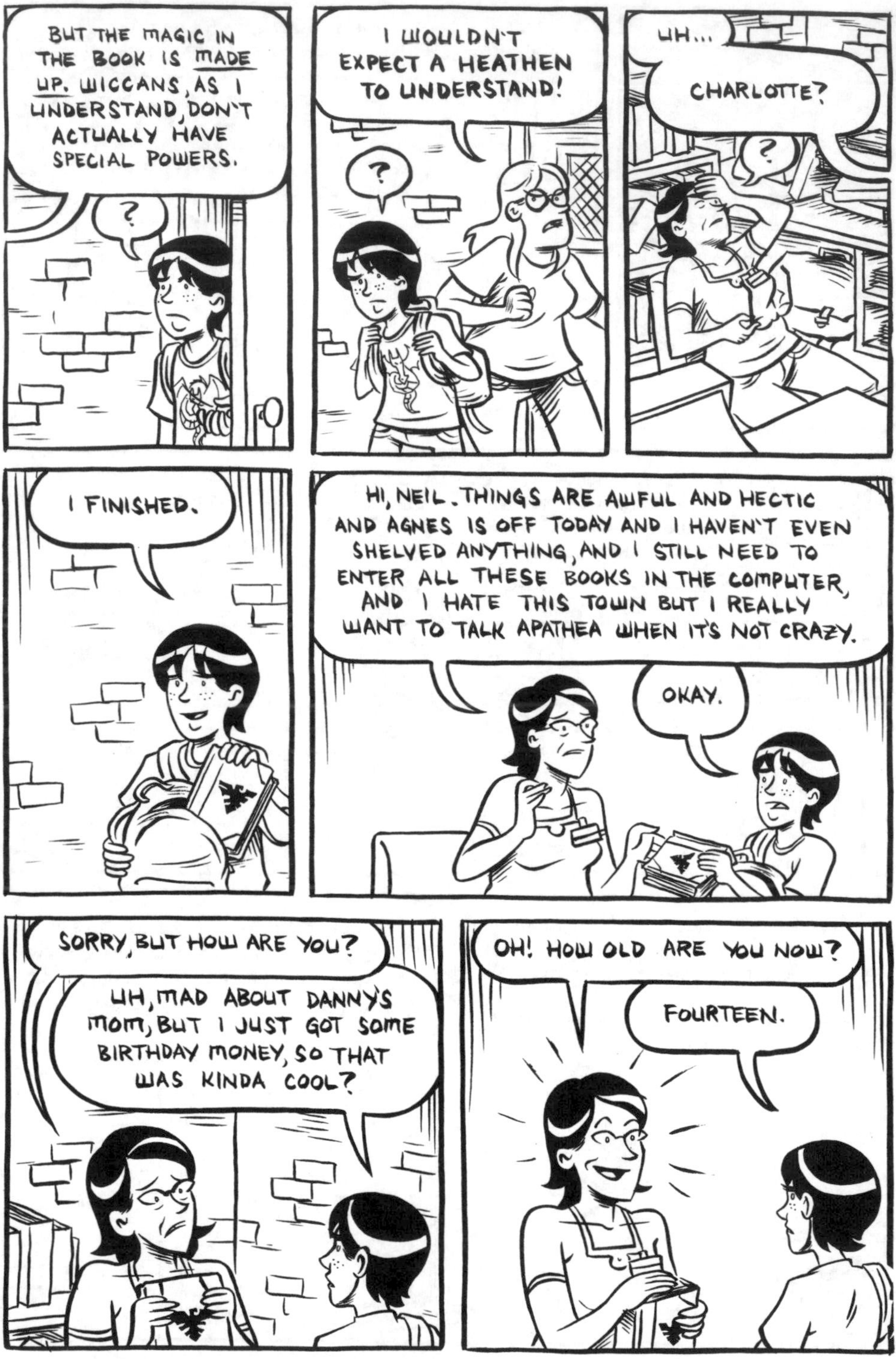
BUT THE MAGIC IN THE BOOK IS MADE UP. WICCANS, AS I UNDERSTAND, DON'T ACTUALLY HAVE SPECIAL POWERS.
?
I WOULDN'T EXPECT A HEATHEN TO UNDERSTAND!
?
UH...
CHARLOTTE?
?
I FINISHED.
HI, NEIL. THINGS ARE AWFUL AND HECTIC AND AGNES IS OFF TODAY AND I HAVEN'T EVEN SHELVED ANYTHING, AND I STILL NEED TO ENTER ALL THESE BOOKS IN THE COMPUTER, AND I HATE THIS TOWN BUT I REALLY WANT TO TALK APATHEA WHEN IT'S NOT CRAZY.
OKAY.
SORRY, BUT HOW ARE YOU?
UH, MAD ABOUT DANNY'S MOM, BUT I JUST GOT SOME BIRTHDAY MONEY, SO THAT WAS KINDA COOL?
OH! HOW OLD ARE YOU NOW?
FOURTEEN.

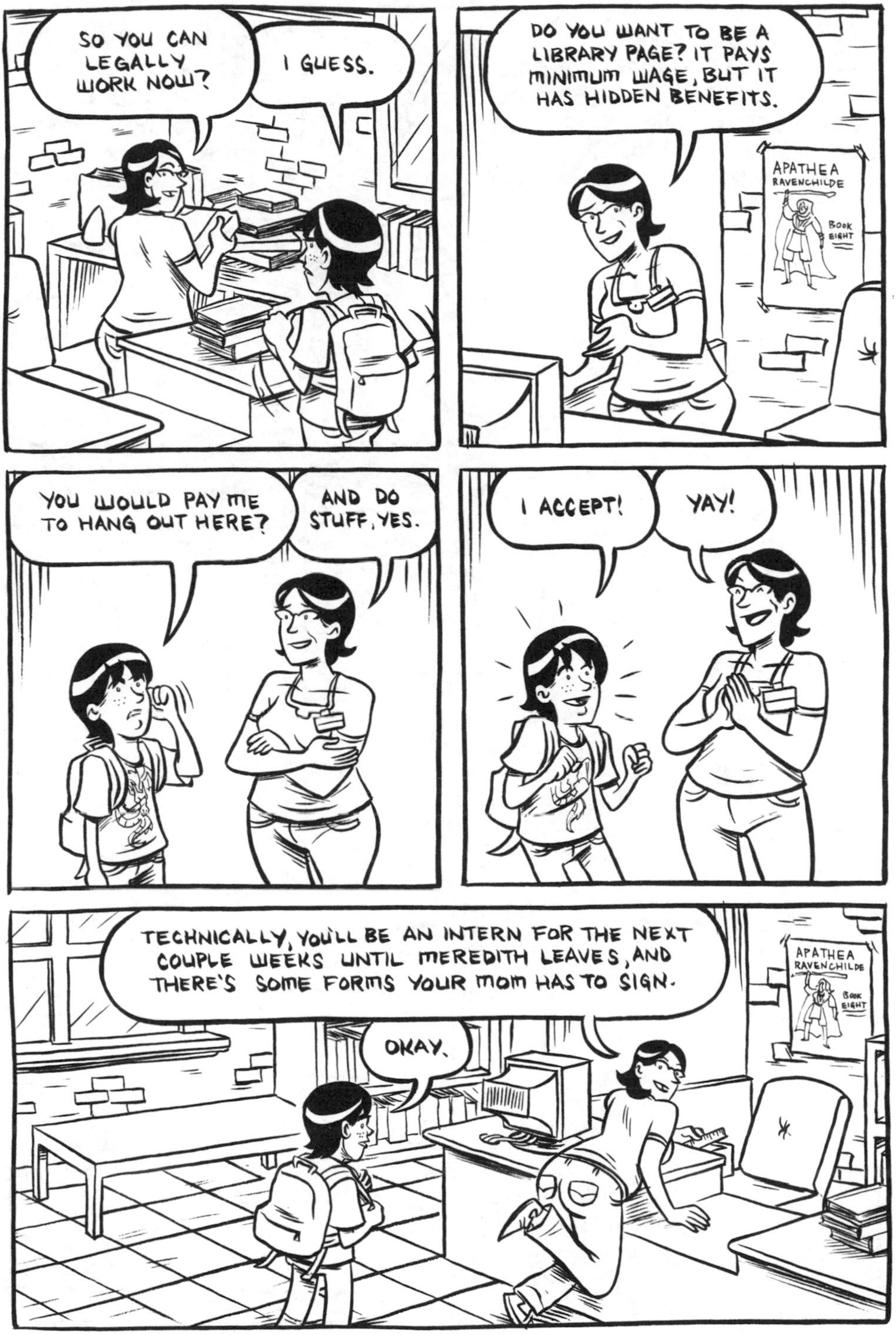
SO YOU CAN LEGALLY WORK NOW?
I GUESS.
DO YOU WANT TO BE A LIBRARY PAGE? IT PAYS MINIMUM WAGE, BUT IT HAS HIDDEN BENEFITS.
APATHEA RAVENCHILDE
BOOK EIGHT
YOU WOULD PAY ME TO HANG OUT HERE?
AND DO STUFF, YES.
I ACCEPT!
YAY!
TECHNICALLY, YOU'LL BE AN INTERN FOR THE NEXT COUPLE WEEKS UNTIL MEREDITH LEAVES, AND THERE'S SOME FORMS YOUR MOM HAS TO SIGN.
APATHEA RAVENCHILDE
BOOK EIGHT
OKAY.

CHAPTER 5

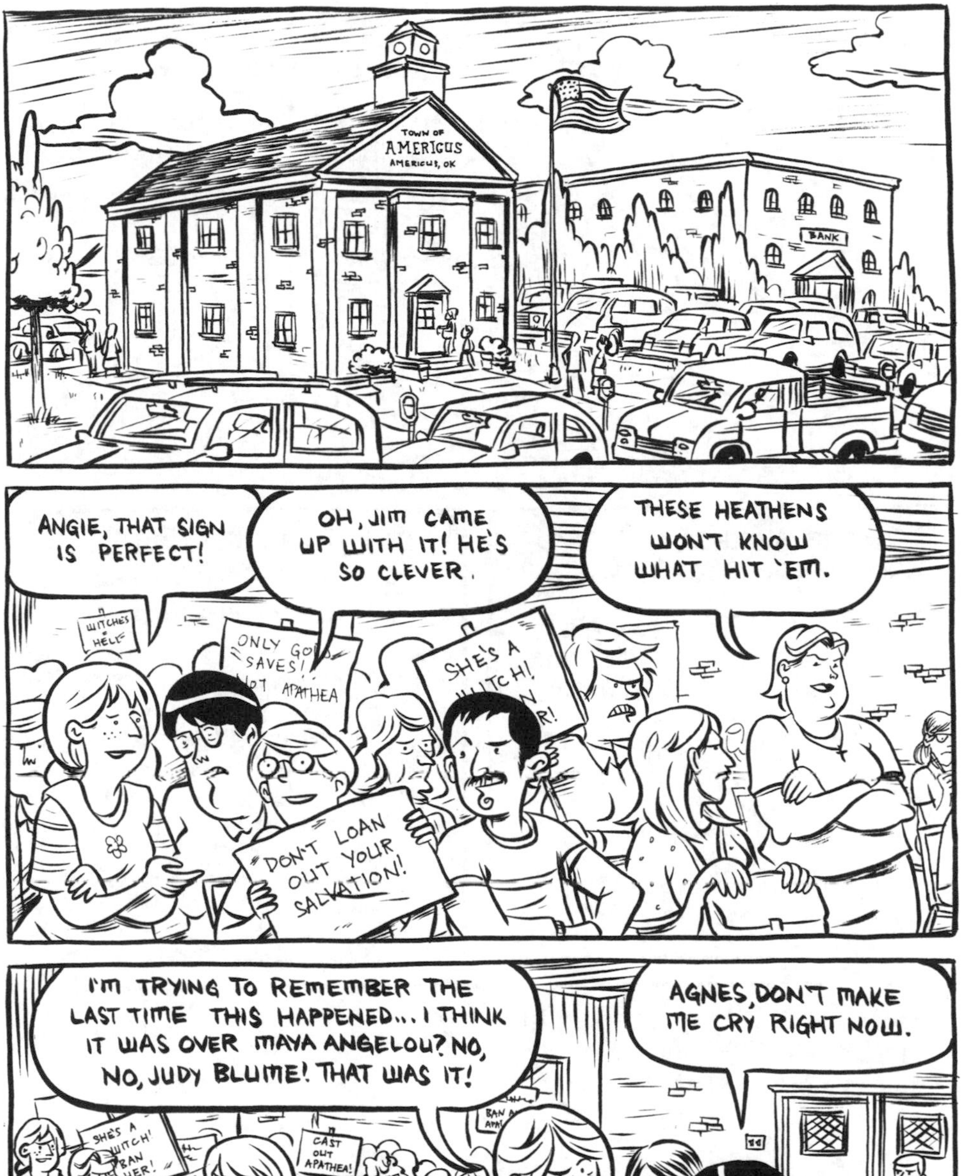
TOWN OF
AMERICUS
AMERICUS, OK
BANK
ANGIE, THAT SIGN IS PERFECT!
OH, JIM CAME UP WITH IT! HE'S SO CLEVER.
THESE HEATHENS WON'T KNOW WHAT HIT 'EM.
WITCHES = HELL
SHE'S A
DON'T LOAN OUT YOUR SALVATION!
I'M TRYING TO REMEMBER THE LAST TIME THIS HAPPENED... I THINK IT WAS OVER MAYA ANGELOU? NO, NO, JUDY BLUME! THAT WAS IT!
AGNES, DON'T MAKE ME CRY RIGHT NOW.
SHE'S A WITCH! BAN HER!
CAST OUT APATHEA!

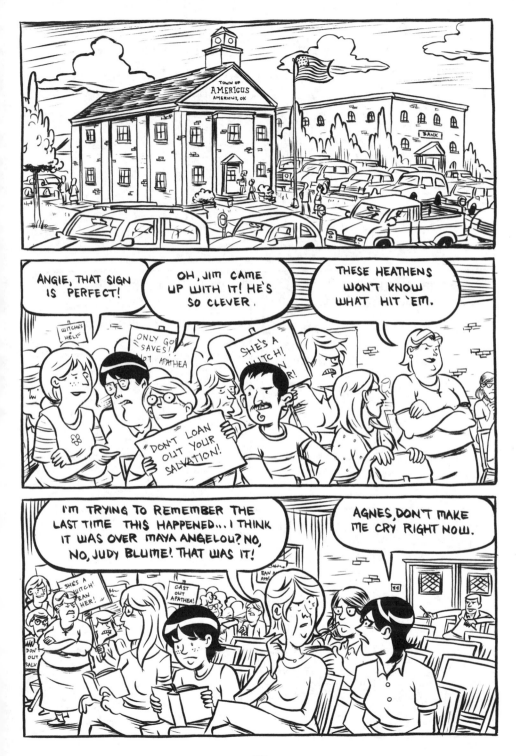

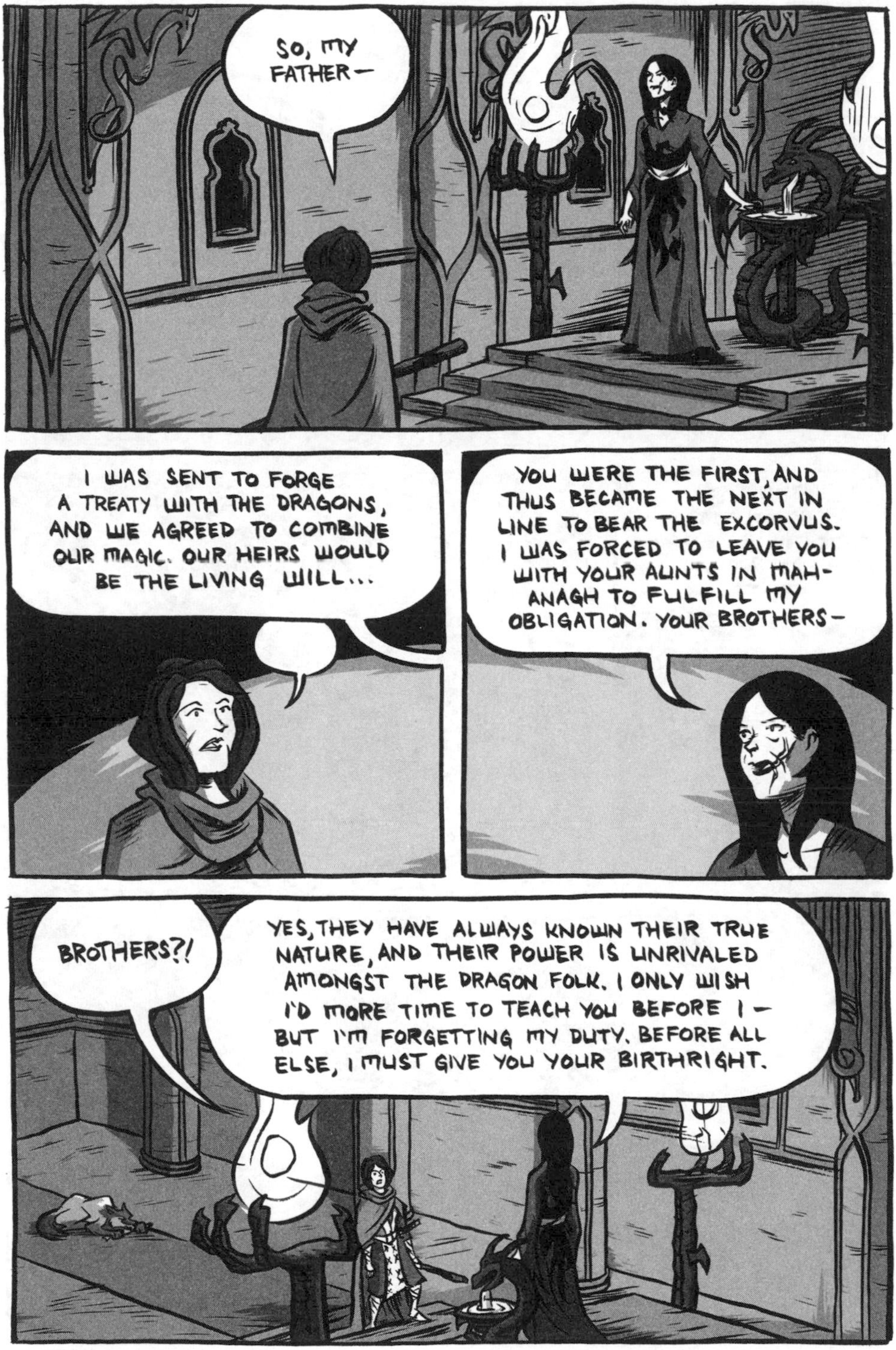
SO, MY FATHER—
I WAS SENT TO FORGE A TREATY WITH THE DRAGONS, AND WE AGREED TO COMBINE OUR MAGIC. OUR HEIRS WOULD BE THE LIVING WILL...
YOU WERE THE FIRST, AND THUS BECAME THE NEXT IN LINE TO BEAR THE EXCORVUS. I WAS FORCED TO LEAVE YOU WITH YOUR AUNTS IN MAH-ANAGH TO FULFILL MY OBLIGATION. YOUR BROTHERS—
BROTHERS?!
YES, THEY HAVE ALWAYS KNOWN THEIR TRUE NATURE, AND THEIR POWER IS UNRIVALED AMONGST THE DRAGON FOLK. I ONLY WISH I'D MORE TIME TO TEACH YOU BEFORE I— BUT I'M FORGETTING MY DUTY. BEFORE ALL ELSE, I MUST GIVE YOU YOUR BIRTHRIGHT.

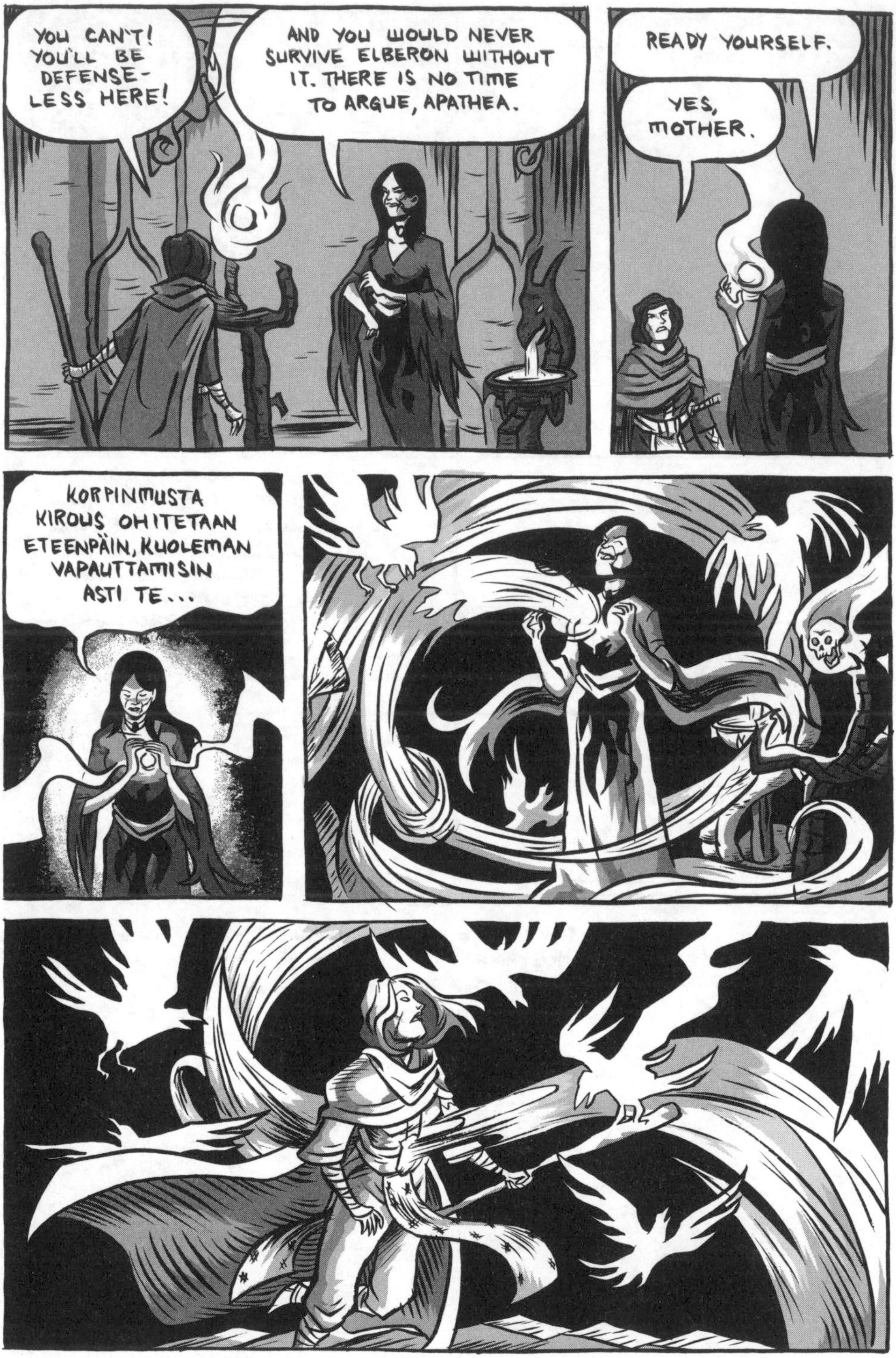
YOU CAN'T! YOU'LL BE DEFENSE-LESS HERE!
AND YOU WOULD NEVER SURVIVE ELBERON WITHOUT IT. THERE IS NO TIME TO ARGUE, APATHEA.
READY YOURSELF.
YES, MOTHER.
KORPINMUSTA KIROUS OHITETAAN ETEENPÄIN, KUOLEMAN VAPAUTTAMISIN ASTI TE...

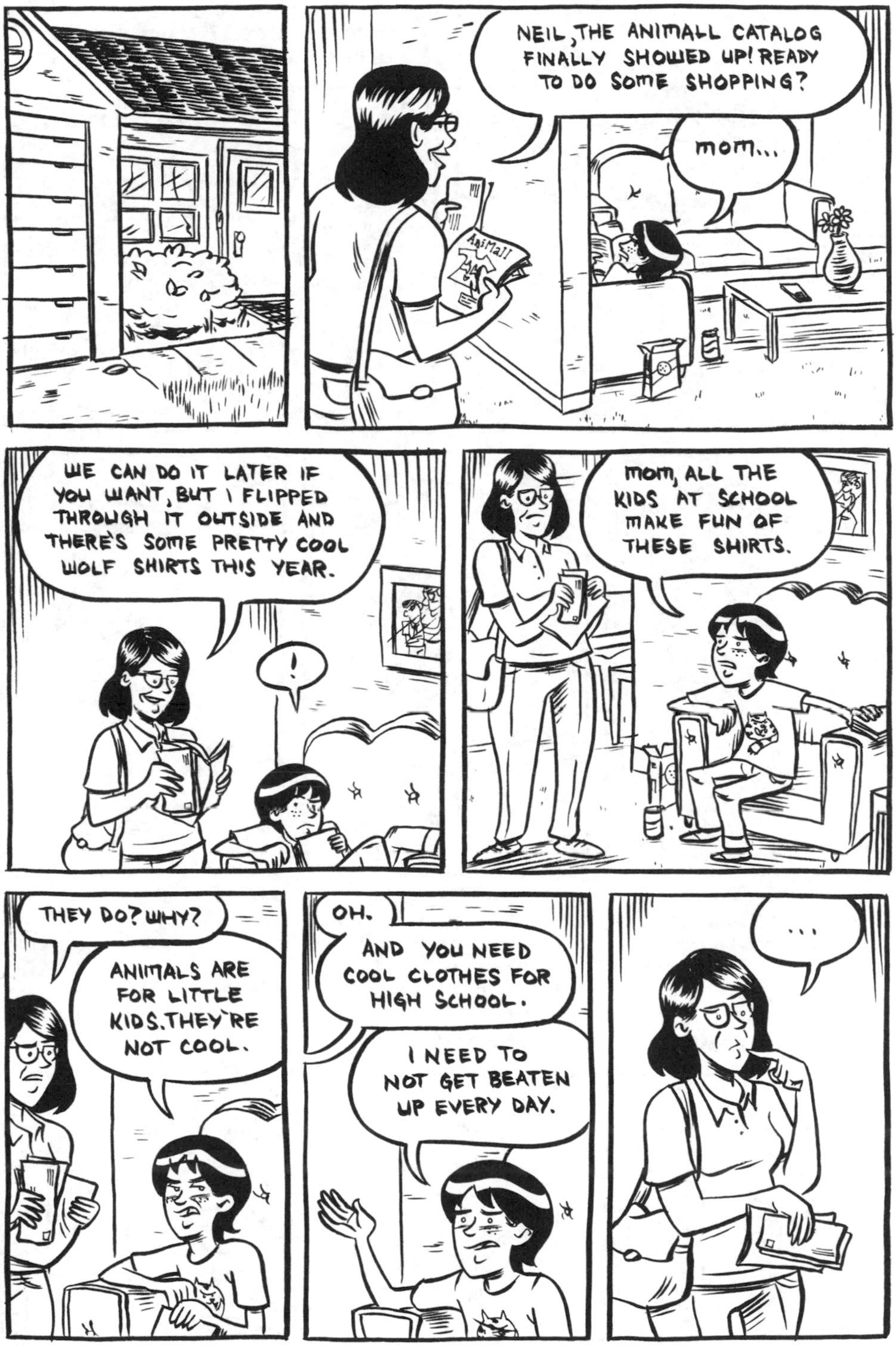
NEIL, THE ANIMALL CATALOG FINALLY SHOWED UP! READY TO DO SOME SHOPPING?
mom...
WE CAN DO IT LATER IF YOU WANT, BUT I FLIPPED THROUGH IT OUTSIDE AND THERE'S SOME PRETTY COOL WOLF SHIRTS THIS YEAR.
!
MOM, ALL THE KIDS AT SCHOOL MAKE FUN OF THESE SHIRTS.
THEY DO? WHY?
ANIMALS ARE FOR LITTLE KIDS. THEY'RE NOT COOL.
OH.
AND YOU NEED COOL CLOTHES FOR HIGH SCHOOL.
I NEED TO NOT GET BEATEN UP EVERY DAY.
...

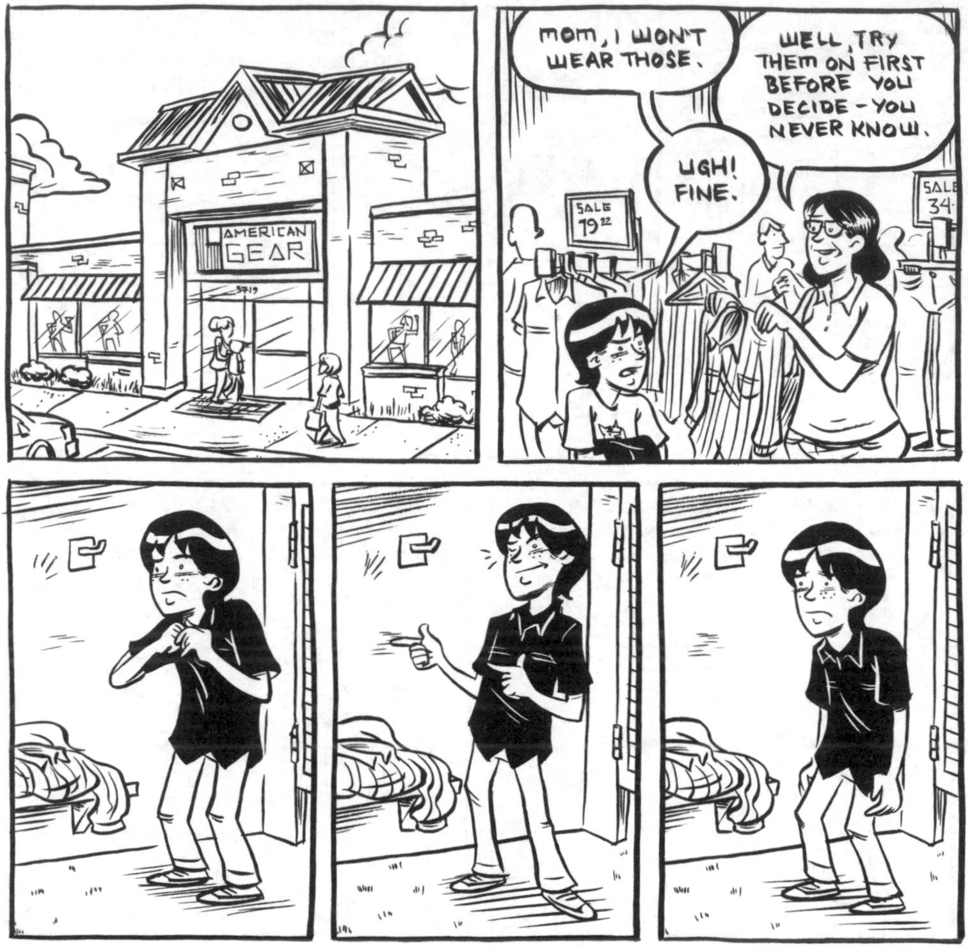
AMERICAN GEAR
3719
MOM, I WON'T WEAR THOSE.
WELL, TRY THEM ON FIRST BEFORE YOU DECIDE - YOU NEVER KNOW.
UGH! FINE.
SALE 19.22
SALE 34.
SO I TOLD CAITLYN BUT THEN SHE TOLD EMILY WHAT I SAID AND EMILY TOTALLY FREAKED OUT AND WAS ALL LIKE, "HOW COULD YOU TELL THEM I LIKED HIM?" EVEN THOUGH EVERYBODY ELSE KNEW ANYWAY!
HUFF
EVERYONE ALREADY KNEW SHE LIKED HIM FOREVER AGO! IT'S SO OBVIOUS!
1
7

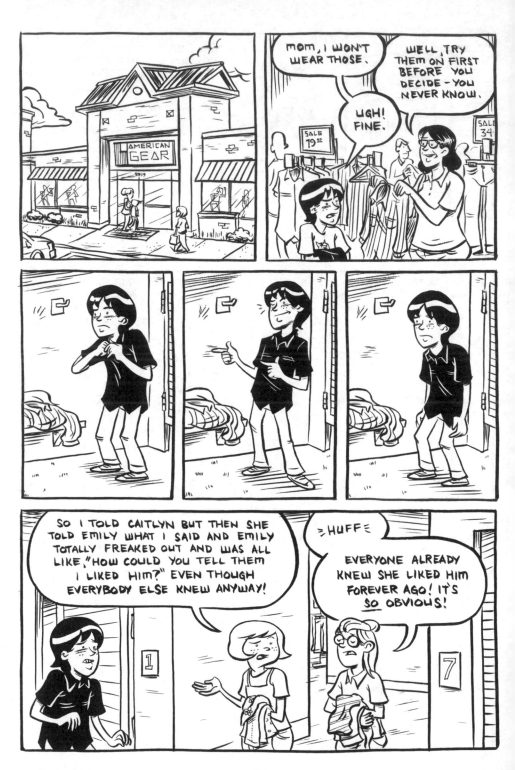

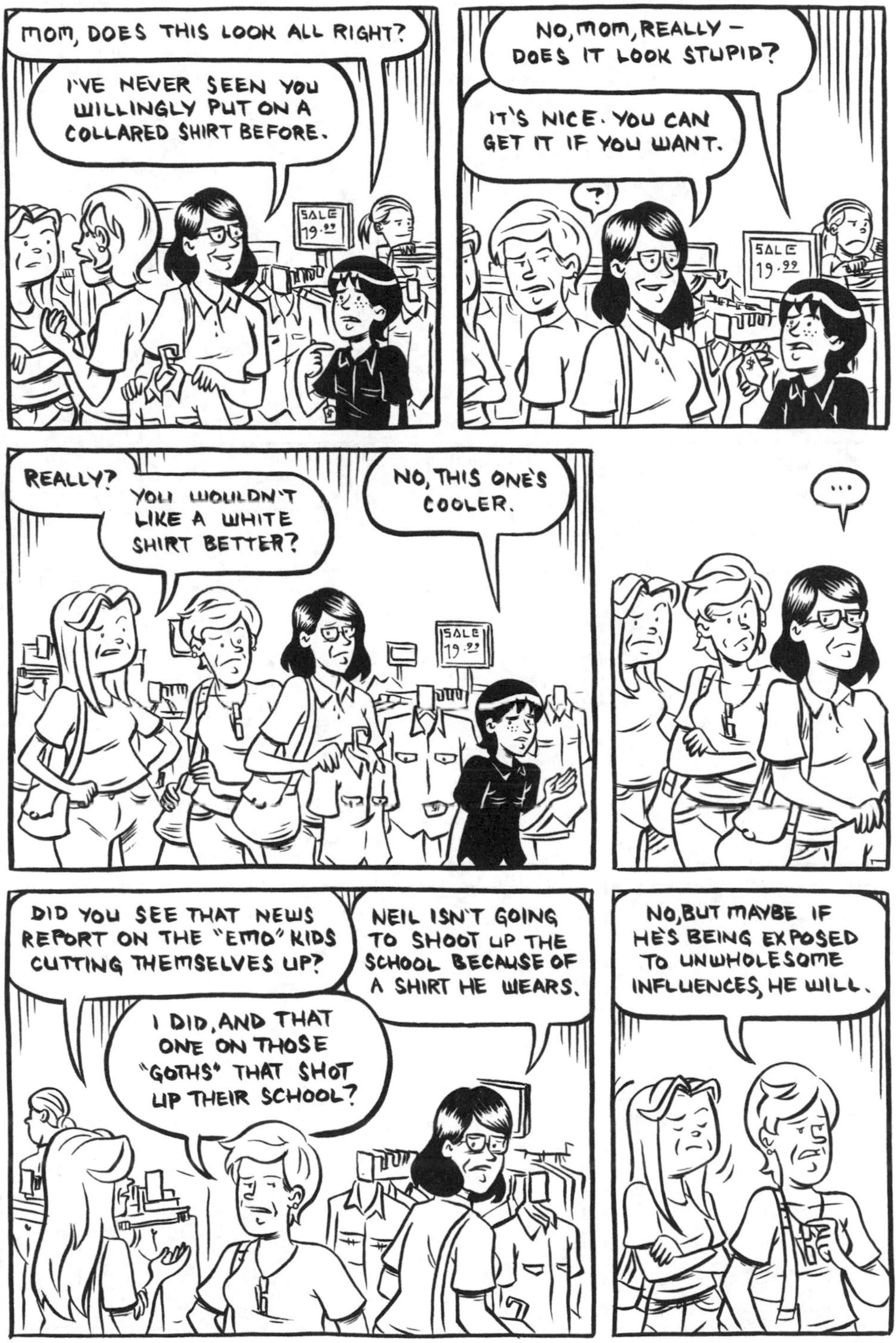
MOM, DOES THIS LOOK ALL RIGHT?
I'VE NEVER SEEN YOU WILLINGLY PUT ON A COLLARED SHIRT BEFORE.
SALE 19.99
NO, MOM, REALLY – DOES IT LOOK STUPID?
IT'S NICE. YOU CAN GET IT IF YOU WANT.
?
SALE 19.99
REALLY?
YOU WOULDN'T LIKE A WHITE SHIRT BETTER?
NO, THIS ONE'S COOLER.
SALE 19.99
...
DID YOU SEE THAT NEWS REPORT ON THE "EMO" KIDS CUTTING THEMSELVES UP?
I DID, AND THAT ONE ON THOSE "GOTHS" THAT SHOT UP THEIR SCHOOL?
NEIL ISN'T GOING TO SHOOT UP THE SCHOOL BECAUSE OF A SHIRT HE WEARS.
NO, BUT MAYBE IF HE'S BEING EXPOSED TO UNWHOLESOME INFLUENCES, HE WILL.

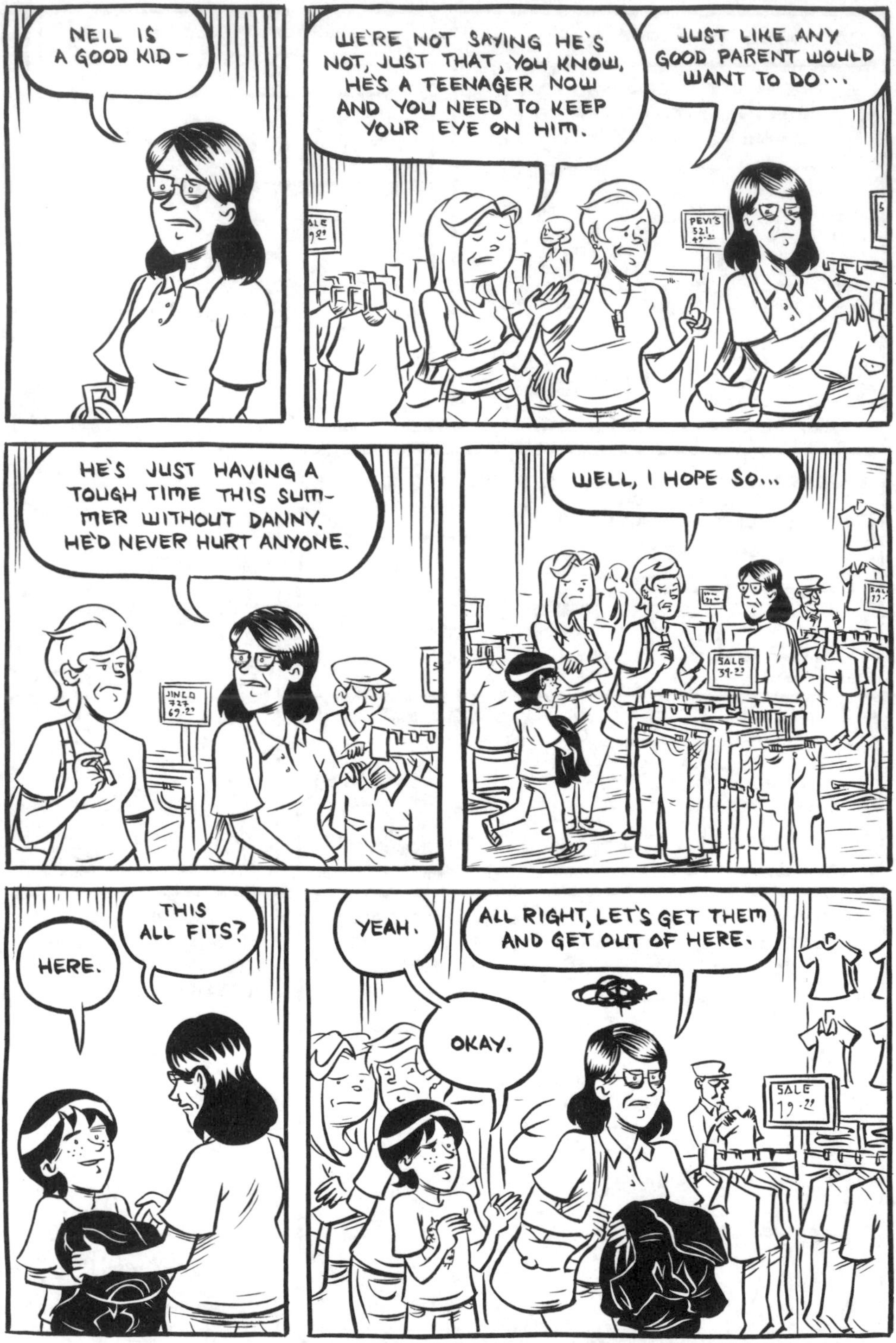
NEIL IS A GOOD KID -
WE'RE NOT SAYING HE'S NOT, JUST THAT, YOU KNOW, HE'S A TEENAGER NOW AND YOU NEED TO KEEP YOUR EYE ON HIM.
JUST LIKE ANY GOOD PARENT WOULD WANT TO DO...
HE'S JUST HAVING A TOUGH TIME THIS SUMMER WITHOUT DANNY. HE'D NEVER HURT ANYONE.
WELL, I HOPE SO...
SALE 39.29
HERE.
THIS ALL FITS?
YEAH.
ALL RIGHT, LET'S GET THEM AND GET OUT OF HERE.
OKAY.
SALE 19.29

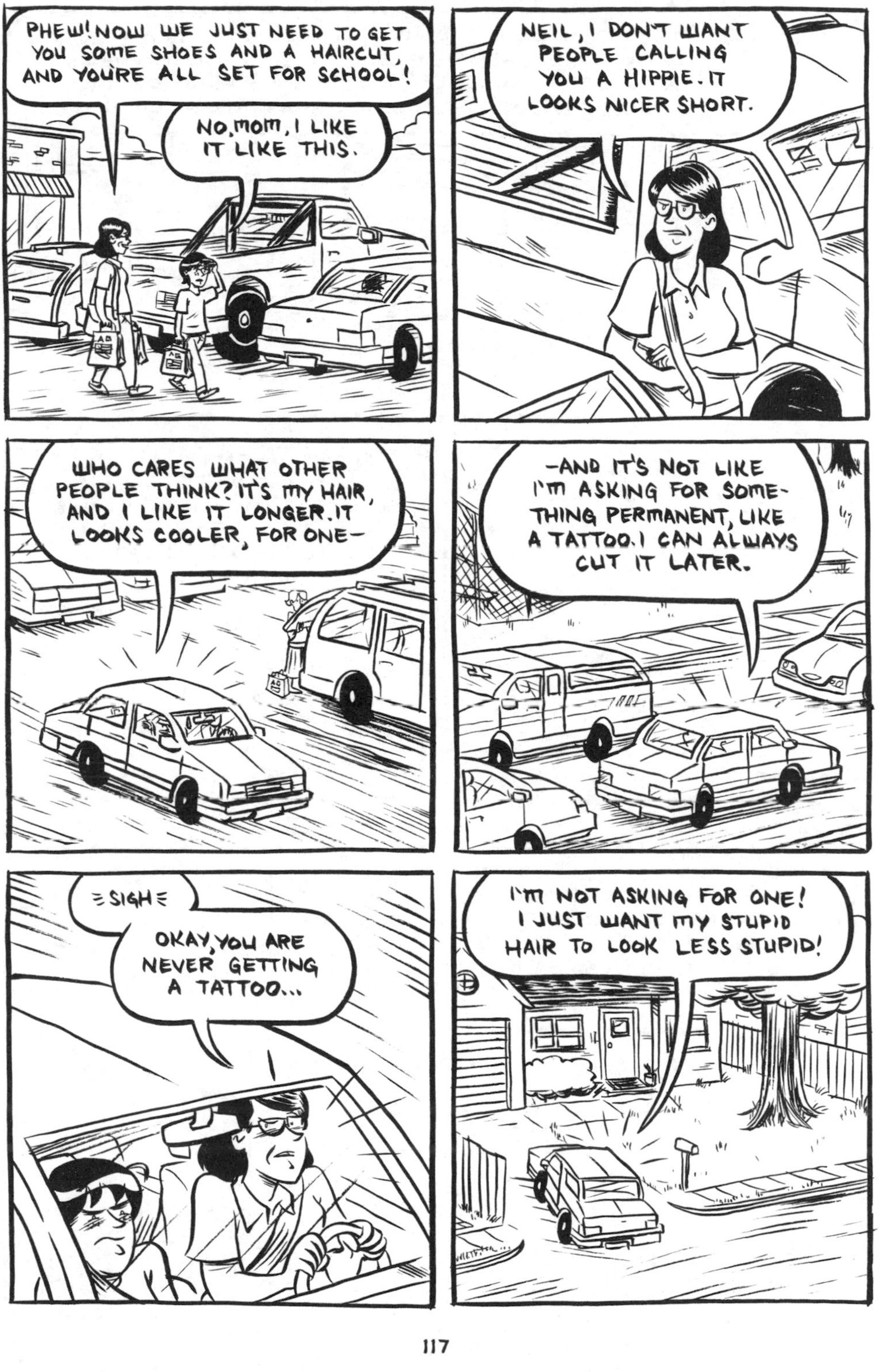
PHEW! NOW WE JUST NEED TO GET YOU SOME SHOES AND A HAIRCUT, AND YOU'RE ALL SET FOR SCHOOL!
NO, MOM, I LIKE IT LIKE THIS.
NEIL, I DON'T WANT PEOPLE CALLING YOU A HIPPIE. IT LOOKS NICER SHORT.
WHO CARES WHAT OTHER PEOPLE THINK? IT'S MY HAIR, AND I LIKE IT LONGER. IT LOOKS COOLER, FOR ONE—
—AND IT'S NOT LIKE I'M ASKING FOR SOMETHING PERMANENT, LIKE A TATTOO. I CAN ALWAYS CUT IT LATER.
≡SIGH≡
OKAY, YOU ARE NEVER GETTING A TATTOO...
I'M NOT ASKING FOR ONE! I JUST WANT MY STUPID HAIR TO LOOK LESS STUPID!

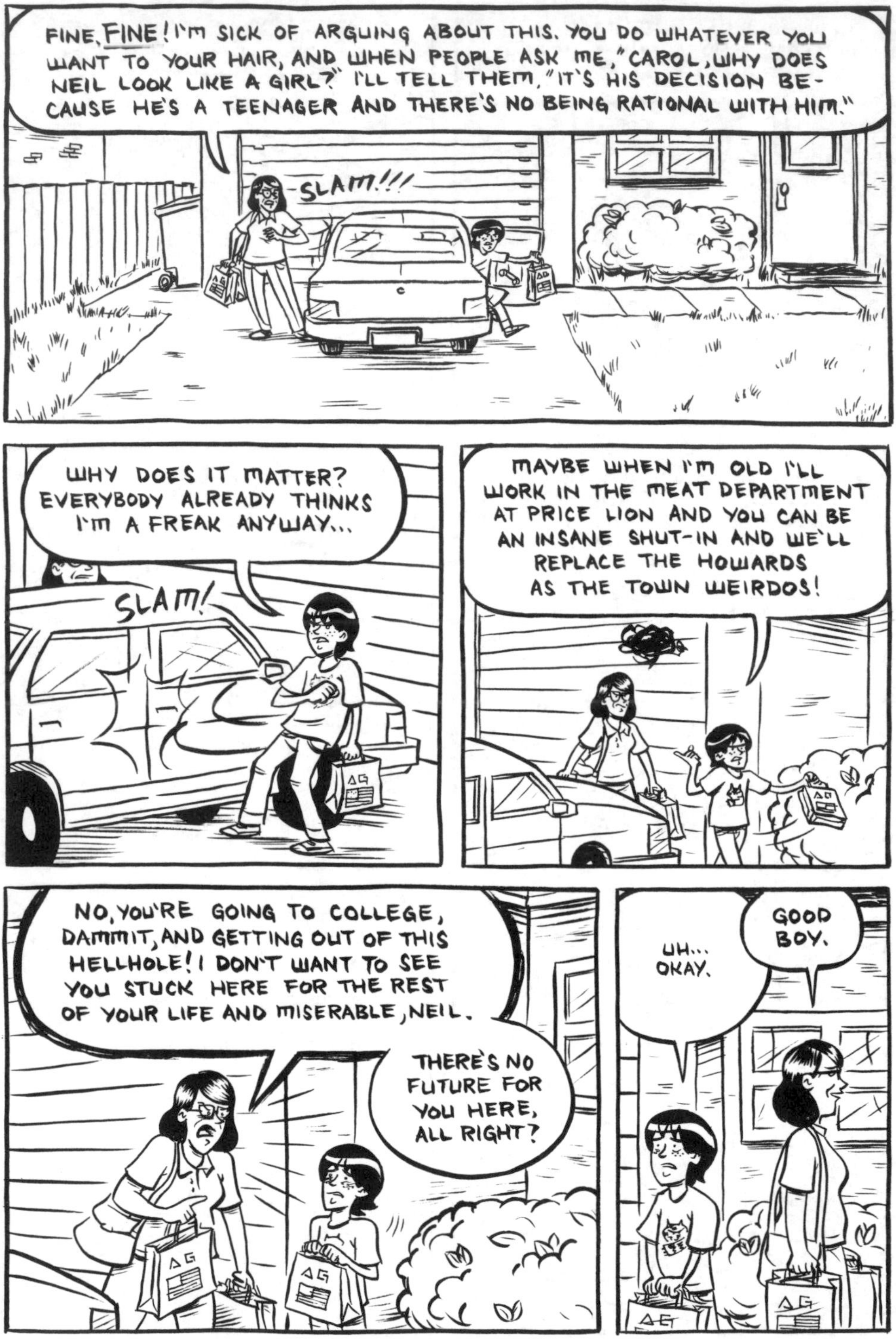
FINE, FINE! I'M SICK OF ARGUING ABOUT THIS. YOU DO WHATEVER YOU WANT TO YOUR HAIR, AND WHEN PEOPLE ASK ME, "CAROL, WHY DOES NEIL LOOK LIKE A GIRL?" I'LL TELL THEM, "IT'S HIS DECISION BECAUSE HE'S A TEENAGER AND THERE'S NO BEING RATIONAL WITH HIM."
SLAM!!!
WHY DOES IT MATTER? EVERYBODY ALREADY THINKS I'M A FREAK ANYWAY...
SLAM!
MAYBE WHEN I'M OLD I'LL WORK IN THE MEAT DEPARTMENT AT PRICE LION AND YOU CAN BE AN INSANE SHUT-IN AND WE'LL REPLACE THE HOWARDS AS THE TOWN WEIRDOS!
NO, YOU'RE GOING TO COLLEGE, DAMMIT, AND GETTING OUT OF THIS HELLHOLE! I DON'T WANT TO SEE YOU STUCK HERE FOR THE REST OF YOUR LIFE AND MISERABLE, NEIL.
THERE'S NO FUTURE FOR YOU HERE, ALL RIGHT?
UH... OKAY.
GOOD BOY.

CHAPTER 6

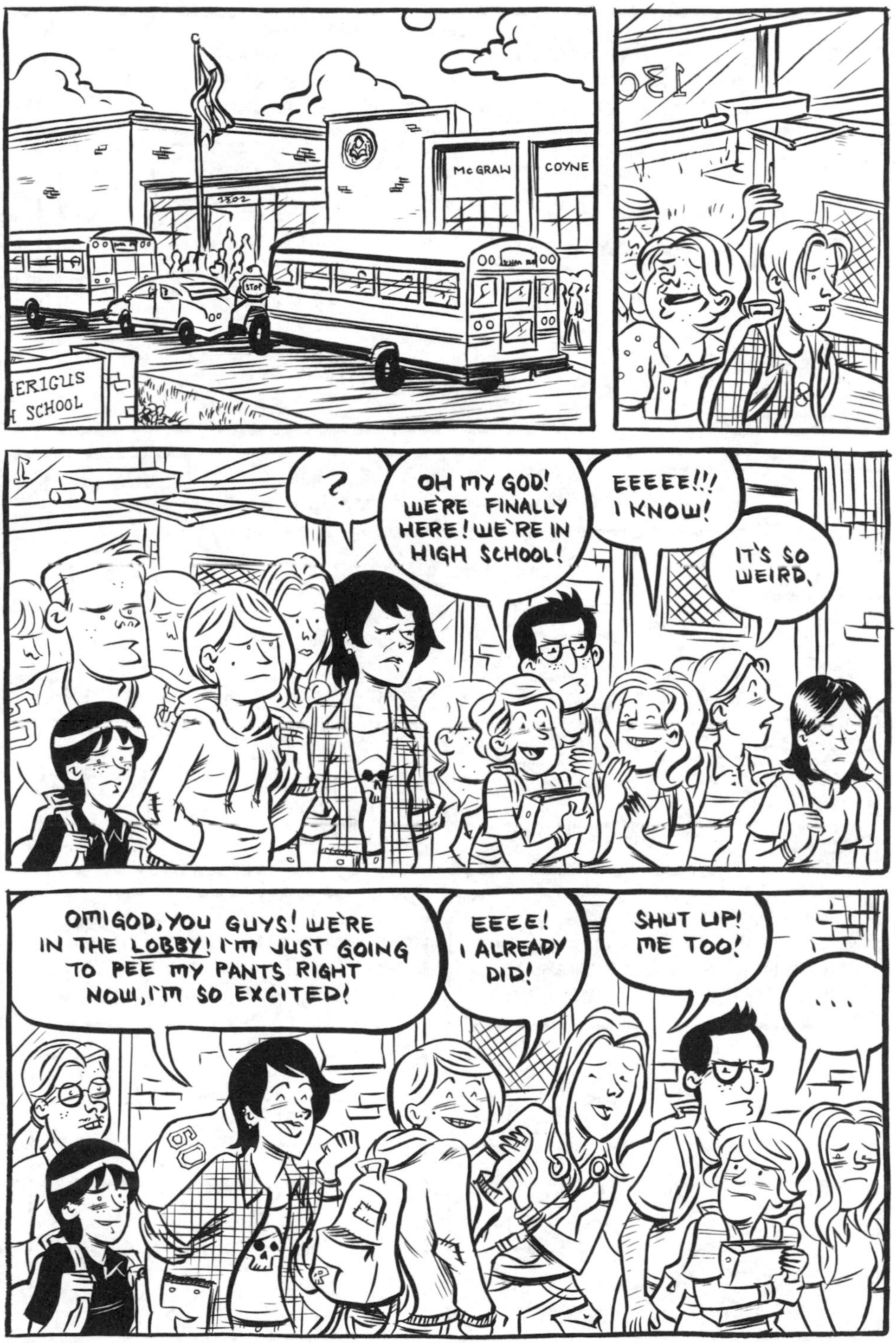
McGRAW
COYNE
ERIGUS
H SCHOOL
?
OH MY GOD! WE'RE FINALLY HERE! WE'RE IN HIGH SCHOOL!
EEEEE!!! I KNOW!
IT'S SO WEIRD.
OMIGOD, YOU GUYS! WE'RE IN THE LOBBY! I'M JUST GOING TO PEE MY PANTS RIGHT NOW, I'M SO EXCITED!
EEEE! I ALREADY DID!
SHUT UP! ME TOO!
. . .

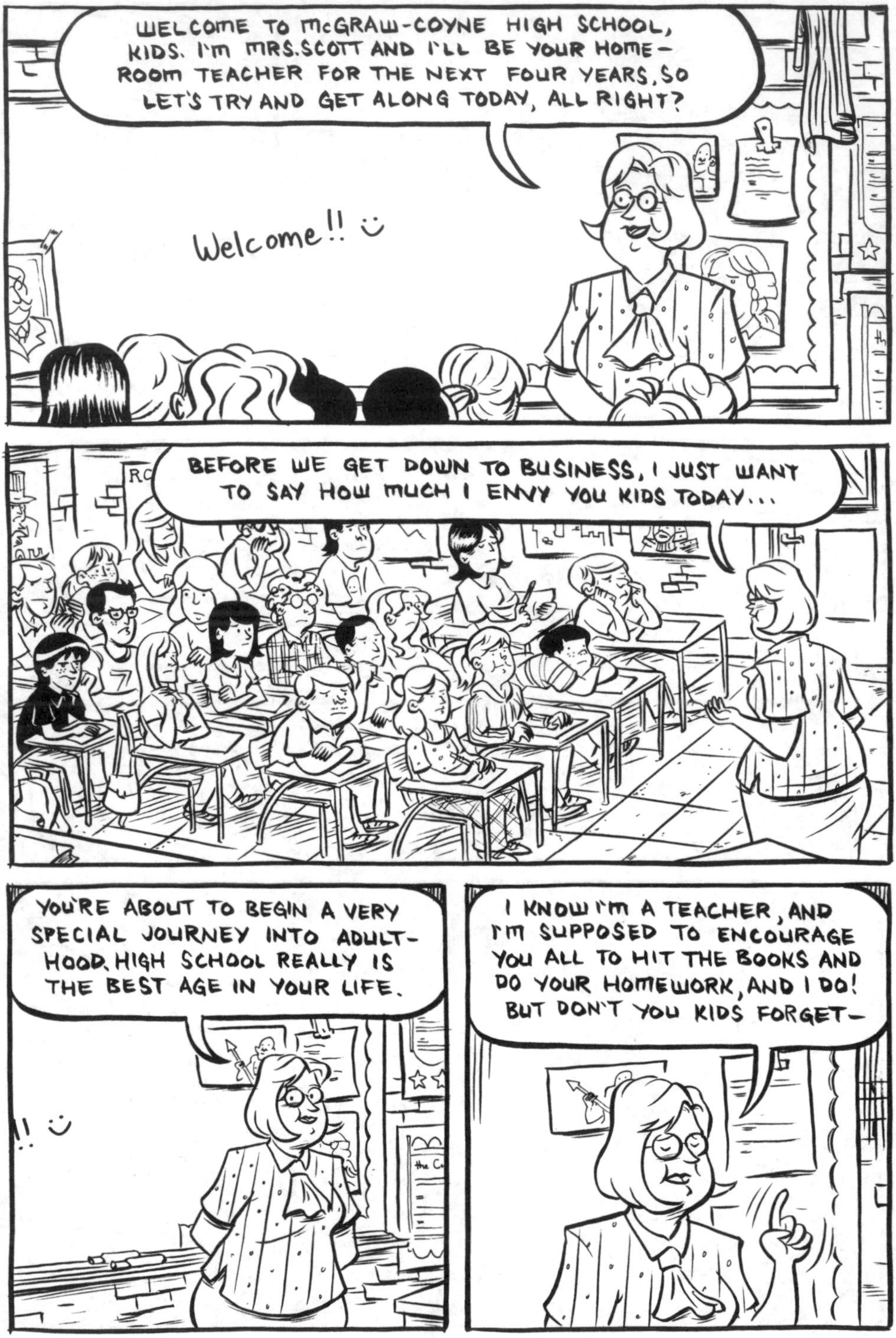
WELCOME TO McGRAW-COYNE HIGH SCHOOL, KIDS. I'M MRS. SCOTT AND I'LL BE YOUR HOME-ROOM TEACHER FOR THE NEXT FOUR YEARS, SO LET'S TRY AND GET ALONG TODAY, ALL RIGHT?
Welcome!! :)
BEFORE WE GET DOWN TO BUSINESS, I JUST WANT TO SAY HOW MUCH I ENVY YOU KIDS TODAY...
YOU'RE ABOUT TO BEGIN A VERY SPECIAL JOURNEY INTO ADULT-HOOD. HIGH SCHOOL REALLY IS THE BEST AGE IN YOUR LIFE.
I KNOW I'M A TEACHER, AND I'M SUPPOSED TO ENCOURAGE YOU ALL TO HIT THE BOOKS AND DO YOUR HOMEWORK, AND I DO! BUT DON'T YOU KIDS FORGET—

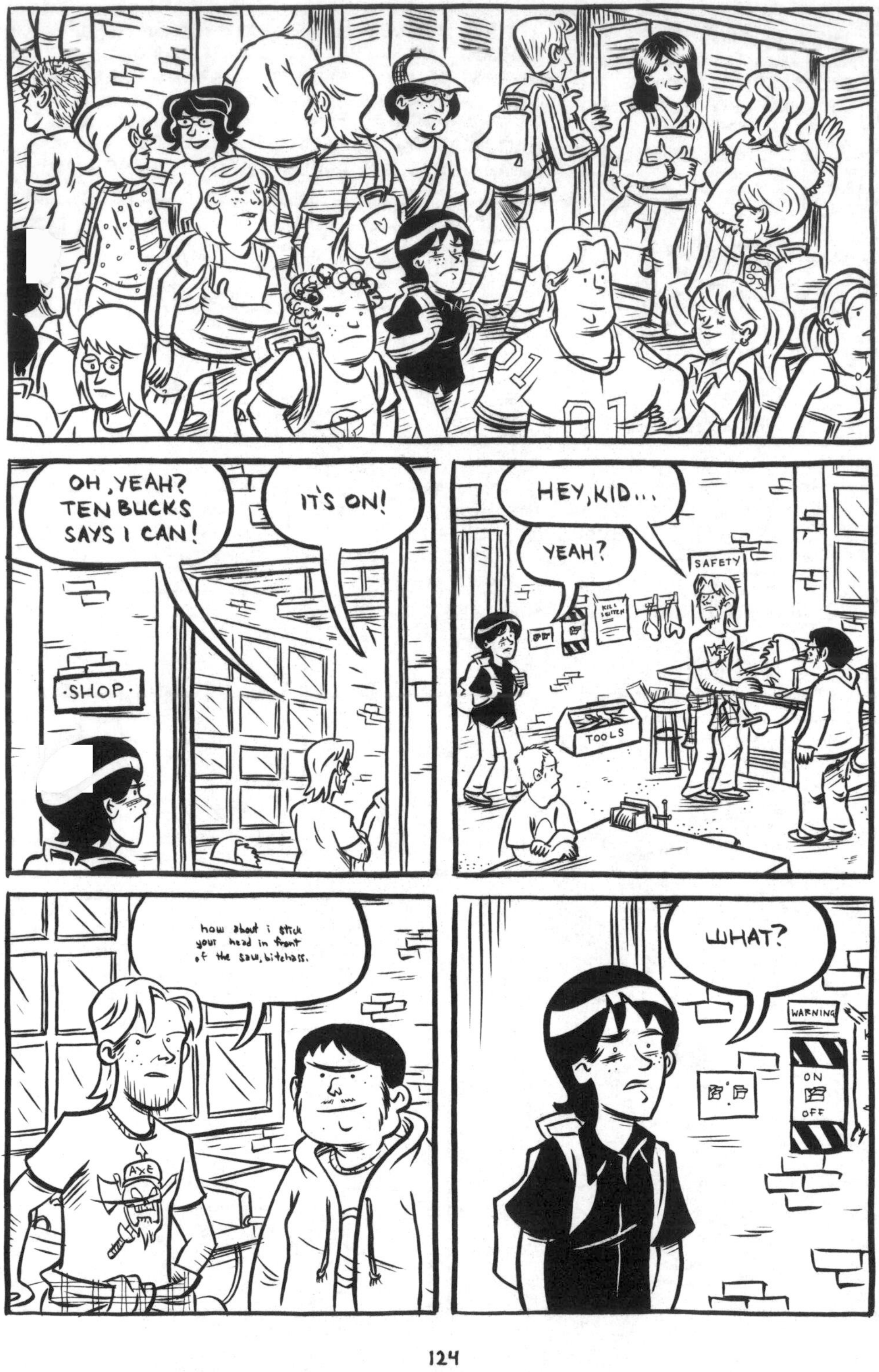
OH, YEAH? TEN BUCKS SAYS I CAN!
IT'S ON!
·SHOP·
HEY, KID...
YEAH?
SAFETY
KILL SWITCH
TOOLS
how about i stick your head in front of the saw, bitchass.
AXE
WHAT?
WARNING
ON
OFF

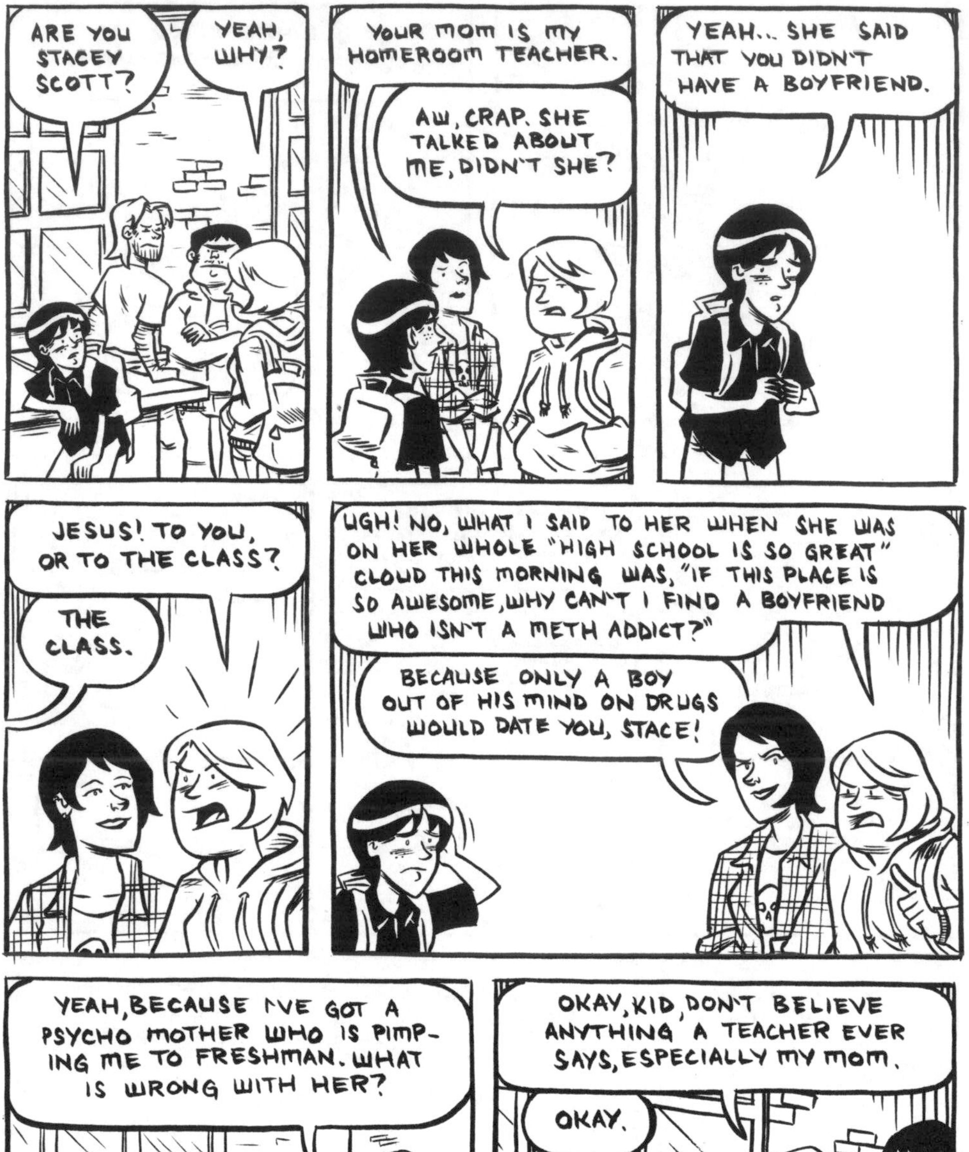
ARE YOU STACEY SCOTT?
YEAH, WHY?
YOUR MOM IS MY HOMEROOM TEACHER.
AW, CRAP. SHE TALKED ABOUT ME, DIDN'T SHE?
YEAH... SHE SAID THAT YOU DIDN'T HAVE A BOYFRIEND.
JESUS! TO YOU, OR TO THE CLASS?
THE CLASS.
UGH! NO, WHAT I SAID TO HER WHEN SHE WAS ON HER WHOLE "HIGH SCHOOL IS SO GREAT" CLOUD THIS MORNING WAS, "IF THIS PLACE IS SO AWESOME, WHY CAN'T I FIND A BOYFRIEND WHO ISN'T A METH ADDICT?"
BECAUSE ONLY A BOY OUT OF HIS MIND ON DRUGS WOULD DATE YOU, STACE!
YEAH, BECAUSE I'VE GOT A PSYCHO MOTHER WHO IS PIMPING ME TO FRESHMAN. WHAT IS WRONG WITH HER?
OKAY, KID, DON'T BELIEVE ANYTHING A TEACHER EVER SAYS, ESPECIALLY MY MOM.
OKAY.

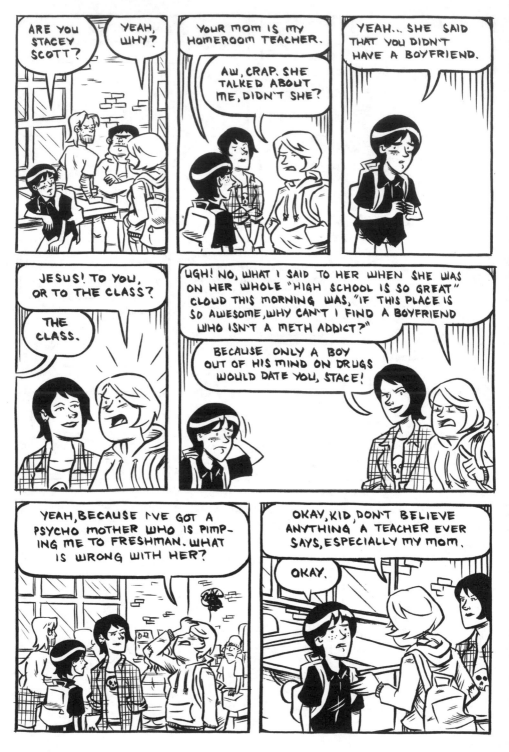

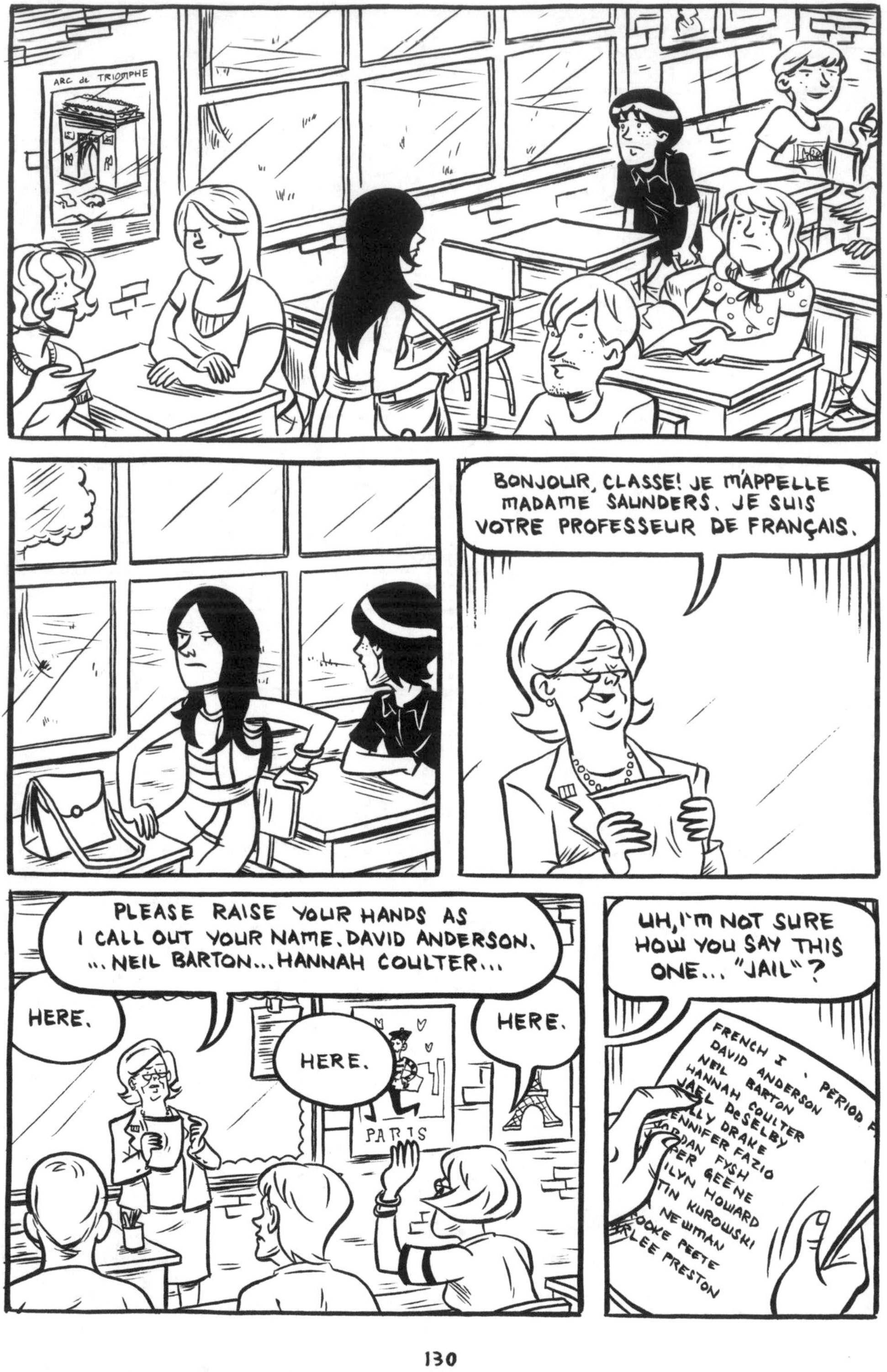
ARC de TRIOMPHE
BONJOUR, CLASSE! JE M'APPELLE MADAME SAUNDERS. JE SUIS VOTRE PROFESSEUR DE FRANÇAIS.
PLEASE RAISE YOUR HANDS AS I CALL OUT YOUR NAME. DAVID ANDERSON. ...NEIL BARTON...HANNAH COULTER...
HERE.
HERE.
PARIS
HERE.
UH, I'M NOT SURE HOW YOU SAY THIS ONE... "JAIL"?
FRENCH I . PERIOD
DAVID ANDERSON
NEIL BARTON
HANNAH COULTER
JAEL DeSELBY
LLY DRAKE
ENNIFER FAZIO
RDAN FYSH
PER GEENE
ILYN HOWARD
TIN KUROWSKI
NEWMAN
OOKE PEETE
LEE PRESTON

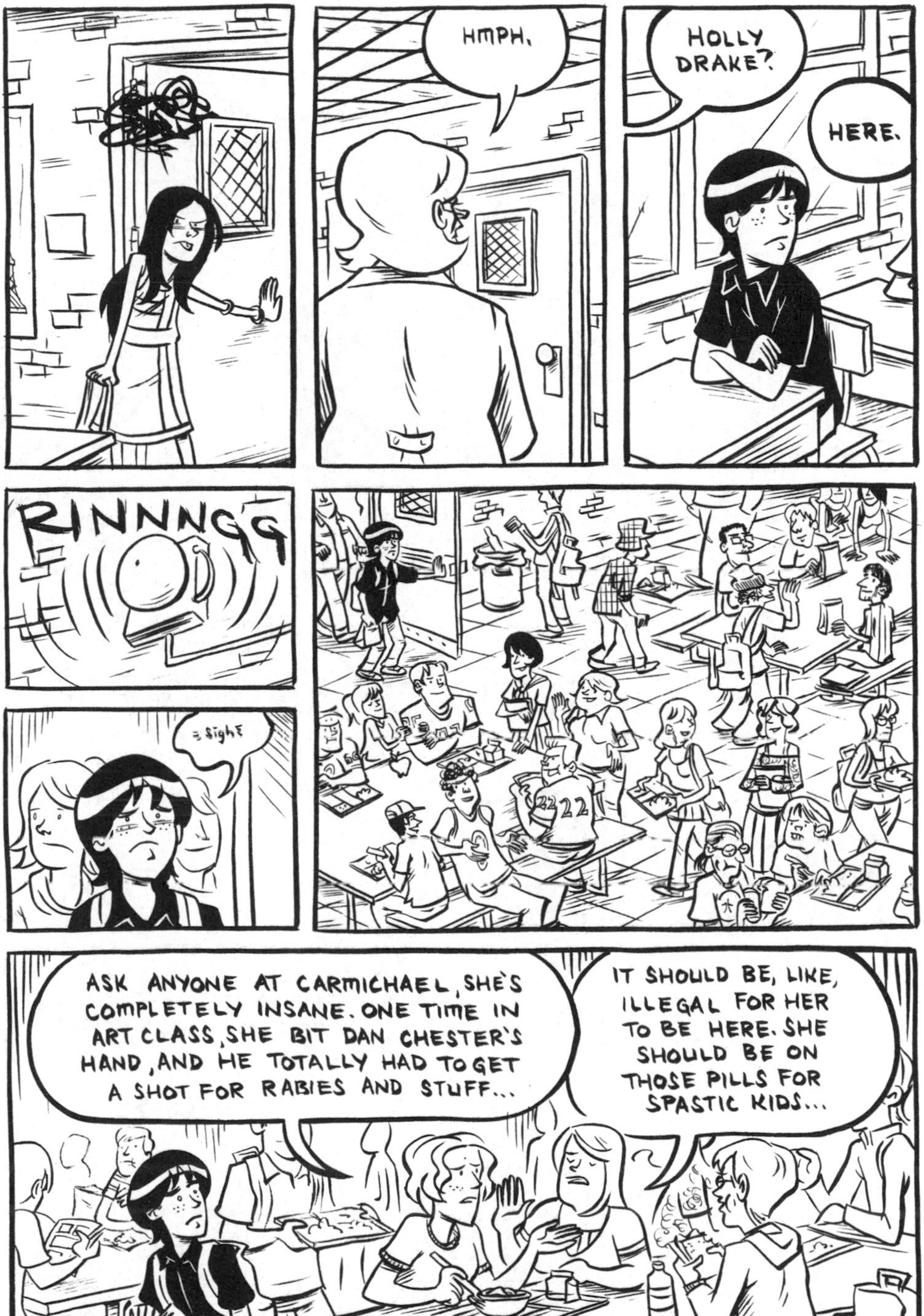
HMPH.
HOLLY DRAKE?
HERE.
RINNNGG
sigh
ASK ANYONE AT CARMICHAEL, SHE'S COMPLETELY INSANE. ONE TIME IN ART CLASS, SHE BIT DAN CHESTER'S HAND, AND HE TOTALLY HAD TO GET A SHOT FOR RABIES AND STUFF...
IT SHOULD BE, LIKE, ILLEGAL FOR HER TO BE HERE. SHE SHOULD BE ON THOSE PILLS FOR SPASTIC KIDS...

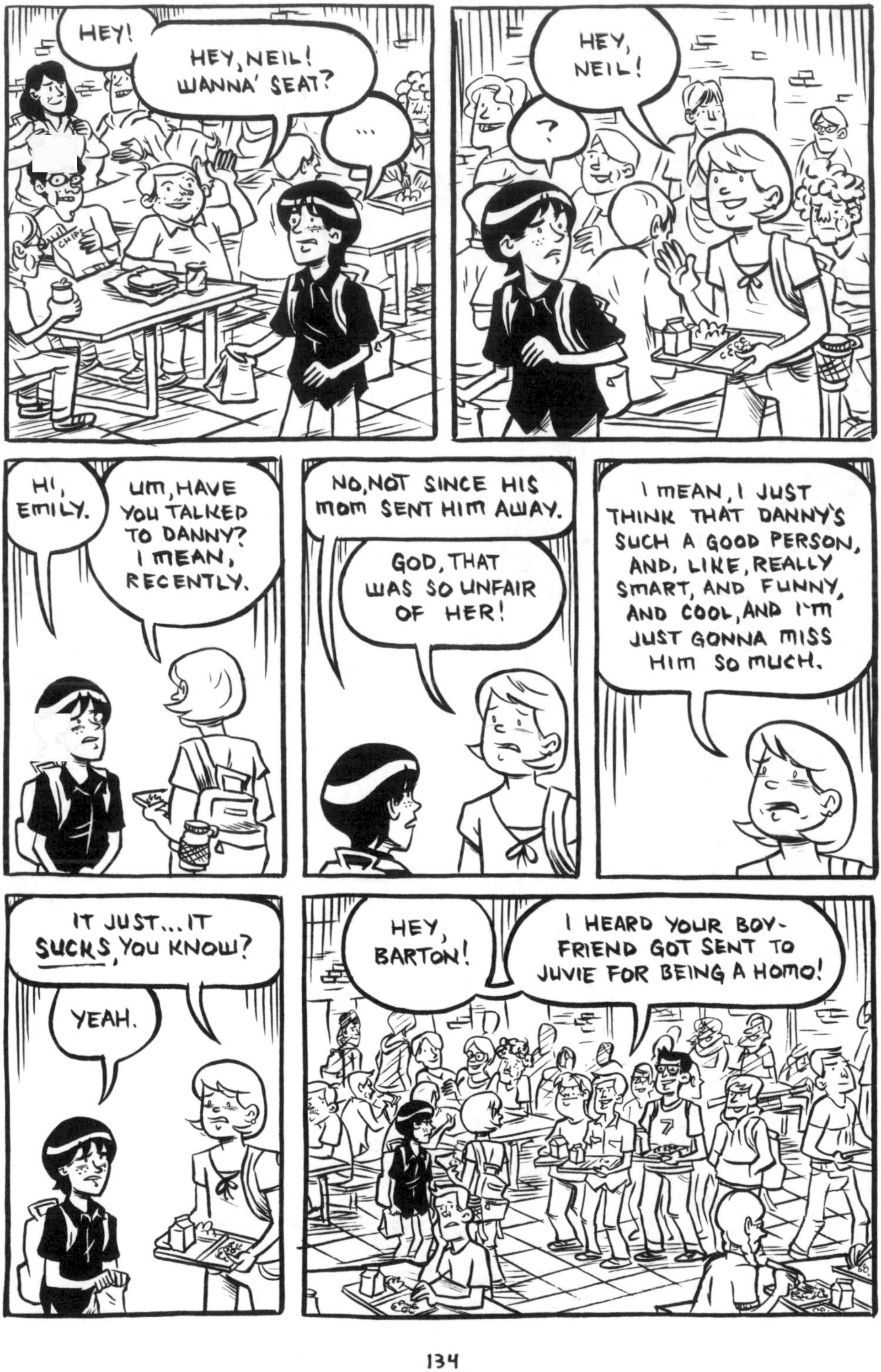
HEY!
HEY, NEIL! WANNA' SEAT?
...
HEY, NEIL!
?
HI, EMILY.
UM, HAVE YOU TALKED TO DANNY? I MEAN, RECENTLY.
NO, NOT SINCE HIS MOM SENT HIM AWAY.
GOD, THAT WAS SO UNFAIR OF HER!
I MEAN, I JUST THINK THAT DANNY'S SUCH A GOOD PERSON, AND, LIKE, REALLY SMART, AND FUNNY, AND COOL, AND I'M JUST GONNA MISS HIM SO MUCH.
IT JUST... IT SUCKS, YOU KNOW?
YEAH.
HEY, BARTON!
I HEARD YOUR BOY-FRIEND GOT SENT TO JUVIE FOR BEING A HOMO!

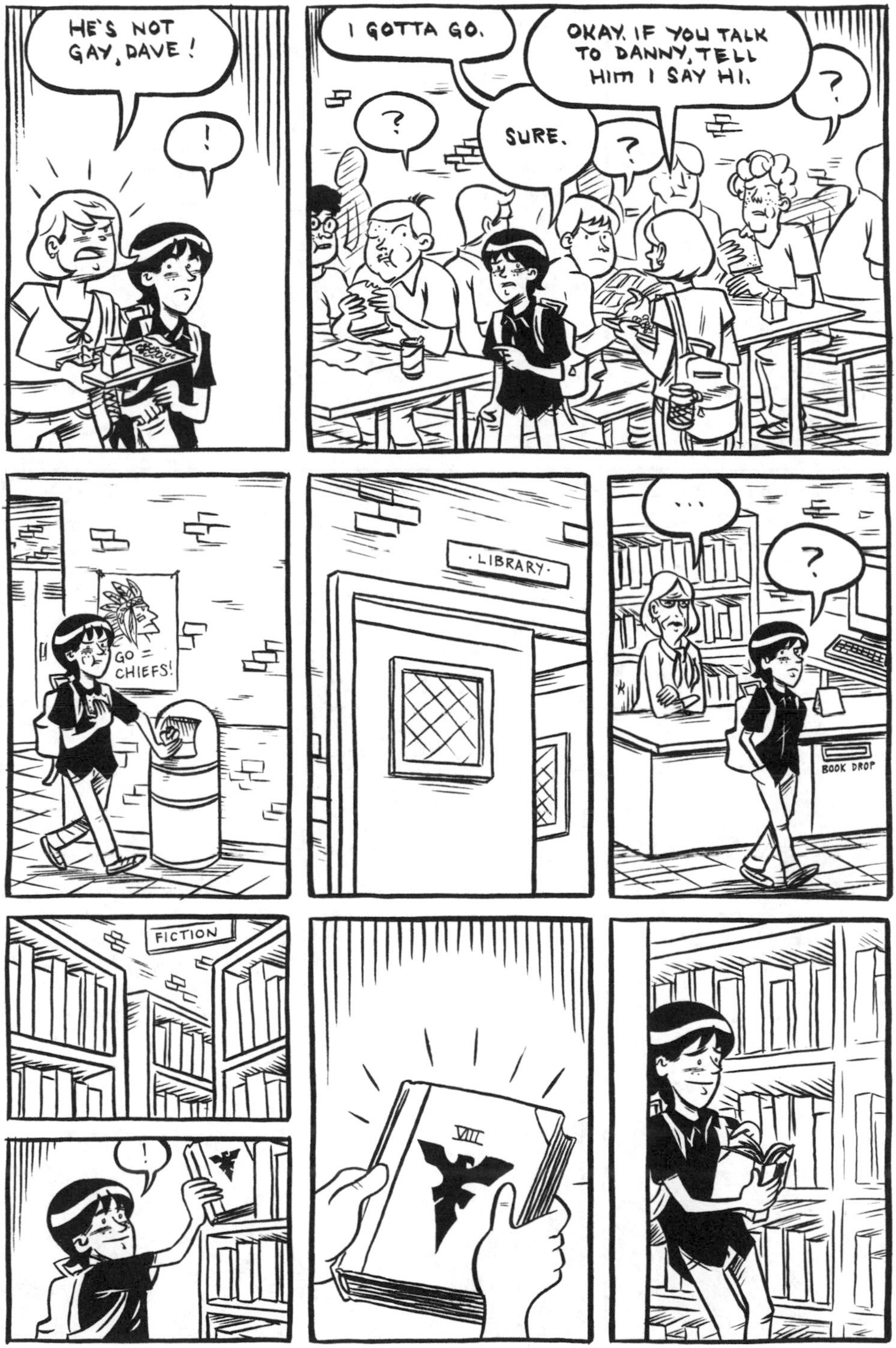
HE'S NOT GAY, DAVE!
!
I GOTTA GO.
?
SURE.
?
OKAY. IF YOU TALK TO DANNY, TELL HIM I SAY HI.
?
GO CHIEFS!
LIBRARY
...
?
BOOK DROP
FICTION
!
VIII

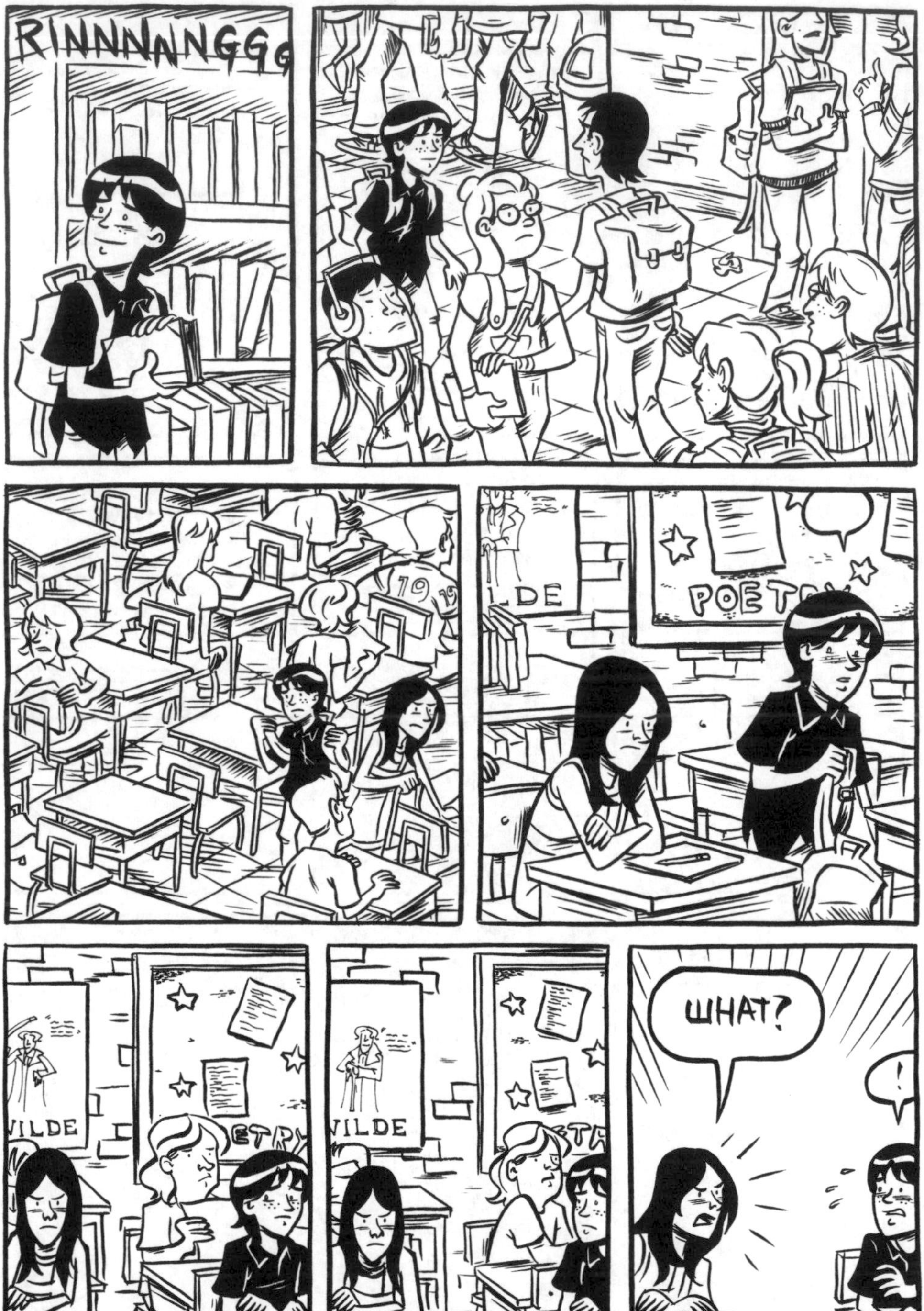
RINNNNNGGG
LDE
POETRY
WILDE
WILDE
WHAT?
!

CHAPTER 7

148

152

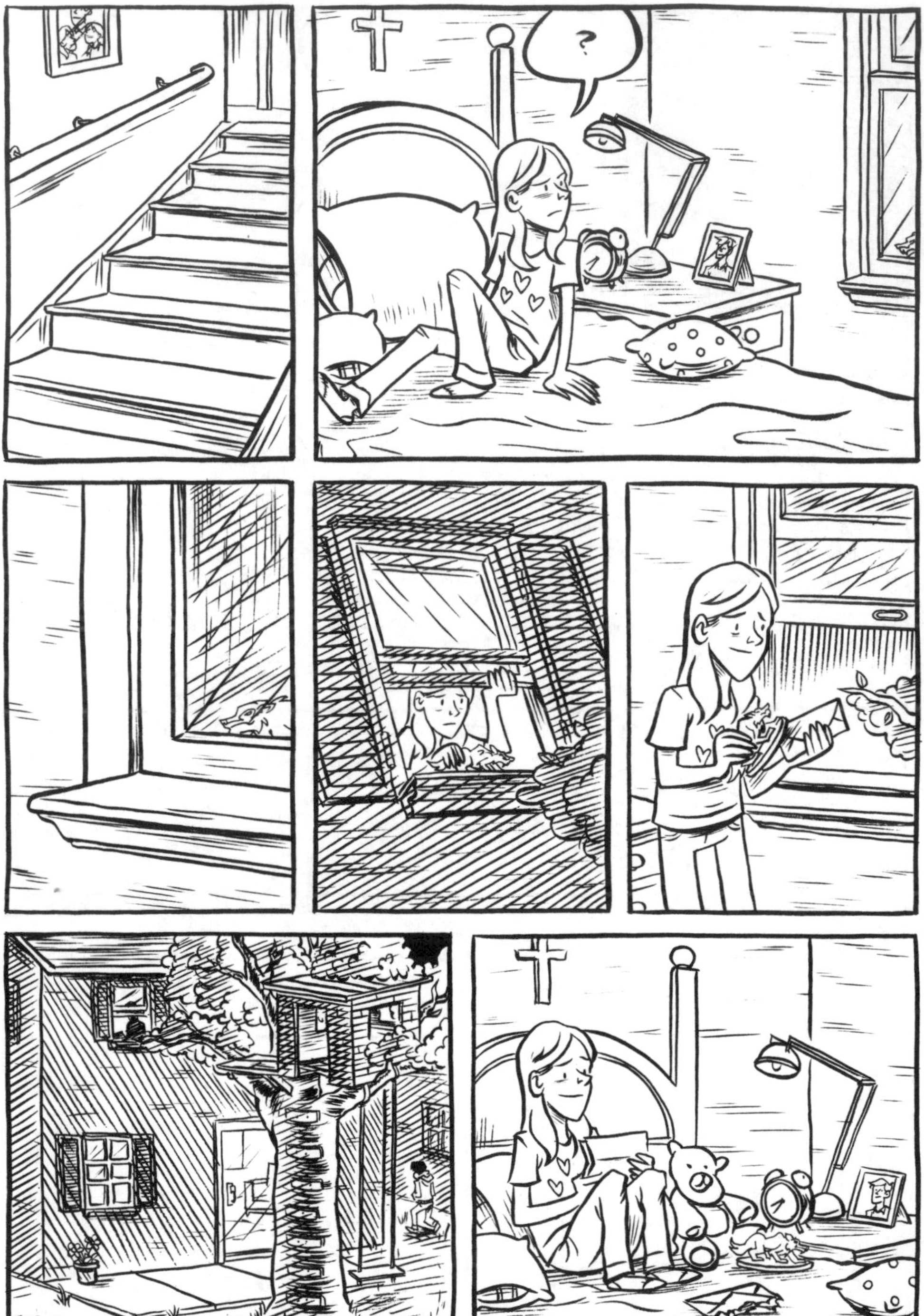
?

CHAPTER 8

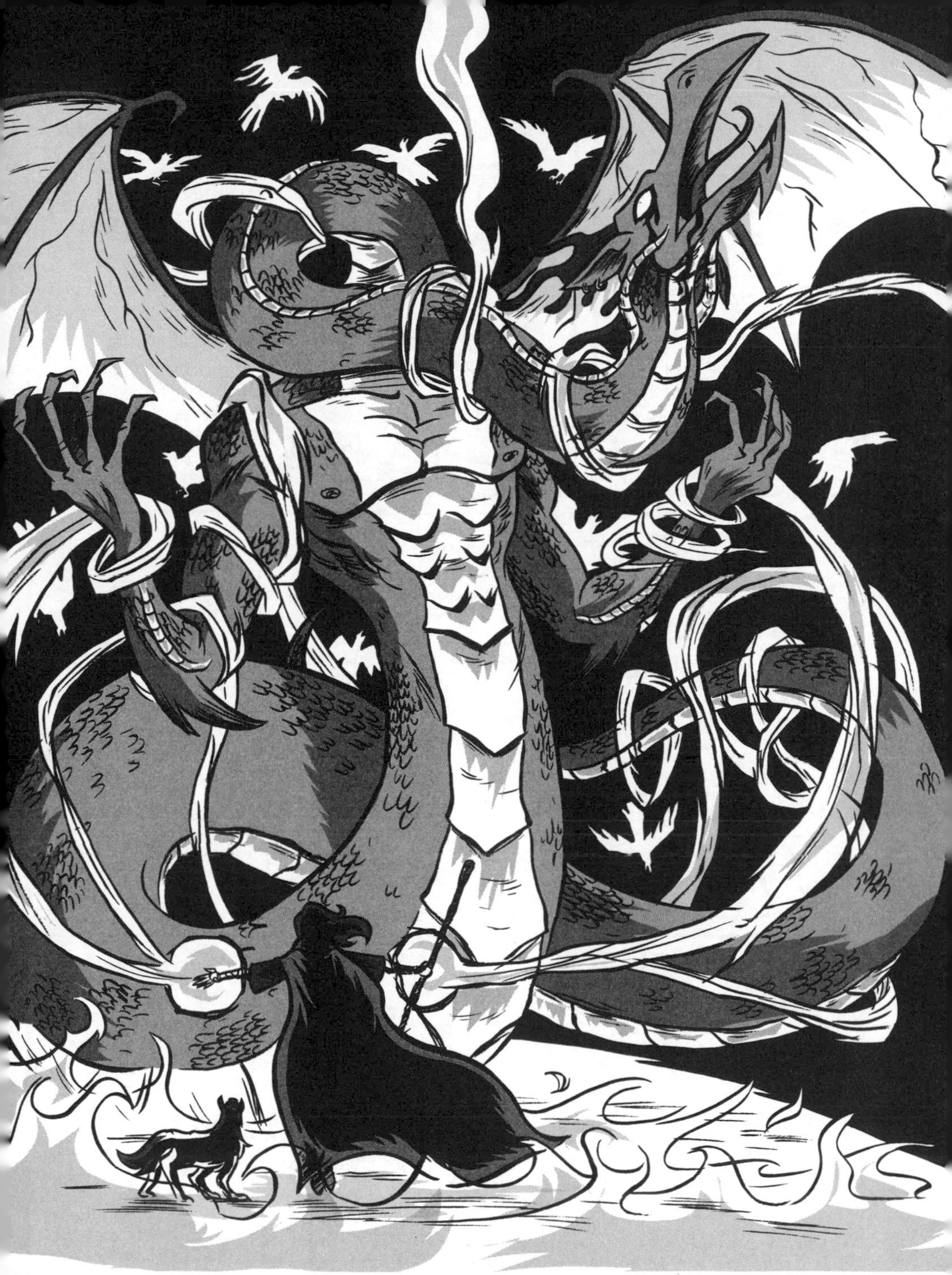

178

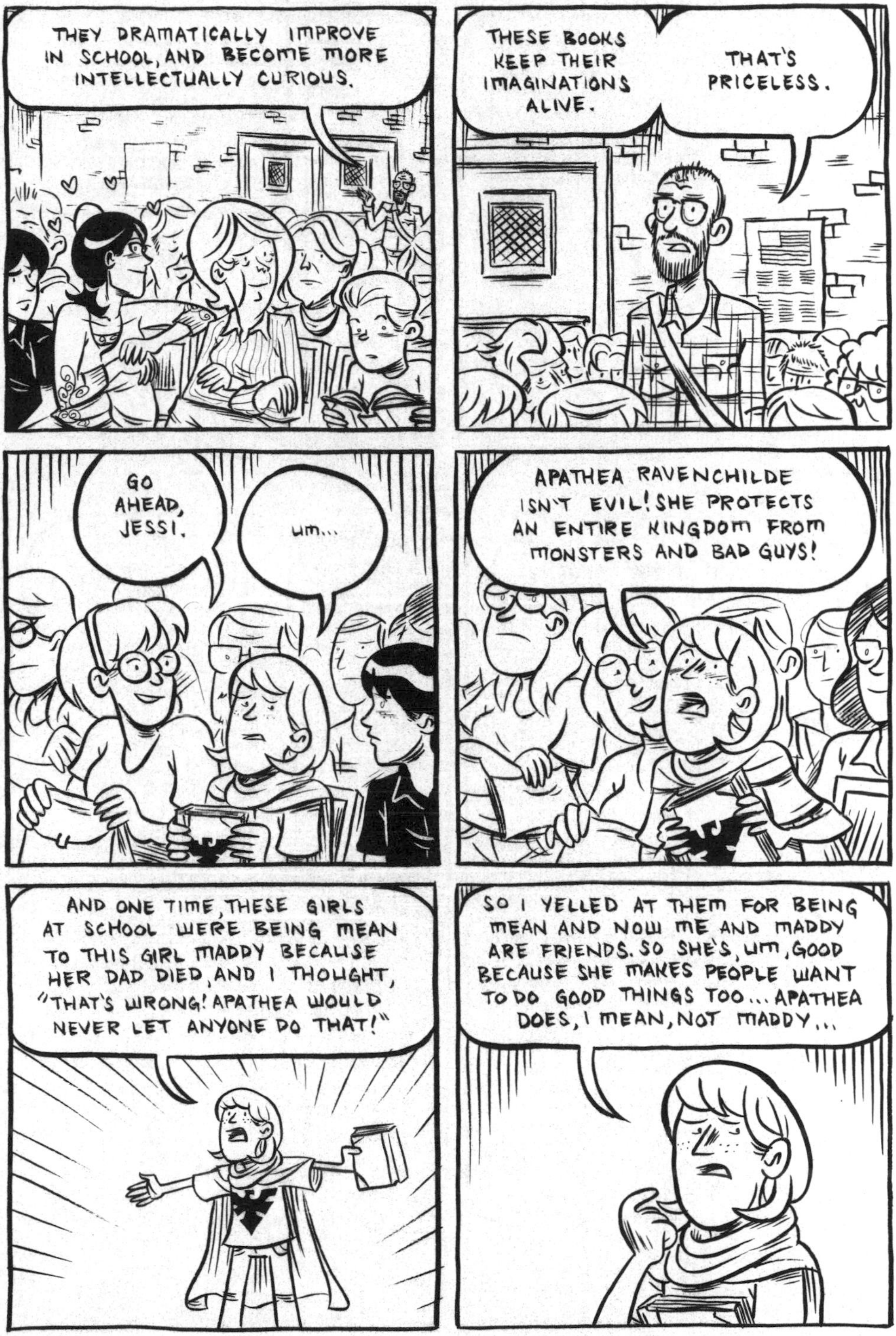
THEY DRAMATICALLY IMPROVE IN SCHOOL, AND BECOME MORE INTELLECTUALLY CURIOUS.
THESE BOOKS KEEP THEIR IMAGINATIONS ALIVE.
THAT'S PRICELESS.
GO AHEAD, JESSI.
UM...
APATHEA RAVENCHILDE ISN'T EVIL! SHE PROTECTS AN ENTIRE KINGDOM FROM MONSTERS AND BAD GUYS!
AND ONE TIME, THESE GIRLS AT SCHOOL WERE BEING MEAN TO THIS GIRL MADDY BECAUSE HER DAD DIED, AND I THOUGHT, "THAT'S WRONG! APATHEA WOULD NEVER LET ANYONE DO THAT!"
SO I YELLED AT THEM FOR BEING MEAN AND NOW ME AND MADDY ARE FRIENDS. SO SHE'S, UM, GOOD BECAUSE SHE MAKES PEOPLE WANT TO DO GOOD THINGS TOO... APATHEA DOES, I MEAN, NOT MADDY...

UH...I'M NEIL BARTON...AND I'M, UM...A PAGE AT THE LIBRARY...

...I'VE READ ALL THE APATHEA RAVENCHILDE BOOKS. THEY'RE MY FAVORITE FANTASY SERIES. AND MY BEST FRIEND'S FAVORITE, TOO.

...BUT HE COULDN'T BE HERE TONIGHT.

EVIL WITCHES!

DON'T SELL SOUL SO CHEAPLY!

I GUESS IT'S KIND OF SILLY TO CARE SO MUCH ABOUT A BOOK.

...BUT IT'S MORE THAN JUST A BOOK TO ME. I CARE ABOUT APATHEA AND HER FRIENDS. I CARE ABOUT LORIAN AND ELBERON AND MAHANAGH AND WHAT HAPPENS THERE.

184

187

CHAPTER 9

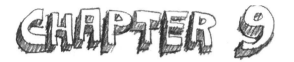

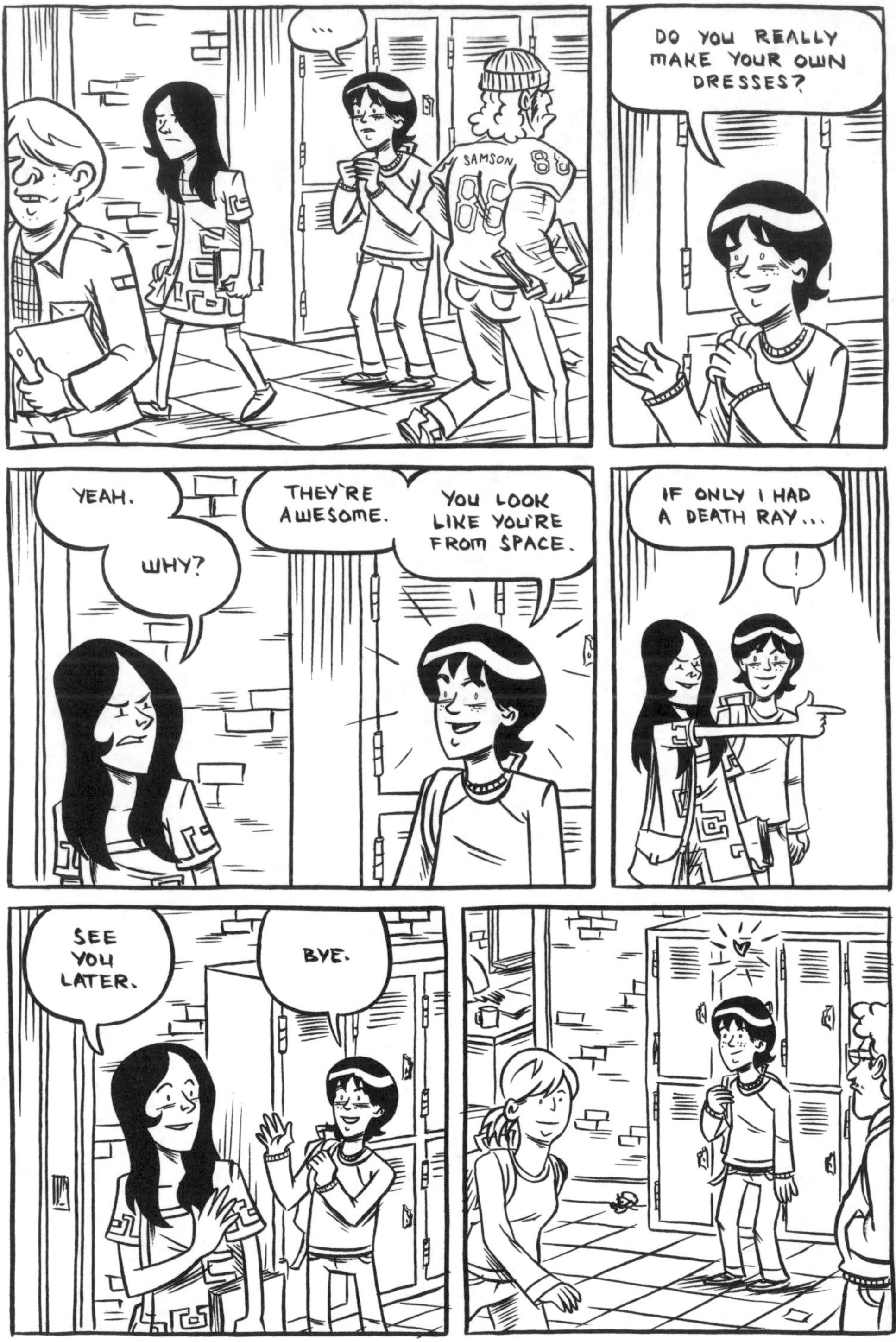
...
DO YOU REALLY MAKE YOUR OWN DRESSES?
YEAH.
WHY?
THEY'RE AWESOME.
YOU LOOK LIKE YOU'RE FROM SPACE.
IF ONLY I HAD A DEATH RAY...
!
SEE YOU LATER.
BYE.
SAMSON
86

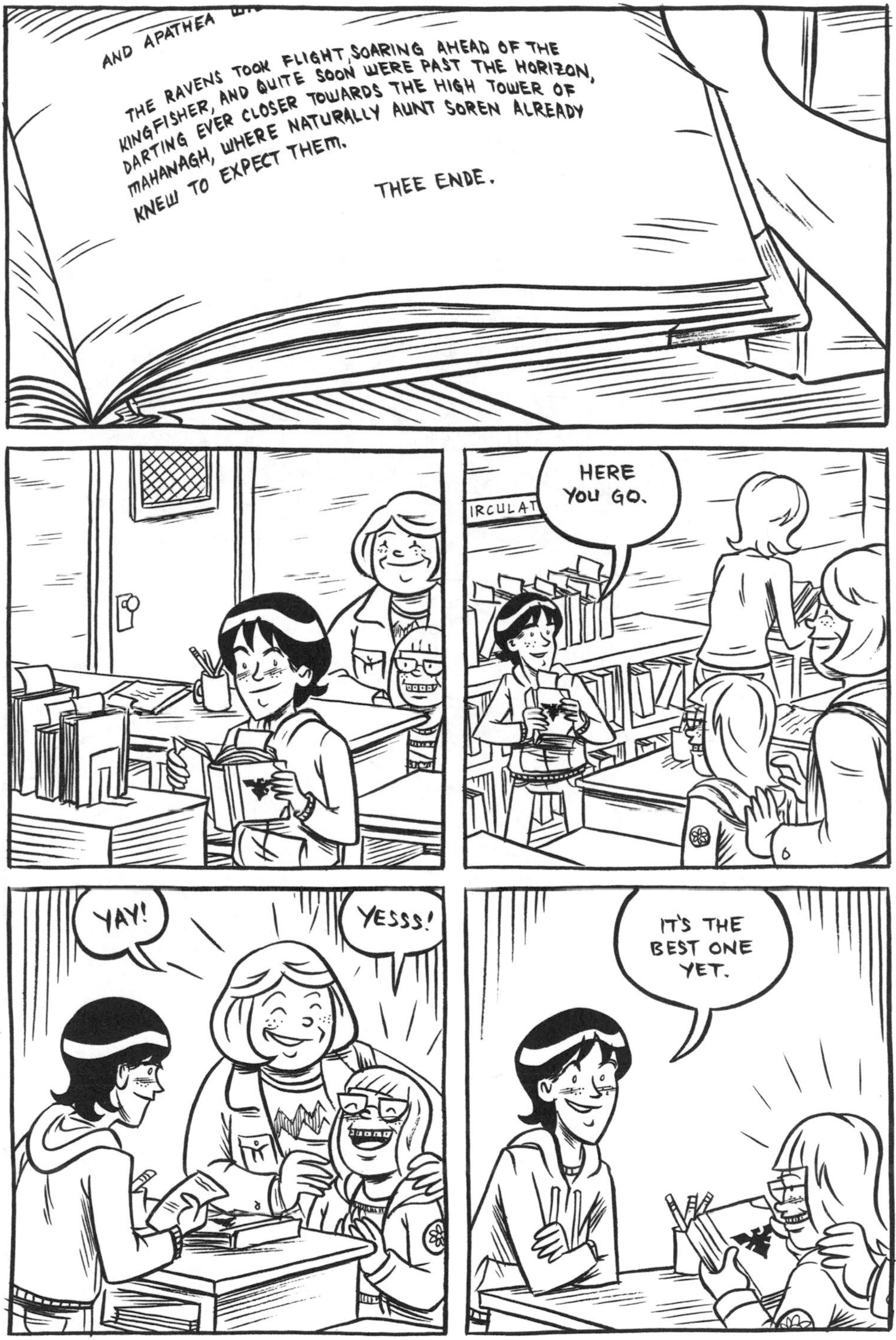
AND APATHEA
THE RAVENS TOOK FLIGHT, SOARING AHEAD OF THE KINGFISHER, AND QUITE SOON WERE PAST THE HORIZON, DARTING EVER CLOSER TOWARDS THE HIGH TOWER OF MAHANAGH, WHERE NATURALLY AUNT SOREN ALREADY KNEW TO EXPECT THEM.
THEE ENDE.
IRCULAT
HERE YOU GO.
YAY!
YESSS!
IT'S THE BEST ONE YET.

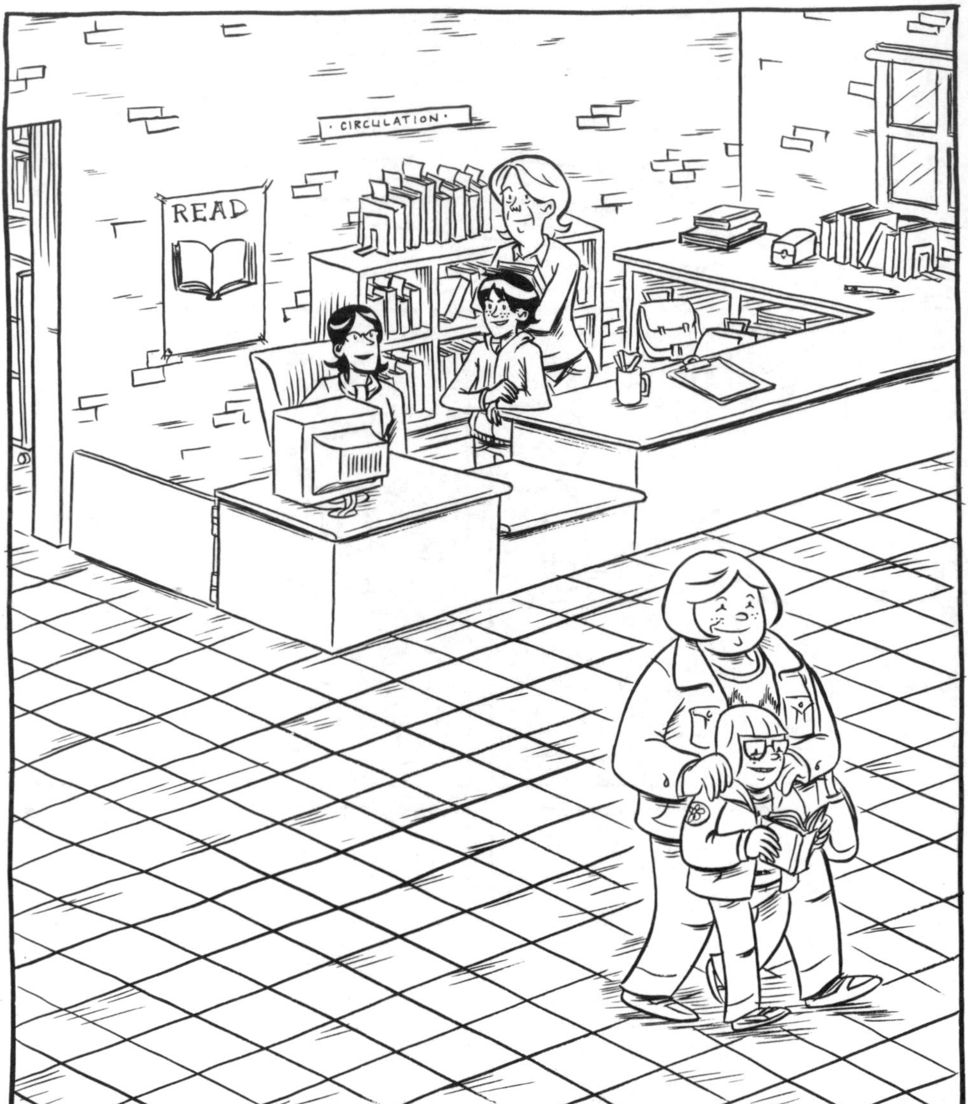
CIRCULATION
READ

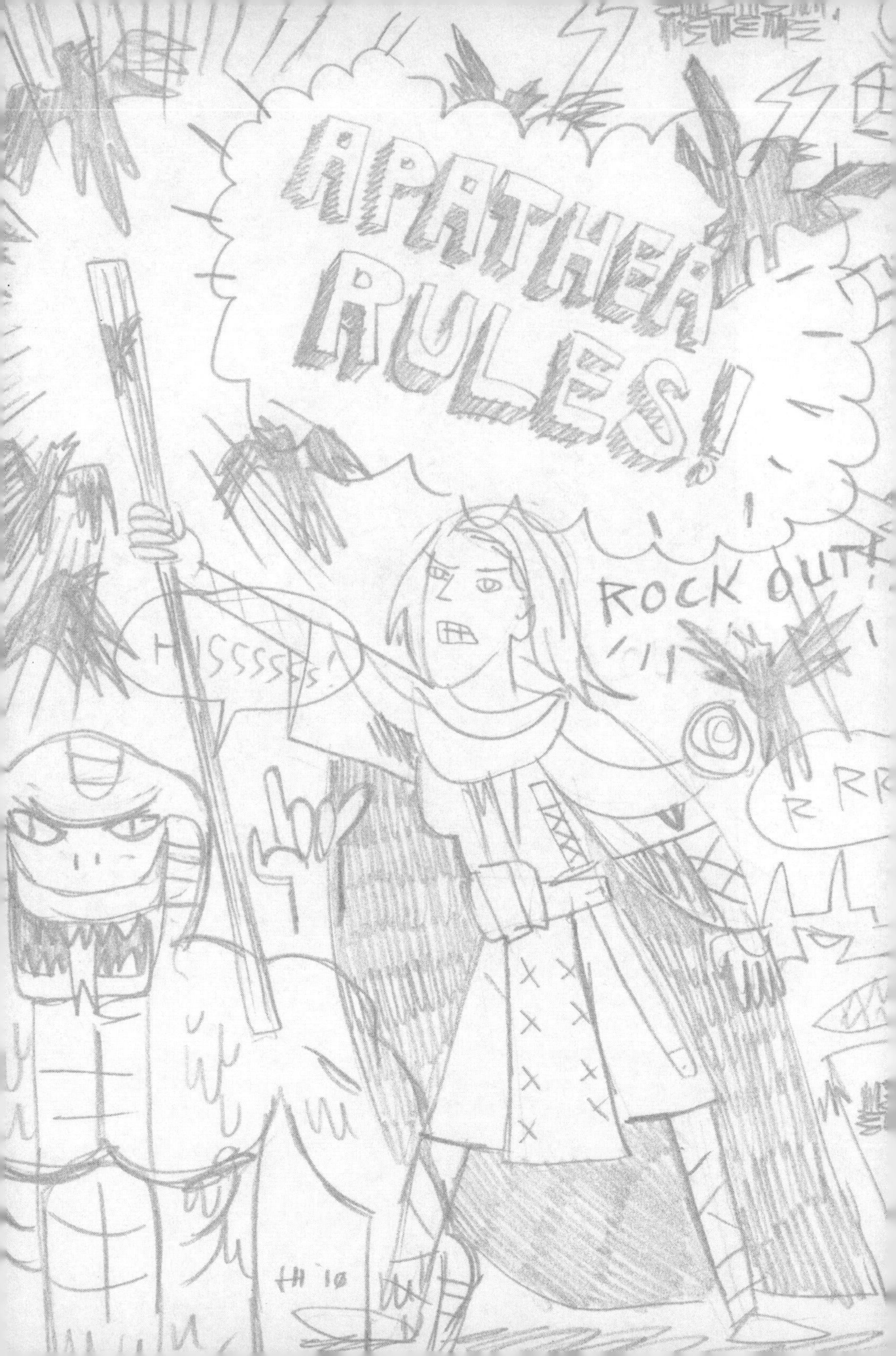
APATHER RULES!
ROCK OUT!
HISSSSSSS!
RRR
FH '10